CAMBAY

Map of the ~ GREAT ~ INDIAN OCEAN

Its Seas, Shores, and Surrounding Environs

SURAT

Arabian Sea

CALICUT

MALABAR COAST

SRI LANKA

THE MALDIVES

The
Adventures
of
Amina al-Sirafi

ALSO BY SHANNON CHAKRABORTY

The Daevabad Trilogy

The City of Brass

The Kingdom of Copper

The Empire of Gold

The River of Silver

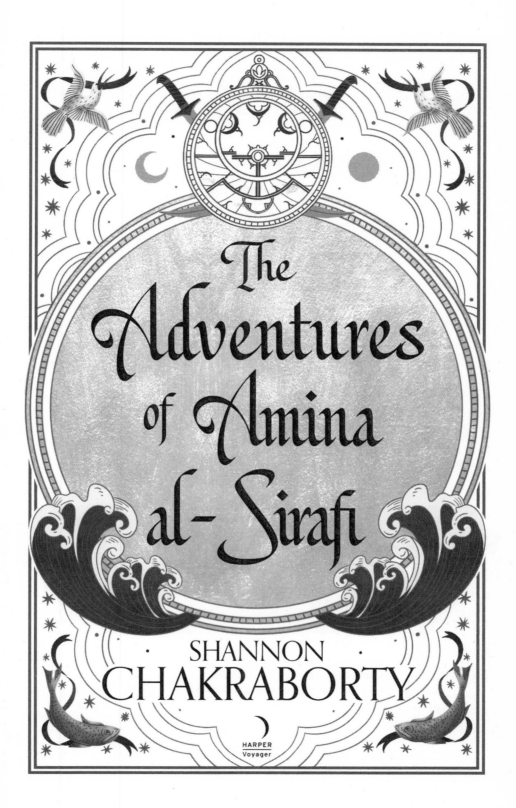

The Adventures of Amina al-Sirafi

SHANNON CHAKRABORTY

HARPER
Voyager

Harper*Voyager*
An imprint of
HarperCollins*Publishers* Ltd
1 London Bridge Street
London SE1 9GF

www.harpercollins.co.uk

HarperCollins*Publishers*
Macken House
39/40 Mayor Street Upper
Dublin 1
D01 C9W8
Ireland

First published by HarperCollins*Publishers* 2023

1

A catalogue record for this book is available from the British Library

ISBN: 978-0-00-838134-9 (HB)
ISBN: 978-0-00-838135-6 (TPB)

MIX
Paper | Supporting
responsible forestry
FSC® C171272

For all those parenting in hardship: during pandemics, through climate crises, and under occupation. For those struggling to keep food on the table, and juggle multiple jobs and impossible childcare. For everyone who's set aside their own dreams, briefly or forever, to lift those of the next generation.

Map of the
GREAT
INDIAN OCEAN
Its Seas, Shores, and
Surrounding Environs

CAMBAY

SURAT

Arabian
Sea

CALICUT

MALABAR
COAST

SRI LANKA

THE MALDIVES

Author's Note

Please note that in the voice of the time and place in which this book takes place, the Latin Christians of Western Europe are referred to as Franks and the Byzantines as the Rum. The novel's twelfth-century, largely Islamicate societies of the northwestern Indian Ocean littoral had their own rich and fascinating way of describing antiquity, their contemporaries, and the wider world, and though I've tried to re-create that here as accurately as possible, this is a work of fiction. A glossary with additional historical and nautical terms can be found at the back, as well as suggestions for further reading.

I clung to the plank of wood, my only refuge in the storm-tossed sea, and berated myself, saying "Sindbad the Sailor, you never learn! After each of your journeys—the first and the second, the third and the fourth, the FIFTH, all worse than that which preceded it!—you swear to God to repent and give up these travels. And every time you lie, swayed by greed and adventure, to return to the sea. So take the punishment that is coming, you deserve it!"

—FROM "THE SIXTH VOYAGE OF SINDBAD THE SAILOR"

A Word on What Is to Come

In the name of God, the Most Merciful, the Most Compassionate. Blessings upon His honored Prophet Muhammad, his family, and his followers. Praise be to God, who in His glory created the earth and its diversity of lands and languages, peoples and tongues. In these vast marvels, so numerous a human eye cannot gaze upon more than a sliver, is there not proof of His Magnificence?

And when it comes to marvels . . . let us delight in the adventures of the nakhudha Amina al-Sirafi.

Yes! *That* Captain Amina al-Sirafi. The smuggler, the pirate. The blasphemer that men of letters accuse of serving up human hearts for her sea-beast husband, and the sorceress—for she *must* be a sorceress, because no female could sail a ship so deftly without the use of forbidden magics—whose appearance somehow both beguiles and repulses. Traders along our fair shores warn against speaking her name as though she is a djinn that might be summoned as such—though, strangely, they have little compunction when it comes to spreading vicious rumors about her body and her sexuality: these things that men obsess over when they hate what they desire and desire what they cannot possess.

I am certain you have heard talk of her. After all, it is tradition for the traveled men of our ummah to share the wonders of the world by creating accounts of their voyages—particularly when those voyages are enlivened by gossip of fearsome female rogues. Many such travelers will swear their accounts are not written to tantalize or entertain—God forbid!—but are intended first and foremost to strengthen the hearts of the faithful and provide evidence of the promised splendor of God's creation. And yet, as Muslims, are we not told to speak honestly? To ascertain what is truth and beware spreading falsehoods?

And dear sisters . . . what falsehoods.

For this scribe has read a great many of these accounts and taken away another lesson: that to be a woman is to have your story misremembered. Discarded. *Twisted.* In courtyard tales, women are the adulterous wives whose treachery begins a husband's descent into murderous madness or the long-suffering mothers who give birth to proper heroes. Biographers polish away the jagged edges of capable, ruthless queens so they may be remembered as saints, and geographers warn believing men away from such and such a place with scandalous tales of lewd local females who cavort in the sea and ravish foreign interlopers. Women are the forgotten spouses and unnamed daughters. Wet nurses and handmaidens; thieves and harlots. Witches. A titillating anecdote to tell your friends back home or a warning.

There are plenty of slanderous stories like *that* about Amina al-Sirafi. She was too relentless, they say. Too ambitious, too violent, utterly inappropriate, and well . . . old! A *mother,* if you can believe it! Ah yes, a certain degree of rebelliousness is expected from youth. It is why we have stories of treasure-seeking princesses and warrior women that end with the occasional happiness. But they are expected to *end*—with the boy, the prince, the sailor, the adventurer. The man that will take her maidenhood, grant her children, make her a wife. The man who defines her. *He* may continue his epic—he may indeed take new wives and make new children!—but women's stories are expected to dissolve into a fog of domesticity . . . if they're told at all.

Amina's story did not end. Verily, no woman's story does. This humble scribe—ah, I should introduce myself: there is a bit more to my name, but for now you may call me Jamal. Jamal al-Hilli. And I have met grandmothers launching new businesses, elderly queens fighting wars of conquest, and young mothers taking up a drawing pen for the first time. Indeed, we may only have Amina's story *because* she was a mother. In our time together, she spoke constantly of her daughter. And though it may be a bold assumption . . . she spoke *to* her daughter. So that her child might come to understand the choices her mother had made. For when Amina chose to leave her home and return to a life at sea, she became more than a pirate. More than a witch.

She became a legend.

This tale will sound unbelievable. What proofs and documents could be collected are reproduced, but when it came to the nakhudha, this scribe felt it best to let Amina speak for herself. To resist the urge to shape and couch her words. But for the sake of honesty, another truth will be confessed. Her adventures are not only being told as evidence of God's marvels.

They are being told to entertain.

Chapter 1

God as my witness, none of this would have ever happened if it were not for those two fools back in Salalah. Them and their map.

—What? What do you mean, that is "not how you start a story"? A *biography*? You wish for a biography? Who do you think you are chronicling, the Grand Mufti of Mecca? My people do not wax poetic about lineage like yours do. We are not even true Sirafis. My father's father—an orphan turned pirate from Oman—simply found the name romantic.

—Don't you think so?

As I was saying. The idiots and their map. Now, I understand the appeal of treasure-hunting, I do. After all, we build our homes upon the ruins of lost cities and sail our ships over the drowned palaces of forgotten kings. Everyone has heard a tale of how so-and-so dug up a jar of Sasanian coins while sowing his fields or met a pearl diver who glimpsed hordes of emeralds glittering on the seabed. It was related to me that in Egypt, treasure-hunting is so popular its participants have organized into professional guilds, each holding their particular tricks close . . . though for the right price, someone *might* be willing to give you some advice. They may even offer to sell you a map! A guide to such fortunes you could scarcely imagine.

The maps are—and I cannot emphasize this enough—remarkably easy to forge. I can even tell you how it is done: You merely need a scrap of parchment and a bit of time. Tonics are applied to darken and yellow the paper, though regrettably, the majority require urine and the best derive from the bile of a bat. The map itself should be drawn with care, with enough details that some geographic locations will be recognizable (ideally directing the mark in the opposite direction of which the mapmaker intends to flee). Symbols can be lifted from any number of alphabets. Many forgers prefer Hebrew for its mystical connotations, but in my opinion, the text off an old Sabaean tomb makes for more mysterious letters. Wrinkle the whole thing up; fray the edges, burn a few holes, apply a thin layer of sandarac to fade the script—and that is that. Your "treasure" map is ready to be sold to the highest bidder.

The map my clients possessed that night did not look like it had been sold to the highest bidder. Though they had been trying to conceal the document along with their purpose—as though midnight excursions to ancient ruins were a common request—a glimpse had been enough to reveal the map was of middling work, perhaps the practice manuscript of an earnest criminal youngster.

But I kept such opinions to myself. That they had hired me to row them out here was a blessing, a chance job I had snagged while fishing. I must have seemed a prime candidate for their mission: a lone local woman a bit long in the tooth and almost certainly too dim to care what they were doing. I made the appropriate noises, warning them that the ruins were said to be haunted by ghouls and the surrounding lagoon cursed by djinn, but the young men assured me they could handle themselves. And as I had spent many a night fishing in the area without encountering even a whiff of the supernatural, I was not truly concerned.

—Excuse me? That "seems sort of naïve"? Do you not recall how we met, hypocrite? Stop talking and eat your stew. The saltah is excellent here and you are barely thicker than that pen you are holding. Another interruption, Jamal, and you can find some other nakhudha to harass for stories.

Anyway. Back to that night. It was an otherwise enchanting evening. The stars were out, a rare sight during the khareef, the summer monsoon that typically mires us in fog. The moon shone brightly upon the ruined fort across the lagoon, its crumbling bricks all that remained of a long-abandoned city locals said had once been a bustling trading port. This part of the world has always been rich; the Romans once called us Arabia Felix, "Blessed Arabia," for our access to the sea, reliable trade routes, and lucrative frankincense groves. Locals *also* say that the lost city's treasury—still bursting with gold—lays hidden beneath the ruins, buried during an earthquake. It was that story I assumed had lured out the youths until one of them loudly clucked their tongue at me in the manner of a man calling a mule to halt while we were still in the lagoon.

"Stop here," the boy ordered.

I gave the black water surrounding us, the beach still some distance away, a dubious glance. During the day, this was a lovely place that attracted flamingos and dolphins. When the wind and tide were just right, water would burst from the rocks in geysers to the delight of children and picnicking families. But during low tide on a calm night such as this, the breakers against the surf were mild, a steady soothing crash and glittering white spray that did little to differentiate between sea and shore. If my clients thought they could swim all the way to the barely visible beach, they were even more foolish than I thought. And I think I've been clear how foolish I considered them.

"We are not yet at the ruins," I pointed out.

"This is far enough." The pair were huddled together at the other end of my small boat, the map spread across their knees. One boy held an oil lamp for illumination, the other a burning bunch of dried jasmine.

"I do not understand," one of the youths muttered. They had been arguing in hushed whispers all night. Though their accents sounded Adeni to my ear, I did not know their names. They had rather dramatically declared that in lieu of offering their names, they would pay me an additional dirham for my discretion, and since I did not actually care, the extra payment was a delightful surprise. "The map says this is the spot . . ." He gestured to the heavens above, and my heart went out to him, for what was written on that map had nothing to do with any star chart I have ever seen.

"You said you wished to go to the old city." I gestured toward the hill—or at least I tried to. But a thick bank of fog had rolled down from the wadi, the monsoon-swollen stream that fed the lagoon, to surround us, and neither the ruins nor the hill were visible. Instead, as I watched, the shore entirely vanished so that we appeared to be floating on an endless, mist-shrouded plain.

The youths ignored me. "We have said the words," the one holding the oil lamp argued. "We have her payment. She should appear."

"And yet she has not," the other boy argued. "I am *telling* you, we were supposed to . . ."

But whatever they were supposed to do stopped concerning me. In the space of a breath, the breeze that had been blowing in from the sea all night abruptly halted, the air turning dead and flat. I stilled, a bead of sweat chasing down my spine. I am a sailor, and there is little I watch more closely than the weather. I lifted a fraying strand from my cloak, but no wind stirred the thread. The fog drew closer, accompanied by a smothering quiet that made thunderous every knock of water against the boat's hull.

There are places in the world where such signs might herald a vicious, dangerous storm, but the typhoons that occasionally struck here typically did not manifest so unexpectedly. The water remained gentle, the tide and current unchanged, but even so . . . there was an ill feeling in my belly.

I reached for my oars. "I think we should leave."

"Wait!" One of the young men stood, waving excitedly at the fog. "Do you see that shadow above the sea-foam?"

It *was* sea-foam, I realized, squinting in the dark. Years of the sun's glare upon the ocean had begun to take their toll on my vision, and I struggled to see clearly at night. But the boy was correct. It wasn't only fog drifting closer. It was sea-foam piled high enough to swallow my boat. As it approached, one could see a reddish-yellow hue to the substance and smell the awful aroma of rotting flesh and gutted fish.

"Give over her payment," Oil-Lamp Boy urged. "Quickly!"

"Forget my payment and sit back down," I ordered as the second youth reached into his robe. "We are—"

The boy pulled free his hand, revealing a large chunk of red carnelian, and two things happened very quickly:

One, I realized that was not *my* payment.

Two, the thing whose payment it was dragged us into the fog.

The boy holding the carnelian barely had time to cry out before the froth rushed to consume him, licking down his neck and chest and winding around his hips like an eager lover. A howl ripped from his throat, but it was not a scream any mortal mouth should have been able to let loose. Rather, it was more the roar of a tidal wave and the death cries of gulls.

"Khalid!" The other boy dropped the lamp in shock, extinguishing our only light.

But fortunately—fortunately?—the seemingly alive and possibly malevolent sea-foam was glowing. Its light was faint, but enough to illuminate Khalid as he bared his teeth like a wolf and threw himself on his companion.

"*You shall not have me,*" he hissed, groping for the other boy's neck. "We will curse you! We will devour you! We will cast you into the flames!"

The other boy struggled to free himself. "Khalid, please!" he choked as more sea-foam—now the crimson of blood—spread over them both. Fanged suckers were blossoming across its surface like the tentacles of a monstrous squid.

I would like to say I did not hesitate. That at the sight of two youths in mortal peril, I flew into action and did not briefly wonder if the malevolent sea-foam might be sated with eating them and leave me and my boat alone. That would be a lie. I did hesitate. But then I cursed them profusely, rose to my feet, and went for my knife.

Now, I am fond of blades. The khanjar that was my grandfather's and the wickedly beautiful Damascene scimitar I stole off an undeserving noble. The small straight knife that hides in an ankle holster and a truly excellent bladed disc from my second husband, who learned to regret teaching me to throw it.

But there's only one weapon for situations like this, one I commissioned myself and never leaves my presence. Made of pure iron, it isn't my sharpest blade and its weight can make it unwieldly. Spots of rust from the sacred Zamzam water I sprinkle over it in nightly blessings pepper the metal, the red flakes making it difficult to discern the knife's inscribed holy verses. But I didn't need the knife to be pretty.

I needed it to be effective when more earthly weapons failed.

I seized Khalid by the collar and ripped him off the other boy. Before he could make a grab for *my* throat, I put my blessed blade to his. "Be gone," I demanded.

He wriggled wildly, sea-foam flying. "You shall not have me. *You shall not have me!*"

"I do not want you! Now, in the name of God, be gone!"

I pressed the knife harder as the bismillah left my lips. His flesh sizzled in response, and then he crumpled. The sea-foam that had wrapped his body hovered in the air a moment then hurled itself at me. I fell as though struck by a battering ram, my head slamming into the boat's bottom.

Icy fingers with bone-sharp tips were digging into my ears, a great weight pinning me in place. But by the grace of God, I was still holding my blessed blade. I struck out madly, and the knife *stuck* in the air. There was a shriek—an evil, unnatural sound like claws scraping over seashells—and then the scaled monstrosity squatting on my chest rippled into sight.

Its glittering eyes were the color of bilgewater, its filthy straw-like hair matted with barnacles.

It screamed again, revealing four needlelike teeth. Its bony hands scrabbled on my own as it tried to wrest away the dagger sunk into its wine-dark breast. Silver blood bubbled and dripped from the wound, drenching us both.

The youths were sobbing and begging God for mercy. The demon was shrieking and wailing in an unknown tongue. I shoved the blade deeper, thundering to be heard over all of them.

"God!" I shouted. "There is no god worthy of worship except Him, the Ever-Living, All-Sustaining!" Holding the dagger tight, I launched into ayat al-kursi, the passage from the Quran I had been taught all my life would protect me.

The demon on my chest howled and writhed in pain, its skeletal hands flying to cover scaled ears.

"Neither drowsiness nor sleep overtakes Him! To Him belongs whatever is in the heavens and whatever is on the earth—*will you get off of me?*" I elbowed the creature hard, and it spit in my face. "Who could possibly intercede with Him without His permission? He knows what is ahead of them and what is behind them, but no one can grasp any of His knowledge—except what He wills!"

Its skin smoking, the demon must have decided it had had enough. A pair of bat-like wings sprouted from its back, and with a gusty flap, it pulled itself off the blade and was gone, vanished into the night.

Gasping, I sat up. The mists were already receding, the youths still clutching each other on the other side of the boat. I held the dagger tight, searching the retreating fog for anything else. Fear coursed through me, thick and choking, as I waited for that familiar laugh. For fiery black eyes and a too-silky voice.

But there was nothing. Nothing but the star-splashed lagoon and the gentle murmur of the tide.

I spun on the youths. "You said you were after treasure."

Oil-Lamp Boy flushed, spots of color appearing in his chalky skin. "Treasure is a concept open to—no, wait!" he cried as I snatched their map and lump of carnelian, thrusting them over the water. "Do not do that!"

I tossed and caught the glittering red gem in one hand. "Do not pretend with me, boy," I warned. "Lie again and I will throw you both overboard. You mentioned payment and a name. What were you trying to summon?"

"We were not trying—Bidukh!" he confessed when I dipped the map into the sea. "My cousin told me about her. She is . . ." He swallowed loudly. "She is one of the daughters of Iblis."

I gaped. "You were trying to summon a daughter of the lord of hell? On *my* boat?"

"We did not mean any harm!" The moonlight had returned, and I could see him cowering. "It is said that if you please her, she will whisper the secrets of love into your ear."

Khalid swayed in his friend's arms. "I am going to be sick."

"Throw up in my boat, and you swim back to shore. A daughter of Iblis . . . may you both be cursed." I hurled the map and carnelian into the lagoon. They vanished with loud splashes amidst the protest of my passengers.

"Hey!" the boy cried. "We paid a lot of money for that!"

"You should be thanking God you did not pay with your lives." I thrust an extra oar in his arms. "Row. Perhaps some labor will knock a bit of sense into you."

He nearly dropped the oar, his eyes going wide as I shifted positions, the movement revealing the other weapons concealed beneath my cloak. I wiped the iron knife clean, placing it back into its sheath before taking up my own set of oars.

Both boys were staring at me with expressions of shock. I could not blame them. I'd fought off a demon, given up the slouch I'd been affecting to reveal my true height, and now rowed with my full strength—a far cry from the quiet, hunched-over old fisherwoman who'd reluctantly agreed to take them out here.

"Who are you?" Khalid asked hoarsely.

The other one gawked. "*What* are you?"

The lagoon was receding, but I would swear I still felt a heaviness in the air. For a moment the water splashing at the rocky beach looked like the yellow-hued crimson of the now-vanished sea-foam, the shadows dancing on the cliffs like tentacles.

"Someone who knows too well the price of magic."

I said nothing else, and they did not ask. But they did not need to. For stories carry, and even if the youths were ashamed to confess their own schemes, the tale of an unassuming fisherwoman who fought a demon like a warrior of God? Who threw off her tattered cloak to reveal an armory at her waist and a form like an Amazon?

Exaggerations, but the truth scarcely matters when it comes to a good tale. The kind of story that spreads in taverns and shipyards. To wealthy women's harems and the kitchens of their servants.

To the ear of a very desperate grandmother in Aden.

Chapter 2

As you might imagine, witnessing a youth being taken over by malevolent sea-foam in hopes of summoning Iblis's daughter was not an experience easily forgotten. If we had awakened some sort of vengeful spirit in the lagoon, however, I did not return to find out. Instead, I fell back into the routines of family and harvest, which meant on the day I returned to a life of misadventure, I was locked in battle with the constant enemy of my retirement: my roof.

Had I held fast to the payment the young men and I had agreed upon weeks ago, I might have been able to purchase a few good boards from a carpenter in Salalah, the town a half day's journey away. Instead, I had taken the boys back to shore for free, moved by their fear and hoping my benevolence would buy their silence in return. A decision I cursed as I laid down a mat of rushes across the latest leak and sat back to assess my work.

It was not an inspiring sight. For nearly a decade, my family had called this decomposing stone house in the seaside mountains home. With commanding views of both ocean and countryside, walls thick enough to block arrows, and a crude escape tunnel hacked into the storage room floor (complete with claw marks and bloodstains on the cramped walls), the place had likely once been the fort of a petty, paranoid warlord. During the khareef, the jungle grew so thick that a screen of greenery hid the house completely, and strange hisses emanated from the surrounding thickets of banana trees. A nearby coconut grove was always cold, too cold, and the crashing waves on the narrow beach sounded like the shrieks of lost souls.

Add the horned stone idol my brother had uncovered while cleaning out the courtyard and you would be correct in assuming locals avoided the place. Which made it perfect for my chief purpose in those years, which was to hide. Less perfect were the endless repairs. Repairs I was required do myself, as I could not bribe workmen from any of the neighboring villages to visit such a haunted abode. The holes in the roof were the worst of them. It was not enough that I had spent my career trying to keep a ship watertight; no, I had to have a house that wanted to be one with the rain and the sea air, a particular curse in the wet season.

"Do you need more rushes, Mama?" my daughter, Marjana, chirped from where she was spinning wool.

"No, little love." I wiped the sweat from my brow, my eyes stinging. "But would you get me some water?"

"Of course!" Marjana dropped her spindle to skip-run away, and I returned to my knots, trying not to despair at the roof's appearance. Between my sailor's stitches and the rushes, it looked less like a roof and more like a reed boat that a shark had devoured and vomited up.

Ever a blessing, Marjana returned with not only a pitcher of water, but a bowl of sliced mango.

"God reward you, my light." I straightened up with care, pinching my brow to keep black spots from dancing before my eyes. House repairs and farming had kept me strong, but my body did not like swiftly moving positions during afternoons so humid it felt as though you could have wrung out the air. I collapsed into a damp hammock strung in the corner and drank directly from the pitcher.

Marjana settled between my feet. "When do you think Grandma and Uncle Mustafa will be back?"

"By sunset, God willing."

"Do you think Auntie Hala will come with them?"

"If she is feeling well enough." Unable to afford a place big enough to host his workshop and his family, my little brother, Mustafa, and his wife, Hala, split their time between her parents' home in Salalah and ours in the hills. But the trip could be an arduous one, and at six months pregnant, with another toddler in tow, Hala was returning less and less.

Marjana wiggled her toes. "If we moved to Salalah, we would get to see her all the time. And I could go to school at the masjid."

The hope in her small face broke my heart. Marjana had been asking about school more often. Though I tried to minimize her ventures to Salalah, my mother was not above spiriting her out for day trips to the market and gossip circles of elderly ladies. "It is cruel to isolate her so, Amina," she would chide. "Marjana blossoms when she is out and about. You cannot let your fears rule her life."

If only my mother knew the depths of my fears. "It is not safe, Jana," I said gently. "Maybe in a few more years."

My daughter stared at me now, a hundred questions in her dark eyes. When she was younger, she would ask them with the relentless curiosity of a child. *Why do we not leave the cliffs? Are there bad people after us? Will they hurt you?* I knew my stammered, evasive answers were never enough, and yet it only made me feel guiltier when she stopped asking them. She seemed too young to have surrendered to fate.

"Why don't we play a game?" I suggested to lift her spirits. Marjana loves her games, inventing her own complicated versions and designing boards and pawns with anything she can get her hands on. "Go find your mancala board."

"Okay!" She beamed, thoughts of school forgotten, and was gone in a flash, her braids bouncing as she raced away.

I pulled off the cloth holding back my hair and mopped my face. A breeze had kicked up, bringing the smell of the sea and rich wet earth more strongly. The khareef was in full swing, patches of light fog cloaking the emerald hilltops. If you have never witnessed the khareef in this part of the world, ah, but it is a wonder. The mountains and valleys undergo an astonishing transformation, rocky cliffs and bone-dry wadis giving way to lush forests and roaring waterfalls. The swiftness of the change and the vivid, ever-present green—a divine hue unlike any other I've witnessed—seems very nearly magical, evidence of God's splendor.

And yet for me, the khareef signified more. The passing of all the seasons did. For if the sea was the heart of our world, the winds were its lifeblood. And when the khareef lifted, so would those winds shift, heralding the beginning of the northeast monsoon. While I labored on this roof, sailors from Kilwa to Zeila were loading the last of the ships to head to Arabia and India with ivory and gold, mangrove poles, and all manner of trinkets; savoring last moments with wives and children. The accountants and overzealous market inspectors of Aden would be absorbed in their tax scrolls, harassing new arrivals if they had anything to declare while the pirate fleets hunkered in Socotra lifted their sails, heading for the unwary and ill protected. On the other side of the ocean, mariners in places such as Cambay and Calicut would be waiting to depart westward, painting the hulls of their sewn ships with fresh layers of pitch and shark oil and checking their sails.

Sailor or clerk, smuggler or trader—this steady calendar has ruled our lives and those of our ancestors since ancient times. They say you can find goods from all over the sea in the ruins of pagan temples and forgotten kingdoms; Indian seal stamps in Bahrain and Chinese glass in Mombasa. Our stories speak of trading cities built and lost before the time of the Prophet, may peace be upon him, and the chants we sing to make ship work pass memorialize the losses of countless perished crossings. My ancestors had attuned their lives to the sea for far too long for me to forget its rhythms.

At least that's what I told myself when it hurt. When watching the winds come and go and not follow them filled my soul with a blazing grief that made me take to my bed. Take to stalking the hills and working the land until my hands bled and sweat poured down my limbs. Until I was too weary to wallow in my memories and despair of never seeing the land recede into watery blue again.

And then Marjana reappeared. And if the grief did not disappear, it did fade. But though her beloved mancala board was in her hands, her gaze was not upon me. She had stopped on the stairs and was looking beyond the edge of the roof.

"Mama . . ." She frowned. "There are people coming up the path."

"People?"

"Strangers."

The word had me on my feet and at her side in the next moment. We did not get strangers. Our location was too remote and removed from the routes connecting Salalah and the coastal villages to attract lost travelers. But Marjana was correct. On the narrow, zigzagging path that cut through the verdant scrubland was a small palanquin being carried by four men. Armed men—they bore swords at their waists. Such precaution was the norm, of course. Bandits and the occasional leopard abound. But these were big men, with a military bearing I did not trust. There were no other cargo animals or people accompanying the palanquin, suggesting the traveler inside intended a short trip.

But a short trip here? Why?

I glanced across the roof. Carefully hidden in a watertight chest was my bow—a gift from a Sohari admirer whose tokens were more appealing than his personality—and a quiver I kept supplied with fresh arrows. The bow is not my weapon of choice, but I am fast with it. Fast enough that I could likely take out two of the men before the others hid. Maybe three.

"Mama?"

Marjana's voice jolted me back to the present. I was not in the world where I shot people first and asked questions later.

I carefully pulled her out of sight. "Stay here and set up the mancala board. I will see what they want."

Her expression was worried. "Should I—"

"You will stay on this roof and not come down until I call you, understand?"

She nodded, still looking a little scared, a sight that made me again contemplate my bow. But I left the weapon where it was, instead picking up the hammer I'd been using to repair the roof. The house was silent as I crept through, the stone walls so thick it was nigh impossible to hear anything beyond them. Despite the hammer in my hand, I briefly considered the blessed iron blade at my waist as I re-covered my hair.

He is gone, I told myself. *Gone. You buried him with your own hands.* Trying to ignore the dread curdling in my gut, I pressed an ear to the barred wooden door.

Whoever was on the other side chose that moment to knock so loud I jumped. But it wasn't the pounding of soldiers preparing to break through. A small band of travelers had simply knocked at my door, a perfectly normal thing to do. I was the one being paranoid.

Keeping the hammer concealed behind my back, I opened the door. "*Yes?*"

Two men stood there, one with his hand raised as if to knock a second time. Slowly his eyes trailed up to meet mine and his mouth opened in a small *o* of surprise. Whether it was my height or my rudeness that took him aback, I did not know. Hopefully one or the other would convince him to leave.

"I . . . peace be upon you," he stammered. "Is this the home of Fatima the Perfumer?"

It was indeed, "the Perfumer" being one of my mother's many attributes. When my family resettled in this land, my mother and brother were anonymous enough to keep their identities. I could not, though it didn't matter. Few people wanted to speak to Umm Marjana, the giant, eccentric widow who rarely left home and prowled the hills like a caged lion.

"My mistress is not in." I was covered in twigs and sweat; perhaps the guise of a gruff, unhelpful servant would make them leave. "I can take a message."

Before the man could reply, the palanquin's curtain was pulled open to reveal its sole inhabitant: a woman swathed in a purple silk jilbab embroidered with delicate opal beads I could tell from a single glance would pay for a new roof. Enough gold bangles to buy another roof and likely all the land I was squatting on ringed her wrists. Though she remained partially hidden in the shadow of the palanquin, she appeared elderly. Her face was veiled, but the hair between her temple and pearled headband was white, her eyes wrinkled with crow's-feet.

Her gaze went from my feet to my head before settling on my face with what looked like satisfaction, as though she had been considering options at the butcher and found a choice sheep. It was a profoundly irritating look and followed up by worse—she began to disembark from the palanquin.

"A message will not do," she announced. Her bearers helped her to her feet.

I moved to block the way. "You should stay in your carriage. The damp air—"

"I find it refreshing." She cocked her head, staring up at me. "My, you *are* tall."

"I—yes," I stammered, uncharacteristically lost for words. The old woman took advantage of my uncertainty to sweep past me and through the door as though she were a sultana entering her own salon. Were it one of her men, I would have slammed their head into the wall and put my blade to their throat for such audacity, but before a frail old woman, I was powerless.

"Sayyida," I tried again. "My lady, please. There has been a mis—"

"You may call me Salima," she called over her shoulder. "And I would be much obliged if you could fetch me a cup of water. Do you mind if my bearers rest in your courtyard?"

I did mind. I minded quite a bit. And yet I could not fathom kicking them out in a way that did not make the situation more suspicious. Guest right was sacred in our land. The moment I saw an old woman stuffed in a cramped palanquin, I should have urged her to come into my home and take respite. Her men were visibly exhausted, with sweat pouring down their faces. An innocent person—a servant, no less—would be falling over themselves to offer relief.

There was also the possibility they would be more vulnerable to attack while resting. I plastered a gracious smile on my face. "Of course not. Please make yourselves comfortable."

It took time to get them settled. I showed the men our well and left them to the shade of the overgrown trees in the courtyard before escorting Salima to our small, sad excuse for a reception room. As we actively avoided entertaining guests, it was not a welcoming place. A steady drip from the leaking roof pinged loudly in a metal tin, and the only light came from a single dusty window. I cleared away sacks of rice and lentils, making a stack of cushions for her to sit upon, and then left to retrieve water and refreshments.

When I returned, Salima had removed her face veil and set aside her jilbab. She appeared about my mother's age, her silvery hair untouched by henna. Though her delicate features were now well lined and flush with exertion, there was no hiding that she must have been a beauty in her youth. She wore a deep blue gown patterned with copper birds and yellow trousers whose ankle hems were so thick with needlework it must have taken a seamstress a year to complete. More gold jewelry, beautifully worked, hung around her neck with ruby ornaments dangling from her ears. From the cut of her clothes to the way she commanded the small room with her presence, everything about this woman spoke of wealth and power far beyond anything I knew.

And far beyond anything that should lead her to seeking out my mother. Granted, in our years here, my mother had cultivated a circle of friends—she always did. She was a survivor, accustomed to her life being hastily uprooted, and she could mend your clothes, paint your hands, and brew up fragrance with a skill that had kept food in my belly since I was small. But we were not remotely in the class of this Salima, who, if she had been inquiring after my mother's skills, would have sent a servant. I set down fruit and water with a lowered head, resisting the urge to study her further.

Salima took the cup, murmuring thanks to God. "When do you expect your mistress back?" she asked after she had slaked her thirst.

"I do not know, Sayyida. It may be very late."

"Is there anyone else in the home?"

My skin prickled. "No. As I said, I am happy to convey a message."

Salima shrugged. "Perhaps later. For now, I prefer your company."

It was not a request I could deny if I wanted to keep up my servile front. "You honor me," I said demurely, cursing internally as I sank to the floor. Even upon her stack of cushions, Salima was still dwarfed by me. I had slipped the hammer into my waistband, the metal head poking reassuringly into the small of my back.

She pulled a small fan from her sleeve and waved it in front of her face. "Muggy day. I was promised that this part of the coast looked like a mirror of Paradise during the khareef, but the *humidity*."

"Where are you coming from?" I asked.

"Aden."

Aden. The most prominent—and notoriously law-abiding—port in the region. "I have heard that Aden puts even our worst heat to shame. Has your family been there long?"

"Nearly thirty years. We are from Iraq originally, but there was more opportunity here." She sighed. "I fear with politics as they are, soon enough my homeland's splendor will live on only in the storytellers of Baghdad."

I clucked my tongue in sympathy. Though I did not intend to confide such a thing to Salima, I suspected my family's maritime history sprouted from similar glory days. My father used to rhapsodize about the splendor of early Baghdad and its Abbasid rulers, when sailors like us would journey from Basrah all the way to China to bring back the silks, books, and spices of a new world, of unknown lands our faith had just started to explore.

But that was long ago. Baghdad was no longer the heart of our world, the city of legend that drew traders and travelers from every distant corner of the ummah. Or perhaps it never had been; the land of my birth had always looked to the sea first, and that sea was *vast*. So vast that it had become uncommon for Arab and Persian sailors to journey beyond India—we did not need to. There were merchants already there, many now Muslim as well, who knew the waters and lands better than us.

Salima motioned to hand her cup back but stumbled. I reached forward to help, and she grabbed my wrist.

"Take care." I gestured to the platter of fruit. "Why don't you eat something?"

"I suppose the journey affected me more than I realized." Salima was still holding my wrist. "Oh my. That must have been a nasty injury."

I followed her gaze. My sleeve had ridden up, revealing the mottled scar that covered much of my right forearm.

"Cooking accident," I lied.

We returned to our seats. But Salima was still staring at me. I could hardly blame her, I present quite a sight. Like many of my class, I have the blood of nearly all who have sailed upon the Indian Ocean. My father's father was an Arab, an orphan who traded pearl-diving for piracy when he stole his first ship, and my father's mother a Gujarati poet-singer who stole his heart, then his purse. My mother's family, though not as scandalous, was no less global, her island of Pemba known for welcoming lost travelers including a number of Chinese mariners, among them her grandfather, who decided taking the shahada and starting a family in a gentle land was better than risking the journey home.

I have a mix of their features and speak enough of their languages that I should have been able to blend in a great many lands. Except I do not blend. Anywhere. I have traveled to more countries than I can remember, yet have never met another woman approaching my height and only a bare handful of men who can best my strength. I may have been retired, but I did what I could to maintain a formidable form—trading sparring and rowing for beating the land into orchards and swimming against the waves every morning.

Salima popped a slice of coconut into her mouth. "Your father must have been a giant. I suspect you could likely bear my palanquin all on your own."

What a compliment to note my worth as it compares to carting her rich ass around. "I was taller than my father," I deadpanned. "But should it become necessary, I would be more than happy to remove you from the house."

Her mouth quirked with what looked like triumph, as if she had enjoyed finally pulling a rude retort from me. It was unsettling—because for the first time, I noticed that there was something a bit familiar about Salima. The way her large brown eyes glinted with amusement and the set of her thin lips. Why did it feel as though I had seen her face before?

She leaned back on her cushion. "This is a very . . . interesting home. But in such a secluded location. Does your mistress not get lonely?"

The roof chose that moment to begin leaking again, water pinging loudly into the pan. "I believe she enjoys the solitude," I said with as much grace as I could muster.

There was a timid knock on the door, and Marjana peered in. "Mama?"

Oh, for the love of God . . . the one time this girl decides to disobey. "Jana, I told you to stay upstairs," I reminded her swiftly, making a shooing motion.

"I know, but I brought food." She lifted a tray with a pitcher of juice and fresh banana fritters. "It sounded like we had guests."

And just like that, my lie began to crumble.

We had guests. The ownership in that phrase and this well-dressed little girl calling me Mama.

Sure enough, Salima turned her shrewd gaze to Marjana, still standing in the doorway. "Is this your daughter?" she asked.

"Yes." I could scarcely deny it; the resemblance between us was obvious. But I tried to salvage the situation, fixing an intent gaze on Marjana. "Thank you for the juice, beloved. This is Sayyida Salima. She came here looking for Lady Fatima, but I have told her the family is away for the foreseeable future. She is just resting a bit before moving on."

"Ah, well, we shall discuss the issue of moving on later . . ." Salima beckoned to Marjana. "Come in, dear one, join us."

Marjana stared at me, confusion blossoming in her eyes. At ten years old, she knew only the vague outlines of what had led our family to live so isolated. She knew that I had sailed many places, that I had done work that led to me wanting to avoid certain people. She knew that in an emergency, there were hiding places she was supposed to go.

I had not told her more. It is a difficult thing to destroy your child's innocence. To tell her the mother she adores is not the "best mama in the world," but a real person who has done terrible, unforgivable things.

My mouth had gone dry. "Sit, Jana," I managed, patting the spot beside me. Salima had commanded it, and no servant would disobey someone so obviously noble.

Marjana set down the platter with trembling hands before folding herself beside me, her body warm against my leg. Salima was studying her with a fascination that made me want to bludgeon the old woman.

"Well, isn't this quite pretty," Salima remarked, reaching out to touch Marjana's belt. "Did you make it? It's so colorful."

Marjana nodded and blushed, running her fingers over the bright blue and green stripes she'd chosen over the traditional red and black. "I like weaving."

"And you are clearly very talented for one so young. It must run in the family." Salima glanced back at me. "Where is your husband from?"

Somewhere I wish I could send you. I did not like Salima's strange little smirk, and it was taking every bit of self-control I had not to snatch her hand away from my daughter's waist. "My village."

"Oh?" She examined Marjana again. "Your daughter is rather fair. I would have assumed your husband a foreigner you met during your travels."

My heart skipped. "I have not traveled very much."

"Is that so?" Salima met my gaze with a disbelieving lift of her brows. "That seems unlikely for a nakhudha."

Well, fuck.

"*Nakhudha?*" I laughed a high, fake laugh, praying the word had been a misstep. The elderly make such mistakes all the time, right? "I fear you must have the wrong family, Sayyida. Neither my mistress nor her son have much affinity for the sea."

"And your mistress's daughter? Amina, is it not? I heard she was a giant. Dark, with her teeth filed into gold-capped fangs and a scar covering much of her right arm, scorched there by naft." Salima tilted her head. "The stories got your size right, if the teeth seem an exaggeration. A pity. I should have liked to see such a thing."

Not an elderly misstep, then.

Another time, Salima's characterization might have irked me. But in that moment, I did not give a shit how a bunch of breathless male writers had described me. Marjana had pressed closer, giving me a nervous look. In the profile of her face, I could see a shadow of the baby she once was, and a surge of something primal, fierce, and very capable of throttling Sayyida Salima flooded through me.

I smiled—widely enough to reveal the gold incisor that had begun that idiotic rumor. "I think this visit has lasted long enough. It is clear our climate is affecting your mind and making you say all sorts of things that are very dangerous."

"On the contrary, I feel quite fine, God be praised," Salima retorted with a challenging air. "Surely you would not wish to turn away such a respected guest. That is the sort of rudeness that makes people talk. And what would your daughter think?"

Salima winked at Marjana, and I snapped. People have this idea of mothers, that we are soft and gentle and sweet. As though the moment my daughter was laid on my breast, the phrase *I would do anything* did not take on a depth I could have never understood before. This woman thought to come into my home and threaten my family in front of my child?

She must not have heard the right stories about Amina al-Sirafi.

"Jana." I touched her hand. "Go upstairs and set up the mancala board. This will not take long."

Her frightened gaze darted between Salima and me. "Mama, are you su—"

"Now, please."

Marjana quickly stood, offered a murmured blessing to Salima, and then slipped through the door.

She was barely out of the room before Salima turned back to me. "I take it we can dispense with the ruse now, Captain al-Sirafi."

I pressed my hands together to stop myself from breaking the pitcher of juice over her head. "I have attempted to correct your misconceptions. I will be clearer. Get out."

"I have proof." She removed a ragged sheaf of papers from her cloak. "Do you think I pulled these details from the air? My son served on your ship and wrote all about you." She thrust the papers at me. "Take a look."

Her *son*? Who in God's name could that have been? I had sailed with dozens of men in my time, but only a few were ever privy to information about my family. On the chance they were a test, I made no move to touch the letters. Tension grew between us, interrupted only by the ping of the leak and the warbles of birds beyond the compound's wall as I contemplated my options. I had little doubt I could make swift, silent work of a single old woman. Her men would be more difficult, but they were weary, napping unaware in the courtyard. I did not relish the prospect—it had been years since I'd taken a life.

However, they had come into my home. They threatened my family.

But Marjana will know. My daughter was no fool. She would hear the death cries, watch from the roof as I removed the bodies. Was I ready to be a killer in my child's eyes? Ready to greet my mother when she returned home with grave dirt on my hands?

Salima called me out. "Judging from the murderous gleam in your face, I will assume I found the right person, but you can put such notions to rest. I made copies of both the letters and my suspicions. If I do not return to Aden by the end of the month, my aides have messages ready to go out to all your enemies."

I scoffed. "My *enemies*? Am I a rival to the caliph that I have foes willing to travel into the hills for some supposed lady pirate on the word of an old woman's ragged letters?"

"For a supposed lady pirate, no. For Amina al-Sirafi? Absolutely. Do not underestimate your notoriety, nakhudha. You seem to have the singular accomplishment of making an enemy not only of every other pirate cartel, but of merchants and sultans from Sofala to Malabar. Why, the emir of Hormuz still has a bounty on your head for the horses you stole—"

"I did not steal anything. I recovered merchandise for a client."

"And the incident at the customshouse in Basrah?"

"Fires start all the time. Nothing to do with me."

"And I don't imagine *you* were the one who poisoned the feast at the trade talks in Mombasa to rob the attendees while they were stuck at the latrines?"

"Never been to Mombasa. Is it nice?"

"Fine." Salima's eyes lit with annoyance. "Would you like a more recent example? Rumor is two boys from Aden recently visited this area only to be abducted in the middle of the night by a monstrous fishwife who dragged them into a haunted lagoon, threatened them with a sea djinn, and refused to take them ashore until they paid her off. A woman who had gold in her teeth and fought like a man."

Oh, is *that* what happened in the lagoon? "You really have quite the obsession with a common dental practice."

The response seemed to break her.

"I know who you are!" Salima shook her letters more furiously. "I tracked you down through your family once. I can do it again and so could others if they learn what I know."

I cracked my fingers. "You need to stop talking about my family like that. When you do, it sounds as though you are threatening us. That makes me very unreasonable, Sayyida."

Salima eyed me like a vaguely irritated hawk. "I have no interest in threatening you. I want to *hire* you."

"*Hire* me?" I assessed again Salima's lustrous silks and the sultan's ransom she wore in jewelry. "What in God's name for?"

She folded her hands neatly over her lap. "My granddaughter was kidnapped. I need you to get her back."

There was a waiting look on her face as if my sole duty in life was dealing with stolen granddaughters. Which I should clarify is untrue. Kidnappings have never been my specialty—either the taking or the returning. I have tried the taking, but no ransom is worth listening to the whining complaints of trussed-up rich folk.

Yet intrigue stalked me, and I hated myself for becoming its prey. "Kidnapped?" I repeated.

"Yes, kidnapped. Two months ago tomorrow." The first hint of a crack appeared in Salima's flinty eyes. She worried the hem of her shayla, crumpling the fine fabric in her fingers. "She was taken from our home in the middle of the night."

"Do you not have guards?"

"Of course I have guards: you just met them. But her kidnappers managed to avoid detection."

Damn, maybe killing the men in the courtyard would be easier than I thought. "How old is she?"

Her expression softened. "Sixteen."

Sixteen. A child, aye, still in the flush of girlhood. It struck too close, and for a moment, I thought of my daughter snatched by strangers in the dark. I imagined her screaming for me, scared out of her mind. I forced the thought away, into that awful corner of a parent's mind where dwell the incomprehensible fates you know would destroy you if made real. This granddaughter was not my concern. But given how determined Salima had been in tracking me down, I thought it best to let her speak.

"Have you had any word?" I asked. "Any demands?"

"No." Hatred bloomed in Salima's face. "But I know who took her."

"Who?"

"Falco Palamenestra." She all but spat the name. If it was a name, because it sounded like foreign nonsense to me, and I speak a half-dozen languages.

"Balamanatrah?" I repeated.

"*Palamenestra*. He is a Frank, God curse them. A former mercenary."

"A *Frank*?" I was not unaware of the wars raging in the north, but I'd never heard of any of the Franks making their way to our lands. "Here?" I asked, flabbergasted. "Did he get extremely lost on his way to Palestine?"

"No. He made it to Palestine but apparently after fighting for both sides—a fact he was quite proud of—it is personal treasure he desires now. He has been traveling the coast, seeking any rare items he can get his hands on."

I frowned in confusion. "How do you know all this?"

"Because he sought me out. My family . . ." The noblewoman paused, seeming to choose her next words with care. "We are fortunate to own a great many artifacts and unique texts from an earlier age. We are normally loath to part with them. But occasionally when the right buyer comes along—"

"You really charged into my home calling me a pirate and yet were willing to sell family heirlooms to some Frankish mercenary?" I nodded rudely at her jewels. "You do not appear hard-pressed for money."

Salima's mouth tightened into an indignant line. "I had no idea who he was. He had a local agent set up the audience under an assumed name, and when I realized he was not only a Frank, but a madman, I had him thrown out." Her voice turned bitter. "I should have had him arrested."

"Why didn't you? Wouldn't someone in a position of authority want to know a Frankish mercenary was sniffing around Aden?" Granted, I had not kept up on politics during my retirement—I generally operate under the principle that all politicians are corrupt, lying dogs—but I *did* have a foggy idea that the rulers of Aden hated Franks. Or were allied with people who hated Franks. Or perhaps had yet to strike a business partnership with the Franks advantageous enough to be worth forgetting the Muslim blood shed during their incursions. Like I said, I don't think highly of politicians. At least we pirates are honest about our goals.

Salima sniffed. "I realize respectability might not rank high in your world, but surely you can understand me not wanting to bring news that I had entertained a possible Frankish spy interested in the occult items my ancestors were fond of hoarding to the attention of the authorities."

The ancestors sounded fascinating, but no matter. "I take it he wants those items as a ransom for your granddaughter?"

"No. As I said there has been no demand for ransom. There . . . there has been no contact at all."

"Then what makes you certain he kidnapped her? She might have simply run away."

"She would never run away," Salima said adamantly. "Dunya is a good girl. She was happy at home."

"Happy sixteen-year-olds are rarer than just kings." I sighed. "Sayyida, it has been two months without word? Without anyone seeing where she went? I do not mean to suggest this lightly, but if he took her in revenge—"

"She is not dead."

I waited, but Salima did not elaborate on her words, and that itself spoke volumes. In a world such as ours, where disease steals away the healthy with little warning and princes play out violent dreams of power with our blood, we rarely speak with such certainty. We invoke God's mercy, couch our hopes and fears with prayer and faith, often the only things we can rely on.

But would I not speak the same if it were Marjana? I would burn down the world to save my daughter, keelhaul any who would hurt her, and do it all until I knew without a shadow of a doubt that she was no longer with us.

Then I'd kill everyone.

"You are clearly well resourced," I said more gently. "Have you asked the governor—"

Salima instantly stiffened. "No. Not the governor. I-I dare not. My husband is dead, and I have no one I trust to press my claim discreetly. If the truth got out, it could ruin Dunya's life."

"It might save her life," I argued, but Salima looked only more stubborn. God save me from nobles and their daft ideas of honor. "To clarify, you came all the way from Aden to badger a retired bandit into investigating a kidnapping you have no proof occurred at the hands of man who has not claimed it. Sayyida, I am sympathetic. I truly am. But I am not in the business of rescuing—"

"You find things," Salima interrupted. "And more important . . . you *get away*. People still trade stories of the wily Amina al-Sirafi. The Chinese envoys who fell asleep on their grand junk to wake up drifting in dinghies, their ship and cargo gone. The treasury at Cambay, plundered under the eyes of at least a dozen soldiers . . ." A little desperation swept her face, and there it was again, the odd sense I'd seen her features before. "Please. I can pay you handsomely."

"I do not need your money."

She looked pointedly around at my creaking, crumbling reception room. A few of the rushes I'd used to mend the roof had fallen through the ceiling, creating a damp bird's-nest-like clump on the floor. The dripping of the leak was softer, but only because the water was now high enough to absorb the blow.

"With all respect, nakhudha . . . you do not appear to have found great fortune in your retirement."

I glowered. "I do not need more *enemies*. You gave me a list of people who would rejoice at the sight of my body hanging in Aden's bay and I am to add a Frankish mercenary to the lot?" I picked up the tray Marjana had brought and stood, meaning to dismiss her. A stab of pain went through my right knee; the ghost of an old injury reminding me of my age in case I was getting any fanciful ideas.

"Surely you could ask around," Salima persisted, her voice cracking. "Falco mentioned having a ship. He would have needed sailors, no? Your class of people. Could you at least come with me to Aden? Ask your compatriots if they know anything?"

"I cannot get involved," I insisted, the heartbreak in her eyes nagging at my soul. "I am sorry, truly. But I would be endangering the lives of my own family if I returned to that world."

Salima grabbed my sleeve. "And what if you never had to worry about that world again? If I paid you enough to start a *new* life for your family, a more financially stable one?"

I shook my head. "There is no amount—"

"A million dinars."

The tray clattered to the ground. I was not even aware of dropping it, the inconceivable number Salima had uttered sending my head into a maelstrom.

"You— you cannot have that kind of money," I stammered. "A *million* dinars?"

"A million dinars. *When* you return Dunya safely," Salima added more firmly. "I will liquidate every one of my family's assets if necessary."

By the Most High. I took a deep breath, my heart racing. A million dinars was a life-changing sum. My family would never have to worry about money again. My *great-grandchildren* would never have to worry about money again. We could buy an estate somewhere far away and the staff and guards to keep it. And Marjana . . .

Marjana would never have to worry about money. About a leaky roof or her next meal; about security or needing to bow to the wishes of some rich woman who used her wealth like a cudgel. Even after I was gone. No matter how long she might live.

No matter what she might become.

Salima must have seen the temptation in my expression. She pressed further. "Surely you realize the money is not all you might win. Falco has been plundering for years; he must have his own treasures. I am not a pirate, nakhudha, and have no interest in stolen loot, only Dunya's safe return. Whatever you recover would be yours."

A million dinars *and* an entire ship of plunder. As if a cruel taunt, a breeze played through the narrow window, smelling sweetly of the ocean. God, it had been so long since I had been at sea. The prospect of standing on the *Marawati* again, of spilling riches before the awed eyes of my crew while making this Frank rue the day he had ventured south and taken one of our girls . . . It was tempting. It was *tantalizing*.

It was *me*. For I have always had a gambler's soul, finding prizes tinged with risk utterly irresistible. But my gambler's soul had gotten innocent men killed. My gambler's soul was now so heavy with crimes that God would have to be most merciful indeed if I was to escape hellfire.

"I cannot," I said hoarsely.

Salima stared at me for a long moment before her expression shifted. "You have not asked his name."

The change in topic threw me. "What?"

She hesitated another moment, like someone forced to play a pawn they had wished to hold back. "My son who served on your ship, the one who wrote about you. You have not asked his name."

No, I suppose I hadn't; though in my defense, "Frankish bandits have kidnapped my granddaughter and I'll pay a wealthy kingdom's annual revenue to get her back" had been rather distracting. "What is his name?"

Salima's gaze did not leave my face. "Asif al-Hilli."

And there it was.

I sucked in a breath. I should have known this change in tack was a trap, and yet not even I was so talented a liar to steel my reaction. *Asif.* A decade later, his name was still a blow. God, no wonder Salima looked familiar.

"I take it you remember him," Salima said stiffly.

"Aye." I struggled to compose myself. "So Dunya . . . she is his daughter?"

"Yes."

Oh, Asif, you bastard. "I-I did not know. He never spoke of a daughter."

She drew back in obvious hurt. "I suppose ignoring our existence made it easier for Asif to run off to sea."

At the charge, a tug of old loyalty sparked in me. "The home Asif spoke of was not a happy one, Sayyida. Your husband—"

"My husband is dead." Salima was trembling now, not bothering to hide her grief. "And Asif was not a child when he left us. He was a married man with responsibilities. His wife died when Dunya was a toddler. I have raised her ever since."

Dunya. The story had been easier to bear when she remained a stranger. A tragedy, no doubt, but tragedies happen. Now she was Asif's daughter. An orphaned girl left fatherless—at my hand.

You owe it to him to chase down a few contacts. It is the least you could do. And honestly, I doubted some Frank could have swept into Aden, stolen a noble girl, and sailed off for parts unknown without people noticing. *My* kind of people, as the Sayyida had so tactlessly pointed out.

"I am old," I said, reminding myself as much as Salima. "Too old for these sorts of adventures."

She lifted her chin. "I've two decades at least on you."

"I am retired. I have no ship, no crew . . ."

"There is no way that the Amina al-Sirafi of my son's letters has rid herself of her ship."

Perceptive old bat. "Sayyida . . ."

"Please. You are my last hope." Salima suddenly looked frailer, which was worse than if she had reverted to threatening me; I hate seeing women reduced to such straits. Asif's ragged letters shivered between her fingers.

I cleared my throat. "Let me see those letters."

Salima handed them over. I took the letters and walked to the corner of the reception room where the sunlight was brightest. Asif's mark at the bottom was instantly familiar, as was his neat, looping handwriting. My own writing is awful, and he'd been a good scribe.

He had wanted to be so much more than a scribe. He had wanted so, *so* much; the kind of wanting that is dangerous. The kind of wanting that draws predators like blood in the water draws sharks.

"His letters—" Salima spoke up. "Just before he died, they got . . . stranger . . ." She trailed off, probably hoping I would fill in the rest: that

I would have answers to the questions that must have plagued her for the past decade.

But there is no power in this world that will make me tell Asif al-Hilli's mother what really happened to him.

I should have turned her away. To this day, I do not know my own heart enough to understand what drove my response. Was it the unexpected chance to seize one last adventure and win riches that would secure Marjana's shaky future? To do right by the family of the young man I doomed? To avoid Salima's wrath and being turned over to a list of enemies?

I suspect only God knows. And perhaps, on the Day of Judgment, I shall too.

Tossing down the letters belonging to the friend whose soul I lost forever, I looked his mother in the eye. "I will give you four months. You have presented me with extraordinarily little to go on, and I will not chase rumors forever. Four months and a hundred thousand dinars, regardless of whether I am successful. I expect ten thousand dinars to be paid to my family before I leave and an additional ninety thousand if I learn where Dunya is being held. If I return her, I get the rest."

It was a ludicrous counteroffer. I could lie, claim the girl was being held anywhere, and vanish with a hundred thousand dinars. Perhaps I even hoped Salima would turn me down and quash the dangerous dreams swirling in my heart.

She did not. "Four months, nakhudha. I will hold you to that."

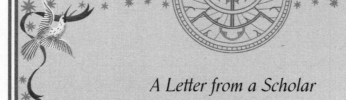

A Letter from a Scholar

We made excellent time out of Cambay, a most prosperous, gentle city. Many goods can be found there, the textile market offering everything from cloth of gold and silk brocade to block-printed cotton in the most vivid hues.

But on our second day at sea, calamity struck. We were besieged by a pirate vessel taking advantage of the dawn fog and soon boarded by the scoundrels, who laughed and spewed invective that would make a God-fearing man pierce his tongue. If a trader of these waters has not yet had an encounter with such outlaws, they count themselves blessed. They are the most violent of all the bandit classes, comprised of thieves, oath breakers, adulterers, poisoners, and con men. Their bathing habits are abominable, their temperaments cursed, and their language an incomprehensible babble of every tongue spoken along the ocean's shores. Though some among the pirates make a weak effort to cling to the path of righteousness, the guidelines of our noble religion are among the first to be cast aside; with prayer irregular and tortuous twists of justification made to consume that which has been forbidden.

This rabble managed to distinguish itself in an even more scandalous way, for they were captained by a female by the name of Amina al-Sirafi, who is gaining notoriety in these parts. We were already negotiating our surrender when it came to light that the nakhudha of the enemy vessel was a woman, for she was built as broadly as a blacksmith and dressed in the turban and robes of a man. She was dark, her origins nebulous, as they are for many of the lower classes of seafolk who care not for the nobility of lineage.

The revelation that al-Sirafi was female caused a great deal of turmoil, as many of the men on my ship protested that they would rather die than suffer the dishonor of surrendering to a woman. After much discussion, during which the rogues threatened to torch us with naft and eat our roasted flesh—may God curse them!— we finally surrendered, losing most of our cargo and all of our weapons.

We had with us a pair of elderly ladies intending to make hajj. They were mercifully left untouched by the pirates but seemed impressed by al-Sirafi's contemptuous wiles, so much that their chaperone wisely kept the women confined for the remainder of the trip to cleanse their hearts. The rest of our journey passed in a more peaceable manner—thanks and praise to He whose Kingdom lasts forever and whose protection is unparalleled!

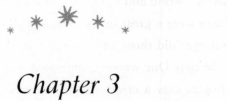

Chapter 3

Sunset found me packing. Lady Salima had hired a cutter to get us to Aden as quickly as possible, but I had to meet her in Salalah early the next morning. Speed would be of the essence in everything we did. If Salima's fears were correct and Dunya had been in the hands of this Frank for nearly two months, he could be long gone. My contacts were good, but the steady stream of trade and pilgrimage ships along our coasts move people quickly. I could only pray Falco had made enough of an impression in Aden to provoke rumors amongst its sailors and laborers.

My mother had put my clothes, my weapons, my tools—all that made me the infamous Amina al-Sirafi—into storage, and unearthing the woman I used to be, carefully tucked and folded away by another's hand, was disorienting. I had once delighted in color and flash, known by reputation to traipse about in whatever royal silks, meltingly thin muslins, and silver headdresses I had recently plundered. Part of it was about cultivating the confidence I needed to survive my chosen profession—a little madness goes a long way in convincing men that you might stab them if they step out of line.

But the rest of it? I had been *freed*. It was a life of banditry born out of tragedy, yes. But in choosing it, I had destroyed any hope of future respectability and was happy for it. Why not wear stolen pearls and a sailor's loincloth? Marry an oarsman I barely knew because he was ach-

ingly handsome and I wanted to fuck him? Drink stolen wine meant for a
sultan across the world and fight duels at midnight?

Well. There were a great many reasons I should *not* have done those
things, *no longer* did those things, and wince when I pray for forgiveness from the only One whose compassion is that encompassing. But as
I ran my fingers over a crimson robe embroidered with clashing green
sunbursts, the sweeter moments returned to me. The cloth still smelled
of sea salt and oil, recalling coir ropes glistening with ocean spray, black
bitumen-painted hulls, and the melodies of sailors against the beat of a
barrel drum.

Salima is paying for your discretion, remember? Not your strolling
about in bloodred robes and flashing a gold-toothed grin. Reluctantly I
set aside the bright garments, selecting plainer options. Then I turned my
attention to far more important matters.

The hinges of my weapons trunk opened with an oiled whisper. My
grandfather's khanjar—the hooked dagger he wore until the day he
died—greeted my eye first. It was a dagger meant for a pirate, its ivory
handle carved into the snarling countenance of a ruby-eyed leopard. His
career even wilder than mine, my grandfather had been known as the
"Sea Leopard," a nickname in which he had taken pride. The two of us
had made an odd pairing—the skinny little girl who couldn't stay still and
the half-blind pirate crippled from a hard life at sea—but we'd been terribly close. My grandfather was the only one who had patience with me, the
one who'd had me jump up and down on banana leaf mats or tie endless
knots of ropes when I couldn't contain the frenetic energy pulsing in my
blood. He talked nonstop, relating not only adventure tales but teaching
me everything he knew about sailing.

It must have seemed harmless at the time—a bored old man chattering nonsense to a girl who'd never need such skills—but as I've grown
older, I wondered if he'd seen something the rest of my family hadn't. If
he'd watched my father struggle to break away from piracy into a more

respectable position, a dream that only added to our debts, and quietly groomed me to one day step into my family's true vocation.

I'll never know, but thank God he did. I pressed the khanjar to my heart, murmuring a prayer for his soul. Beneath the khanjar was my sword, a stolen Damascene beauty, and my shield, a gift from the only husband with whom I parted on good terms. They both needed some care: polishing and new bindings on the grips. But that was work I could do while traveling to Aden, the sight of which might disincline others from bothering me.

It was at the exact moment my arms were laden with weaponry that my mother burst in.

She took one look at me, inhaled like an arrow being drawn back, and shouted, *"Have you lost your mind?"*

I set the weapons down. "Peace be upon you, Amma."

She glared. "Do not wish me peace and then have me arrive home to news you are off to chase Franks. What is this Marjana is saying about a stranger from Aden hiring you?"

I sighed. Marjana's sharp hearing and inability to engage in even the slightest duplicity was a dangerous combination. Her father might have been the most treacherous creature I'd ever met, but Marjana cannot lie to save her life. My mother was still standing in the doorway, dressed in black traveling clothes. Though she and Salima were likely near in age, my mother had none of the noblewoman's frailty. She was tall like me; thin but tough as steel, as if the years had boiled away all weakness in a way that made her only more impressive.

And intimidating—even to her fully grown former pirate of a daughter. I glanced past her shoulder. "Where is Mustafa?"

"Back in Salalah. Hala was not feeling well, so they decided to spend the night with her parents."

A small blessing. I did not wish ill-health on my pregnant sister-in-law but knew my little brother well enough to know he would have sided with our mother in the battle to come.

My mother crossed her arms over her chest, casting a meaningful glance at the packed saddlebag and pile of weapons. "Explain yourself, daughter."

I made—I will always claim—a valiant effort to do so.

"The stranger from Aden is the mother of one of my late crewmen. Her son sailed on the *Marawati* for many years, and we were close. She came because she needs my help . . ." Not wanting to worry my family, I decided against mentioning that Salima had originally threatened me, instead offering the least worrisome version of a Frankish kidnapping I could manage. "All the Sayyida requests is that I return with her to Aden and ask some questions of my old contacts."

"Ask questions about the whereabouts of one of the butchers of Palestine and Syria, a foreign mercenary who has managed to make his way to our land?" Genuine fear colored my mother's face. "Absolutely not. The Franks are animals, Amina. Animals who leave nothing but slaughter and ash in their wake."

I'd feared this sort of reaction. My mother *did* stay up-to-date on politics, and she had very strong, very personal opinions on the wars in the north. She'd been a girl when Jerusalem fell, and stories of Frankish atrocities and pleas for assistance from survivors and refugees had carried far in the scholarly and religious circles her family frequented. Indeed, they'd struck such a note that her beloved elder brother had been moved to answer the call for jihad. He'd been in Palestine less than a year before he was killed—not while saving Muslim lives, but as a pawn in a local power struggle between so-called Muslim princes taking advantage of the chaos to expand their own territories. (See? This is why I don't trust politicians.)

On my part, I had never met a Frank; theirs was a world far away from mine. Highbrow sorts often spoke of them as backward barbarians, and I knew their attacks made northerners nervous because those attacks *were* increasing. Nearly every local merchant with a far-flung family had stories of relatives forced to flee Frankish incursions. First, cities in al-Andalus began to fall. Then Sicily. Their various marches through the land of the Rum, past Constantinople and into the House of Islam for a city the Franks claimed was theirs. A land they said Muslims, Jews, and misguided local Christians had profaned, as though it wasn't filled with families shortly to be erased by their bloody hands.

Now, I am not ignorant of war, of conquest. Kingdoms rise and fall and are swallowed and spit out in different shapes so often that at times, I am genuinely uncertain to whom I would owe taxes if I cared about such a thing. But the people typically remain. Why would we not? There is more profit to be made in us living and paying tribute and trading all the nice luxury goods new rulers desire. It is not clean. There is death, almost always paid by those who have no choice, and there is sacking. But as a people, we endure.

That is not what happened when the Franks arrived.

The first invasion was decades ago, and the bloodletting in Jerusalem and Antioch remains of a scale that still haunts. Their leaders were not content to take over as figureheads; instead, their armies put to the sword entire surrendered populations and roasted women and children on spits. The Franks were said to have barricaded the Jewish population in their temple, where they prayed to God and brought their babies, and set it ablaze; to trail Muslim blood in the Haram al-Sharif and host pigs in its sacred corridors. There are even whispers they tortured and ate the victims of Maarat al-Numan when that city finally fell.

It is a brutality I do not care to try to understand. Not at the hands of anyone. Maybe it's because I'm a criminal with no political loyalties . . . or maybe it's because I come from the class of people who'd be left to die while their leaders fled. I have no doubt in their faraway homelands, lands rumored to be harsh and cold and unforgiving, there are thousands of people who are concerned only with putting food in their children's bellies, people who would be horrified to learn what those of their creed did. I have traveled widely enough that I take everything written about "foreigners" with doubt and know better than to judge a community by their worst individuals.

But the Frank who visited Salima boasting how he'd fought on both sides? That's a man with blood on his hands. A man who might now have Asif's daughter.

But I was never going to convince my mother of the righteousness of fighting Franks, not after what happened to her brother. So I said the only thing I could: "Salima is offering a million dinars for the girl's return."

My mother went still with shock. "Impossible."

"I said the same, but she promised to liquidate her estate if necessary. Theirs is one of those old Iraqi families, the ones who have been rich since the days of Harun al-Rashid. She has ten thousand dinars waiting in Salalah to be paid upon my departure. A hundred thousand if I learn where the girl is being kept. That is not money we can turn away."

My mother's face clouded in suspicion. "It could be a lie. All of it. Besides, first you said you merely intended to ask a few questions of your contacts. Now you speak of stealing the girl back?"

Damn, I should have known she would catch that. I raised my hands in a gesture I hoped conveyed reassurance rather than surrender.

"Amma, I have no desire for a fight. If I am blessed to find this Frank and he is keeping Dunya in a situation I cannot easily pluck her from, I will sell that information to Salima and walk away. With a *hundred thousand* dinars. I am long overdue for a check on the *Marawati* anyway. I will go to Aden, ask a few questions, and return a wealthy woman."

My mother gave me a level look. "The last time you went to check on the *Marawati*, you ran off to become a criminal and I did not see your face for fifteen years."

"This is not like that," I tried to argue. "I swear."

But my mother wasn't listening. Instead she turned to pace the floor, the open window catching her gaze. I'm not certain my mother realizes how often she stares off in the direction of the sea. Perhaps after spending years waiting for her loved ones to return, it became instinctual.

"I should have gone back to Pemba after your father died," she said softly. This was how my mother's regrets always began, with her wishing she had returned to the parents who disowned her for marrying him. "I should have tried."

"Amma, it has been decades," I said gently. "We would have lost the *Marawati*. And I do not regret my career."

She spun back on me. "How can you *not* regret it? I might have given you a normal life. Instead, you have blood on your hands, crimes on your soul, and men on every shore spreading rumors so vile I cannot even speak them aloud. Men who would do anything to hurt you." My mother looked torn between protectiveness and throttling me herself as she wrung her hands. "God curse that grandfather of yours. Him and all his stories."

Without my grandfather's stories, we would have been destitute. I would have never had Marjana, my greatest blessing. But my mother and I had been arguing about my path since the morning I left at sixteen to beg mercy from my father's creditors and instead stole the ship and cargo intended to pay his debts. I did not wish to resume such quarrels now.

Especially when the truth was that we were struggling. That may surprise you. I know the stories tell of an Amina al-Sirafi who plundered treasure ships and retired to a golden castle. But the thing about fame is that it often rests on lies. I never knew wealth. I knew *comfort*; I knew being able to ensure my family had a solid roof (once), enough to eat, and a good education and apprenticeship for my brother. But boats are expensive to maintain, particularly when you chase smuggling jobs instead of steady clients. I paid my crew well, both because it was my responsibility as their nakhudha and because I needed to make damn sure they stayed happy with the female captain who carried a price on her head. We had fabulous scores and adventures aplenty, but I was careful not to overstep.

There was also the gambling, but the less said about that the better. I am reformed.

If I had retired with more forethought, I might have set up proper investments instead of paying off my men, handing over my ship, and walking away with no plan. But such laments can join a long list of regrets. And that was the avenue I settled on now, knowing my mother to be more clear-headed when it came to our survival.

"Amma, we are not in a position to turn this money away. Tinbu only takes legitimate jobs with the *Marawati* now, and that income isn't enough to sustain a family. We farm land that could be taken away at any moment and have made a home in a house we have no rights to." I gestured to the crumbling roof. "Even that is coming apart around us. With the new baby . . ."

"We will find a way," my mother insisted. "We have survived far worse. God provides."

"And He has! He has provided us with Salima and a fortune that could change our lives! Amma, the amount she is offering just for information . . . a *hundred* thousand dinars. We could buy Mustafa a house and workshop in Salalah to get his business off the ground. We could hire proper tutors for the kids and get them into any profession they want. They could be doctors, they could be scholars, they could thrive in ways we never could. You could *rest*, instead of breaking your back in the garden." My God, it hurt to even say all these things aloud, the ambitions and dreams I tried to deny blossoming to light in my heart. "Amma, we could be stable. We could have security, real security. Marjana would never have to worry about money. She would never have to worry about *anything*."

"Marjana would have less to worry about in the future if you would let her live in the present. If you would allow her go to school and meet people outside our family!" she burst out. "Amina, this woman has filled your head with such fantasies that you do not see the risks. Why do you think she is offering so much money?"

I ignored the first part—my mother had no idea the extent of my worries when it came to Marjana—and answered what I could. "Because Salima is desperate to get her granddaughter back in a way that maintains her reputation. Rich people, Amma? They aren't like us. They throw as much money as they can at a problem, assuming the greater the amount, the more they can rely on it to protect them. It usually does," I added, a bit more bitterly.

My mother stared at me, her dark gaze both worried and furious. "And if something goes wrong? You . . . Amina, you were *broken* when you finally returned. You barely spoke. You barely ate. You would lay in bed all day and stare at the wall. You were not the daughter who had written so assuredly throughout all those years."

My mouth went dry. "I-I had just had a baby. I was exhausted."

"It went beyond having a baby. I know you. Something happened out there, and you were never the same. For a long time, I assumed . . ." My mother had been crossing the room but suddenly stopped, seeming to startle. "Salima's son . . . is he Marjana's father? Is that the reason—"

"No!" But she had struck close, and it was difficult not to react, my heart perilously near to being laid bare. For something *did* happen. But it wasn't something I could ever confide if I wanted my mother to look upon me the same. "Marjana is not Asif's daughter. But he died on my ship, and it has weighed on my soul. I owe this to his family."

"Money and honor, what fine motivations," she said acidly. "How carefully you have constructed this argument. So that any concerns I express will sound like the fretting of an old woman. As though I do not know how often you polish your weapons and pour over Tinbu's letters." The anger was gone from her voice, replaced by the same sadness with which Salima had spoken of Asif. "As though you haven't been looking for an opportunity to leave us for years."

I dropped my gaze, ashamed. My mother was not entirely wrong. My mind was already on the *Marawati*, my blood rising with an excitement I had not felt in years. I was not doing this just for Asif. But I wasn't doing this on a lark either, and for a moment I urgently wanted to tell her the truth, to divulge my fears for Marjana to the person I respected most in this world. The person I so desperately did not want to think I was a terrible mother for embarking on such a dangerous quest.

But I could not.

I took a deep breath, clasping my hands behind my back and steadying myself as though I were already standing before my crew. "Amma, I love you. I respect your opinion. But I will not let a blessing like this slip through my fingers. It is one job. Just one job and we shall never have to worry about money again, God willing."

My mother held my stare. "You speak of security, and I understand. I understand wanting the world for your child. But Marjana, Amina? She only wants you." A warning laced into her voice. "And it would destroy her if something were to happen to you."

The words were pulled from her quiver with care, and they struck true once shot. For a moment I saw it: My mother collapsing at the news. Marjana sobbing, wailing for me again and again. It would break her heart in a way that would never entirely heal.

But then it was replaced by another vision. Marjana older and alone, death having come for me no matter what. Marjana older than a human had any right being, bewildered and afraid, with a strangeness that might grow. With a strangeness that might frighten.

How much easier her life would be if she were rich. For while the pious claim money doesn't buy happiness, I can attest from personal experience that poverty buys nothing. It is a monster whose claws grow deeper and more difficult to escape with each passing season, with even the slightest misstep setting you back years, if not forever. Add Marjana's . . . *unique* heritage, and it painted a frightening future in which I wouldn't always be around to protect her.

This is for the best. "I know how to keep myself safe, Amma," I said firmly. "This is my world. I've taken more dangerous assignments. If things turn sour, I will walk away."

"Then we have nothing else to say to each other." My mother's expression was so thick with disappointment and sorrow that it tore my heart. "I would rather not part with anger between us, but you will not get my blessing." She turned away. "I leave it to you to say farewell to your daughter."

◆

Marjana was in the bedchamber we shared, my favorite room in the house. Its three windows faced the sea, and the wooden floorboards were soft underfoot, creaky from all the pacing I did while rocking her to sleep as a baby. My mother and I had painted the walls; she'd chosen traditional patterns and stars while I'd opted for cheerful spots of color with sea creatures and plants. A delicate glass mobile of discarded shards from Mustafa's work sparkled in one corner, while across the room, green shelves lined the wall, heavy with an assortment of souvenirs from my travels.

I found my daughter kneeling there now, her back to the door. Marjana has always been fascinated by the shelves' treasures. Small enameled animals from Kashmir, fine porcelain jugs from China, wooden miniatures from Persia, ceramic lamps from India, tiled mirrors from Basrah, trick-boxes from Sofala . . . remnants from trips half remembered, physical reminders of the life I had abandoned. She was worrying a small ebony turtle with an abalone shell in her hands. When she was very little, she would crawl on her hands and knees to make it travel across the floor.

My footfalls made no sound, but it didn't matter—my daughter always seemed to hear everything. Without turning around, she asked, "So you're going to Aden?"

I hesitated, wondering how much of her eavesdropping she had understood. "Yes. The Sayyida's granddaughter has gone missing, and I know some people who might be able to help."

"What do you mean, 'missing'?" Marjana dropped the turtle and it clunked on the floor. "Is she in danger?"

I sat heavily on the bed and made circles with my wrist, rubbing away an ache from my work on the roof. "I pray not. Sometimes . . . sometimes important people will hold other important people until their relatives pay a certain amount of money or grant some sort of promise. It is nothing to do with you or people like us, understand? But I know a lot of sailors in Aden and may be able to find out where they took her. Besides, it has been a long time since I have checked up on the *Marawati* and our affairs. It is a good excuse to do so."

Marjana finally glanced my way. "So . . . it is like a business trip? Like when Uncle Mustafa went to Mutrah?"

I could not think of a less likely comparison than my brother's short fellowship to an elderly glassmaker who taught him how to blow roses, but I simply nodded. "Something like that. It should not take me longer than four months, God willing."

Marjana stared back at me, her wide eyes filled with unasked questions. Is there any stare like that belonging to your children, the kind that fills you with love and responsibility at once? Those eyes steady upon my face have been my constant companion since she was a baby. Looking for reassurance, for answers, for attention.

"But that is a long time," she whispered, her voice quavering. Indeed, for a child, four months must seem like forever. For her mother too. "And so far away."

I pulled her close. "I know. But Grandma and Bubu will have you hopping all over the place," I said, naming my toddler nephew. "And the time will pass before you know it. Maybe I can get you some new games in Aden. Or wool for the loom? You would like that, yes?"

Marjana toyed with the end of one of my braids, her soft cheek brushing mine. "Can I go with you?"

"No, little love, I don't think that's a good idea."

"Is that because it's not safe?" She pulled back to look me in the face. "Is it because you are going on a boat? Can you not travel another way, Mama? I don't want you to go on a boat."

Her fear took me aback, as did this sudden concern about boats. "Why not?"

She dropped her gaze. "Because that's how Baba died."

My heart fell. "Marjana . . ."

"I-I'm sorry," she rushed. "I know you don't like to talk about Baba. But if Sayyida Salima's son died, and Baba died . . . Mama, maybe sailing is too dangerous." Her gaze was bright with unshed tears. "I don't want you to die."

"Oh, love . . . Come here." I opened my arms and Marjana crawled wordlessly into them, tucking her head under my chin, her body folded into mine as if she were a girl half her age.

I stroked her hair as she stifled a sob. "My life, my beloved." I wiped away her tears. "There is no need for this. I grew up on boats! And Aden is just a quick trip along the sea; we are not taking a ship across the ocean. It is all perfectly safe."

Lies upon lies. And yet what else was I supposed to say? Is it not the job of parents to reassure their children?

Marjana clutched me tighter, her next words muffled against my chest. "Don't go, Mama. Please."

There was genuine terror in her voice, and I frowned. Marjana is on the quiet side—far quieter than I was at her age—and rarely prone to such fears. I held her out again to look her over and saw that her nose was running, her gaze darting everywhere to avoid mine.

"Are you truly so worried about me sailing?" I asked gently. "I told you, love, it is a small trip."

"Not just about sailing."

"Then what?" As her fingers twisted in the folds of my shirt, I realized she was shaking. "Marjana . . . Marjana, look at me. What is it?"

The room had darkened, one of the lamps flickering out. In the dim light, my daughter's eyes were enormous and black as coal, blacker than the eyes of any person I've ever met.

Well, save one, of course.

She bit her lip. "I have a bad feeling."

I went entirely still.

From another child, "bad feelings" upon a parent's departure might not be things to worry over. But Marjana is not an ordinary child. And before I could stop it, a memory rose in my mind. A laughing, husky voice against my ear and hot fingers sliding between mine on the steering ropes.

"This way," he said, closing his beautiful black eyes and pulling east.

"There is nothing that way," I had argued. "Nothing but the doldrums. We will find no ships and may risk our own."

"Trust me, nakhudha. It will be worth your time. I have a feeling."

"A feeling?"

"A feeling. Good feelings, bad feelings . . . how else do you think I direct your kind toward prosperity?" He had waggled his eyebrows with a mischievous grin. "Or toward calamity."

It had sounded like a joke, though I already knew by then that he was not human. But Marjana . . . Marjana is not that. She is not *his*, not in that way. I had looked for signs since she was laid in my arms, perfectly warm and sweet and innocent. The shadows do not warp when she enters a room. When she falls, she scrapes her knees, and though she loves her games, there is no streak of good luck that sees her a constant winner.

I steadied my voice. "What sort of bad feeling?"

"I just . . ." Marjana looked away again, flushing with embarrassment. I could see she was struggling to compose herself, wanting to be older and braver. "Never mind," she mumbled.

For a moment, I paused, uncertain whether to press. But I had made my decision, had I not? So I forced myself to dismiss the warning, perhaps both of us lying to make the other feel better.

I hugged her again. "You have nothing to worry about, my love," I promised, pressing my face upon the soft crown of her head. "It's just one job. One job and then I will be home, God as my witness."

◆

It was dark when I woke, dawn a distant shade of rosy ash outside the windows. I hadn't slept well, a mix of nerves and Marjana's tossing and turning keeping me awake. She'd snoozed firmly snuggled against my armpit, and I hadn't the heart to move her: a decision I knew my aching shoulder would punish me for today. I disentangled her carefully, sweeping a sweaty lock of hair off her cheek.

Shivering despite the morning's humid warmth, I made my ablutions, splashing water from a basin over my face and neck. I changed into an amber-hued robe of soft cotton and bound up my braids, draping a light scarf over my head before turning my intentions to prayer.

If the criminal past didn't alert you, I have not always been a very good Muslim. Drinking and missing prayer were among my lesser sins, and if I tried to straighten myself up every year when Ramadan rolled around—a new life of piety easy to imagine while dazed with thirst and caught up in the communal joy of taraweeh—I typically lapsed into my usual behavior by the time the month of Shawwal had ended.

But then Marjana was born. And Asif was . . . lost. And if one of these events made me feel as though I had no right to ever call upon God again, the other filled with me a driving need I could not deny. So I keep my daily prayers, even if I feel unworthy the entire time.

I pressed my brow to the ground in a motion ingrained upon my soul and recited the words I've known nearly all my life. I added my personal supplications last, imploring that both my family and Salima's wayward granddaughter remain safe. While I prayed, I listened to Marjana's soft breathing. Though dawn had arrived, a few ribbons of remaining moonlight still banded across her sleeping body, illuminating the rise and fall of her chest.

There is to be an eclipse soon, I recalled, the dying lunar glow jostling my reminiscence. If this had been the old days, I would have known the eclipse down to the very night; sailors are a superstitious sort, and like many nawakhidha, I paid every year for a glimpse at the copies of astrological tables and almanacs drawn in the great courts of whatever city I was in, to learn of both auspicious and inauspicious dates and signs. Though I no longer took note of such happenings, my brother, Mustafa, had been clucking his tongue over the eclipse, fearing the event would cloud the birth of his second child, just over three months away now.

A birth I might miss. Four months I had promised Salima, and the implications suddenly struck with such force it left me breathless, the plans I had so fervently defended wavering. What if Marjana got hurt in that time? What if the new baby came early and they needed help with the delivery?

A million dinars, I reminded myself. A fortune that could change the course of all our lives. Marjana would be in good, loving hands while I was gone, and my mother could handle the matter of new babies far better than me. Four months of missing each other was nothing compared to a lifetime—life*times*—of security.

I planted a single kiss on Marjana's smooth cheek. "God protect you," I said softly. Fearing my resolve would fail if I tarried a moment longer, I stole a final glance at my child, then made my way downstairs.

My mother was busy in the kitchen as I knew she would be. If the stack of waiting tins was any indication, she'd probably been cooking all night.

"Amma, you did not need to do this," I protested. "There is enough food here for an army."

"What else I am to do when you insist on running off to risk your life? At least you will not starve." She picked up a pale porcelain dish. The water inside was tinged blue, from the dissolved ink she had used to write holy verses. My mother had no doubt been praying herself. Had probably snuck into my room to sprinkle Zamzam water on my bags and watch Marjana and me sleep. "Drink this."

I obeyed.

She quickly wiped her eyes, pulling me into an embrace. "Be good, Amina. Be *careful*. No amount of money is worth losing you."

"I will be careful, I promise." I kissed her hands. "Take care of Marjana."

Then I picked up my bags and was gone. I could feel my mother watching from the doorway, but I didn't look back to watch the dawn light warm the home I had built: the little enclave in which my daughter had grown up safe and blissfully unaware of our violent past, of her own origins. I was not sure my torn heart could take it.

I had made one new decision, however, swayed by my mother's pleas and my daughter's tears: I would not travel to Aden, not straightaway. They wanted me safe?

Then I would go to the most dangerous person I knew.

A Missive to the Wali of Basrah

[A note for the reader: Several sections of this report, recovered from a burnt fragment of parchment, appear to have been scrubbed out. What has been possible to reproduce has been done here through the grace and mercy of the Almighty.]

—take heed! Ahmad al-Danaf, I know well you are a stalwart man of God, and I have little doubt your prefect consists of equally experienced police, but I pray you listen to my warning: Let this murderess pass through. Close the markets, warn your people to stay indoors, but make no attempt to seize her or interfere with the ransom on her head from the gang she has betrayed. Her lot are the most cunning and violent of the criminal guilds under the banner of the Banu Sasan, consisting of all manner of illusionists, pretend dervishes, vagabonds, and highwaymen. They lie as they breathe, having no shame as they feign to be lepers, preachers, blinded prisoners of war, or helpless maidens—only to turn without warning on the one who would aid them, plundering him for all that he is worth. At best, they abandon their victims naked and destitute on the side of the road. More commonly, they leave them with slit throats.

[scrubbed-out section]

—and if that is the truth of the matter between them, I cannot blame the outlaws for their pursuit. God preserve us, this is why women are to be guarded! Better they are kept

safe at home and rightly guided rather than running about the streets becoming daughters of the Banu Sasan. Either way, beware this "Mistress of Poisons." It is recommended she not be touched with bare skin; nay, I would go so far as clearing out the area she is perceived to be in or advising face coverings. When she was last cornered in Mosul, she took out an entire squadron with some sort of knockout gas. It is rumored she carries sleeping cakes on her person, poison tablets in the ribbons of her headdress, and needs only the barest few drops of liquid to activate the fumes in either . . .

Chapter 4

With a hastily scribbled note informing Salima I would meet her in Aden after . . .

—Wait, is that a *map*? What are you doing with a map? I already told you I wasn't sharing the name of my next port of call.

—"For a better understanding of geography"? Have you lost your wits, Jamal? You want to risk coming to the attention of our world's most notorious criminal gang for a better understanding of *geography*? Fool, no one is listening to sailors' yarns about pirates and wizards to learn about fucking topography. Put that damn map away and let's try this again.

An *unspecified amount of time* after Sayyida Salima intruded upon my home, I stood before a skinny shop in a forgotten town between Salalah and Aden, sweat stinging my eyes. The sun was high overhead, that most sweltering point of the day when anyone with sense is resting in the coolest spot of shade they can find. The building was purposely innocuous, surrounded by foul-smelling tanneries, dye shops, and barbers who must have specialized in bloodletting and flesh-branding, judging by the stench. Greasy mats of tightly braided reeds covered the shop's windows, and the battered door was devoid of any markings that might have indicated the building's purpose.

"We are friends," I reminded myself under my breath, working up some courage. "And friends do not murder each other without warning." With a whispered prayer, I knocked on the door.

It swung inward on a pair of rusty hinges, revealing a yawning black hole.

"Hello?" I called out. "Is anyone here?"

There was no response. My heart racing, I stepped inside. The room was exceedingly small and bare, the only furniture a low wooden bench. Just beside the bench was another doorway. A patterned red curtain had been drawn across it and a ceramic plate inscribed with religious verses hung above.

"Nakhudha?"

I jumped and spun around with a curse. A small woman now stood between the outer door and me, having appeared seemingly out of thin air. Dressed in an ash-covered blue tunic rolled to her elbows, she was so short that she barely rose to my chest, the dim light casting a greenish hue across her golden-brown skin and making her face look delicate.

"Dalila!" I greeted brightly. "Well . . . look who has gotten more beautiful with retirement!" This was a lie. Dalila has always possessed a kind of alarming beauty, but right now her dark chestnut hair was so snarled it resembled a bird's nest, one of her eyebrows appeared to have been recently singed off, and she was squinting, giving her expression a more manic edge than usual.

"Amina al-Sirafi." Without warning, Dalila lunged forward to wrap me in a tight hug. "My friend, you have finally come to visit!" She grabbed my face, her nails digging into the back of my skull as she kissed my cheeks. "My goodness, I was beginning to fear you'd forgotten all about me! It was beginning to hurt my feelings!"

Fear galloped through me. I glanced down to see if the linen cap covering her head was her infamous one—the one whose ribbons are festooned with poison tablets and glass vials of death fashioned to look like pretty baubles.

I couldn't tell. Damn. "No. No, of course not," I replied, forcing a laugh. "How could I forget my closest friend?"

"Tinbu is your closest friend. He got your ship."

"Tinbu did not *get* my ship. He sails under my leave. Because he is a sailor and not someone who refused to learn anything about boats."

Dalila straightened, bringing all her petite form up to bear. "I could have learned."

I tried to change the subject. "So your trade nowadays . . ." I glanced around the bare interior. "It is what exactly?"

She smiled for the first time, a devilish gleam in the dark. Closer now, I could see silver streaks in her hair and a few fine lines tracing out from her eyes and lips. "Pharmaceuticals."

Pharmaceuticals. I choked. "I did not think you had any . . . training in that."

"Oh, I don't. But it is largely the same principle as poisoning, no? Just in reverse." Dalila winked. "The ladies here love me. So many terrible husbands dying in their sleep. It must be something in the water."

God preserve me. "I am, ah, happy you are finding your place in the world."

"One has little choice when they have been abandoned by those they considered their closest comrades."

"I literally paid you off. Generously."

Dalila took my arm, and I tried not to tense. "Generosity is a matter of opinion, my dear nakhudha. Come, I will show you my work."

Somehow she made that sound not quite like a threat, and we swept through the curtained entrance into a room four times bigger than the false entry that made immediately clear—no matter her griping—that Dalila had invested her final payoff well. Repurposed shelves and sturdy tables were covered in stoneware dishes and clay jars. Some were filled with the herbs, oils, resins, and such one would find in a proper apothecary, but there were also stranger, more lethal ingredients hinting at her true profession: blacksmith's filings and powdered glass, pickled nightshade berries and dried oleander flowers. The strong stench of chemicals rose from a corner of the room dedicated to simmering liquid-filled metal pots set over a trio of braziers.

Taking great care not to touch *anything* and casting a wary eye at a complicated apparatus with glass bulbs, copper tubes, and what looked like blood splashed in its interior, I let out an impressed whistle. "Nice workshop. Certainly appears you've kept yourself busy."

"The quiet life of being ignored by my companions has otherwise done me well, and staying in one place lets me run experiments longer." Dalila gave an affectionate tap to a suspended burlap sack dripping purple ichor into a glass flask. "I have been doing some truly astonishing new things with knockout gas."

"You're going to permanently knock yourself out one day with one of these experiments if you're not careful." There seemed distressingly poor ventilation in her cramped workplace.

"What is a little risk compared to the possibility of advancing the poison arts?" Dalila raised her singed eyebrow. "You know what my sheikh says."

"'He who dares does while he who fears fails,'" I said, repeating the mantra of the Banu Sasan. "Not to insult your guild's beliefs, but perhaps we could talk somewhere away from knockout gases?"

With a disappointed roll of her eyes, Dalila led me to a small courtyard boxed in by the looming, windowless walls of the surrounding buildings. Save the deadly experiments, her personal possessions were few. A low rope bed covered in a patchwork quilt stood in one corner, and an icon of Maryam and baby Isa, peace be upon them both, was set reverently in a niche in the bricks nearby. Upon a single trunk was her staff, a slender length of polished hardwood I'd seen crack more than one man's skull.

It was a far cry from my warm, bustling home filled with family and souvenirs, and upon taking it all in, I did feel a measure of guilt. Or perhaps Dalila had guided me to such guilt. Like any youngster, I grew up on tales of the Banu Sasan. Stories of thieves who break into homes by digging tunnels under the foundation and murderers who can cut a man's neck so cleanly his head won't topple off. Some people say the Banu Sasan are the criminally talented descendants of Persian kings chased into the mountains centuries ago; others claim they're just con men with clever tricks that make for easily exaggerated gossip. Either way, they inspire wonderful stories, this brotherhood of terrifying brigands and scoundrels, their tales so audacious they seem impossible to believe.

Then Dalila joined my crew. Or rather she blackmailed my crew into spiriting her out of Basrah by stowing away in the cargo hold, poisoning my navigator, and withholding the antidote until we had cleared the Persian Gulf. It was a complicated recruitment process. But becoming the boon companion of an actual devotee of this supposed Sheikh Sasan has not enlightened me as to the mysteries of the Banu Sasan, or Dalila herself, in the slightest. She is a Christian, a proud one who makes a quiet point of looking out for her people when she can, but I could tell you nothing more than that. We once had a particularly obnoxious linguistics scholar turned hostage who tried to wheedle more information out of her, claiming he could tell from her accent and rituals where her people were from. After he smugly declared her to be an Assyrian from Mosul, Dalila smiled and prayed Christian invocations in a dozen different languages, changing her inflection, accent, and gestures for each, and we all stopped bothering her about her origins.

"Sit, sit." Dalila waved me toward her bed and then busied herself preparing two glass cups, steeping and straining dried red dates with some sort of chopped root and shards of amber jaggery.

She handed me one of the cups. "My newest creation. Like nothing you will ever drink again." She sat down on the other side of the rope bed, and it was as though a spirit had alighted, her weight not shifting the cushions in the slightest.

I regarded the honey-colored concoction and her expectant expression. Surely she was only teasing me. Dalila had always had a disturbing sense of humor. And we were friends, right? At least the closest approximation of friendship I thought Dalila capable of.

I sipped my drink. "It is good," I said, trying to pretend I could taste anything while she watched me with her cat eyes.

"Not too bitter? You know, you still have a price on your head. A high one."

I stared at her. If Dalila wanted to kill me, she didn't need to poison my drink. That would be so obvious it was almost insulting to her abilities. She had already kissed my cheeks, touched the back of my neck, and taken my arm in hers—more clever, more elegant delivery methods. More her style. We used to joke that of the three of us, I could kill you up close, Tinbu could kill you from another ship, and Dalila could kill you from a different city three days later.

I drank back the entire cup.

She cackled. "Oh, nakhudha, I have missed you."

"Enough to stop jesting about my death?"

Dalila shrugged, finally taking a sip from her own cup. "That depends. How's my baby?"

"Marjana is flourishing, God be praised. She is lovely and kind and nothing like either of her parents."

A hint of relief flickered in her face. Dalila was the only person I allowed to attend Marjana's birth. The only person I trusted to do what was necessary if my worst fears came true. "I am glad to hear it."

"What about you? Have you a life beyond trying to burn down your workshop in an experimental blaze?" I glanced around. "I see no evidence of a husband."

Dalila laughed again. "Men are your weakness, Amina. Not mine."

"Come now," I persisted. "Companionship has occasional benefits."

"You do not need men for companionship. And Kamran tried to stab you. *Twice*."

"Yes, but in my defense, it was my first marriage, and he was distractingly pretty."

"You threw the second one off the *Marawati* stark naked."

"We were at port, it was warm, and he was an excellent swimmer. Besides, I upgraded to Salih after, and he was lovely. Even you liked him."

"He was an extremely impressive cutpurse," Dalila admitted. Then she gave me a pointed look. "And the husband after Salih?"

I cleared my throat. "Never mind marriage. Still . . . being cooped up in here must get dull, no? You are perhaps desiring an adventure beyond alchemy and poisoning the neighborhood grooms?"

Dalila leaned against a cushion. "How abruptly you puncture the illusion this visit was prompted by friendship."

"I apologize for my rudeness. Asif al-Hilli's mother came to visit me."

The humor left her eyes. "What? Does she—"

"No," I said quickly. "It wasn't about . . . about what happened to him." I hesitated, my heart still a mess when it came to Asif. "He had a daughter, Dalila. A wife."

"Ah." Her lips thinned. "I guess they got left out of those stories about how terrible his family was."

I grimaced. "That's not fair. He was young."

"He was a fool." But her blunt words were tinged with grief. "A fool who made a deal anyone else would have seen was a trap."

It was difficult not to flinch at that—Asif wasn't the only fool. "He didn't deserve what happened to him," I said instead.

Dalila sighed, returning to the matter at hand. "So, Asif had a daughter and wife he walked out on, and now his rich mother has tracked you down. Why?"

"You may have to steady yourself. She believes his daughter was kidnapped by some Frank prowling about Aden."

Dalila went completely still. "A Frank? A Frank prowling about Aden?"

I frowned. "Have you heard of such a man?"

"You might say that." Dalila rose to her feet, heading for a trunk in the corner. "A man matching that exact description wrote to me last year."

I gasped. "He wrote to *you*? How? I didn't think anyone else even knew where you were."

"You are bold to assume such a priority in my life. There are a few others who know how to contact me, but none I could imagine foolish enough to share that information." Dalila unlocked the trunk and rifled through a messy stack of letters and broken scrolls before plucking one out. "Yet this foreigner was able to get his note into my hands."

"What did he want?"

"It is best heard directly from its insane source." Dalila brought the letter to her face, squinted, and then held it farther out to read aloud. "'To the Mistress of Poisons, I have heard great tales of your feats and accomplishments. I, too, am a Seeker of Truth and' . . . well, here he mostly brags about himself for a paragraph, comparing his intellect to Aristotle's and his fighting prowess to Samson's—"

"Modest."

"Yes, he is quite humble. He continues: 'I will pay most handsomely for your expertise in the manner of vapors and humoral sciences in both coin and knowledge. If you are interested in peering past the mysteries of the Veil to see the Unseen and quench thy thirst on the magic of the Hidden Realm, I would be delighted to guide you. I look forward to your response.'"

"He sounds like a drunk witch." I grimaced. "I don't like it. You know how I feel about magic."

Dalila waved off my concern. "These are the sort who see a card trick and believe it an act of the greatest sorcery. The Frank said he intended to visit Aden last spring and that if I desired a meeting, he had an agent by the name of Layth."

"Salima said a local agent set up their meeting as well. And Aden in the spring would put him in the city when Dunya was kidnapped." I quickly related the rest of Salima's story.

Dalila looked skeptical. "Ransom?"

"None, which has been gnawing at me. Salima said there has been no further contact."

"So she has no proof this man is involved?"

"That was my response as well. But the family apparently has quite the treasure trove of talismanic items. If Falco is the same man who sent you that ridiculous letter, I could certainly see him being interested in their stash."

"Still, it is strikingly slim evidence to have lured you out of retirement." Dalila gave me a knowing look. "What did she offer?"

"A hundred thousand dinars if we learn the girl's location." Despite the circumstances, it was impossible not to grin. "A *million* if we retrieve her. As well as any plunder we recover from the Frank."

Dalila let out a soft breath: not even a daughter of the Banu Sasan could remain stone-faced at the prospect of such a sum. "Do you believe she has that kind of money?"

"She gave me ten thousand as a deposit. For ten thousand dinars, I am happy to go ask some questions in Aden and check on the *Marawati*. We shall see what we uncover and take it from there."

"Oh, is it 'we' already? I do not recall agreeing."

"I mean, if you fear your skills have deteriorated . . ."

"Amina, you nearly jumped out of your sandals when I appeared. Do not insult me out of pretense." Dalila squinted at my face again. "Does it not seem a bit coincidental that this Frank has learned of two different members of your crew?"

"It is far too coincidental," I agreed. "Which is even further motivation. You should come with me to Aden and make sure we thoroughly investigate matters."

Dalila rolled her eyes. But then she paused. "I used to wonder, you know, what would finally bring you back. Whenever a strange message showed up, whenever an unexpected shadow fell over my doorstep, I would think, 'This is it. She has some new score, some new scheme.'" Dalila met my gaze, her face carefully expressionless. "But then one year turned into two. Five. A decade."

I opened and closed my mouth, lost for words at the unexpected confession: Dalila and sentiment had always seemed enemies. "I didn't think any of you wanted to see me again," I said. "Not after how things ended."

"That end wasn't your fault, Amina. Maybe if you had bothered to write, I could have assured you of such and you would not have spent the past ten years as a hermit, ignoring the rest of us." I flushed with shame, but before I could apologize, she changed the subject in her abrupt, enigmatic way. "Though I suppose I shouldn't be surprised it would be the most dangerous of jobs that would tempt you back."

Even more heat crept into my face. "Yes. Ah . . . that is actually why I came to you first," I admitted, feeling extremely sheepish. "You know how I have a tendency to misjudge risk?"

She snorted. "You are an excellent judge of risk. Your problem is that you run toward it."

"I can't this time. I promised my mother and daughter that I'd come home safe. That I'd walk away if things got too dangerous." I attempted some groveling. "Dalila, I have never met *anyone* with your skills. If there's anyone who can help me keep that promise, it's you."

"I understand." Something almost compassionate flickered in Dalila's face. "You will give me a bonus from your cut."

So much for affection. "See? This is why Tinbu got my ship."

Dalila ignored my response, screwing up her eyes again as she studied her laboratory. "I will need to pack; I have some promising projects I'd like to bring along."

"Wait." Acting on my own suspicion, I walked across the courtyard and raised a hand. "How many fingers am I holding up?"

"Two."

I dropped my closed fist. "Not even close. Are you having problems with your eyesight?"

"Just when I read," Dalila replied dismissively. "It is a small thing."

"You were not reading just now!" I gasped. "You make *poisons*, Dalila. Can you even see the labels on those vials you've been mixing up?"

"I can see well enough to notice *your* limp, Amina. Are you sure you can fight with such an impairment? It could be very dangerous were you to lose your balance at sea when no one was around to help you."

"Are you threatening me already?"

Dalila gave me a wicked smile. "Of course not, nakhudha. Especially not when you're worth a million dinars. Now help me pack. We both know your true love awaits in Aden."

Chapter 5

A h, Aden. What can I tell a collector of tales about Yemen, that most glorious and blessed land, that they do not already know? I suspect you can spout plenty of verses extolling the wealth of the famed kingdoms of Saba and Himyar, and know by heart the epics of the warrior-king Sayf and his djinn companions in these lands. And at first blush, one might think Aden—Yemen's most valuable pearl—would embrace the bewitching legend of its countryside. Perched upon the sunken crater of a long-dead sea volcano and ringed by jagged peaks that tear at the sky, the city's very location seems out of a book of myths. There is but a single pass through the mountains, one said to have been carved by Shaddad bin 'Ad himself during his conquests of the world before Islam. Curved around a bright blue bay, Aden gazes down upon its harbor like an eager audience in an amphitheater, with three forts, a new seawall, and numerous gates adding to its already fearsome natural fortifications. It is though the Almighty Himself decided to protect it. Sailing past its ancient breakwater—the stones said to have been set there by giants—you might feel as though you have entered a mythical port of magic from a sailor's yarn.

You would be sorely mistaken.

Aden is where magic goes to be crushed by the muhtasib's weights, and if wonder could be calculated, this city would require an ordinance taxing it. It is a den of number-crunching scribes, overly zealous accountants, and tax clerks who have you locked up if you so much as jest about bribes. There is money to be made for people like me: you can charge an excellent rate to smuggle goods around the city's onerous customshouse. But to what end if there is not a tavern in which to spend your hard-earned coin and the only company to be found is with a bunch of law-abiding bureaucrats?

Dalila and I had chosen to make the trip overland and through the main pass rather than upon the sea, where those in charge of clearing travelers were more thorough (and by "thorough," I mean they hire ladies who inspect *everything*). We had another reason for traveling discreetly as well. Though I couldn't entirely blame Salima for how she approached me, Dalila had been less than pleased to learn how prepared the elderly noblewoman had been to reveal my location to my old foes. And by "less than pleased," she called me a fucking idiot and went into a great harangue about the management of risk that convinced me she regularly murdered curious neighbors.

Nonetheless, by the time we arrived in Aden, we had a new plan. Salima was no doubt impatiently awaiting my arrival, but we would not go to her right away. Instead we would meet up with Tinbu and the *Marawati* and spend a few days taking the temperature of the city and inquiring after our mysterious Frank. Politics shift swiftly around here, and I did not wish to get caught in a situation unawares. For all I knew, Salima was working with the governor himself to set a trap for me.

All right, yes, all that came from Dalila as well. See? This is why I recruited her first. Sometimes one needs a paranoid poisoner at their side.

As it was, we made it through the pass and into the city unbothered. I insisted on going to the *Marawati* straightaway, and as we strolled onto the beach I could not help but marvel at the difference a decade had made. One of the blessings of age is the waning of certain men's eyes, of that stare that fixes upon you when you are a girl too young to notice. The men who do not lower their gaze as is commanded by our faith, but instead

steal second and third glances; the men who hiss the vulgarest of obsceni-
ties and when called out, blame their behavior on your clothes, your smile
or lack thereof, your pretty eyes, your very existence.

The men who always seem very surprised to be knocked on their ass
and splitting bloody teeth when attempting such tricks on ill-tempered
lady pirates. But happily past forty and dressed in the mended garments
of fishwives, Dalila and I might have been invisible as we strode across the
hot sand. We passed the seawall, and I paused to admire the unobstructed
view of Sira Bay.

Aden's harbor was gentle and the expanse of azure water—a sailor's
dream, clear of the coral and shoals that make most of the ports north
of here so deadly—was dotted with about twenty ships, mostly the big
sanabiq that carry trade goods to the East African and Indian coasts. A
few more boats had been dragged onto the narrow beach for repairs, the
muddy flats crowded with sweating laborers tightening hull stitches, making rope, and mixing sealant. The smell of coir and pitch combined with
the salty breeze and reek of fish guts on the humid air to make a smell
only a sailor could love. New mansions and promenades glistened in the
distant hills, where their wealthy inhabitants could enjoy stunning sea vis-
tas and pleasant breezes, but Aden's newest construction boom appeared
to have missed its poor: the palm frond huts on the sweltering beach—
huts I spent a not-insignificant portion of my childhood in—looked as
miserable as ever.

I fanned my face with the end of my turban as we made our way
through a maze of wooden hulls, shark-oil-filled barrels, carpentry tools,
lengths of rope, and flapping sails. The hot sand crunched beneath my
thin sandals, and I was drenched with sweat in moments. Longing to
spy my *Marawati* and plunge into the ocean, I stopped in the shade of a
large sunbuq framed by stilts. Still, no one had bothered us. God, give us
a couple tins and we could have boarded a ship claiming to be delivering
food to hungry husbands and stolen it.

But I did not want any stolen ship, I wanted *my* stolen ship. I shaded my eyes, the sun's glare upon the water fierce, and scanned the boats drifting in the bay.

"Do you see it?" Dalila asked.

"No. Though knowing Tinbu, she is likely nigh unrecognizable." There is no one who knows his way around boats like Tinbu, my former first mate and the man who has been captaining the *Marawati* in my stead since I retired. He can break a ship down and build it anew in ways one would never imagine. "Look for similarly sized hulls."

"Mama!"

On instinct, I turned and spotted a little girl running across the sand, her black braids bouncing behind her. Giggling, she crashed into a group of women mending nets and dropped to the ground, her hands full of oyster shells.

My heart panged. I was trying to preoccupy myself with work, but I could not go an hour without thoughts of Marjana, and the sight of any child made me ache. Was my daughter eating enough and staying safe? Did she miss me or had she gotten distracted in the blissful way of children? I watched the girl settle into her mother's lap, the smiles exchanged between them driving a knife of loneliness through my chest.

"Amina." Dalila tugged on my sleeve. "Can you see what is happening over there?"

I followed the direction of her glance. On the southern side of the harbor, closer to Sira Island, a group of people had gathered on the beach. There seemed to be some sort of commotion; their gazes were directed at the sea and excited chatter drifted our way. I glanced back upon the boats I had already examined thrice, but my *Marawati* was not there.

Nor did I like the energy of the growing crowd, an ill premonition knotting my belly. "Let us check it out."

The crowd had gathered upon a sloping sand dune that made it difficult to see anything of the sea beyond glistening shards of water. I pulled the tail of my turban across the lower part of my face in case the years had not aged me into anonymity, and Dalila and I separated without a word, melting into the group.

"—think they shall find anything?" a man coated in wood dust whispered to his companion.

"Heard their throats were slashed to the bone, crabs crawling out of their mouths—"

I jostled past two boys, one hoisting the other to peer over the shoulders of the men in front of them. With an elbow to the ribs of a sailor and a rude shove to a matronly looking woman who let out an offended squawk, I was free of the mob with a clear view of the commotion.

And there, swaying in the gentle waves like a comely dancer, was my *Marawati*.

I praised God under my breath, my soul eased at the sight of my first love, at the ship I'd have cast all my ex-husbands overboard to save. She was a true beauty, India-made with a narrow hull of the finest dark teak. Her name was original, though I've little idea what it means; my grandfather was as cagey about the *Marawati*'s name as he was regarding the no doubt illegal way he obtained her. She was not overly large, but with a full complement of oarsmen and a deft hand controlling the vast sails and two rudders, she was one of the swiftest vessels on the sea, capable of fleeing far bigger warships.

Not that she looked like it at that moment. The oars and the rails that held them were nowhere to be seen, the decked platforms where we launched weapons were dismantled, and the rudder and stern ornaments had been changed. The hull and masts had been painted an ugly yellow-tinged green that looked like it needed to be refreshed twenty years ago, and between the fraying nets and rusty chains, the *Marawati* looked less like a speedy smuggling vessel and more like a fishing boat used to coast along the shore. The one thing Tinbu had not altered—my sole request—

were the wooden rondels my grandfather had carved along the captain's bench.

However, my eyes had barely settled on my beloved ship when said heart-easing abruptly ended. For you see, my *Marawati* was neither alone nor at peace. It was being actively searched by soldiers and pinned between two large—armed—galleys.

When . . . *in the name of God* . . . had Aden gotten warships?

"Two dirhams they find nothing," a man behind me declared. "No one would be reckless enough to rob an Adeni vessel and then put in here for repairs."

"I will take that bet," another answered. "Never underestimate men's carelessness. And whoever killed those poor souls was a monster. Such thieves have no shame."

"Nor do the two of you, gambling over the dead," chided a third man. "God deliver us from such perversion."

A triumphant cheer sounded from the *Marawati*; several of the soldiers were hefting metal-hued ingots in the air. There was an indignant—and familiar—cry of protest, and then Tinbu, my most trusted first mate and sweetest of friends, was hauled out from the cargo hold.

I watched, my heart in my throat, as Tinbu was pushed before two figures in official-looking robes and turbans. Gesticulating wildly, my friend appeared to be arguing or perhaps pleading. I was not sure which option concerned me more. Tinbu is excellent at striking pacts with criminals, so practiced he forgets that civilian authorities occasionally have different responses to being bribed. The other men looked stern, their arms crossed over their chests. Tinbu raised his hands in an imploring fashion . . .

And was promptly smashed in the back of the head by a sword hilt.

He crumpled, and pandemonium broke out. A merchant-looking fellow in a striped blue and yellow shawl rushed to Tinbu's side while around them, furious sailors threw themselves on the soldiers in a blur of fists.

But the fight was over as quickly as it started, Tinbu's band outnumbered. Aghast and helpless, I watched as they began arresting the crew, binding the men with ropes and shoving them toward one of the warships.

"Well." Dalila reappeared at my side as though stepping out of an invisible realm. "This changes things."

I pulled at my turban in despair. "Why are there warships?"

"Yes, that is also an unpleasant development." Dalila clucked her tongue. "We will need to find an alternative way to travel."

A pair of guards dragged Tinbu between them. I watched as he attempted to lift his head and was rewarded with a punch to his stomach.

An old, dangerous anger lit inside me. "We follow."

"Amina, 'we follow' plays no part in obtaining very large sums of money for discreetly—"

"No sum of money is worth such a loss to me."

Dalila grunted in annoyance. "I knew he was your favorite."

"I was talking about my ship. Now *follow*."

◆

Tinbu and his crew were marched directly to Aden's prison, a former warehouse beside the muhtasib's office. Whatever crime my friend was accused of must have been serious, for a crowd of onlookers awaited him at the prison as well. They were swiftly dispatched and replaced by a pair of baton-wielding soldiers who installed themselves outside the muhtasib's door.

Fortunately the surrounding streets were busy, and so Dalila's and my loitering was easy to miss. After so many years of isolation, I found the bustle of a proper city invigorating. I have always liked meeting new people and seeing new places, and quickly set to chatting up various vegetable buskers, leatherworkers, and a rather charming juice vendor who gave me a cup of pressed date nectar in exchange for the gossip I shared of the beach.

The juicer lowered his voice to a hush after my whispered recollection. "The wali is keeping it close to his chest, but rumors are a ship that normally carries pilgrims between here and Jeddah was smuggling iron ore and went missing a few weeks ago. Some say it was an accident and the boat must have broken up on the reefs, but others are claiming the bodies that washed ashore had their throats cut."

"Pirates?" I clutched a hand to my chest. "So close to Aden?"

"Only God knows." The juicer pursed his lips in annoyance. "The muhtasib is new and looking for any reason to seem important. But there is not much in Aden for him to crack down on save women visiting tombs and the occasional vendor letting their sugarcane juice ferment a bit too long. I imagine the prospect of murderous pirates, real or imagined, would be tantalizing."

I liked this fellow. "Now, brother, surely you are not suggesting a government official would invent such a heinous crime for his own amusement and career advancement?"

He blushed prettily above his salt-and-pepper beard, and I was reminded just how long it had been since I enjoyed a man. "God forbid."

I winked, finished my drink, and returned to Dalila. She had spread a mat on a patch of street that gave us a clear view of the prison, displaying a sad array of bruised fruit for resale that we'd bought in case anyone asked what we were doing.

"Done flirting?" she greeted, shooing away a pigeon.

"For now. How is business?"

"Poor. My boss is a fool who is wasting my time on a side venture when a riper prize beckons." Dalila stabbed her knife into a melon, carving out a section and offering it to me on the blade. "That will be a million dinars."

Taking the fruit, I asked, "Any updates?

"I have not heard screaming, so presumably he is not being tortured."

"Tinbu would stay for you," I pointed out as I squatted beside her.

"I would never require saving."

There was little argument I could offer against that, so instead I studied the prison. It looked secure; the stone building had probably been there for at least a hundred years and its few windows were little more than narrow, barred slits. I had already scouted the perimeter, but a rear entrance was bricked over, leaving the guarded door as the only way in or out. We could tunnel below; we'd done so with similar buildings before. But tunneling took time and equipment, and we had neither.

I turned my attention to the nearby streets. This was a commercial neighborhood, crowded with workshops and offices, along with shops and food stalls that catered to hungry laborers and clerks needing to run errands before returning home. The closest mosque was distant, its minaret hazy above the maze of rooftops. In all, it seemed like the kind of place that emptied out at night. I rose on my toes to peer farther down the street, and my gaze fell upon a foul scene. A young girl, barely older than Marjana, was being crudely examined by two men dressed in rich garments several buildings away. She wore a sackcloth tunic that skimmed her thighs, her hair hanging in loose, uncombed waves. One of the men motioned for her to open her mouth so he could check her teeth, the other squeezing her belly as though evaluating a fatty piece of meat. I hissed.

Dalila glanced up to see what had earned my ire, and her expression grew stormy.

"Hypocritical bastards," she said in disgust. "Those men would probably die of shame before allowing their wives to take a lover, but force yourself on a girl who has no say because you bought her and suddenly all is fine and permissible before God."

"I do not believe that," I said firmly. And I don't. Slavery is an abomination, no matter what excuses we find for it. There are people who will say the Quran allows such bondage; that many slaves are sold by their own parents and leave primitive, famine-struck villages for lives of ease and advancement in palaces and mansions and the enlightenment of God.

I wonder how many such defenders have spoken to those enslaved? Because I have. My crew never consisted of fewer than a third freemen, and they had more horror stories than pleasant memories. I have stowed away girls whose hands were still wet with the blood of masters who raped them and seen lash scars on sailors' backs so bad they could no longer move without pain. And yes, I know what the Holy Book says— but does it not also tell us to use our eyes and our hearts? How can one say Paradise lies under the feet of a mother if one may steal away the child in her arms?

Dalila touched my hand—I had reached for my dagger without meaning to. "You cannot save them all." Indeed, the men were already exchanging coins and leading the girl away. "Dunya, Amina. *Tinbu.*"

Tinbu. Another who had been enslaved, taken captive in a raid when he was a teenager. My friend was a cheerful, lighthearted man, but he rarely spoke of those years, and I could only imagine how he felt now, shackled again.

I dropped my hand with a curse. Dalila was right. I couldn't save everyone, but I would be damned if I left Tinbu in prison. "Does that mean you'll help me break him out?"

Dalila made a sour face. "This is probably a trap."

"You think everything is a trap. Perhaps God has placed us here on purpose."

"If you are naïve enough to believe that, I would like to go back to my workshop."

Raised voices came from inside the prison.

"I am telling you Tinbu was not involved in such a heinous crime!" It was the man in the striped shawl who had rushed to Tinbu's side on the boat. A soldier was escorting him forcefully to the door, followed by an older man in officious dress. "You cannot charge him without proof!"

"What we can or cannot do is not your concern," the older man rebuked. "Were he Jewish, he would be released to your community to handle. As he is not, I will get the answers I need." He lowered his voice. "Think of your family's reputation, Yusuf. Steer clear of this."

They shut the door in his face.

The man—Yusuf—stood there, wringing his shawl. He was thin, his skin the pale brown of a man who did not spend his days toiling in the sun. His clothes were of fine flax, the hems embroidered with dancing hares in silver thread, and his beard tidily groomed. A well-off man, from one of the Jewish merchant families that had long held prominence in Aden, if I had to guess. He looked about a decade younger than me, and if he wasn't traditionally handsome, there was an earnestness in his green eyes I suppose would be endearing if that was your type.

It was not mine—I make terrible decisions and thus prefer men with a bit more mischief, which has only ever turned out well. But I knew another who preferred his paramours sweet and soft, and so when Yusuf stalked away, looking heartbroken and miserable, I met Dalila's gaze and we rose wordlessly to our feet.

We followed him through Aden's narrow winding streets, deep into the city and through the pleasanter parts, which rose away from the humid beach and busy market. Here the homes were larger: stone mansions with windows and doors framed in lovely intricate designs of whitewash, their interiors so thickly perfumed that the smell of frankincense and bakhoor scented the neatly swept avenues. The adhan rang out, the muezzin calling for maghrib prayer, and we took advantage of the knots of men strolling from the pavilion overlooking the harbor to the city's main mosque.

Yusuf was not behaving as though he suspected he was being followed. He turned down a skinny lane that cut between two buildings so tall they blocked what remained of the sun's dying light. A quick glance revealed no windows and no other passersby.

"Wait here," I whispered. Dalila fell back, stationing herself casually at the foot of the lane, and I hurried forward, affecting my best weary stoop.

"Sir!" I cried. "Please, might you spare a coin for a hungry old woman?"

Yusuf sighed but stopped to reach into his purse. Oh, bless him. "I do not have much, but—"

I was there the next moment, my dagger at his throat.

"Do not scream," I warned. "I have no interest in harming you, but if you cry for help, by the time it arrives, you will be dead, and I will be gone." I shoved him forward, deeper into the shadows. "Walk."

His eyes burning with indignation, Yusuf nonetheless obeyed. I waited until there was no possibility of being overheard and his back was against a wall before I dropped the dagger a fraction away from his throat.

"Tell me of Tinbu," I demanded.

Yusuf drew up with a furious, outraged air. "Who are you?"

"I am asking the questions. Is Tinbu hurt?"

His glare did not lessen, but he answered. "Tinbu is alive. He took a nasty blow to the head and seems confused, but that has not stopped their interrogations."

"And what exactly are they interrogating him about?"

"He was caught carrying iron ore he found in the shallows north of here. The authorities claim it belonged to a ship that went missing several weeks ago. The ship has yet to be recovered, but the bodies of some of the passengers washed up. What was left of them anyway," Yusuf clarified, going pale. "The wali says they were murdered."

So it was as the juicer said. Damn. "Do they intend to charge Tinbu?"

Trembling, Yusuf nodded. "With murder and brigandry."

My heart dropped. Murder and brigandry were the most severe charges that could be levied against my kind. Piracy is a tricky, complicated business in these parts. The merchants and princes who rain curses upon our heads are often the very same ones who hire us to protect their ships, smuggle them through customs, and steal from their competitors. I have never met a sea-thief who relishes ending a human life, if not for the sin of it, then for the risk of punishment beyond a fine or brief stint in the stocks. Too much death and we were a scourge to be eradicated instead of a business resource. Taking to the sea is terrifying enough. Should you step out of line, there is no authority who won't hesitate to make an example out of you.

And the examples . . . they are gruesome. The punishment for murder and brigandry, for "cutting the sea lanes," is crucifixion, bisection, and having what's left of you hung at the city gates. It has been the punishment since the time of the Romans, if the stories are to be believed, and perhaps even longer.

"Did Tinbu confess to illegal salvage?" I asked, recalling his pleading on the *Marawati* just before getting knocked out.

"Not at first. He, ah . . . suggested that if he could not account for the iron ore's past, perhaps they might all agree to share its future."

I groaned. "The fool has cut his own throat."

"But he did not kill those men! I know Tinbu, and he is no murderer. I mean, he does not always conduct himself strictly within the law but . . ." Suspicion stole back into Yusuf's voice. "Why are you asking me these things? Were *you* involved with these men's deaths?"

"Not in the slightest. I too am a friend of Tinbu's and hoped to recruit him for a job. A job that he has already put at risk, which is remarkably fast even for him." I pinched my brow. "Are his men being charged as well?"

"I do not know. From what I gather, the wali is keeping them locked up without food and water while they consider their loyalties."

Wonderful. A friend accused of murder and a crew of thirsty men. "And what of those galleys in the bay?"

Yusuf's expression turned sourer. "They are new. The governor thought warships would make for a good deterrent after the pirate attack a few seasons ago. Raised our taxes only to use them for personal pleasure cruises thus far."

Unsurprising yet promising—perhaps the men who manned them were novices at sea fights. "What kind of soldiers do they carry?"

"Some Mamluks imported from God only knows where. I could not understand the language they were speaking amongst themselves on the ship."

"And what shape is the *Ma*—is Tinbu's ship in?" I asked, correcting myself. "Is she seaworthy?"

Yusuf blinked. "I have no idea, I'm not a sailor. I know Tinbu brought her ashore for repairs a couple weeks ago, but he has not started loading cargo for his next trip yet."

That was both good and bad news. The *Marawati* would be light, but for all I knew the sails were full of holes and the oars traded away for supplies.

But no . . . that wasn't Tinbu's style. He was reckless with officials, never with ships. No one with as many years as he had on the ocean was reckless with ships. There was a reason I had placed the *Marawati* in his hands.

I would have to pray he had earned it.

However, there was still the matter of getting him out of prison. "The wali and the muhtasib . . . Do you believe they'll act swiftly?" I asked.

Yusuf began worrying his shawl. "Yes. They seem to genuinely believe they have their man, and even if they did not, he's an unbeliever who makes for an easy scapegoat. They will make fast, awful work of him to put other travelers' minds at rest."

"What news?" Dalila asked.

Yusuf jumped. "Oh, God, there's another one of you."

I gave her a grim look. "Tinbu is being charged with murder and cutting the road and therefore will be shortly tortured and executed."

"Ah." Dalila's voice was blunt. "Then I reiterate my earlier point. We need another ship."

"And I will reiterate *my* earlier point: we are not leaving him behind."

Shocked hope blossomed in Yusuf's eyes. "Are you saying you can help him? Do you have evidence to prove his innocence?"

Evidence to prove his innocence . . . oh, but this man did not know the seafarer he was defending so ardently. "Who are you to him?" I prodded.

Yusuf blushed, instantly confirming my suspicions. "I am one of his clients. He has been carrying cargo for my family to Calicut for a few seasons."

"And you defend all your contractors with such ferocity?"

The blush deepened. "We have become friends."

Oh, I bet. "Does that friendship extend to risking yourself to save his life?"

The merchant hesitated. "I would have to remain anonymous—I cannot put my family in harm's way—but I will do what I can."

Dalila grabbed my wrist. "You cannot seriously be considering this. Breaking a man out of prison is the exact opposite of 'being discreet.' We will have to flee Aden. Salima—the woman who can track down your family, remember?—will be furious. And any information we might have learned here will be gone."

"Do you think I don't know that?" I snapped. The promises I made to Marjana, to my mother, to Salima were ringing in my head . . . and yet to leave Tinbu to such a fate was unconscionable. "We will find another way, we always do. But right now, we're getting our friend out of prison, and I'm getting my ship back from those fucking Mamluks in the bay."

"*Your* ship?" Yusuf seemed to take me in anew, his eyes tracing my height and then going very, very wide. "By the Most High . . . they say her first mate was an Indian, but surely you cannot truly be—"

"No, surely I cannot. Let us leave it at that, yes?"

Yusuf opened and closed his mouth. "All right."

"Excellent." I glanced at the darkening sky with apprehension. I've never liked swift action. A proper job takes time to plan. The best take weeks of preparation for but a few hours of action. But Tinbu did not have weeks. I doubted he even had days.

I thought fast, contemplating my options. "Dalila, my light, do you remember the gold market in Kilwa? Could we get those materials in an hour?"

Dalila crossed her arms, giving me a severe look. "Obtaining those materials is not the same as blending them, and I have yet to agree to this idiocy."

"Oh, for God's sake, I will give you another percentage of my share, all right? Is there enough time?"

"Theoretically. The mixture does better when it's had a full day to simmer."

"If we wait a day, you will have to row instead of the crew."

She made a face. "Fine. But we have no elephant."

"We will make do with another distraction." I glanced at Tinbu's merchant, who was looking at us as though we had gone mad. "Yusuf . . . how is your acting?"

Exposé of the Tricks of Those Who Work Knockout Drugs and Other Stupefacients from The Book of Charlatans by the Learned Jamāl al-Dīn ʿAbd al-Raḥīm al-Jawbarī

Now listen here and I will tell you further of the worst poisons of the tribe of charlatans who call themselves the Banu Sasan. This is their most prodigious trick and the classiest of sleeping pills— "Blue Cretan" henbane. To concoct the most effective possible knockout drug, they take five dirhams by weight mature blue henbane, four dirhams black poppy seed, three dirhams opium, four dirhams euphorbium, five dirhams black seed, six dirhams agarikon, four dirhams lettuce seed, two dirhams basil seed, five dirhams mandrake apple, and two dirhams datura nut. All of this is pounded together, kneaded with leek juice, and made into pills, which are then fumigated with blue sulfur; the pills can be made only after it has been crushed to a powder. To drug a person, they give it to him in some food, drink, or halvah, and he falls asleep on the spot and has no idea of what's been done to him till he's revived by the administration of vinegar via the nose or is given blue tinder to sniff, after which he vomits up the drug. This is the most effective things of its kind I've come across. So wise up! Be mindful of what you consume, especially at the hands of suspicious characters.

Chapter 6

By midnight I was sequestered on Aden's newest promenade, an expensively constructed pavilion of alabaster and imported wood that fronted one of its wealthiest neighborhoods and offered stunning views of the crashing black waters of Sira Bay. With the moon a bare sickle, lamps and torches had been lit to chase back the night. By now most families had retired, pulling sleepy children home, but knots of men still ambled this way and that, chatting amicably and occasionally tossing a coin to the last beggars. A few vendors and buskers were beginning to depart as well, selling remaining portions of grilled fish and fried sesame pastries for a bargain.

But there was still enough of a crowd for me.

"Take a chance!" I cried, spreading my hands to display the three clay cups overturned on the rattan crate before me. My pot sat at my knee, an oil lamp burning brightly to show off the glittering coins inside. "Three fils, three chances to win!"

A group of youths wearing well-made clothes and finely embroidered belts had been watching me and nudging one another. They came over now.

"I shall take that bet," one boasted, his beard little more than a few hopeful black hairs on his chin.

I did not need to cheat to defeat his hopes and yet I did so anyway because old habits are hard to lose, and I had grown protective of my winnings. Switching the three clay cups round and round, I tucked a walnut in my little finger, slipping it back and forth as the boy chose wrongly to the disappointed groans of his fellows.

"Do not lose poorly!" I shouted at their retreating backs. "Come, try again!"

"I will play if you would have me." It was Yusuf. Tinbu's "client" now looked like an entirely different man from the fretful merchant I had accosted earlier. No longer dressed in Adeni fashion, he wore the loose robes and draped headcloth of a traveler from the interior. A foreigner, perhaps one unaccustomed to urban ways and local rogues.

"I would be delighted to have you, sir," I said magnanimously. "Have a seat. Do you know the rules?"

Yusuf settled himself with a regal air that was almost immediately undone by the quivering in his hands. "I . . . ah. Refresh my memory," he said, handing over three copper fils.

I held out the walnut in my palm and then placed it under one of the cups. "Watch closely when I move them. If you guess correctly which cup has the nut, my pot goes to you. Incorrectly and your coins stay with me. Understand?"

He nodded. "Go ahead."

I began swapping the cups around, my hands a blur of movement. I did not bother cheating this round—I was more preoccupied with ensuring my fingers slid over the clasp of the gold cuff Yusuf wore around his wrist.

Finally, I stopped. "Choose."

Without any hesitation, Yusuf tapped the leftmost cup—the one that had the walnut hidden underneath—and met my gaze with utter knowing in his eyes.

Well, didn't someone have depths? I was about to accuse him of cheating when a shrill female cry broke the air.

"That is her! That is the thief!"

I glanced up in practiced annoyance to see Dalila storming toward me, her wooden staff held before her like a queen's scepter, two policemen in her wake. She was as transformed as Yusuf, wearing her finest dress and veiling her face with a length of sheer embroidered cloth held in place by a pearled headband. Bangles and anklets of fool's gold and glass painted to resemble precious gems sparkled and chimed from her wrists and slippered feet.

"My boy came home saying he played her little game and lost far more than three fils—she stole his signet ring." Dalila flapped a bejeweled hand at my head. "I want her arrested!"

I feigned a look of affronted innocence. "I did no such thing."

"What's all this, then?" One of the cops nodded rudely at the cups and kicked over the pot of my winnings. "Some sort of gambling?"

"Search her!" Dalila clutched her jilbab below her chin. With a few artfully escaped tendrils of midnight hair and tears streaking her lovely kohl-lined eyes, she was the picture of noble suffering, beautiful and tender in a way men always needed to save. "*Please*. That ring has been in my family for generations. It is my only remembrance of my father."

"Curse your father for raising a liar!" I shouted.

A scandalized silence stole over the policemen. But only for a moment, until with some excitement, they realized they had a new reason to harass the poor.

"On your feet, wretch!" One grabbed me roughly, and I let slip the gold cuff I had stolen off Yusuf's wrist.

The cuff clattered to the dusty ground, and Yusuf's mouth fell open in genuine shock. We had not practiced that part; I find the occasional surprise in a confidence job makes the reaction of my coconspirators all the more authentic.

He made a choking sound. "Th-that is mine!" Quickly he caught up, glaring at me. "Thief!"

"Liar! All of you are! Trying to take advantage of a poor old woman with your spurious charges and aye—*do not touch me*!" I tried to pull free of the soldier's hands, falling against his body in a swift effort to assess if he carried anything at his waist besides a baton and dagger. No. Excellent. "Let me explain! By God, what is this world coming to when such dogs manhandle grandmothers on the street! I bet none of you are even local! A fine thing, for our foreign overlords to import men to harass honest Adenis! Is this what we pay taxes to support?"

I have not, in the entirety of my life, ever paid taxes. Or customs fees. Or fines of any sort (I do pay my zakat and give sadaqah, of course, for the Divine Authority is the only one I respect). But the words I was ranting were chosen with enough precision that truly honest Adenis were starting to stop and watch the confrontation.

The cops seemed to notice.

"Enough," one hissed. "All of you are coming to the police prefect. He can sort out your . . . by the Most High, what is in this *bag*?" He brought the saddlebag that had been underneath my crate near his face and then gagged, thrusting it toward his fellow. "It smells worse than an unwashed stable."

The second one danced away. "I don't want it!"

I lunged for the saddlebag. "Give that back!"

The first officer slapped me, and I stumbled, as a frail old woman might.

"Probably more stolen trinkets," he said dismissively. "Or just garbage. She sounds like a madwoman."

"She looks like a giant." His companion squeezed my bicep. "By God, woman. What do you eat to be built like some sort of warhorse?"

"Your father's—"

This time they hit me hard enough that I shut up.

We were led directly to the prison warehouse. The three of us made for a sorry lot: me getting prodded unnecessarily and cursing them all, Dalila fretfully weeping, and Yusuf looking like he regretted agreeing to this scheme in the first place.

Only one man stood guard outside the prison now, frowning as we approached. "What have you got here?"

"A thief and her victims."

"Alleged thief!" I corrected as I was shoved inside. Cushions lined one wall, and a low floor desk sat in the center of the office, crowded with papers, weights, and a large set of brass scales, the red-gold metal gleaming in the dim light. I took a moment to scan the room, judging what items could be used as weapons. An open doorway led into the yawning dark corridor of the cellblock—though I could see nothing in its lightless gloom. Save for two bored young men playing backgammon on the floor under the glow of an oil lamp, the room was empty, the officials having gone home.

Five men—unless there were additional guards in the prison itself. Not the greatest odds. I glanced at Yusuf out of the corner of my eye, wondering if he was good in a fight. He was the color of chalk and visibly trembling. Probably not.

One of the soldiers playing backgammon, his face marked by pox scars, glanced up. "What's all this?"

The soldier holding my bag pushed me to my knees. "Found a vagrant stealing from civilians down by the sea pavilion."

"I stole nothing, you impotent mule. Where are your witnesses?" I insisted. "I have such a right!"

"My cuff plainly fell out of your sleeve," Yusuf pointed out.

"Then perhaps it should not have been there!"

"God curse you." Dalila ran her hands down her face, fluttering her eyelashes, and three of the four soldiers took the opportunity to gaze upon her too long. "If you have induced my son to wickedness, I will see you charged. I will see you punished."

"Search her," the pox-marked officer said wearily.

They immediately set to doing so, patting me all over in a manner that was most inappropriate. When the poking and prodding was over, three sets of onyx earrings, the signet ring, four ivory bangles, a silver hair ornament, an embroidered bridle, and a bone penknife with tiny carnelians lay on the desk.

There was a moment of disbelieving silence.

I raised my hands, taking a more conciliatory tone. "I swear I can explain."

"No doubt you can." The cop pulled over a wooden writing board and pot of ink. "It's enough to hold her until the wali comes in tomorrow. The witnesses will need to make statements but . . . what is that *smell*?"

"Me," I said urgently. "I try not to bathe more than once a month. It keeps the bodily humors balanced."

"It's this bag," the officer still holding the saddlebag said, ignoring my excuse. "The vagrant was carrying it on her person."

He tossed the saddlebag to the floor, and the jarring motion sent up a thick, grassy waft of foul air. The man with the pox marks recoiled in disgust, but his companion stilled. There was a flash of suspicion—intrigue—in his expression, gone the next moment when he glanced up at the officers who'd brought us in.

"We shall take it from here, boys," he said smoothly, ignoring the confused look from his partner. "You can return to patrol."

He waited until the others had left before shooting me a cool, mocking grin. "Open it."

I made no move toward the bag. "I cannot. I am fermenting apricots in there. Best cure for gas, but if you expose them to air too early—wait!" I cried as the second man reached for his baton, clearly meaning to beat me into obedience. "*Fine.*"

I opened the bag. Nestled inside were two large, dark, sticky bricks of compressed herbs and resin.

The pox-marked soldier inhaled. "Is that what I think it is?"

"Sweets for my grandchildren," I lied. "Best halwa around."

"If that is halwa, I am the sultan of Iram," the other officer remarked. "I *thought* it smelled like hashish."

"But it's so dark," his fellow officer mused, picking up one of the bricks and bringing it to his nose. He inhaled with a shudder. "Oh. Oh, my. I bet that's strong."

"This is how the rich are said to take their hashish. I heard they dissolve it in sweet wine that they sip from the navels of dancing girls at their parties." The officer cut a glance at me. "Is that what you are, then? Some sort of drug runner for the nobility?"

"I am nothing of the sort," I said defiantly. "That is fertilizer for my garden. I confused it with the sweets for my grandchildren."

The man snorted. "Before or after you confused it with the fermenting apricots? You can't even keep your lies straight. Deceiving the police, vagrancy, theft, drug running . . . and here I thought the homicidal pirate would be our only excitement for the month."

"Still, perhaps we should try it," the pox-marked officer suggested. "Just a taste to confirm her story," he added more hastily.

"It is not hashish!" I sneered. "And if it was . . . how would a pair of country bumpkins such as yourselves even know? Tell me, for you have not a hair on the chin between the both of you, have your balls dropped yet? Or did your members, knowing they would never be inside a woman, not bother to mature thus?"

Their eyes flashed in anger at the crude insult to their manhood. And we all know where this is going, yes? I do not need to recall the snippy bits of rising invectives that led to the inevitable?

The soldiers tasted the cake.

A sliver had barely passed the lips of the first when he swooned, his eyes going glassy. "I . . . I do not feel right."

"I feel amazing," his fellow whispered. "I feel as though I could fly among the birds and compose a dozen verses and—" His eyes rolled upward and he crumpled to the floor

The other soldier stared at him, tilted his head, and abruptly keeled over.

Yusuf clasped a hand over his mouth. "God preserve me . . ." His voice was muffled through his fingers. "Did you just kill them?"

"No. But be silent." I grabbed one of the soldier's batons and headed for the door. I pressed my back flat against the wall, nodding to Dalila.

"Save me!" she cried, hefting up her staff and positioning herself near the doorway leading to the prison cells. "Oh, please help! She's gone mad!"

There was a flurry of motion and then the soldier who'd been standing guard outside rushed through the door. He was barely over the threshold when I cracked the baton over his head and knocked him out. In the next second, I rushed to join Dalila, but no soldiers emerged from the dark prison.

I waited a long, tense moment and then stepped back. "I think we are alone."

"*This* was your plan?" Yusuf sounded aghast. "What would you have done if they did not taste the cakes?"

I checked the pulse of the man I had knocked out, quickly binding the wound on his head. He would wake with a demon of a headache, but he likely would wake. "Yusuf, my dear, if I have learned anything in my years of work, it is to never underestimate the pride of young men. The moment I insulted them, they were going to taste the cakes. And if not? Well"—I held up the baton—"there are always contingencies."

"Contingencies," he repeated weakly, tiptoeing around the cakes as though they might lunge up and hurl themselves into his mouth. "Do I want to know what is in those?"

"You better not want to know anything." Dalila glared at him, possessiveness stealing into her voice. "That formula is *mine*. It took me years to perfect."

"He's not going to steal your formula," I assured Dalila. "Stay here and keep watch. Search the men and the office and take everything we can carry. Waterskins, weapons, food, and supplies. In that order. Yusuf"—I rooted into one of the soldier's pockets, pulled out a set of keys, and tossed them to the merchant—"time to free your lover."

Holding the wooden baton in one hand and an oil lamp in the other, I slipped through the door to the prison block. There were four cells: cramped places with barely enough room for two people each. That had not stopped the police from cramming in the twenty or so men making up the *Marawati*'s crew into the narrow lockups. Most were curled into tight balls on the floor, some sleeping, others looking dazed with thirst. A few straightened up when I passed, letting out soft sounds of sluggish surprise.

But I only had eyes for Tinbu. My best friend was not in a cell, he was shackled to the dirty floor at the end of the corridor, bleeding and alone. He'd been stripped to his waist and flogged, swollen lash marks crisscrossing his skin.

"Tinbu!" Yusuf rushed forward with the keys, swiftly unlocking the manacles around Tinbu's ankles.

"Yusuf . . ." Tinbu croaked through cracked lips. "You should not be here."

"It is all right," Yusuf replied. "We are here to rescue you."

Tinbu's bleary eyes blinked open. "*We?*"

I stepped forward. "We." I cut through the ropes binding his wrists with the knife the police had been too incompetent to find sheathed at my thigh. "Good to see you, my friend."

"Amina," Tinbu exhaled noisily. "Am I dead? Not even your timing could be this good."

"So, you do know each other." Yusuf stiffened. "You might have mentioned being the right hand of the most notorious female bandit of our time, Tinbu."

Guilt swept his face. "I was trying to go legitimate."

"You were *just* caught with illegal salvage."

"Yes, but . . ." Tinbu sat up, grimacing in pain. "I did not kill those men, I swear."

"Hey!" one of the imprisoned crew members called out. "Hey, lady! Pass over those keys, I beg you!"

"The two of you can hash this out another time," I hissed under my breath to Tinbu and Yusuf. "What is the shape of the *Marawati*? Is she seaworthy? Have you taken on provisions?"

"Provisions, no," Tinbu replied. "Not really. The water in the cistern is more vinegar than anything and I have no doubt the soldiers stole our food and anything else they could get their hands on. Seasonal repairs are done, and the ship is seaworthy, but the sails are tied up and the oars hidden under a false bottom."

I lowered my voice further. "And the crew?"

"Loyal and disreputable enough to be tempted by whatever you offer." Tinbu's bloodshot eyes met mine. "I assume you have something to offer?"

"I always do."

Yusuf and I hauled Tinbu to his feet. By now the rest of the crew had awakened, and with our escape appearing imminent came more pleas alongside a few offers of sexual innuendo that would have to be put down. They pressed themselves to the bars of the overcrowded cells, their sweaty faces shining in the light of my oil lamp. They were a diverse crew like the majority that ply these shores, their garments and tongues suggesting homelands in Ethiopia and India, the most southern reaches of East Africa and north to Aqaba. More were likely of mixed coastal heritage like myself, and around my age as well. There were a handful of youths and older men, the elders reliably sporting the missing limbs and milky eyes associated with a hard life at sea and the young ones looking like spry babies.

I had no doubt Tinbu had vetted them carefully. But if I've learned anything in my career, it's that men often respond to vetting differently depending on whether it is a man or a woman they are supposed to serve.

"Hey. Hey, lady. Big Lady." It was the first man who had spoken, his Arabic reminding me of Red Sea ports and his garments stained with cooking grease. "Let me out. I will make it worth your while, I swear."

"Oh, will you?" I handed Tinbu the oil lamp, my friend cringing as I strolled closer to the other man's cell. "How will you make it worth my while?"

He gave me a leering smile. "You are a good deal larger than the women I typically go for, but . . ." His gaze traced down my body and he leaned close, his teeth gleaming near the bars. "I am certain you still taste—"

I smashed the hilt of my dagger into his mouth. He let out a screech of pain, blood and at least two teeth flying. Before he could recoil, I grabbed his belt and yanked him against the bars.

I pressed my knife where his legs met. "The first offense costs a tooth. The second, something far dearer. So shut your fucking mouth and listen to me." I shoved him back and he fell into a pack of now very wide-eyed and utterly silent sailors.

I paced the cellblock, boldly meeting their eyes and examining them with brusque assessment. "I have little time so I will make this quick. I am the nakhudha known as Amina al-Sirafi. You have been crewing on my ship, the *Marawati*, a task Tinbu says you have performed somewhat competently. I am in Aden because I need my *Marawati*—and a crew—to steal something very precious for a rich old woman who has promised to shower all those who take part in the endeavor with gold."

"Bullshit." It was a skinny youth who shrank back when I turned on him. "I mean, respectfully. No one has seen Amina al-Sirafi in ten years. How do we know you are truly her?" He glanced at Tinbu. "What say you?"

Tinbu bowed his head, knowing better than to talk in my defense. I would not work with anyone who needed a man to speak for me. "She is my nakhudha," he said simply.

"And I return for my own," I added. "But none of you are my men, and truthfully, the smaller the group, the easier it will be to sneak away." I frowned, as though reconsidering my offer. "Can any of you even row an oared ship?"

There was a moment of hesitation and then they broke.

"*Yes,*" a stout man with a heavy Persian accent said breathlessly. "I have been rowing for years. I know the patterns well and can teach others."

"And I am willing to learn!" the skinny youth said quickly. "I'm a great lookout too, best eyes on the ship."

I clucked my tongue with doubt. "You would need to decide together. That is how my crew does things."

As you might imagine, the choice between "stay behind to face possible crucifixion for piracy" or "escape with the large, armed woman promising riches" was not a difficult one. We freed the men swiftly and slipped out, stepping over the crumpled bodies of the now very naked cops.

Tinbu glanced between the bare bodies, the *completely* stripped office, and the hashish cakes before glancing at Dalila and bowing his head. "Mistress of Poisons . . . glad to see you have not let your skills deteriorate."

"Idiot." Dalila smiled sweetly. "She came to me first."

"It is not a competition, Dalila," I said. "Should I ask why the cops are naked?"

"A professional thief leaves nothing behind," she replied, tying up the last bundle. "But there were no weapons besides the soldier's batons and daggers. And only a single skin of water."

"Pass the water around. Each man gets a sip. Tinbu, you said the oars were *underneath* the deck?"

Still leaning on Yusuf's arm, he nodded. "They can be pried loose, but oared galleys of the *Marawati*'s size tend to make port authorities skittish, and I've been trying to pass her off as an old fishing ship."

"How long would it take to free the oars?"

"Not long; I made sure the planks concealing them could be easily pried off. But getting them out and laid is going to be loud. If those warships are still there . . ."

"They are," Dalila confirmed. "I saw them when I went to fetch the police."

I swore. Those oars were our only chance of escaping Sira Bay. The sails would take even longer to set up and there was little wind tonight either way.

Tinbu spoke again. "There is, ah, something on board that might help us. Something I found when I salvaged the iron ship. I hid it before we were boarded, but I doubt the soldiers found it. The wali would have added its possession to my charges."

"Tinbu, you are *deeply* worrying me."

He raised his hands in the same imploring gesture that had gotten him knocked out by the police. "Just listen. I have an idea."

Chapter 7

We slipped out of the office in knots of two and three, making our way through Aden's midnight streets. Dalila and I had stashed our traveling bags in an adjoining alley, and I retrieved my sword and my grandfather's khanjar with haste, feeling better the moment they were back on my person.

It was an astonishingly dark night. By the time we reached the beach, the water was a blur of churning blackness marked only by the crash of silver surf and the shattered light of moonbeams rising and falling with the waves. It was impossible to distinguish between the horizon and the sea, let alone make out the contours of the harbor and distant seawall. The *Marawati* was a bobbing cutout of stars and shadows marked by the faint light of a few torches burning on the warship anchored at her side. There was only one vessel there now, the second lurking God only knew where.

I glanced at Tinbu. "Do you think you'll be able to swim?"

His voice was laced with pain, but he nodded. "You'd be amazed the things I can do when fleeing prison."

"Then this is where I leave you," Yusuf said softly.

Tinbu spun to face him. "Come with me."

"I cannot." Even in the dark, I saw the heartbreak writ across the Jewish merchant's face. "I could not abandon my family like that."

"What if we kidnap you?" Tinbu pleaded. "Then it wouldn't be your fault."

"I doubt they would appreciate the difference." Yusuf touched Tinbu's cheek. "We will see each other again, I know it. Nakhudha-whose-name-I-am-avoiding, you will take care of him?"

"I will," I promised. "And thank you for your assistance. You have a future in the cups game should you be interested."

Yusuf shuddered. "I have had enough adventure. God be with you all."

Lovers parted, we crept across the beach and entered the water with as little movement as possible. Though the *Marawati* wasn't anchored too far offshore, our swim was long and purposefully slow. I drifted more than swam, my soaked traveling clothes heavy and my bags floating around my shoulders. The water this time of year was warm, the salty taste rushing over my lips as I watched for any movement on the *Marawati*'s deck. Had the moon been brighter, we might have been visible, but the sea was black as pitch.

We gathered in the water at the stern end, the men clutching the twin side rudders as they bobbed in the tide's pull. I swam for the anchor chain and started to climb, my heart in my throat. It was dark, yes, but if any of the soldiers glanced over, I would have an arrow in my chest before I could drop back into the sea.

My arms were aching by the time I finally slipped aboard. I had an irrational urge to hug the *Marawati*'s worn wooden railing, to press my brow to the damp hull as I reunited with my beloved ship for the first time in ten years. It felt like this moment should be more momentous, more solemn. Then again, having to sneak on board was probably more fitting given our history. I dropped into a crouch, surveying what I could. The *Marawati* had been trashed, supplies and belongings tossed everywhere. But with the crew imprisoned and a warship nearby, the authorities must have felt confident, for they had left only a single soldier sitting on my captain's bench. He was awake, thumbing the beads of a misbaha as he murmured his way through dhikr.

I hesitated. It was a great sin to attack a fellow Muslim at prayer, and yet what choice did I have? If I failed to act, I risked the lives of all my men. So I snuck up behind him, clamping a rag over his mouth at the same moment I pressed my khanjar to his throat.

"I have no wish to kill you," I whispered. "Stay silent and you will survive this night." Granted I did not give him much choice, stuffing the rag in his mouth as I divested him of his weapons and bound him with rope. Once the soldier was secure, I motioned silently to the men waiting in the water.

They moved fast, crawling over the deck like spiders, taking their places as we had planned as the ship swayed and dipped with the movement of the midnight ocean, every knock of water against the wooden planks making my heart race. My instincts were on high alert, waiting for the cry of alarm I knew would eventually come from the other boat. But it didn't, not yet. Aden was a law-abiding place, the prospect of people sneaking onto a vessel floating beside a galley full of soldiers likely so ludicrous they were barely watching the *Marawati*.

Tinbu joined me at the captain's bench. "Do not be angry with me," he began, always a promising start. "It was the most secure place I knew." He slid apart a series of panels beneath the bench that had not been there when I last sailed to reveal a shallow, hidden space and started removing objects: his bow and quiver, a leather coin purse, a well-wrapped rectangular parcel . . .

"Is that my rahmani?" I breathed. "You put *my family's navigation manuals* in with—"

"Would you rather they have been seized by the wali?" Far more gingerly, Tinbu lifted out a medium-sized wooden crate and set it down between us. He pried open the lid, clearing away the cotton batting that had been used to cushion the four cylindrical objects nestled inside. They were brass bowls wired into coconut-sized spheres, and I could already smell what was hidden at their core: the acrid aroma of pine resin and sulfur that sours the belly of any sailor. The scars on my wrist itched.

Naft.

Few weapons are more feared on the sea than naft, a substance of near-mythic origins. There are many Rum who believe naft is sacred, a miracle granted to their people to fend off the would-be conquest of Constantinople centuries ago. An oily substance, it ignites with water and does not cease to burn until there is nothing *left* to burn. In their Mediterranean Sea, mercifully far to the north, their warships carry great pumps, astonishing marvels of technology that spew naft over a burning flame to create lethal jets that can incinerate an enemy across the waves.

In its deadliest form, naft is a zealously guarded state secret, one both scholars and spies have died to protect. We do have copycats, various recipes for a pitch that can be stuffed into canisters and hurled by catapults or by hand, or that arrows may be dipped in. It is not enough to incinerate invading navies (though to be fair, we do not really have "invading navies"—the Indian Ocean is either too vast or northerners more querulous, God alone knows best). Some of the wealthier trade ships and many of the warships around here carry at least some form of the concoction, which they typically cobble together themselves in an effort that has never, ever gone wrong and burned down their own vessels.

A carton of *that* was what Tinbu had found floating amongst the iron ore he had salvaged.

Dalila joined us. The three of us had been on enough misadventures that no one needed to speak as our eyes met above the box of fiery death, but Dalila did so anyway because she believes in murdering hope whenever possible. "What if it does not work?"

"What if it *does* work?" Tinbu countered. "Why must you always be so cynical?"

"Being cynical has kept me out of prison. How has being naïve worked for you? And what if those warships have their defenses up?"

There *were* defensives against naft. Vinegar-soaked surfaces were usually impenetrable, and sand could smother small pockets of it. And if we had been pirates about to raid a vulnerable merchant vessel in the open sea, I might have been concerned.

But we were facing a warship in the most secure port in the western Indian Ocean. Aden did not fear invaders from the sea; the sole attempt had been years ago and resulted in the attackers being butchered on the beach. These ships and their soldiers were here to deal with smugglers and bandits—an attack on *themselves* would have been suicidally foolish. Clever pirates stayed far away from properly armed foes, preferring easier prizes.

"They have no reason to be expecting such an attack," I argued, trying for more confidence than I felt. "But keep two of the devices back."

"Why?" Tinbu asked.

"For when the second warship inevitably turns up. Take your places and wait for my signal."

I returned to my captain's bench, taking command of the *Marawati* for the first time in a decade and setting my gaze upon the horizon. I had been studying the stars all night, orienting myself to the layout of the sea, letting memories long buried rise to the surface. There was a time I knew Sira Bay like the back of my hand. Knew its currents and sandbars and the breakers against the ancient seawall. A time when I was brashly confident in my abilities as one of the best—most feared—nawakhidha in the Indian Ocean.

I prayed I could be that person again.

Taking a deep breath, I whispered a prayer and glanced down, meeting the expectant gaze of the broadly built Sumatran sailor—named, inexplicably, Tiny—who everyone had agreed had the most accurate throwing arm. I nodded.

Tiny raised his arm, rolled back his entire body, and hurled the brass projectile of naft at the brightest light burning on the warship. I swear to the Almighty that time itself seemed to slow as the incendiary sailed through the air toward a large glass lantern hanging from the stern ornament—and then completely missed, instead smashing into the stern ornament itself with a thunderously loud crack that promptly woke every soldier on the ship.

"What was that?" a distant voice cried, followed by exclamations in whatever tongue the imported warriors spoke back home. The naft that had been in the smashed projectile glistened and dripped in the firelight, but it was too far from the lamp to catch flame.

"There are people aboard the Indian's ship!"

Well, there went discretion. "Again!" I cried. Tiny did not need to be told twice; he threw the second projectile with all his might and this time it struck true, shattering the lantern and bursting into flame.

"Now!" I shouted.

With the zeal of men fleeing crucifixion, bisection, and the hanging of body parts, my new crew tore into the *Marawati*.

Hammers and crowbars, penknives and bare hands, they ripped into the false floorboards and smashed through the painted bark panels concealing the oar frames. At the same time, another pair of men began hauling up the front anchor as Tinbu set the side rudders at the slant I had indicated.

Chaos engulfed the warship. In the time it took us to break out the oars, the Mamluk soldiers had attempted to put out the fire with their cloaks and waterskins—accomplishing nothing but spreading it farther. Panicked voices cried out in confusion as the soldiers raced about the ship. Arrows had not started flying yet, but I knew they would soon enough.

It was a credit to Tinbu's ingenuity and training that the crew had the oars out and set up so quickly, but as I took over the rudders and he raced to lead the men in rowing, alarm spiked through me at their messy, uneven lines. The *Marawati* is not a large ship; the oars are light enough that they require only two men each rather than the giant galleys with a team per blade. However, several men were hugging the oar to their chest instead of holding it by the handles, a couple facing the wrong direction altogether.

"Nakhudha!" It was the outspoken Parsi youth, Firoz. He gestured wildly at the burning warship, and I glanced over just in time to see the spreading fire overwhelm their mainsail.

This had two consequences:

One, with naft burning in multiple locations, most of the soldiers jumped overboard, preferring to chance the short swim to the beach and possible dishonor to a fiery death.

Two, the soldiers who stayed behind were that lethal combination of stupidly brave and well trained enough to pick up their bows and start shooting at us.

"Heave!" I cried, ducking an arrow that whizzed past my face. "Stay low! Pull fast!"

The *Marawati*'s sides were high and curved to protect the oarsmen, but my heart climbed in my throat as the few men not rowing rushed to take shelter. Mercifully after a few false starts, the *Marawati* began to move. Achingly, *agonizingly* slow at first. But as the men fell into a rhythm, we gathered speed. We were not going *fast*—not without the sails. But the burning warship lagged behind, the arrows less and less frequent until they fell away altogether.

Now I just had to get us out of the harbor.

I followed the stars, adjusting the rudders to lead northward out of the bay and searching for the waves crashing against the breakwater that walled off the harbor and would mark where I could make my exit. But the sea was calm, and it was not until we were quite close that I spotted the ancient stone causeway.

Along with the second warship, moving to block our escape.

Cursing, I tried to gauge the distance to the other vessel and our speed. Beyond the warship beckoned the open ocean, where our small size would make us nearly impossible to catch in the dark. And while the warship was not large enough to block the entire waterway, it had the advantage of a side position by which to loose an entire cavalcade of arrows as we approached.

I contemplated my options. None were great.

Dalila joined me. Her warning was low, for my ears alone. "They are watching you."

She did not need to say anything else. The nervous, expectant eyes of my crew glimmered in the dark. I could feel the weight of their doubt, their fear. They might have been willing to cut a deal to escape prison, but now their fate was in the hands of a stranger. A woman. I have felt that tension too many times in my life, that knife's edge where it would take very little to tip into mutiny and a grisly death.

I glanced at Tinbu. "Speed up."

He let out a soft sound of surprise. "Nakhudha?"

"Do it." I raised my voice, knowing it would carry along the water to the approaching soldiers. "*RAM THEM!*"

Hamid, the cook who had spoken out of turn in the prison and lost two teeth for his trouble, took exception to this plan.

"*Ram* them?" he repeated. "Are you out of your mind? We will sink both ships!"

"Whether or not we sink both ships is up to them. Because by the time we get close, we shall be going too fast to stop. Our choice is between freedom and a brigand's death. They know that." I glared at him. "And a brigand's death will be kinder than the one I will serve you should you question me again."

Hamid glanced desperately at Tinbu. He was not the only one, the crew looking to their old leader to step in.

But Tinbu was mine before he was theirs. "The nakhudha has already saved you once, has she not? Speed up!" He let out a howl, clapping his hands. "Let those dirt-loving horsemen know the ocean's sons are coming to drown them!"

I feel like I should clarify, for I have insulted them now at depth: the Mamluk soldiers stolen from distant lands who can barely tread water are genuinely admirable warriors. Terrifying ones—when they fight Franks or rulers who don't pay them. They are astonishingly skilled riders, knowledgeable in weapons I've never even heard of, and well disciplined.

But they're not locals. They're not seafolk. And facing off against crazy sailors and divers who could swim before they lost their milk teeth in the middle of a midnight bay?

I had made worse gambles.

"Speed up! Ram them!" Tinbu's cry carried, the men adding their own shouted threats and wild hollers. Nearly all were rowing, but those who were not stomped their feet, hurling insults.

The wind was flat, but we seemed to fly across the water, the men finally falling into tempo. The oars rose and fell with great splashes that broke the black water, its spray drenching.

"Get down!" I ordered when we were within arrow range. "Move, you bastards," I added under my breath, praying whoever was in charge on the warship saw wisdom. I wasn't confident; there was great commotion and confused yelling aboard the other vessel. A few arrows were loosed our way—some of which were flaming. But our ship was already soaked, and they were quickly smothered.

However, the galley still wasn't moving away. I spotted men at their oars, but the order must not have been decided.

Well then, I could give them something else to consider. "Tinbu, get your bow and a dry flint."

He obeyed, returning with a handful of arrows already prepared. He gestured to the crow's nest. "I will take the shot from there. It offers the clearest view."

I took the bow from his hands. "I will take the shot."

"Amina . . ."

Tinbu's voice was low, but I hushed him further. "Trust me, I know

which of us is the better archer. But you're injured and it needs to be me."
I was not customarily one to let pride dictate such matters: one cannot be
a nakhudha without knowing when to delegate.

But I wanted to make damn sure the crew knew who they owed their
lives to tonight.

I slung the bow over my shoulder and climbed the mast, clutching
the worn rope ladder as my heart skipped in fear—I have always hated
heights. Pulling myself into the crow's nest, I stood, bracing my feet.

Tinbu raised a pot of pitch-soaked arrows up the rig. I lit them carefully, relieved our own sails were still tied back. The swaying of the ship
and the salt-dried wooden mast were risk enough. I pulled back the bow.
The string whispered against my cheek, the fiery arrowhead cracking and
hissing. The warship—which had seemed so close, the wall we would
break ourselves upon—now looked much smaller, a moving target on a
churning midnight sea. I had only six arrows.

If he *were here, you would not miss. That other ship would have already lost you in the blackness or the wind would be ripe for the sails.*

But he was not here, and I had learned the hard way not to rely on a demon's luck. I let loose my arrows and by the grace of God, they flew true. I
was not as talented an archer as Tinbu, but enough arrows struck the warship's mainsail that soon it was aflame. That must have been enough for
the soldiers aboard to decide being rammed by a bunch of crazy pirates
and drowning in the dark was a worse fate than obeying a power-hungry
government official. Their oars began moving in the firelight and so did
their ship, leaving a clear path for us to escape.

"God be praised, they are retreating!" A cheer went up from among my
men. "The nakhudha did it!"

"The nakhudha did," I muttered, lowering the bow and murmuring a
prayer of thanks. I leaned back against the mast, catching my breath as
we surged past the breakwater, the deep ebony of the open ocean pulling
us into its concealing embrace.

Behind us, the ships were burning bright enough to light up Sira Bay, to light up Aden itself, the powerful city in which I was supposed to have met Salima and hunted down clues of her missing granddaughter. Discretion, I had promised the Sayyida. A few careful questions of trusted contacts, I had sworn to my mother.

That night should have been a sign that this would only get worse.

Excerpt from a Warning about the Malabar Coast

"... sales have been bountiful, praise be to God, and a full inventory of cargo will follow this letter. The nakhudha tells me he intends to take on additional archers and fighting men for the return journey. Apparently, the raiders off the Malabar Coast have been more of a plague than usual, some say because harvests in the region have been poor. I saw no such pirates on the trip here but have heard plenty of tales. While the people of India practice a great diversity of faiths, old communities of Muslims, Jews, and Christians along with those who worship local deities and various Brahmanical devotions—all disavow the crafty Malabar pirates who till their fields in one season and 'till' the seas in other; if by 'till' one means taking to the ocean in a vast flotilla of rafts, dugouts, and speedy cutters to harvest any merchant ship that strays too close.

It is a family affair, the villages emptying out and wives and children doing their part. The raiders are astonishingly clever with boats; there is nothing they cannot make seaworthy; it is said some of them have survived months floating upon but a bare piece of lumber, so talented they are in maritime endurance. They can row for days and send an arrow through the eye of a lookout from a frightening distance away.

As their children are born into such a life, they make for prized captives, as worthy as a steppe-lad who being placed in a saddle from toddlerhood makes a most excellent Mamluk. Our nakhudha says he once owned such a slave, a Malabar youth seized when he was an adolescent who grew into the most talented boatman the nakhudha had ever known. In the raiders' hearts, however, deceit cannot be rooted out. After a decade of service, the slave turned on his master and the straight path of guidance he had offered in favor of some cursed crew of bandits led by a woman. The ingratitude of it all!"

Chapter 8

We rowed through the night, eager to put as much distance between us and Aden as possible. Shortly before daybreak, the wind picked up enough for the sails to be raised, God be praised, and I left my captain's bench to check on Tinbu.

I had ordered him to rest in the small galley, one of the few places on the *Marawati* where one could enjoy a bit of privacy, but found him awake and arguing with Dalila as she attempted to apply a foul-smelling poultice to the lash marks on his back.

"—I am *moving* because it stings like a hundred wasps are attacking me. There are times, Dalila, that I think you enjoy—Amina!" Tinbu's eyes lit up as I ducked inside the galley to join them. "Save me. Dalila says she is here to help, but I'm fairly certain I'm being experimented upon."

"You know the price for my skills," Dalila chided. "If you don't like it, stop getting caught so easily."

Tinbu grumbled and I took a moment to look him over in the dawn light filtering through the cracks in the wall. Other than his wounds and the morose look in his brown eyes, Tinbu appeared criminally un-affected by the last ten years, his waist trim and his arms well muscled from ship work. His glossy black hair was thick as the day I left, now streaked with a dashing stripe of silver. The only other change was a jaunty mustache, the curled tips of which I could tell from a glance he oiled every morning.

"Nice mustache," I remarked. "Is that to impress the pretty-eyed merchant?"

Tinbu's expression grew even glummer. "Would it be so wrong to kidnap him?"

"My friend, he just found out you're a criminal. Give it a little time before you commit a crime *against* him. Speaking of which . . . what were you thinking, attempting to bribe a new government official? You know they need a few months to become properly corrupt."

"He was winking at me!"

"You were on a boat in the middle of the day," Dalila pointed out. "Did it not cross your mind that he was blinking in the sun?"

"It was entrapment."

"Sure it was." I sat across from Tinbu, leaning against the galley's thin wall of woven branches as the *Marawati* crested a gentle swell. "I trust you are otherwise well? How was the visit with your family?"

"Like all such visits. My parents are healthy and hale, but did I know how much happier they would be if I returned home for good? Especially since so-and-so has a daughter looking to wed." Tinbu sighed. "My brothers and sisters have provided them with a dozen grandchildren. You would think they would be content."

I gave him a sympathetic look. Like me, Tinbu hails from a long line of sea raiders, though if mine were wandering pirates, his were scavengers who rarely strayed from their homeland on the Malabar Coast, preferring to plunder the rich merchant ships when they passed by, then returning to their crops and villages for the harvest. It is a lucrative but risky profession—Tinbu was captured during a raid gone bad when he was a teenager and spent ten years as a slave before our paths crossed.

"Perhaps it is less about grandchildren and more about wanting their son safe at home," I argued gently. "I can scarcely blame them."

"I know." Tinbu winced and sat up so Dalila could finish his bandages. "But I cannot live the life they want, and I spent too many years serving the whims of another to cage myself again. This is best. They get money and occasional visits; I get pretty-eyed merchants. But I know you did not come to Aden to harass me on my parents' behalf, so let's talk about this job."

"Has Dalila filled you in?"

"Less than I had to," Dalila cut in. "Tinbu had his own run-in with Falco."

"*What?*" I was immediately tense. Falco had tracked down Asif's family and gotten a letter to Dalila. Now he had also learned of my first mate?

Tinbu held up a hand. "It wasn't as bad as she makes it sound. His agent sought me out, that was all. An old acquaintance of mine from Hormuz by the name of Layth. He used to work for the pirate princes out of Kish, but he must have run afoul of someone because he's been on this side of the peninsula putting crews together for captains with less-than-savory business."

I glanced at Dalila. "The letter you received from Falco . . . his agent had the same name, no?"

"He did," she answered. "But it wasn't Tinbu whom Falco was seeking. It was *you*, nakhudha."

"*Me?*"

"You," Tinbu confirmed. "Layth said he had a Frank who was looking for a captain and gotten his heart set on Amina al-Sirafi. Falco apparently spoke of your exploits day and night, saying he had been promised you were the best smuggler in the Indian Ocean and there was nothing you couldn't steal." He paused, a hint of apology in his eyes. "He seems to believe you are blessed by the supernatural."

Blessed. A sour taste bloomed in my mouth, the word lodging in my gullet. Granted, such gossip had long swirled around me. Men find it easier to believe they have been swindled by a witch than outwitted by a woman. I used to find the stories entertaining, the more outrageous the better.

I stopped finding them entertaining a long time ago. "What does he want with me?"

"He probably hopes you will take him to new places to plunder," Dalila suggested. "You heard his letter. He's a treasure seeker, out to collect all the shiny, fascinating things that catch his eye."

"Regrettably, I am not feeling very collectible," I said curtly. "What did you tell him, Tinbu?"

"The usual lies. That last I heard you'd retired somewhere beyond India to surround yourself with wine and jewels and beautiful men. Layth seemed to believe it; he said he'd already told Falco that no one had seen Amina al-Sirafi in years."

"Did you not think to warn me?"

Tinbu gave me a pointed look. "You were with your family in peace, Amina. Perhaps I did not want you to be tempted by his offer."

I scowled, but his was not an entirely unjustified point, considering Salima had already lured me out.

Dalila started pacing, tugging at the cross around her neck, something she did only when she was truly worried. "I don't like this. It's been a decade since we were active and there are a dozen other captains he could have hired. Amina is notorious enough to attract idle gossip, but the rest of us . . ."

"The Frank isn't working off idle gossip," I realized, the insight sending a finger of ice down my spine. "He's been speaking with someone who knew us. Knew us well." I paused, not wanting to say the name. "A candidate comes to mind."

The insinuation landed like a thunderclap. We all knew who I meant.

"It would fit," Dalila agreed. "He never did like me very much."

Tinbu's expression grew stormy. "Majed would *never* sell us out. I know you two didn't part under the best terms, but he wouldn't betray us."

"Didn't part under the best terms" was an understatement. What happened to Asif shattered my crew in different ways, but for Majed—my navigator and a man who had once been like an elder brother—it was an end a long time coming.

"I'm not saying Majed willingly sold us out," I clarified. "But what if the Frank gave him no choice?"

"Falco could have killed him for it," Dalila offered unhelpfully. "Majed was never very good in a fight."

Tinbu shook his head. "I had a letter from Majed last month. He sounded fine."

I was immediately, unjustifiably stung. "Majed writes to you?"

"He does. I have visited his family in Mogadishu."

His family? Now I felt like an ass. "I didn't even know he had married."

"Oh, yes. To a widow from one of the local clans. They have a young son and a baby girl." Tinbu rolled his eyes. "Beautiful family, but the man has gone completely, violently, *annoyingly* straight. He's been on hajj multiple times and cares for a whole bunch of orphans with a, get this, *government* job. He reports directly to the muhtasib, though I believe he still does a bit of mapmaking on the side."

I shuddered. Majed reported to the market inspector? *The market inspector?* That was as close to turning traitor as I could imagine. "Has he ever taken the portion I set aside for him?"

"No. He said it's the devil's money."

"Stubborn idiot. All right." I rose to my feet, swaying with the movement of the *Marawati*. Through the cracks in the wall, I could see the golden-brown line of the distant coast, the rising sun sparkling on the pink water. "So if not Majed, who else could have told Falco about us?"

Dalila threw me an annoyed glare. "Maybe if we had not triggered a prison escape and lit multiple warships on fire back in Aden, we would be able to ask around. As was our *original* plan."

"Ah, but then you would not have rescued me from a dire fate," Tinbu pointed out cheerfully. "Besides, I might have a lead."

"Which is?"

"Layth, Falco's agent. We got to talking quite a bit. As I said, I knew him from back in the day, and he sounded like no matter how good the money was, he was getting tired of dealing with Falco's shit. He mentioned that once he'd found Falco a ship and a captain, he was thinking about going to Zabid to spend his earnings."

My spirits brightened. Zabid was farther north but not too far away. And finding Falco's recruiter sounded more promising than chasing gossip in Aden. "Clearly breaking you out of prison was very worth it," I said, giving Dalila a victorious smirk. "We'll head to Zabid after picking up supplies."

Tinbu smiled. "See, Dalila? Nothing to—oh! Payasam!" Tinbu dropped to his knees, recent wounds be damned, to peer through a stack of crates. He rubbed his fingers together, making a soothing sound. "Come on out, beautiful girl. I was getting worried about you!"

There was a loud, pitiful meow, and then the most bedraggled ship's cat I had ever seen emerged. A skinny, rust-brown thing the color of a tool left in the sea air, its fur stuck up in clumps and it was missing an ear.

Tinbu rushed to collect the cat, cuddling it close to his chest. "Did those nasty soldiers scare you?" he asked in a singsong voice.

The cat made a sound between a death rattle and a wheeze in response, knocking its head so hard into Tinbu's chin it had to hurt.

"Your . . . mouser?" Dalila asked, sounding doubtful.

Tinbu flushed. "We are still working on the 'catching mice' part. But Payasam noticed a spider the other day. Even put a paw on it!"

He shared this accomplishment with the pride of a father announcing his child's marriage, and I rubbed my temples, feeling a headache come on. "Tinbu, please tell me that you did not choose the only cat incapable of catching mice to bring aboard my ship. What does it eat? Because its name better not indicate you are wasting rice and sugar on it."

The cat gave me a doleful look.

Tinbu crossed his arms defensively over the creature. "Payasam is not an 'it,' and *she* eats from my rations alone. The crew is very fond of her; she has brought us only good fortune."

"You were all about to be crucified for murder and brigandry."

"Until—in an astonishing bit of luck—my best friends turned up to save me." His eyes danced. "And now that you have connected *with* me, I am to lead you directly to Falco's own agent." Tinbu snuggled the cat to his face and kissed it very loudly. "My lucky, million-dinar cat."

Chapter 9

Once we were supplied with fresh water for the cistern and food from an accommodating fishing village used to looking the other way, we headed for Zabid. The wind was mostly favorable, giving us plenty of time to return the *Marawati* to its beautiful self in a blur of wood dust. The broken boards and torn matting used to conceal the oars and oar ports were repurposed, fashioned into sturdy fighting platforms and shooting barriers. We strung fishing line behind the ship and made a big drum from a broken barrel and canvas to scare away the aggressive sharks and whales that make the waters near the Red Sea their home. But except for a ship's cat that did not actually hunt mice (and which—in the manner of its species sensing human dislike—took a violent love of me), Tinbu had kept the *Marawati* in prime shape, and there was little to complain about.

Despite my dismay upon learning it had been stored alongside naft, the ship's original rahmani—the nautical notes my grandfather had begun, my father had edited, and I had expanded—were also well-preserved. Our family's rahmani were priceless, among the most comprehensive captain's journals in the Indian Ocean, replete with carefully annotated maps, star charts, and anecdotes that detailed everything from the currents around Comoros to the reefs outside Jeddah, the best mangrove forests to hide in in Malabar and a concealed smuggler's cove outside Sur. It was not as comprehensive as Majed's collection of rahmani—I doubted anything was—

but Majed himself had gone through these notes countless times, making observations and corrections in his precise handwriting.

I had made a duplicate of the rahmani, copying its pages over the years and sending them along with the money I forwarded to my mother, but I hadn't the heart to take the original notes when I retired. They belonged with the *Marawati*, a decision that felt even more right when I reviewed them now, reading about our past adventures from the captain's bench as seabirds squawked and my new crew sang work shanties.

As for that crew, I did not sit on laurels for having saved them in Aden. I trusted Tinbu to select men carefully, but knew better than him how frequently a man can feign respect for a woman only to turn on her. I was the nakhudha, their provider and protector, and if I needed to play up some of the old legends of Amina al-Sirafi, so be it. The sailors who've served me most loyally have always done so with a healthy mixture of fear and love; it is only a rare few I've ever taken into my true confidence. I was strict but fair, making clear my expectations.

Bonding with a new crew also meant sitting with them, learning of their families and traditions, the sort of casual discussions over chores and rest that never fail to bring me delight. Those of us who make the sea our home carry libraries in our head, a fact I have tried to impress upon many a land-dwelling intellectual. The scholars who travel the world to study could learn just as much if they would speak to the sailors, porters, and caravan hands who ferry them and their books to such faraway lands. My crewmates had lived fascinating lives, sharing tales of tapping for sap in forests so deep and dark one needed a torch to see, and of fending off sharks with spears as they dove for rare mollusks off islands with unfamiliar names.

A few of the men had also heard stories of our Frankish treasure hunter, and their gossip painted a troubling portrait. A noble like Salima might regard Falco as a gullible, indecorous brute, but from my sailing brethren, there was wary fear. Supposedly several men under his employ had gone missing, and people whispered that he had access to magic, an inner eye that knew things it should not. There were more gruesome rumors as well: that he'd bathed in so much innocent blood he'd forged a devilish armor that could not be penetrated. That he was more beast than man and had the claws and teeth of a wolf. That he made his followers sign their marks to magical squares that promised retribution if they betrayed him.

Now, I knew too well how such ridiculous legends grew. How could I not, hearing that I myself was half djinn, married to the king of an island that appeared only at the full moon, and that together we delighted in sucking the marrow out of our victims' bones? But that night on the lagoon kept returning to me. My own life had taught me that true magic is rare, much rarer than people would believe, but also deadlier. Salima had not mentioned the sort of talismans Falco sought and Dalila had dismissed his interest in the supernatural as that of a naïve mark. But Dalila was a professional charlatan used to running tricks and Salima was intent on protecting her family's reputation—might their biases have prevented them from sensing a different kind of danger?

However, in those early sun-filled days back on the *Marawati*, it took more than murky rumors about mysterious Franks to dampen my joy at being at sea again. As I finished praying one afternoon, the scent of salt and teakwood coming through the fabric of the cloak I pressed my brow against, the *Marawati* rolling and creaking in the water as I shifted positions, my soul was suddenly filled with such pleasure it brought tears to my eyes. Salah has always had a different quality out here, a rawer one. There is a great vulnerability in being entirely at God's mercy, a position akin to a worm upon a floating splinter that with the slightest ripple may be lost forever.

It's a vulnerability that brings to the surface truths long buried in your heart. And the truth was that Frankish kidnapper or no Frankish kidnapper, I had *desperately* missed this life. I had missed praying at sea. I had missed jesting with my beloved companions and falling asleep after a hard day's labor to the gentle rocking of the current. I had missed the ocean's briny air in my face and the too-bright glare of the sun. And yes, although doing so had spectacularly blown up our original plans, I had enjoyed the brazenness of breaking the *Marawati*'s crew out of prison. In saving innocent—yes, that's relative—men from a horrific fate because some blasted civil servant wanted to look important. Indeed, it was difficult not to see God's hand in setting me in Aden the very day Tinbu needed me. I am a believer, after all, and we are told to look for signs.

What did it mean if those signs pointed to a path I had sworn to disavow?

I sighed, turning my head from right to left, greeting and apologizing to the overworked angels recording my deeds, and then winced as I accidentally pressed my bad knee against the deck. I was hardly the only Muslim needing a bit of extra maneuvering while praying, but the reminder of my age was not a welcome one.

You are too old for these adventures. You should be home with your family. Home with your daughter. As swiftly as pleasure had lightened my soul, it was swept away by guilt. How could I enjoy being on the *Marawati* if it kept me from the daughter I loved more than life? I ached to hear Marjana's happy humming and spy her sweet little face. And though I would never have dared brought her on such a dangerous mission, I knew she would have delighted in being at sea: searching for dolphins and lying flat on her belly to peer at the colorful fish dashing through the deep corals.

But by the time we were approaching Zabid, I had put personal fretting aside to focus on the job at hand. We anchored offshore, south of the town itself, along a stretch of coast whose high cliffs and unfavorable rocks made it unpopular with ships who were not trying to stay hidden. Tinbu went ahead in the *Marawati*'s dunij, the small boat we used to ferry cargo and people across the shallows, on the guise of buying supplies to see if this supposed agent was around.

He was—but the news was not encouraging.

"Layth is here," Tinbu said, climbing back aboard. "But he also claims he's done with the Frank, forgive me— that 'demon-snake of an infidel.' I said I had a client looking for information and he said he hoped you had deep pockets."

"How fortunate that I do." And whether that meant it held coins, my fist, or a knife, I'd yet to decide. I'd already dressed, choosing the rough woolen robe of a Sufi mendicant. I suspected news would carry of two women orchestrating a prison break out of Aden, and I had little desire to look like the foul-mouthed busker with poisoned hashish cakes. The loose-fitting garment would also better conceal the sword and dagger at my waist, an agreeable side effect.

"It was strange, though," Tinbu continued. "Layth was jumpier than usual, like he was expecting someone might come for him."

"To murder him or buy information?"

Tinbu frowned. "I don't know. Just something about his demeanor made me uneasy."

"Something about his demeanor made me uneasy" led to *me* leaving Dalila behind. I needed somebody I trusted to look after the ship, and if that person was someone with a history of poisoning jumpy informants when she got impatient, all the better. Tinbu and I rowed to shore, and then he led me around a winding rocky pass to a roadside tavern well outside Zabid proper where Layth had agreed to meet.

The tavern was a sorry place, one that all but announced it preferred gamblers and highwaymen to merchants and pilgrims. Constructed from a motley assortment of scavenged black tents, patched sailcloth, and palm fronds that had been stacked, nailed, or otherwise tied to crumbling mud-brick walls and scorched wooden columns, it looked like the previous building had died a violent, fiery death and had a ghoul of one resurrected in its stead. There was a smell—burned hair? dead fish?—emanating from the open entrance and vomit stains splattering the dust.

"Falco Balalamata must pay well," I noted dryly.

"His last name is *Palamenestra*, and you have taken me to worse places." Tinbu ushered me through the open doorway. "Come."

The tavern wasn't any more appealing on the inside. Perhaps it kicked up when traders visited for some nighttime licentiousness, but right now it was occupied by about a half-dozen sleepy men in various states of intoxication and poor hygiene. Fish bones and nutshells cracked underfoot, the smell of hashish and sweat heavy in the stale air. The poor construction and threadbare roof meant the light was good, however, a benefit in a place that looked like patrons often got knifed in shadowy corners.

Good unless you were the one who needed to do the knifing, that is.

I followed Tinbu to a low table in the back. Surrounded by stained cushions and half hidden by a threadbare curtain, it all but declared "come here to plot your harebrained criminal conspiracies!" My estimation of Layth fell to lower depths.

Layth appeared to hold similarly misinformed expectations of me, however, for I had no sooner stepped around Tinbu than Layth's eyes rose in slow horror to take in my head nearly scraping the low ceiling.

He jerked back. "Tinbu, you fucking liar. You told me you had a *client*, not the sea witch herself!" He shot to his feet. "I'm leaving."

"You're staying." I swept my robe aside to reveal the weapons at my waist. "And be warned that the sea witch does not like when people speak of her as though she is not there. Nor does she enjoy learning those same people are spreading coin to hunt her down for a foreigner." I pressed him back into his cushion with little effort. "*Sit*."

Layth sat, shooting me a look I believe was intended to be rage but mostly appeared as though he was trying not to shit himself. Damn, either the stories Falco and his people had heard about me were particularly creative or there was more to this situation than Tinbu suspected. I could read a mariner's hard life in Layth's features: his skin was mottled and prematurely lined by the relentless sun, and his gnarled hands and joints were swollen with arthritis. One eye had turned cloudy, and he had the gaunt, uneven body of a man whose diet had swung between feasting and malnourishment. His hair and beard, both unruly, were entirely white.

My grandfather had looked much the same at the end of his life, but he had people to care for him. In a sweat-stained jubba in need of mending, his body hunched in suspicion, Layth did not strike me as someone with people. He looked like someone sick of all this, ready to exchange a life of criminality for a quiet hut by the sea. I settled on the opposite cushion. The old leather creaked beneath me; God only knew what might have been crawling out from between its fraying seams.

"Tinbu, get our guest something for his nerves." I didn't take my gaze off Falco's former agent, and when Tinbu left, I continued. "Now, I mean you no harm. Indeed, nothing would please me more than to leave you a newly wealthy man. But we are going to talk no matter what, understand?"

Layth was visibly fuming even while trembling. "I want a hundred dirhams. A hundred dirhams or nothing."

It was a ludicrous sum to demand for a few moments of his time. Salima had paid me enough of a deposit that I could spread some of it around, but I had not come *that* prepared. "I can give you twenty now and then get the rest from my ship. Deal?"

Layth glowered but said nothing, crossing his arms over his chest and jutting out his chin like that was supposed to impress me, until I reached into the purse hanging from my belt and he jumped again.

I dropped two silver coins on the sticky table between us. "Asshole, it would take little convincing for me to leave you with a blade between your ribs instead of dirhams. So. As I said earlier . . . we are going to talk, yes?"

Layth swallowed loudly and plucked up the coins. "What do you want to know?"

"I want to know why the hell some Frank is so interested in me and my crew."

"Because he wants to *hire* you, lunatic. You and the rest of your band of merry thieves. Falco fancies himself some sort of scholar of the occult and has visions of sailing all over the Indian Ocean building a collection of magical talismans. A source had convinced him you could all but walk on water and that there was no nakhudha as skilled a tracker."

A *scholar of the occult?* My skin prickled—I did *not* like the sound of that. "Who?"

"Who what?"

"Who was Falco's source?"

Layth rubbed his throat. "God only knows. He is a violent, unpredictable man who likes his secrets and has surrounded himself with even more violent, more secretive men. It could have been one of his fighters or it could have been a stranger in a brothel. Falco did not say, and I did not ask."

Tinbu rejoined us, handing Layth half a coconut shell filled with a muddy liquid I didn't bother trying to identify: I've learned the hard way in my travels that people will attempt to ferment anything at least once (and sometimes only once if the results are dire). The smell of this concoction was enough to roil my stomach.

"His *fighters?*" Tinbu asked, sounding alarmed.

"His fighters," Layth confirmed. "He has a pack of them, the nastiest soldiers for hire he could find." He gulped down half of his drink and immediately began coughing.

I leaned back to avoid the spray of spittle and considered all that. The news about more vicious mercenaries aside . . . who in God's name could have been Falco's source? Dalila was the most enigmatic person I had met in my life, trained from childhood to cover her tracks. Tinbu had concealed his past even from Yusuf, a man he clearly loved. Asif was dead nearly ten years, and though he might have been foolish enough to share details in his letters home, he hadn't ever seemed to have anyone in his life besides us and his family. Of our core group, that left only Majed, but as Tinbu had said, my old navigator probably would have cut out his own tongue before selling us out.

So who, then?

Layth took another sip from his cup and shivered as if it had gone down with a burn. "By God, what do they put in these drinks?" He glared at me like it was my fault. "Get to the point, al-Sirafi. We both know what you're after."

That was news to me, but I decided to play the hand he offered. "I'm looking for a girl he is rumored to have kidnapped."

Layth burst into choking laughter. "Oh, is it the *girl* you're after?"

"You know of whom I speak?"

"The little rich girl out of Aden?" Layth withdrew a rag and made a disgusting wet hurking noise as he coughed something foul into its depths.

Hope rose in my chest. "That's the girl, yes." When Layth glanced pointedly at my purse, I rolled my eyes but handed over another two dirhams. If he could give me solid information about Dunya, I would happily shower him in silver. "Tell me what you know."

He snatched up the coins. "I know the family is from Iraq, though all that's left of them is a bitch of a grandmother and the girl. One of those old clans trying to restart in Yemen by selling off their treasures, you know? Such treasures supposedly included the kind of artifacts Falco liked, so I set up a meet."

"And how did that go?"

"Spectacularly wrong. Had the grandmother been spryer, I think she would have tried to run Falco through with a sword when she realized he was a Frank. She started shouting about him being a spy and ruining her family's reputation. We were lucky her guards settled merely for throwing us out. I figured she was a dead end, but then the granddaughter tracked us down in the street. Said she wanted to make a deal."

My mouth nearly fell open in shock. "The *granddaughter* wanted to make a deal?"

"Falco was just as disbelieving, trust me. The girl was rambling about needing to leave, suggesting all sorts of prizes she could give him. We tried to shake her off . . . but then she offered something that halted me in my tracks."

"Which was . . ." I prodded when Layth fell silent.

His taunting bloodshot eyes met mine. "The Moon of Saba."

There was a long moment of stunned silence between us.

Tinbu spoke first. "Horseshit."

"Ah, so tales of the Moon have made it to Malabar?" Layth snorted. "Falco knew only a little—I suspect it was my reaction that stopped him cold. Convinced him to listen and then strike her bargain. I'm still not certain he understands what he's after. But you, al-Sirafi . . . I bet you know the stories."

Of course I knew the stories. Everyone along these shores grew up on legends of the Moon of Saba. The largest pearl in the world; a miniature moon said to have been snatched from the sky by a lovelorn fairy and gifted to Queen Bilqis, who made it the centerpiece of her crown. A gem believed to bestow upon its owner countless wishes, supernatural sight, and unending good fortune. A pearl that had brought mighty empires to their knees, foolhardy kings to madness, and had finally been lost when warring sea djinn destroyed one of their island kingdoms in a battle to possess it.

There are dozens more stories. Hundreds—especially among the pirates and fortune-seekers with whom I've spent my life. We all love a good tale of blood and treasure.

Asif used to talk about the Moon of Saba. Not often; it was only one among the many ridiculous stories he told of his family's supposed past, his nostalgic waxing about how his ancestors used to be great, how they had served emperors and shahs. A dreamy history he had so desperately longed to recover and emulate. A way to make his parents proud.

I hardly knew what to question first. Did I ask just how developed—and possibly dangerous—was Falco's interest in the occult? Inquire deeper in the supposed mythical treasure Salima had failed to mention? Demand proof that instead of Dunya's being kidnapped, she had apparently willingly joined the Frank?

I started with none of that. "*Where?*" I growled out. "Where did they go?"

"A place whose name was enough to put me off his employ for good. A damned fool quest across dangerous terrain for a gem that is more likely than not a lie? No thank you." Layth leaned back like he wanted to project confidence but then began coughing again, his face getting ruddier by the moment.

"Are you all right, man?" Tinbu reached for his waterskin. "Do you need some water?"

Layth grunted. "I'm fine. Let's finish this." His red-limned gaze fixed on mine again. "You want me to tell you where to find Falco? Then hand over that entire purse right now." I hesitated, and he sneered. "I'm the only one who knows, al-Sirafi. The rest of the men bought into his nonsense and left alongside him."

The prospect of putting a blade in Layth's ribs was growing more tempting by the moment, but we both knew I had few cards to play. I could not kill the *one* person who knew where Falco went.

I tossed the purse on the table. "Talk."

Layth took the small bag, hefting it in his palm as though to evaluate the weight. "An island."

"An island?"

"A big one."

I smiled as though we were joking—and then lunged for his throat, putting my dagger to his neck. "I'm going to need more than that."

But give the man credit, he didn't back down, wheezing instead, "You promised me a hundred dirhams. This purse is not that. Get the rest of your money and then you'll get your details."

"Son of a whore, you'll have drowned in your own spittle before—"

Tinbu laid a hand on my wrist. "It's fine, Amina. Go back to the ship for the remainder. I will stay with him."

Resisting the urge to slap Layth upside the head, I shoved to my feet. His hacking cough and smug expression followed me as I stalked out, burning with rage.

I did not get far.

There was a strangled, raspy groan and then—"Amina!" Tinbu cried.

I whirled around. Layth had fallen to his knees on the dirty floor and was clutching his throat. His eyes were wide with panic, foam gathering on his darkening lips.

Fuck, was he *actually* choking now instead of just gargling his own backwash? I rushed over. "What was in the drink you gave him?" I asked urgently.

"Alcohol?" Tinbu spun on a small squirrelly man who had frozen across the tavern. The barkeep, judging from the dusty brown jug and coconut shell cup he'd been filling. "What did you give me?"

"J-just date liquor," the barkeep stammered, giving me and my khanjar a terrified look. "The same as them have been drinking!"

Layth's face was turning red. I hauled him up by the shoulders and rolled him over my knee, cuffing his back with my fist to try to dislodge whatever was stuck in his throat. "Did he put anything in his mouth?"

"Nothing I saw." Tinbu joined me in pounding Layth's back. Falco's former recruiter couldn't speak and was scrabbling so desperately at his throat that he was gouging his own skin, blood dripping down his fingertips. His eyes bulged, his visage an ominous, purple-tinged crimson.

I struck his back once more, and a small object finally flew out, landing in the dust. Blood and mucus coated its silvery surface, but the shape was instantly recognizable.

It was a single silver dirham.

With what seemed like a last burst of strength, Layth shoved a finger down his throat, but it did nothing. With a final gurgle, he collapsed in his own sick, his eyes vacant and staring. His lips fell open, silver glimmering past his teeth. The bulges beneath the skin of his swollen neck . . . They were all coin-shaped.

It isn't possible. It isn't. My heart galloped with fear, but I had to know. Swapping my dagger for my blessed iron knife, I prodded Layth's dead hand with the blade, teasing free the object still clutched between his fingers.

It was the purse of dirhams I had given him. The now-*empty* purse of dirhams.

A scream wrenched me back to the present, the nearest man having looked up from his hashish-induced stupor long enough to take in Layth's grisly appearance.

Tinbu gasped. "Amina—"

But then the barkeep screeched as well, the rest of the patrons shoving closer. Before anyone could stop us, I seized Tinbu's arm and yanked him to his feet. This tavern might be on the rougher side, but I was not getting caught with a man who'd choked to death on a dozen silver coins. We were out the door the next moment.

Tinbu stumbled at my side as we hightailed it down the sandy road.

"Amina, wait. Amina, *stop*!" He pulled from my grip, staggered into the bushes, and promptly vomited.

I spared a single glance to make sure no one else was around and then collapsed myself. I sat in the dirt, my head in my hands, until Tinbu rejoined me, falling to the ground at my side.

"Oh, fuck," he said hoarsely. "Those coins he choked on . . . were they *ours*?"

I could barely speak but managed, "I think so."

"*How?*"

"I don't know." But then some of the crew's wilder gossip returned to me. Falco was supposedly obsessed with loyalty. People said he made his men sign all sorts of magical pacts, or something. Promising retribution if they . . .

"*Betrayed him*," I whispered. "Layth was betraying him. Some of the men . . . th-they said there were rumors the Frank had unnatural powers."

Tinbu gave me a wild look. "*You think Falco did that?*" he asked, jabbing a hand in the direction of the tavern.

The dry desert air teased at my face, a mocking whisper on the breeze. I wanted to tell Tinbu no. I wanted to retreat into denial about what I had just witnessed—the death I might have unwillingly caused—and flee back to my ship, to the world I knew.

But I was the nakhudha. I did not get to run from situations I had brought others into.

I swallowed loudly. "Yes. I fear the rumors about his interest in the occult may have been understating things just a bit."

Tinbu looked like he was going to be sick again. "Gods, Amina . . . what did we get ourselves into? You hear stories about witchcraft like that, but before Rak—"

"Don't say his name," I burst out. "Please. Not now."

Tinbu looked away, wringing his hands. "Then what's next? 'Large island' could mean a hundred such places. Do we report back to Lady Salima? Do you think *she* knew the Frank could do th-these *things*? Or about the Moon of Saba? Maybe that's what she's actually after."

My mind was still spinning. The revelation about the Moon of Saba had been immediately dwarfed by the revelation that Falco-the-aspiring-sorcerer was suddenly less aspiring and more lethally capable. I mean, yes, the Moon of Saba—if it existed—would be an astonishing score, worth far more than a million dinars. But Salima didn't strike me as the type to dream about legendary gems. She had her gaze firmly set on the here and now. On Dunya's safety and her family's honor.

And the Moon of Saba hadn't been Layth's only surprise.

"No," I said slowly, anger coursing through me as I realized it. "I think Salima offered that money because of what Layth said about Dunya cutting a deal with Falco." I wiped the bloody knife against my leg and rose to my feet, helping Tinbu up. "And I think it's time we check in with our client about what else she's been keeping a secret."

The First Tale of the Moon of Saba

If you will permit this scribe's intrusion, I believe it may be time to relate the first tale of the Moon of Saba.

First you must understand that there are a great many tales. Stories do that, don't they, branching out like a sapling searching for sunlight? By the time centuries have passed and that sapling is a mighty tree, there are more branches than can be counted, sprawling in widely different directions. You will find, as our dear nakhudha was to learn to her later chagrin, that the Moon of Saba fits this metaphor most aptly. But we shall begin first with the tale most popular along the shores where Amina al-Sirafi once prowled, and it opens very simply.

There was and was not a queen who bewitched the moon.

A great many songs and holy verses have extolled the magnificence and clever mind of the Prophet Suleiman, peace be upon him. A wise king, blessed and beloved of God, who was granted mastery of animals and djinn alike. But it is the woman alternatively called his consort and his companion, his queen and his ally, whom I shall speak of today. We're all familiar with her name and her story—Queen Bilqis of Saba, a prosperous and gentle land, lush with wealth and an ancient heritage. Rumored to be the daughter of a human king and a djinn mother, Bilqis herself was touched by magic long before meeting Suleiman.

We know well too their famed first meeting, brought about when Suleiman's wily djinn servants transported Bilqis's throne across vast deserts and mountains in the blink of an eye, landing the startled queen in the palace of a foreigner. And yet Bilqis was so moved by the marvels of Suleiman's court—by the glass floor so wondrously constructed over a pool of swimming fish and dancing seagrass she lifted her hem to cross—that the queen gave up her pagan ways to worship God alone, may He be praised! Suleiman and Bilqis shared the wisdom of rulers, traveled widely, and, depending on the teller of the tale, eventually married.

But that is not the account I like.

I prefer the stories that have them part sweetly as the dearest of friends. The stories that have Bilqis return to her homeland with a company of djinn retainers, a gift from Suleiman. They would serve her as devotedly as they had attended to Suleiman, and perhaps—if I am permitted to speculate—in a more familiar way, seeing her as a beloved cousin. With her djinn companions, Bilqis built vast palaces and libraries, fortresses and gardens, some of which still stand today. She ruled wisely and independently for decades to come, surrounded by grandchildren and perhaps a handsome djinn consort or two. She was cunning and beautiful, a monarch so beloved that Yemen's later queens would call themselves "little Bilqis.'"

So cunning and beautiful that she captured the attention of the moon itself . . . or rather an aspect.

Now, we are not sailors like Amina, reliant upon reading the lights of the night sky, so perhaps I should clarify what I mean by an *aspect*. As you trace the movement of the stars and planets over the horizon, so too does the moon travel across them all, taking residence in a different location or manzil every fortnight.

Practical people read such signs to cross oceans, devise
horoscopes, and predict the weather; whimsical souls
such as myself with too much time and audiences to please read
them to entertain with tales of centaurs and scorpions.

There are eighteen named manazil and we may forget all save the
fourth, al-Dabaran. It is said while the moon was in the manzil of
al-Dabaran, it spied upon Bilqis and fell instantly in love (do
not ask me how moons can do such a thing, I am a simple scribe).
Al-Dabaran longed for Bilqis, the many months he spent in darkness
a torture. Not content to be with her only two weeks out of the
year, al-Dabaran one day managed to manifest himself, appearing in
the form of a large celestial pearl.

Delighted to meet her lunar admirer, Bilqis made the pearl the
center of her diadem and was said to enjoy the company and
advice of al-Dabaran throughout the rest of her years. Considering
al-Dabaran is the manzil of strife, ill will, spirits of discord, and
revenge, I am not certain how that favored her. Then again it is
apparently an excellent time of the year to purchase cattle and
dig ditches, so who I am to question the accumulated wisdom of
centuries of scholars?

As to the fate of the pearl (called the Moon of Saba from then
on) after Queen Bilqis surrendered to death and returned to her
Lord . . . ah, that is where our already complicated tree of tales
branches off with a profusion of blooms unrivaled in its fertility.
I have heard dozens—scores!—of stories relating its fate. Some
say al-Dabaran drove waves over her palace in a massive tide
to retrieve his manifestation; others say the great conqueror

Alexander stole the diadem from a mausoleum now lost, broke off the pearl, and used its magic to conquer Persia. There are tales of it being plucked away by a fairy who accidentally dropped it into the ocean, whereupon it transformed into the island of Comoros, and other tales of a great sea dragon with a leering bone face swallowing up a ship of human thieves who tried to ferry the pearl to the emerald heights of Mount Qaf. I have met pirates and princes, fishermen and porters from lands as far away as Madagascar and Malacca who laugh at my stories and correct me—for you see, the Moon of Saba ended up in *their* lands, tied to another further dozen fates and hiding places yet uncovered.

It is a bewildering chaos that seems almost . . . purposeful. As though long ago someone or some persons, well trained in the disposal of dangerous magical artifacts, sowed the seeds of a bewildering cacophony that would end up making the Moon of Saba sound even more ridiculous than the rest of the fanciful items treasure hunters seek. As though they feared the Moon of Saba falling into the hands of someone who lacked Bilqis's wisdom and had only avarice in their hearts. As though . . .

Well, I suppose to go on further would be getting ahead of things. And truthfully it seems a bit rude to rush past our dear nakhudha, who was already getting pulled into situations not of her making and which she, as she told me many a time, "would have fucking avoided." (God forgive such language, but I did promise to honor her voice.)

So let us return to Amina al-Sirafi, now determined to get some answers of her own.

Chapter 10

"Y ou are doing it again. Amina; if you insist on going in alone, at least stop *caressing your dagger.* You remember people are looking for us, yes?" Dalila hissed as she raced to keep up with my long strides.

I did remember. I also did not care. We had taken caution sailing back in the direction of Aden, but filled with a blinding rage since Layth's death when I realized Salima had lied to me about Dunya *and* possibly duped me into facing off against a fucking wizard, I'd thought of little but confronting her.

Fortunately Salima did not live in Aden proper, but in the neighboring garden city of Rubak, where many nobles kept second apartments and pleasure homes. We anchored on the other side of the peninsula from Rubak—keeping the *Marawati* even farther from Aden—and then Dalila and I made the trek by land. Rubak was a quieter town, and I followed the directions Salima had given me weeks ago to a large stone mansion on a clean-swept block facing the sea. Heavy teak doors carved with climbing roses barred the entrance.

Dalila grabbed my sleeve. "Are you sure you want to do this?"

I shook her off. "What choice do we have?"

"We could *leave.* I want the money as badly as you, but the ten thousand deposit she left with your family is no miserly sum. We could take the *Marawati*, take Tinbu and your family and go somewhere far away until the Frankish sorcerer who kills traitors with blood magic and was *already looking for us* finds another part of the world in which to play treasure hunter."

It was not the first time Dalila had suggested fleeing and not the first time I had considered it. But whether it was the vile, greedy whisper of a million dinars still floating around my head, the duty I owed to Asif, or the fact that I did not want to rip my family away from the home we had built—based only on Layth's words—I could not yet make that call.

"Let me try talking to her," I said. "See what she knows."

Dalila ran her fingers through the glass vials hanging from the ribbons of her cap. "I wish you would take one of these."

"I need to *talk* to her, Dalila. Not melt her face off."

My Mistress of Poisons looked even more dubious. "If you're not out of there by nightfall, I'm coming in. I hope you have something to cover your nose and mouth."

"Around you? Always." Of the many Banu Sasan tricks Dalila had mastered, knockout gas was her favorite.

"And don't get *distracted*. We were hired for a job under false pretenses. That is what you are here to correct."

God, had I brought along my mother or a former assassin for all this lecturing? "I am not distracted," I insisted. "I am murderously focused."

"Right. So the fact that you've been muttering about giant pearls in your sleep is a coincidence?"

My face went hot. "Stop watching me sleep. It's creepy. And the Moon of Saba is a myth. I haven't given it a second . . ."

But Dalila was already gone, vanishing in her typical fashion. With a sigh, I turned my attention to the al-Hilli residence. Their house was two stories tall, and though there were no windows on the first floor, a narrow second-story balcony loomed overhead. Covered with intricate wooden screens, it was likely from there that the women inside gazed upon the world, watching the street and its people from the seclusion of their family home.

I regarded the balcony, a window into a life I could scarcely imagine. I hail from fishwives and singers, maids and those who ready brides. Seclusion is not an option for us, neither its privileges nor its hardships. We are the women in the streets the others watch from behind their screens. Accordingly, we are often granted less honor, our bodies assumed to be available for the right price or simply invisible. I have cast a judgmental eye straight back, dismissing the rich women behind the screens as pampered dolls.

Now, though, they made me wonder. Had Dunya been happy here?

From the picture Salima painted, it didn't sound like Dunya had wanted for much. It was no doubt difficult to be an orphan, but Salima clearly adored her granddaughter, indulging her interests and eccentricities enough that she became quite learned, even at her young age. Had Dunya been content with that life, enclosed in her wealthy bubble of books and tutors? I knew her father wouldn't have been. Asif was always dreaming of more—a new adventure, a new land. He dreamed so much his desires drove him into the arms of a monster.

Praying the same fate had not been visited upon his daughter, I knocked on the entrance.

The doorman was rude, the guard he summoned to toss me out of the neighborhood even more obnoxious until I mentioned being the "woman from Salalah," and they both paled, the doorman scurrying off to find his mistress.

He returned to lead me through a home that felt like an eerie contrast to my own. Where my house was falling apart, Salima's mansion was splendid, the walls covered in tapestries from all over creation and finely polished silver mirrors. Here and there were painted porcelain vases and ivory carvings set upon rosewood tables inlaid with mother-of-pearl designs. The rugs were soft and expensive, depicting dancers and feasts. Lushly planted lime trees and date palms grew in the large courtyard, surrounding a fountain decorated with brightly painted tiles. The perfume of flowers and frankincense competed to delight the nose, a nightingale singing sweetly from one of the trees.

And yet as rich and magnificent as the house was, it felt hollow and haunted in a way that made the hairs on the back of my neck rise. I saw not a soul besides the two men escorting me. The flowers in the vases were dead, the fruit from the courtyard trees left rotting on the ground. The longer one listened, the more the nightingale sounded like it was in despair, calling for a lost mate. Two of the silver mirrors were smashed and a game of chess abandoned in the middle of play, the pawns gathering dust. It looked like the sort of family home Asif had claimed to come from: one of faded grandeur he had been determined to reclaim. I struggled to connect it with the fiery, determined grandmother who'd hunted me down and badgered me into helping her. Maybe losing Dunya had torn out the home's heart.

I was beginning to feel sympathetic until they led me to the kitchens. If the kitchens had been staffed, the cooks were nowhere to be seen; the place was as neglected as the rest of the mansion. The clay oven was cold, the hanging copper pans tarnished. A basket of garlic had green shoots snaking out from the withered skins, and a bowl of overlooked prunes was the only food on a yawning wood-block table that could have held the ingredients for an entire neighborhood's iftar. A mouse raced off its length, fleeing our approach.

The guard gestured to a bench. "She will meet you here."

"In the kitchens?"

His eyes skimmed my body, from my roughly spun turban to my patched dress and unembellished trousers. Like many women of my age and class, I didn't cover my face.

His voice turned frosty. "Is that a problem?"

It wasn't for me, since I'm not a wealthy snob who looks down upon kitchen work. But on Salima's part, it *was* an insult, a rather petty one. Did she think I needed to be put in my place? She had rested in my reception room and eaten food my child had prepared. Besides, the house was empty; it was not as though we needed to hide our relationship.

I smiled graciously at her servant. "Not at all."

Salima was at least prompt in arriving, joining me in the silent kitchen only moments later. Her servant pulled out a stool, upon which she primly sat, and then he vanished, leaving us alone and me on my feet.

"Nakhudha," she greeted flatly. Despite the house's somber air, Salima was impeccably turned out in a muslin gown of deep violet, patterned with pale green diamonds and silver embroidery. A sheer shayla of the same hue draped her perfectly coifed hair, framing emerald and pink pearl earrings.

"Peace be upon you, Sayyida." I touched my heart in respect. "Apologies for the unexpected visit. I figured I would return yours in kind."

Salima eyed me severely. "I am simply glad to see you. I was starting to fear you had absconded with my money to wreak havoc in Aden. That was you, was it not? The woman who poisoned the soldiers at the wali's office, freed a crew of homicidal pirates, set a score of ships on fire, and fled the harbor in the middle of the night?"

"I would never confirm such a thing and put you at risk of consorting with criminals. But it was two ships, not a score. I wouldn't wish to encourage exaggeration."

Her face lit in outrage. "I told you to be *discreet.* I will not have you ruin things for my granddaughter."

My temper flared at the charge. "Oh, did *I* ruin things?" I challenged. "Odd, that. Because I doubt I could harm Dunya's reputation any more than she did herself when she ran away with a Frank."

Salima didn't even blink at the accusation. "Dunya did not run away. She was kidnapped."

I crossed my arms over my chest. "Falco Palamanas—Palametes—the *Frank's* agent told a different story. He said Dunya went running after his master after you kicked them out, begging to go along."

The words were chosen to offend Salima's pride and throw her off-balance, and they did, spots of colors blossoming in the old woman's cheeks. "You believe the word of an infidel-serving wretch over my own?"

"I believe you have been lying to me from the beginning." I stepped closer and I did not miss her alarmed gaze flicker to the door. "And I would like you to tell me, Sayyida, what your granddaughter knows about the Moon of Saba."

The first hint of genuine shock rippled across Salima's face. "How do you know about that?"

"Because the Moon of Saba is what Dunya offered Falco in exchange for him taking her along."

Salima dropped her gaze to her lap. Her hands were shaking, but I watched as she smoothed the tulips decorating the hem of her shayla, as though to collect herself. "She did not run away," she said, her voice quiet but no less firm. "She was kidnapped."

I threw up my hands in frustration. "Sayyida . . . I have no interest in airing your family's private matters. No interest in ruining Dunya's reputation or harming whatever marriage prospects you have arranged for her. But I was once sixteen. You would be shocked how determined a teenaged girl who wants her freedom can—"

"My *granddaughter* is nothing like you." Salima drew back, her lip curling in disgust. She looked genuinely appalled at the prospect. "Dunya is a noble-born scholar who's never been so much as alone with an unrelated man. You . . ." She raised a shaking finger in my direction and the guise of unshakable matriarch briefly fell away, replaced by something wild and grief-stricken, as though by yelling at me, she could deny the truth of what I had laid at her feet. "You are a thief and a murderess who has slept with sailors in every port from Aden to Kilwa. You know *nothing* about Dunya."

Her words landed with a thunderous air, shattering our previously tense but restrained exchange. I've had far worse insults slung at me, of course. But as I glanced around the dusty kitchen chamber again, the only place she had deemed acceptable to meet someone of my ilk, I felt the connections that tied Salima and me together vanish. It didn't matter that we were both mothers, that we had both loved Asif. The Sayyida might have pulled on those strings of sentiment to convince me to take this job—no, she *had* pulled on them, successfully; I could admit that weakness now.

But it was damnably clear Salima had never forgotten who I was. *What* I was. And that was beneath her.

To hell with her. To hell with all *of this.* Salima wasn't going to tell me anything useful about Falco if she wouldn't even admit her granddaughter had run away with him. But she wasn't the only one with relatives to worry about, and I'd sworn to *my* family to return, to step away if things got too dangerous. I'd already saved Tinbu's life, rescued my crew, and had ten thousand dinars sequestered at home. Not for the first time, I realized Dalila had been right.

It was time for this adventure to end.

I was sorry for Dunya, truly. But I'd watched Layth die in an unspeakably grisly manner from magic I didn't understand at the hands of a predatory Frank who was already too interested in me and mine. And she had chosen to follow him.

I stepped back. "Then I am done. You wish to hold on to your secrets? Fine. But I will not risk my crew or myself to find a girl who does not want to be found, nor go up against an enemy I do not understand."

My response seemed to rock the old woman; maybe she didn't think thieving murderesses who'd slept with half the Indian Ocean made those sorts of decisions. "You-you're *quitting*?"

"I'm quitting. I will keep the money you have given me thus far. Falco's agent said they were headed to a large island. I have no further details because the coins I paid him to betray his master somehow wound up *in the agent's throat* and choked him to death."

Salima went parchment pale. "*What?*"

"You heard me. I do not know what sort of man you invited into your home, but I want no further involvement with him. God be with you. Truly."

"You cannot leave—nakhudha!" she shouted as I turned my back. "You go out that door and I swear . . . *I swear* . . . you will never see your daughter again!"

My fingers stilled on the doorknob.

"*Excuse me?*" I glanced back, half thinking Salima was having a stroke. She *better* be having a stroke. "What did you say?"

Salima was clenching her hands so tightly the bony knuckles had gone white, but however frail she appeared, there was nothing but bitter determination in her gaze. "Dunya is my world. I lost my son to your ship, a death I can tell *you* are not being entirely forthcoming about. Now you remain my best, possibly my sole hope of recovering the only family I have left. If you walk away, I will destroy yours."

I had drawn my dagger and stepped closer before I even realized it. "I assume grief has driven you to madness to threaten me like that," I hissed. "I could kill you right now and be gone."

Salima laughed, a shattered sound. "Are you naïve enough to think that would stop me? I am no fool, nakhudha. I told you back at your home: If something happens to me, letters go out to every ruler on this sea. Your enemies will find you. They will find your family. You won't even have time to return home."

I was shaking with rage. *You fool. You absolute fucking idiot.* How had this gone so wrong, so fast? "I do not believe you."

"Then try me," she challenged. "I've had guards watching your house since your stunt in Aden. I meant them to apprehend *you* if you were trying to run off with my money, but I am certain they can make far swifter work of your family."

It was my turn to rock back, the brutal threat shocking me to my core. "You met my child," I whispered, still disbelieving I had misjudged Sayyida Salima so badly. "You . . . you ate by her *hand*."

Salima flinched. Perhaps she was not entirely heartless. But she pressed further. "I did. And she seems like a blessing, a true one, but you're forcing me to do this, Umm Marjana. So let's cease this talk of quitting and make sure you return to her." She pulled a small purse from her robe and tossed it at my feet. "Finish the job."

The purse was red velvet with silken tassels, far finer than the purse I had given Layth, but the message it sent was clear.

Salima had me trapped. Her world of letters and connections was not mine, and I had no idea how to stop the flow of information she might have set in process; if she had lawyers or clerks or perhaps simply powerful friends waiting in the shadows. But it was suddenly, horrifically clear that if she chose to level her privilege and wealth against me in a true vendetta, I would be crushed. My family would be crushed. My daughter, an innocent child who had smiled and brought her fruit, would be crushed.

Have I ever told you what happens when you capture a ship? People paint such bloody, terrifying portraits of pirates you would think passengers would be begging for their lives, for mercy? Sometimes they do, and I grant it. I have never been a killer and always preferred smuggling to outright piracy.

But on the occasions that I did capture ships, let me tell you: I could judge the wealth of a passenger by their outrage. By their *fury*. Men and women who were more offended at the audacity of a poor local demanding a cut of the riches they built on our sea than by the possibility of losing their lives. How *dare* we? Did we not know that our place was to shut up and stay silent? To beg at the masjid if decades of ferrying them from place to place, diving for their pearls, and making their goods left us crippled. To hush our starving children when they travel past our reed huts draped in jewels and silks. To bite our tongues when the traveling scholars who owe their lives to our boats toss the food we've prepared them in the sea because they deem it unclean.

For the greatest crime of the poor in the eyes of the wealthy has always been to strike back. To fail to suffer in silence and instead disrupt their lives and their fantasies of a compassionate society that coincidentally set them on top. To say *no*.

Salima wanted her granddaughter back. In her eyes, I was not a mother myself then, I was a tool, a draft animal to be beaten into obedience if I balked at her command.

The coins inside the purse clinked gently when I picked it up. I could barely think through a haze of rage, but the threat to my family cut through everything, cold and piercing as the sharpest blade. Ten years ago, I would have told this woman to burn in hell and risked running. But I would not risk Marjana. Not ever.

I cleared my throat, struggling to speak. "Where does she think it is?"

Salima blinked at the change in topic. "What?"

"Where does Dunya think the Moon of Saba is?" It sounded ludicrous to even ask. "People have been searching for the Moon of Saba for hundreds of years. Kings, scholars, professional fortune-hunters . . . all have failed. Tell me how some teenaged girl has gotten it into her head that she knows the location of a mythical, magical gem no one has seen in millennia."

Salima took a deep breath. I did not miss her posture relax at my question: how relieved she must have been to threaten the recalcitrant pirate into submission. "If there were ever a teenaged girl to uncover such a thing, it would be Dunya. Recall that I already told you our ancestors had an interest in ancient texts and talismans."

Ancient texts and talismans. How vague and unthreatening it sounded. I decided to be obnoxious. "Asif said your people were some sort of necromancers and exorcists in the jahiliyyah, the time of ignorance before Islam."

Salima did not look pleased to have her ancestors called necromancers, but she continued. "Dunya has been obsessed with our family's lore since she was a child. I encouraged her originally—at least, in the academic and historical matters. Her talent with languages is astonishing and I believed further study would be beneficial. She had no parents, no siblings, no cousins, and she was never happier than when she was poring through the old books in our library. I indulged her, let her write to other scholars, enough that she garnered a reputation for her skills." Regret stole over her face. "And then she learned of the Moon of Saba and became obsessed. She says one of our texts mentions it being hidden and sealed away. The text was encoded, but Dunya worked for years to decipher its clues."

I frowned, needing a moment to adjust to the realization that hope was apparently not lost. "Where is this text? It may tell me where she and Falco went."

Salima hesitated. "The text is gone. I can tell you some of what her notes said."

"You mean give me more half-baked information? No. You are black-mailing me for my knowledge of the seas and its shores, which is bad enough. At least let me do my fucking job and read her notes myself."

"You cannot."

I snarled in anger. "I can read perfectly well. In four different languages, if that—"

"I burned them."

It felt as though I'd been punched. "You did *what*?"

Salima glanced away, faltering. "I tried to tell Dunya that the Moon was an unhealthy fixation. That she needed to start living in reality and preparing for her marriage. She could have her studies! But she needed to give up this interest in illicit magic before she ruined her reputation. She would not listen. So I-I burned the text she was translating and the notes that accompanied it."

A wave of coldness swept through me. "You burned her work and *still* don't think she ran away?"

Salima wrung her shayla between her hands. "I had no choice."

I pulled at my chin, pacing in despair; the sliver of hope that had glimmered so sweetly yanked away. "God save me, woman. What *do* you remember of her notes?"

"Dunya said the Moon of Saba had been hidden on an island, one believed to be often inaccessible. There were some sort of marks—carvings perhaps—on the surrounding rocks. And a passage, one she liked to quote."

"A passage?" I repeated, feeling like I had fallen into a nightmare.

"Yes. Dunya said that the Moon would 'sleep until the Day of Judgment, guarded by white snakes and hidden behind a veil of water that never saw the sky.'" A haunted expression stole over her face. "Dunya said it was very poetic in its original tongue and she . . . she always loved her languages."

A remote island of white snakes and hidden water? "Please tell me you remember more than that," I begged. "That you have saved some of her records or there are other books . . ."

Salima grimaced. "That is all I know. We have a library of texts and tablets, but you would need a specialist to decipher the majority and it would take months, if not longer. And that is assuming they say anything about the Moon of Saba. If Dunya is truly the first one to have figured this out, I do not imagine its location is information easily gleaned."

I swore. "Then I need to see Dunya's quarters. And this library where she was working."

"Why?" Salima asked, suddenly suspicious. "Why her quarters?"

"Because some old woman has sworn to destroy my family if I do not find her granddaughter, and I have no other leads!" I did not bother checking my anger. "You have to give me *something* to work with, Salima."

"Fine," she relented. "Usman will show you the way. I . . ." There might have been a hint of remorse in her expression, but it was gone the next moment, and I frankly did not give a shit if she felt sad for threatening me. "It is difficult for me to visit her rooms."

"I am also going to need more than this," I said, shaking the purse. "I have a ship to maintain and a crew to feed."

"I will give you enough money to keep searching. Please find her, na-khudha. I understand I am putting you in a difficult position, but Dunya is my world. Bring her home to me and all this business will be behind us. You will return to your own family a wealthy woman." Salima's gaze met mine, more sincere this time. I had no doubt she meant those words.

I also had no doubt she would carry out her threat if I tried to disobey her again.

Hating myself for having to do so, I bowed my head. "Understood."

◆

The rude servant named Usman led me out of the kitchens, through twist-ing corridors and up two flights of stairs, all shrouded in dust and loneli-ness. My attempts to make conversation went ignored. No doubt Salima had coached him well.

We stopped outside a heavy wooden door. Usman the Grim unlocked it and motioned me through, seeming prepared to wait in the corridor.

"Are you not worried I will rob the place?" I asked mildly.

"Anything removed from there would be a blessing." Usman scowled, as if he had forgotten speaking to me was below him, and stepped back.

Compared to the rest of the house, the furnishings in Dunya's room looked maintained. There were fresh roses in a vase beside a large plush bed covered in embroidered pillows, and the windows that overlooked the courtyard had been thrown open to let in light. The furniture was polished mahogany, the rugs of Persian design. Imported luxuries for a girl who had been encouraged to dream, only to be returned abruptly to reality. A door on the other end of the bedchamber was half open, reveal-ing bookshelves.

Had Dunya slept alongside a library? For a scholarly minded soul, that must have been a dream. I decided to search the bedroom first, starting at one end and working my way outward, shaking out the folded blankets and running my hands around the grooves of the massive bed. I examined drawers and chests, finding nothing but the occasional filigreed comb and mislaid bangles. Dunya had enough clothes and shoes to outfit the wedding trousseaus of a dozen brides, so it was difficult to tell if she had taken anything with her. Her sleeping quarters were otherwise bare of anything that seemed personal. Whether that was because she had the forethought to bring such effects with her or had preferred to spend her time in the library, I did not know.

But there was one thing, the sight of which stole my breath.

On a sunlit window shelf sat an exact replica of Marjana's jade turtle.

Like a woman possessed, I approached it, picking up the sun-warmed toy and feeling all the ghosts of my past swarm me. How was this *here*? But then I remembered: the turtle back home had not originally belonged to Marjana. I had bought it for Mustafa when he was still a child. Asif had been with me then, hadn't he? Had he watched me purchase the little turtle for my kid brother and quietly done the same for the baby daughter he had abandoned? It was difficult to imagine Asif as a father; he had always seemed so young to me.

"I wish you had stayed home," I said softly. Here in this opulent house with a mother who had clearly loved him, it was impossible not to judge Asif's choices. Or my own. I wish I had kicked him off the *Marawati* instead of being won over by his earnestness.

I went to put the turtle down and then noticed that it hadn't been sitting on the window shelf itself; it had been set upon a slim pamphlet. I picked up the pamphlet and leafed through the pages, growing a bit confused if not slightly amused. They were satirical poems—some quite bawdy—about the most legendary of the early Abbasid caliphs.

"I guess Salima isn't the only one interfering in her descendants' lives," I mused, glancing over several ribald verses on a well-worn page relating how al-Amin's mother ordered dancing girls and page boys to swap garments and effects in hopes of sparking the caliph's desire. Apparently more than a few enjoyed it.

But neither the sentimental turtle nor historical gossip was going to help me find Dunya, so with a sigh, I headed for the library.

In retrospect, I don't know what I was expecting. A rich family with scholarly tastes would almost certainly boast a decent collection of hadith literature and Quranic commentaries, biographies of the Prophet and his companions, peace be upon them, and texts of Islamic jurisprudence. Because of Dunya's interest in history and linguistics, there was probably also a prized assortment of translations and ancient scholarly works from Indian, Persian, Chinese, and Greek sages. Maybe a half-dozen or so books on alchemy, astrology, and esoterica—something by Abu Ma'shar or Jabir ibn Hayyan, names even a commoner like me knew.

Instead the moment I stepped inside, I understood Usman's comment about removing items being a blessing.

It looked less like a library and more like the crowded den of a master of the occult sciences. Hundreds, nay *thousands*, of books and scrolls filled four walls of groaning shelves. Where the shelves were not holding books, they displayed bizarre objects and artifacts I could scarcely make sense of: ceramic bowls with lines of foreign script encircling monstrous figures, wax-stoppered brass bottles that appeared as though they'd been dragged from the bed of an ancient lake, scarab amulets of lapis lazuli, hanging lines of knotted strings, and dried animal skulls painted with silver and given eerie glass eyes. Neatly labeled rows cataloged amulets of winged demons with snake phalluses and clawed hands, dog-faced dragons and fanged fish people wielding spears. A life-size stone relief of an ibis-headed man wearing a loincloth anchored the western corner of the room, a reed pen in one hand and some sort of looped cross wand in the other. There were coins stamped with the names of djinn kings sharing space with masks and idols in all sizes and shapes and materials. Carnelian beasts with bull heads and hooved feet, sandstone fish women, and marble cocks—and yes!

Those kinds of cocks.

—What's that you're muttering, Jamal?

—*Oh?* I don't need to dwell on the details? What, is this not an "integral part of the historical record" or whatever such nonsense you like to natter about? *You're* blushing? How do you think I felt being stared at by the glass eyes of a dozen long-dead creatures and surrounded by stone penises all day? We'll get back to things, yes?

Now, listen . . . I'm not an easy woman to shock. I'm a sinner very much relying on the "Most Merciful" aspect of my Lord. I'm a former *pirate*—do you know some of the things I've seen in my career? I'm aware, as well, how common the small magics are in everyday life. A pendant with a wolf's claw and a bedtime rhyme to keep djinn away. Auspicious letters and numbers set in squares to bring good fortune. Dream interpretations and love knots. I've not gone near any of it since Asif's death. (Well, no, that's a lie . . . Like most desperate new parents, I was not able to resist the siren call of the spells and talismans people swear will help your baby sleep. All failed. Fussy babies answer to no authority.)

However, *this* . . . my eyes grew wider as I ventured deeper into the library. I had never seen anything like this collection in my life. And the books! Not just a few texts of magic—*hundreds*. What seemed like the entire *body of work* by Abu Ma'shar, Ibn Hayyan, Maslama al-Majriti, and Ibn Wahshiyya. Of the little I could decipher, there were manuscripts of protection spells and spirit summoning. Faded astrological charts of such complexity that I—a sailor who has been able to read the stars since I was a child—could only blink at them in bafflement. Treatises on lunar conjunctions, celestial navigation, and planetary indicators were stacked alongside intricate magical squares with letters and numbers in a dazzling variety of languages and foreign scripts. Maps had been tacked to a wall, marked with pinned scraps of parchment and ribbons indicating routes. In one corner, a solid mahogany cabinet held columns of fired ceramic tablets covered in a scrawl of minuscule, wedge-like characters.

No wonder Salima had dismissed the prospect of hiring a scholar to look through these materials; at this point I could hardly blame her for wanting to keep her family's eccentricities discreet. Who *were* the al-Hillis? This place didn't have the feel of a library meant for mere scholarly curiosities.

It felt like the base of operations for people who saw these objects as tools. I could only assume the Frank knew nothing of this collection, else he would have murdered anyone standing in his way of obtaining all its treasures. I gripped the hilt of my blessed iron blade, glaring at every suspicious book, idol, coin, and weird bowl in the library.

"As a word of warning to any possible spirits creeping about . . . I am not interested in you," I told the otherwise silent room. "You leave me in peace, and I shall do the same."

Whether my words were received by invisible djinn or my own nerves, I could not tell. But since this library was the only clue I had, I muttered a prayer for protection, took a deep breath, and settled into unraveling the mystery behind the girl whose father I had killed.

If there was a mercy, it was that the library was neat. The desk was crowded with papers, but they were organized, and indeed, one of the few things I could recognize was placed there: an almanac still open to a discussion on the date of the upcoming eclipse. Little surprise: to someone like Dunya, such an ominous celestial event was probably a more exciting prospect than her own wedding.

But nothing I could read seemed to have anything to do with the Moon of Saba. And as the day grew longer, it became clear how hopelessly out of my depth I was. A number of books were in Arabic, yes, but the language was so esoteric and specialized that they might as well have been recorded in the same cuneiform as the stone tablets. By dusk, I was openly despairing of ever finding anything that had to do with legendary pearls, "large" islands, or lovesick lunar aspects and had resorted to pulling back the carpets and peering between floorboards when a chance glance revealed a piece of parchment that had fallen in the narrow crack between the desk and a side table.

My heart in my throat, I carefully plucked it free. The scrap was barely larger than my palm and badly scorched. I carried the paper to the window and tilted it to the light. It contained mostly tiny drawings: what appeared to be part of a constellation along one burned edge and bizarre sketches of a stick figure man with antlers, a crude boat, and a half-dozen cruciforms. Here and there were a few words in a language I could not identify, but written neatly in Arabic was a single fragment:

". . . *veil of waters and guarded by white snakes, he sleeps beneath a ceiling of stone hands, forever separated from the celestial abode.*"

The passage Salima had related returned to my mind. Something about a hidden veil of water as well, yes? And she had mentioned rock carvings . . . I quickly grabbed a stylus and an inkpot from Dunya's desk, adding what I remembered.

Then I stared at the piece of parchment, my brief flush of hope dying out. I had a burned scrap of paper with outlandish drawings and fairy-tale words. Falco had access to magic that had killed a man while he dwelled in an entirely different land.

I had nothing.

◆

It was dark by the time I left Salima's house with the parchment and several pieces of jewelry hidden beneath my dress (listen, old habits die hard; no one was using them, but in retrospect, such female finery was clearly undesired). Usman the Grim sent me off with two additional purses courtesy of Salima, but the blackmailing noblewoman herself did not appear.

I suppose it was unseemly to bid safe travels to the dishonorable bandit whose life you had threatened to destroy.

Dalila materialized at my side barely a block away. "I was beginning to fear I would need to rescue you. It would have lost you another percentage of your cut." She frowned when my only response was a grumble. "You look angry and thoughtful. That is not typically a good combination."

"I am murderous and despondent." I handed over one of the purses. "Take this in case we need to split up."

The purse vanished into her garments. "Your meeting must have been somewhat successful if it resulted in more money."

"The money does little to make up for the additional threats and useless information that accompanied it."

Dalila gave me a sharp look. "What threats?"

In the past, I wouldn't have told her everything. But I was weary of secrets and could not see a path out of the maze I had gotten myself trapped in. And so I spoke more freely than usual, relating the entirety of my confrontation with Salima as well as the disturbing search of Dunya's quarters.

Dalila's expression grew more lethal as I spoke. "I did try to warn you. The moment she mentioned being Asif's mother, she knew she had you. The old Amina al-Sirafi would never have—"

"Yes, yes. I know, all right? I am aware I fucked up." I caught sight of the sea as we turned a corner, and suddenly wanted nothing more than to flee toward it. To thrust myself into the vast watery expanse I had always relied on to save me. I was a good sailor. The *Marawati* was a fast ship. Was there a chance I could beat Salima's messengers? Slip past the guards she said were watching my house . . .

And what if you fail? Images of armed men bursting into my home swam before my eyes. My mother being seized, Marjana screaming for me as she searched for a place to hide . . . I let out a choked sound, swaying on my feet.

"*Amina?*" Dalila grabbed my elbow. "What is it?"

"Salima said she has people watching my home," I whispered. "Letters ready to go out to all my old enemies. She blames me for Asif. Told me that if she loses Dunya as well, she'll make sure my family pays the price." Dalila's dark eyes turned positively murderous at that, and I seized her hand before she could vanish to do something rash. "*No.* She said it was already too late. That if I killed her, I'd only be condemning them faster."

Dalila swore but stayed put. "Then what do we do?"

Her choice of words didn't miss me. I stared at my most inscrutable of companions, her wild hair blowing in the dusty wind. "This isn't the job you signed up for. If the Frank—"

"I signed up for the million-dinar reward, and the Frank has already tried to track me down." Her voice was firm. "So where do we go next, nakhudha?"

Nothing in Dalila's expression allowed for disagreement. I sighed and fingered the small piece of parchment with its obscure figures and broken constellations, clues I could not dream of piecing together. There was only one answer.

"Mogadishu," I said softly, returning my gaze to the gleaming sea. "I need Majed."

Chapter 11

Needing Majed and getting to Majed were different matters. It would be at least a fortnight before the winds changed, the northeast monsoon beginning, and with it the southerly route from the Arabian coast to East Africa opening up. Like any sea-thief of renown, I *can* make voyages against the prevailing season. It requires a skilled crew, a lot of tacking and coasting, and more than a bit of luck. But with a new team and a barely provisioned ship, I decided to go first to al-Mukalla, a dull if well-supplied port town used to readying ships for the journey down the East African coast.

Along with unexpected bonuses courtesy of Salima's blackmail money, I gave the crew a week of leave to replace their sacked possessions and purchase small items they could sell or barter along our voyage, such as tins of ghee, glass beads, and striped Yemeni cloth. I set Hamid, the cook, off with instructions to not only be generous in replenishing our food stocks, but to buy the fattest sheep he could find so we could properly feast before setting out.

Tinbu received similar largesse to buy matching sets of tubban and jubba for the crew, recruiting another half-dozen mariners among the pearl divers returning from the harvest in the Persian Gulf. Oared galleys often drew suspicion, and I hoped the appearance of a uniformed, well-nourished crew might set the minds of passersby at ease that we were not pirates (which happened to be true, on this voyage, at least). Add in the fact that Mogadishu was a genuinely fantastic city to visit—as cosmopolitan and exciting as Aden, but with better weather and fewer market inspectors—and most of the crew seemed happy when we departed, delighting in their new clothes and full bellies.

I spent the entire trip contemplating murder.

"I should have killed that woman the moment I laid eyes on her," I groused, watching from the captain's bench as my men adjusted the sail. It was our second day at sea, the Hadhramaut coastline long vanished behind us. I pulled on the ropes for the left rudder. "Shot her and her guards from the roof and dumped their bodies in the sea."

"Too obvious," Dalila countered, not glancing up from the small pouch of black powder she was measuring into a clamshell. Whatever it was smelled terrible and acerbic, but she had ignored my efforts to pry into its contents. "You should have slipped a poison into her food. Something long-lasting so she could have returned to Aden before dying of what would appear to be natural causes. You would have gained a small fortune and never needed to leave your home. Alas, you did not bother to stay in touch with me. I would have sent you samples."

Tinbu climbed onto the deck, holding a large parcel of Abyssinian leather. He set it down on the bench and unwrapped the leather mat to reveal a battered brass platter of grilled fish and pickles, spiced rice, and a few rehydrated ka'ak biscuits.

"For the record, *I'm* still happy you took the job," he pointed out. "You know, on behalf of me and the rest of the crew not being crucified, cut in half, and hung at the gates."

"There is that," I agreed miserably. "Now just tell me what 'large island' is guarded by white snakes, and we shall be squared up."

"It could be anywhere. Kish. Socotra. Dahlak. Maybe even Madagascar—you don't get much larger than that. Can I take some of this, by the way?" Tinbu asked, nodding at the platter.

I snapped a pickle, pretending it was Salima's neck. "Go ahead."

Tinbu parceled out some of the rice onto a wooden dish, dousing it in ghee and then climbing up to set the offering in a small shrine he kept on the galley roof. My friend had returned to his faith after escaping slavery, not caring for the advantages conversion might have afforded him in this far more Islamized western half of the Indian Ocean. Indeed, he had initially been wary of continuing with me, fearing a Muslim nakhudha would forbid him his rituals.

But I was not that sort of a nakhudha. Both my grandfather and father had impressed upon me from an early age that we shared the sea with countless other peoples; if God had not meant for such diversity, he would have made us all alike. There was also the very practical fact that bigoted nawakhidha did not often last long among the multiethnic crowd that made up most crews.

And yet . . . "Tinbu, is that for your Lord Varuna or Payasam?" I asked after he finished praying. Though I didn't see the blasted cat now, it had become fond of napping on the galley roof, and because it was the least graceful feline God had ever put on this world, *falling off* the roof when the *Marawati* rolled too much.

"Lord Varuna, among others." Tinbu jumped back down. "The gods are less picky than Payasam and we could use all the boons they have to spare." He wrinkled his nose at Dalila. "Do I want to know what you are doing?"

"Not in the slightest," she replied.

I pulled the platter closer, familiar enough with Dalila's experiments that I could eat and ignore them. Hamid's cooking was decent, the rice slightly brackish from the mix of salt and sweet water used to boil it, the fish tossed with vinegar and cumin. I glanced up to see Hamid doing a poor job of pretending not to watch me eat.

"He feeding the men the same?" I asked, popping a ball of fish and rice in my mouth.

"As per your command." Tinbu lowered his voice. "You broke them out of prison and gave them all bonuses. They are appropriately enamored of their new nakhudha."

"God be praised." I nodded an affirmation to Hamid, who beamed a nervous smile in response that revealed the gap where I had knocked out his teeth. "Speaking of being nakhudha . . . I need to have words with you."

A hint of nervousness flickered in his eyes. "I thought we had agreed the carton of naft ended up being a good thing."

"This isn't about the carton of naft. I wanted to tell you, despite questionable decisions regarding illicit salvage, you have done an admirable job as nakhudha in my stead. The *Marawati* is in excellent shape, the crew is well trained . . . I am proud of you, my friend."

Tinbu beamed so brightly it made me fear I didn't compliment his work enough. "Thank you. That means a lot, Amina. Also, please consider staying on, because I despise the responsibility. The constant fretting over every detail. And the *navigating*. Do you know how complicated your charts are? I would rather maintain ships and be told where to sail them, not stare at the stars all damn night."

I snorted, returning to my food as I gazed upon the blue-green horizon and my bustling ship. The sea was calm and my crew in good spirits, some singing as they finished with the sail, others making rope and trading items from their new personal chests. It was a hot day, and I could not help but notice several of the men had shucked off their new cloaks, muscled limbs glistening with sweat.

"Uh-oh." Tinbu laughed. "Maybe you *are* staying on as nakhudha. You've got the look."

I glanced at him. "What *look*?"

"The I-wonder-which-of-these-fine-men-might-make-for-a-good-husband-number-five look," he cackled. "Don't deny it. I know you too well. What about Tiny? He's very sweet, and I can attest the name does *not*—"

"Oh, shut up," I said with a flush. "I am denying it. I'm done with husbands." But claiming I was done with husbands was one thing; controlling my eyes when I hadn't touched a man in ten years and now spent my days surrounded by some particularly well-formed ones wearing nothing but sailor's briefs was more difficult. A woman can lower her gaze only so often without tripping over her feet. "What pleasures men bring are not worth the trouble."

"I've heard that before." Tinbu sat beside me, helping himself to a biscuit and watching Dalila, still absorbed in her work. She had bound up the clamshell with the black powder inside, a piece of twine stuck out like the long tail of a rat. "All right, Dalila, my curiosity has gotten the better of me. What *is* that?"

"Chinese salt mixed with a few additions. I'd been hunting after some for quite a while and recently found a supplier." Dalila placed the clamshell on the edge of the railing and then stepped back. She touched a burning twig to the twine.

I glanced up from my lunch. "Wait, isn't Chinese salt what they use to—"
The clamshell exploded.

It happened so fast I could scarcely make sense of it. There was a resounding bang, a burst of fire, and then the two halves of the shell went whizzing apart as though they had been struck by a bolt of lightning. One hurled itself into the sea while the other flew directly underneath the main yard, narrowly avoiding punching a hole through the sail. Several of the sailors shouted in alarm, and Tinbu leapt back so fast he fell off my bench.

Dalila let out a cheer. "It worked!"

"It *worked*?" I gaped in disbelief. "You intended to make some sort of . . . of *fire explosion* on my ship? My *wooden* ship?"

She was already retrieving the pouch of black powder. "Yes."

I lunged for the pouch, then thought better of touching it so violently. "God curse you. Is this why you only have one eyebrow? Get rid of it. *Now.*"

"I think I know of this black powder." Tinbu picked himself up, sounding traitorously fascinated. "In China, they shoot it into the sky for grand celebrations. I've heard it showers down in lovely sparks of light like a whole flock of falling stars."

"They shoot it into the sky?" Dalila repeated, clearly intrigued.

"Indeed. Perhaps if we fastened it to a projectile . . ." His eyes *lit up.* "What about one of my arrows?"

I threw a fish bone in his direction. "Stop encouraging her!"

Dalila shot me an annoyed look. "You got to keep your naft."

"It is not *my*—" Payasam chose that moment to leap down from some hidden spot on the galley and landed directly on my platter, scattering fish and rice everywhere. "Damn it!"

Tinbu quickly scooped the cat away. "Do not mind her," he cooed. "Once she has the Moon of Saba, she will be a lot less grouchy."

Dalila groaned. "I knew you were going to fall for that Moon of Saba rubbish. It is nothing but a charlatan's tale."

"You've always been too quick to dismiss magic," Tinbu chided. "Does a charlatan's tale cause a man to choke to death on coins that mysteriously appear in his throat? Was the last husband Amina set her sights on a character out of a charlatan's—"

"My last husband was a *monster,*" I cut in harshly. "And the reason I do not care whether or not the Moon of Saba exists. If someone was to wave it before my eyes, it would not matter. We are not getting any more involved in the supernatural than we already have."

That silenced them both for a moment, the dark reminder of the worst night in our shared history dimming the mood and making the sun-filled day and melodies of the sailors seem distant.

Finally Tinbu spoke. "Then how do we fight a man who might have such power?"

It was a question that had haunted me since I watched Layth die. I had no answer.

"We outwit him," Dalila said firmly. "We *trick* him. We fight in ways he could not see coming." She tapped her bag of black powder, and I could not help but flinch, remembering the explosion a tiny fraction of it had just caused. "Ways like *this*. Amina, you were the one to claim I had *skills unlike anyone else you know*. Let me use them."

Tinbu glanced my way. "She has a point."

I attempted to level my best nakhudha's glare on them, but neither appeared particularly cowed—they knew me too well. And Dalila wasn't wrong. If Falco had access to the kind of blood magic that had killed Layth . . . we were going to need every bit of criminal ingenuity we had.

"Fine," I gruffly relented. "But no experimenting on the ship. And absolutely no mentioning fire explosions to Majed. This reunion is going to be difficult enough."

A Notice to Suleiman Batawiyna on the Dissolution of the Apprenticeship of His Son

"Let it be known that Majed ibn Suleiman Batawiyna is no longer affiliated with either Ibrahim Shirazi, master cartographer to the Sultan of Kilwa, or Sheikh Dawud al-Hasan, having abandoned his teachers, his duties, and all manner of respectability. Furthermore, should he return to Kilwa, he is to be brought immediately to the local qadi for questioning as to his relationship and possible criminal assistance to the accused smuggler Saad al-Sirafi. For his failure to complete assigned work, the debts of his board and supplies will be transferred to his family, a bill amounting to eighty-four dirhams to be presented to Suleiman Batawiyna posthaste . . ."

[written in a different hand and scrawled beneath]

Suleiman, I have tried my best to rein the boy in and salvage his position, but no amount of pleading will change their minds this time, and I cannot blame them. I do not believe your son has turned to lawbreaking, but his willingness to go off on any vessel in his efforts to explore have embroiled him too often with suspect nawakhidha. I fear he may be lost for good this time. If you manage to entice him home, tie him to a trade and a wife as far from the sea as possible. For Majed no sooner gets a glimpse of a ship, than he packs up and is gone.

Chapter 12

The wind and sea cooperating, we made good time to Mogadishu. Save a brief storm that put us into shore, the journey was otherwise gentle, the Somali coast ambling past in a blur of sloping sand dunes, pale yellow cliffs, and quiet fishing villages. Mogadishu, however, was no fishing village, and the corona of boats plying its waters snarled us in sea traffic before the city's forts and mosques were even visible. We maneuvered and bullied our way past jilab and sanabiq, qunbar and dugouts, each belonging to seemingly every group of people with a toe upon the Indian Ocean. I took care to watch for any ships with official markings or soldiers, but saw mostly merchants and fishermen. We were far enough from Aden that I was not terribly worried about being pursued (the excellent thing about living along an ocean of a hundred different kingdoms is being able to commit crimes in one and flee very quickly to another), but it did not hurt to be paranoid, particularly when Salima kept reminding me I had a price on my head.

A few local agents paddled out to the *Marawati* with welcoming words and silver trays of roasted goat. Were we legitimate traders, we would have gone off with one of them to find lodgings and the best place to sell our goods. As it was, we were masquerading as a charter: Dalila posing as a wealthy widow traveling to Mogadishu to visit a cousin and check on investments. Back in our criminal days, that had been a typical ruse for us. One of the many benefits of Dalila and me being female was taking advantage of men's discomfort and fear of impropriety when interacting with ladies outside their household. Decked out in false jewels and pretend silks, Dalila could imitate the most noble, untouchable Sayyidas out there. Everything in her haughty, veiled silence screamed that to approach her would be horribly disrespectful; to actually *question* the documents a hushed Tinbu handed over on her behalf would be unthinkable. I did what I could to maintain the façade, acting as her servant and chaperone— feigning respectability is not among my skills.

Dalila's story passed muster with both agents and inspectors, and soon we were free to anchor outside Mogadishu and proceed to the city in the dunij. But if I imagined my friends intended to provide a united front before Majed, I was sorely mistaken.

"I am not going with you," Tinbu declared. "I know better than to involve myself in that fight. Besides . . ." He patted his now-hefty midsection, his robe hiding several items he did not wish to pay customs on. "I have goods to sell."

I made imploring eyes at Dalila.

"I am not going to help your case with Majed," she said plainly. "He has never forgiven me for the manner in which I joined the *Marawati*."

"You poisoned him and refused to administer the antidote until we got you out of Basrah," Tinbu reminded her. "That's difficult to forgive."

"I hope he's in a merciful mood," I said bleakly. "Or at least accommodating enough to hear me out before he slams the door in my face. But sure, go shop and smuggle, you unreliable traitors."

Tinbu winked and tapped a purse of cowries. "Come, Dalila, my crafty. Let's make some money."

It was a Friday, and Mogadishu's main road was packed not only with the pious headed to jumu'ah but with vendors hawking everything from glass bottles of camphor and pickled chilis to polished tortoise shells and stacks of mangrove poles. Children ran around a group of women examining local cloth, making my heart pine for Marjana. Several nawakhidha were gossiping in the shade of a tree, and I ducked my head to avoid them, not needing any fellow shipmasters to identify me. The sun blazed overhead, but with plenty of awnings and a fresh breeze off the ocean, the heat was manageable. The aroma of roasting spices and freshly squeezed juice enticed me in the direction of the food stalls, but I was not permitted to eat or loiter in the market until after I had approached Majed.

And yes, I was rewarding myself with food and incentives like a child.

But even the brief venture brought me enjoyment. I love traveling, and it had been fifteen years since I last visited Mogadishu. Bustling then, it had grown into a metropolis now that easily rivaled its sister ports. I had scarcely gone two blocks when the sound of drums and trumpets forced me to stop for a magnificent procession. Soldiers with gleaming weapons and perfectly draped uniforms—qadis and wazirs and all manner of clerks, each better dressed than the next—paraded by, preceding a royal palanquin adorned with a rainbow of colored silk. Gold birds with pearl eyes and silver talons were perched upon the corners of the palanquin. Inside, all I could see of their king as he passed was the furred mantle and emerald hem of his fine Jerusalem brocade.

I craned my neck to watch the parade depart, only to chide myself for the distraction. I was not in Mogadishu to play ogling tourist, and so I followed the directions Tinbu had given me to a pleasant neighborhood of lofty homes. They were not the grandest mansions in the city but spoke of respectable professions and carefully cultivated wealth, the houses of physicians and international traders. Tinbu had said Majed married into a local merchant clan, and it showed, the sort of respectable life Majed's family had always wanted for him.

I stopped outside a home with cheerfully painted blue doors, balancing the presents of Egyptian paper, Yemeni glass bangles, Indian block-print cloth, and sugar I had brought for Majed's family. Beyond the door, children were laughing, and guilt snarled me at the sound. Of my companions, Tinbu was my most trusted sailor and Dalila was . . . well, Dalila.

But Majed had been with me the longest. I would not have become the nakhudha I was without him; he crewed with my father and was the only one to stay on when I took over the *Marawati*. If any of them were family to me, it was Majed.

Like any siblings, we've had our disagreements, but he is a good man. I should have known he got married; I should have known he had children. Our families should have visited and enjoyed holidays together. Marjana should have thought of him as an uncle, and I should have showered him with gold upon his children's births. That our relationship had soured was on me, and I was nearly as nervous as when I'd been bluffing with the warship in Sira Bay.

Whispering God's name, I rapped loudly on the door.

A small boy dressed in a blue thawb so clean he must have just come back from Friday prayer opened it. He could not have been more than seven, his wide-set curious eyes so like my friend's, I knew in an instant this had to be Majed's son.

"Peace be upon you, little one," I greeted warmly. "I'm looking for Majed of Kilwa."

"Upon you peace." The child rocked back and forth on his heels like I had pulled him from a game of chase. "Baba!" The chatter of an unseen courtyard increased, and he raised his voice. "BABA!"

"I am coming, I am coming." I heard Majed's drowsy voice before the door was pulled from the boy's hand. And then he was there, my old navigator, very much wearing his years in a beard that had gone silver and a paunch his striped thawb was not quite hiding. He had a sleepy ease I'd never seen in the man I knew as high-strung, and he squeezed the boy's shoulder with gentle affection.

Then his gaze fell on me.

Majed jerked back like he had been doused with a bucket of cold water. He quickly scooted his son away. "Return to your game, Ahmad."

I waited until the boy was gone and then offered my most innocent smile. "Greetings, Father of Maps."

Majed stared at me. Then he slammed the door in my face.

So much for hearing me out. "Oh, come on, Majed . . ." I shoved my weight against the door before he could throw the locks, keeping it a tiny bit open. "You cannot still be angry at me!"

"I absolutely can be!"

I wedged a foot in the door. "I just want to talk."

He stomped on my toes. "Go away!"

"You stubborn son of a . . ." I got an elbow in, not entirely accidentally jabbing him in the eye. "I only need a moment."

"I am not giving you any moments." There was a pleading insistence in his voice. "I am normal now. Normal!" He attempted to shut the door on my wrist, but I was faster. I reached in and seized him by the collar, to which he responded by kicking me in the shin.

There was a shocked gasp.

"*Majed?*"

We both froze. I peered in to see a tall Somali woman down the corridor, wearing a brightly patterned red and white home dress. She was about my age, with a willowy grace and kind eyes. Majed's son peeked out from behind her back, his fingers hooked in her skirt. A little girl was balanced on the woman's opposite hip, the toddler's tiny, tufted brows drawn up in a perfect mirror of her father.

My heart warmed at the sight of my navigator's lovely family—even as I took advantage of Majed's panic to yank the door open and step completely inside. I patted his shoulder as though I'd merely tripped and grabbed him for balance.

"Thank you for catching me, cousin. Old knees . . . one cannot trust them!" I beamed at the woman. "Oh, but this must be your wife! Peace and blessings upon you, my lady."

She looked perplexed but returned my smile. "Upon you peace." She glanced at Majed, and though her smile did not waver, I could read a dozen questions in her pointed gaze. "You didn't tell me you had family visiting."

A mix of terror and outrage swept his face. "I did not. I mean, she is not—"

"Family? No, not properly." But I was already crossing to kiss her cheeks. "My, you are stunning, mashallah! I am Umm Lulu. Majed and I had the same milk mother back in Kilwa."

"Oh . . ." She still sounded slightly confused but motioned me forward. "I'm Nasteho. Please, come in. Make yourself at home."

"She is not staying," Majed said hotly. "There has been a misunderstanding."

Nasteho shot him a look. "Of course she is staying. I will not have people speak poorly of my family's hospitality." She took my arm in hers. "Come, sister. You can tell me if my husband was this rude as a child while I show you around."

"God bless you, that would be wonderful!" Arm in arm, off we went together, to Majed's horror.

Inventing a story about why I was there and Majed's and my idyllic childhood in Kilwa—a place I did not step foot in until I was twenty—was easy enough. And yet I could have held my tongue, for I was introduced to a barrage of people—children, in-laws, traveling cousins, long-lost friends, and misplaced relatives—each chattier than the next. Nasteho's family was from a local tribe, but like many mercantile clans, they had intermarried widely, and I met spouses and neighbors hailing from Cairo to Cambay, Malacca to Muscat, the courtyard a cacophony of different languages. There were children everywhere, some belonging to the family and others who were fostered orphans. One uncle had a full class of youngsters practicing their letters, while in another area, women and children packed meals for the poor.

It was all so wholesome and perfect that by the time I heard how Majed had personally saved a group of pilgrims on his third hajj, I would have started to suspect I was being conned—if not for the alarm Majed was barely concealing. They pulled me into their Friday celebrations, and I was feted with blessings, rose water poured over my hands, and offered the choice pieces of stew. The food alone was worth the trip: fine dishes of local vegetables, fish, chicken, and meat fried in ghee and served over spiced rice, green bananas simmered in milk, and a delicious concoction of sour dairy, ginger, mangoes, cured lemons, and chilis.

I hadn't eaten this well since Mustafa's wedding, and I thoroughly over-indulged, to the point that when betel leaves and areca nuts were being given around, I moaned, the prospect of anything else passing my lips unbearable.

Nasteho chuckled and patted my shoulder before pulling her daughter from my lap. The little girl had become fascinated with my gold tooth, clambering over to try and touch it at every opportunity. "I will make a bed up for you," she offered.

"Oh, that will not be necessary," I assured her, staggering to my feet. I had eaten with the women but did not miss Majed reappearing behind his wife's shoulder like a worried ghost as though afeared I had spent the meal scandalizing the pious souls around me with recollections of our misadventures.

"Then come. You two should speak properly."

I followed them down a quiet corridor to a small room. It must have been Majed's office; a low table was crowded with half-drawn maps, scrolls and nautical calculations scattered everywhere. A drafting desk overlooked a large open window through which the sea could be admired.

The office was not empty, however. Ahmad was lying on his belly upon a woven rug, his head buried in a book.

"Reading anything interesting?" I asked the boy.

He peeked up, kicking his feet in delight. "I'm learning about India.

Did you know they have over three thousand different kinds of snakes there? Some have horns the length of a man and can fly between cities!"

I checked the name on the book and smiled. "I think the nakhudha al-Ramhormuzi may have slightly exaggerated. There are two thousand kinds at most."

Ahmad's expression grew serious. "I will have to find out."

"Ah, do you want to be an explorer like your father?"

"I do!" He grinned, his eyes crinkling with excitement. "He says I can take his maps and go anywhere I want."

"I said you can take my maps *if* you pay attention in your lessons," Majed corrected. "A good explorer needs all the cleverness they can get."

"Ahmad, love, let's give your father and his guest some space." Nasteho ushered the boy out and then glanced back. "Perhaps I can bring the children to see the *Marawati* tomorrow?"

I blinked in surprise. Well, I suppose Majed had not kept his wife entirely in the dark about his former life. "I would be glad to have you."

Finally Majed and I were alone. He shut the door, locked it, and then for good measure, shoved a trunk in front of it.

"No," I deadpanned. "Nothing suspicious about that at all."

He whirled on me. "I am going to cut out your heart and feed it to a shark."

"Now, brother, does that sound like the language a proper triple hajji would use?" I wandered deeper into his office, studying his effects. "And *relax*, all right? I did not travel all this way to get you in trouble with your extremely perfect family and law-abiding job. My heart to God, I am happy to meet your children. They are beautiful, and your wife is quite the catch, mashallah. I like her very much."

His expression thawed just a bit. "God has blessed me."

"It seems He has. She knows you are a pirate?"

"I am not a pirate," Majed huffed. "I am a cartographer with a checkered past."

"Yes. A checkered past of piracy."

"A checkered past I have *given up*," he added more firmly. "In exchange for the straight path once again. Nasteho knows about the *Marawati* and my time with you, but no one else in her family does. And if you say anything—"

"Yes, yes, I know. The cutting out of my heart and feeding it to sharks. A perfectly normal threat for a cartographer to make."

Majed crossed and uncrossed his arms, looking torn between throwing me through the window and continuing our chat. "And you?"

"Me?"

"You are . . . *well*?" he asked, sounding the word out like it might bite him. "Tinbu said you retired with your family."

Retired. How peaceful it sounded. I had fled from my past and hid like a roach. "Something like that. We are back in Oman. My brother is married with a second child on the way and his business flourishing."

"His business." Majed sounded briefly nostalgic. "Mustafa seemed barely older than my Ahmad when last we met. And your mother?"

"Happier than I expected to have me returned. Healthy as well, God be praised. If anything, the years have only made her sharper."

A semblance of a smile finally broke across his face; Majed had known my family long before I took over the *Marawati*. Indeed, it was he who started corresponding with my mother when I was first too ashamed to do so myself.

"I am glad to hear it," he said sincerely. "So you're truly out of the business, then? No smuggling?"

"None."

"Drinking?"

"Not in ten years."

"Gambling?"

"Life is a gamble, brother."

His smile faded. "Tinbu told me you had a child. Is she . . . thriving?"

"Her name is Marjana," I said, defensiveness bubbling up in my voice at the carefully phrased question. "And yes, she is thriving. She is the sweetest, kindest child I have ever known, a gift from God."

"She sounds like a blessing. And is she . . ." Majed faltered. "Does he—"

"She's *my* daughter," I said fiercely. "That's all that matters."

Majed sighed, his expression softening. "Amina, we are misunderstanding each other as we do so often. I am asking if she is *safe*. If he knows of her?"

"He is dead."

Majed shook his head. "I was there. We don't know that. Not for certain."

"We watched the tide wash over the spot where we buried the chest. None could survive that." I turned away and started rummaging through his half-drawn maps. "Working on anything interesting?"

"You're changing the subject."

"Be glad for it. Unless you would prefer to speak of demons where we could be so easily overheard by your wife's family?"

Majed gave me an annoyed look that I knew nonetheless signaled defeat. "New approaches to Madagascar to better handle the currents and avoid the rocky coastline at Mahajanga," he answered in an exaggerated professional tone.

I was intrigued. "How?"

He pointed to a small depression on the map. "There is a lagoon a bit farther north that cannot be seen from the sea. It is accessible only a couple of nights during the highest tides, so very few people know of it and even fewer dare it, but with the right map . . ."

I shook my head in bemusement. "I do not know how you find these places."

"I read about it in a book and sailed past with your father." He shrugged. "My mind has an inkling for storing these things."

That was a mild way of putting it. Majed was never a natural sailor, but he has a talent for maps like no one else. When we were together, the routes we would plot might cause another nakhudha to faint with fright.

And yet . . . "Is it the rocks at Mahajanga or its customs fees that your clients are trying to avoid?"

"What people do with honestly obtained knowledge is not my concern."

I snickered. "Bet that checkered past comes in handy." Majed glared at me, and I raised my hands in a gesture of peace. "An observation, not a judgment. Has your work taken you any place new?"

"No." He returned the map to one of the narrow shelves that lined the wall. "I have not traveled farther than Mecca since I departed the *Marawati*."

"*What?*" I asked, unable to hide my astonishment. The Majed I knew was an explorer before anything else. He had been working his way around the Indian Ocean since I was a child. "You have not gone *anywhere* else? What about China? That was your dream. When you left, I figured—"

"Dreams are for young men. And fools." There was no bitterness in his voice, just a note of sad acceptance. "God has given me a brilliant wife, healthy children, and mostly honest work. I ask for nothing else."

"Amen." I tried to crack a smile. "You certainly did better than me when it comes to spouses."

I meant it as a joke to lighten the tension from our near spat about Marjana, but Majed flinched. I could not blame him. I also wanted to flinch when thinking about my last husband.

He sighed. "You didn't come all the way to Mogadishu to discuss maps with me. You have had the moments you requested, many of them. Speak your business."

"In truth, I did come to discuss maps. I am looking for Asif al-Hilli's daughter."

"Dunya?" Wariness stole into Majed's voice. "Why? What do you want with her?"

"You *know* of her?"

"Aye, though I am hardly surprised you did not." Majed ran a hand over his beard. "Asif only spoke of her a few times. Toward the end. When he was getting . . . stranger. I think he had all but stopped sleeping. At night when I took watch and it was just the two of us, he used to ask me all these questions about God. About salvation and . . ." Majed swallowed hard. "About what the Quran says about souls."

What the Quran says about souls. If that was not a punch in the gut. I dropped my gaze, picking up a brass astrolabe from the desk. I doubted Majed wanted me pestering all his belongings, but it was easier not to look him in the eye. "Is that when he told you about Dunya?"

"It was. He confessed that he had gotten married less than a year before joining us. Asif said his family forced him to wed—it was a political match they could not turn down. But he never visited his wife and daughter after joining the *Marawati.* He said he hadn't been ready to be a husband and didn't know how to be a father."

"What did you say?"

"I told him to go home."

I set down the astrolabe. "You told him to leave us?"

Majed's expression was heavy with grief. "Asif was so lost, Amina. He was chasing ambitions and glory beyond reason. I told him that he had had adventures aplenty. It was time to take his earnings and go home to his wife and his child."

"I wish he had listened to you," I said quietly. "I really do."

Remorse hung between us a moment, but then mercifully, it was Majed who changed the subject. "His daughter must be nearly grown by now. Why are you looking for her?"

"Because she has run off with a Frank. Or been kidnapped by one, depending on who you ask."

Majed's mouth fell open. "A *Frank?* When? *Why?* Where did he—?"

"I was hoping you could help with that last part." I pulled free the scrap of parchment I had taken from Dunya's room. "Anything about this look familiar?"

Majed took the parchment and read the words aloud. "'Beyond the hidden veil of waters and guarded by white snakes, he sleeps beneath a ceiling of stone hands, forever separated from the celestial abode.'" He gave me a baffled look. "Is this a riddle?"

"Yes. To the supposed location of the Moon of Saba."

He swore and collapsed into a cushion on the floor.

"My God," he whispered, tracing the figures with a finger. "That ridiculous magical pearl Asif was always going on about? The one that was supposed to belong to Queen Bilqis? How did you *learn* of this?"

"His mother tracked me down." I hesitated, rubbing the back of my neck. "I . . . Dalila and Tinbu are with me. They are here, in Mogadishu, selling contraband as we speak."

Majed stilled. "I had wondered if they might be. Why did they not come here with you?"

"They feared we would kill each other." His eyes met mine, and my next words came out in a rush. "I did not wish to involve you. Truly. I still do not. But . . . I am *lost*, brother. Chasing down clues has only turned up more questions and this Frank she is with—" I shivered. "He can do things. Like what happened to Asif."

Majed dropped the parchment to his lap. "Then walk away, Amina." For all that had happened between us, there was still a protective urgency in his voice. "You have your own family to protect."

"I know," I said bitterly. "That's why I can't walk away. Asif's mother threatened them." When Majed swore again, I hurried an apology, cursing this trip in my head. "I'm sorry. I shouldn't have brought this upon you." I reached for the scorched page. "I will go—"

Majed grabbed my wrist. "You will stay."

The words hung heavy in the air. It was the same thing Majed had said to me over twenty years ago on the deck of the *Marawati* when everyone else on my father's old crew deserted. When they abandoned me, stealing away on the dunij with everything they could carry as the emirs of Kish closed in. When I realized the only thing standing between me and a ghastly death was my grandfather's ship and a strange cartographer who dreamed of China.

He released my arm. "Sit, nakhudha. Sit and tell me whatever it is you are trying so hard not to say."

And so I did, starting with Salima's surprise visit and the way she had framed Dunya's kidnapping. I told Majed of the prison break in Aden and the bloody death of Falco's ex-recruiter. Of how it was becoming horribly clear the Frankish man had not only succeeded in obtaining some of the magic he ached for, but held a frightening interest in me, my crew, and the *Marawati*. Of the way Salima had shut down my questions and threatened my family when I tried to quit. Of the wild things I had discovered in Dunya's library that spoke of a girl who knew far more than she should have and held ambitions that might have already led her to her death, if not worse.

Majed listened intently through it all. He occasionally pulled his beard in contemplation or stood to pace, but he stayed silent. Even after I finished, he stayed quiet, simply staring at his feet for a long moment.

Finally he spoke, the paper scrap in his hands. "I should have shut the door faster. If I had done so immediately, I could have thrown the locks before you shoved your way in."

I lunged for the parchment. "You know what . . ."

He ducked, keeping it away. "I said you could stay and talk. Not that I would hold my tongue. Good God, Amina. You *would* come back under circumstances like this. A Frankish sorcerer and the Moon of Saba. A Frankish sorcerer hunting *us*, in particular. And Asif's daughter . . . of all the people he could have taken."

"I know." I waved a hand at the parchment. "Does that mean . . . anything to you? No pressure, but you are my absolute last hope."

Majed's brow furrowed in concentration. "An island, yes?"

"A large one. That is often inaccessible, to make this even more of a nightmare."

"That might be a more useful clue than you realize. Give me a few days."

I rose to my feet. "Should I return?"

"No . . ." Majed was already pulling a scroll from one of his chests, getting absorbed in this new cartological mystery. "Do not come back here. You are very loud, and Nasteho's family overly curious. I will come to you."

I could hardly judge him for his caution; indeed, I was just pleased this hadn't ended in bloodshed. "Thank you, brother."

"Do not thank me. We are family. It is what we do for each other." His voice gentled. "Asif was family too. Which makes his daughter one of ours. I will try to uncover what I can, God willing."

Asif was family too. "Of course," I said, a wave of fresh shame washing over me. "God be with you."

Chapter 13

Nasteho came with her children the following morning. I took the dunij to retrieve them from the beach and granted the rest of my crew the day off so Majed's wife and children could explore the *Marawati* to their heart's delight. Nasteho had brought more of her family's excellent food, and we spread a picnic while Ahmad raced around the ship, shrieking with glee and climbing everything he could.

"So this is the life he gave up for us," she mused, watching as Ahmad tugged eagerly at the left rudder under Tinbu's watchful eye and shouted about going to India to search for snakes. "What a wondrous experience to go anywhere you wish with only the wind."

I laughed. "You'd be surprised how fickle a partner the wind can be. Sometimes it conspires with the current to take you in an entirely different direction from which you intended. Majed and I once set out from Zanzibar for Muscat and ended up in Madagascar."

"Still, it must have been exciting."

"Aye," I said softly. "We had some times."

Nasteho picked up a mango and began slicing it, handing the fleshy pit to the toddler to suck on.

My heart twisted at the sight. "Mangoes are my daughter's favorite too. I used to let her gnaw on the pits like that when her teeth were coming in. Made a terrible mess, but it was the only thing that helped."

"Ahmad only ever wanted to gnaw on *me* when his teeth came." Her gaze flickered to mine, and whatever she saw there gentled her expression. "How long has it been since you saw her?"

Salima's threat hissed in my mind. *You go out that door and I swear you will never see your daughter again.*

I managed to speak past the lump that rose in my throat. "Two months."

"You must miss her terribly."

"I wish to God she were here." My heart a mess, the answer slipped out before I could check myself in front of a woman who was still a stranger to me. "Well, not necessarily *here*, sharing the . . . ah, job with which I've been tasked. But I would enjoy having her on my ship, playing with your Ahmad."

Nasteho looked surprised. "Have you never brought her aboard? Majed says you grew up on the *Marawati*."

I hesitated, uncertain how much Majed had told her about Marjana and the circumstance that had led to my "retirement." "No," I confessed. "This is the first time I have been at sea since she was born."

"Ah." Nasteho glanced at Ahmad, who was now begging a visibly stressed Tinbu to let him climb the mast. When she spoke again, her voice was contemplative. "After my first husband died, I used to go to my father's office in town once a week to check the books. I am better with numbers than my siblings, but it was boring, mindless work. And yet I loved it. The chance to be alone for a few hours and accountable only to myself. To have lunch on the beach and watch the waves come in without anyone needing me. It was a respite I did not realize until I married a second time and Ahmad was born. I love my children with my whole heart, but . . ." She met my gaze, understanding there. "Part of you must be overjoyed to be a nakhudha again."

Yes. However, it wasn't until Nasteho said it that I really let myself accept that truth—guilt had kept me from making the same connection. For how could I enjoy being on the *Marawati* if it kept me from Marjana? Especially on a mission so dangerous?

But I did. I loved it. I had always loved it. I loved being on my ship, the wind in my face and the salty damp in my clothes. I loved taking pride in running a tight vessel and a capable crew, jesting with my companions and rising each dawn to see a new expanse of water stretching toward the horizon. Seafaring had been stamped into my soul long ago; there was no rooting it out.

"I'm not sure I ever stopped being a nakhudha," I finally replied. "Our hearts may be spoken for by those with sweet eyes, little smiles, and so *very many* needs, but that does not mean that which makes us *us* is gone. And I hope . . . part of me hopes anyway that in seeing me do this, Marjana knows more is possible. I would not want her to believe that because she was born a girl, she cannot dream."

But the last words rang slightly false. For what use was it giving Marjana an example of female independence if I rarely let her leave the house and refused to send her to school out of fear? Yes, that fear was deeply justified . . . but I suspect similar sentiments had led Sayyida Salima to sequester Dunya so thoroughly. And look how that worked out.

Nasteho's eyes danced with mischief. "What if Marjana dreams of being a pirate?"

"God forbid." But I seized the opportunity to change the topic. "Has Majed ever admitted we were pirates? I must know."

"Oh, never. He is far too talented at dancing with his words." She hesitated. "I am terribly fond of him. There is no way my parents knew his true past when they suggested the match, but discovering the seemingly staid cartographer I married was actually Amina al-Sirafi's navigator made for a very exciting surprise on my wedding night." She met my gaze again, her expression more serious. "This job you're on, searching for your friend's daughter: Is it dangerous?"

The bloody memory of Layth choking on silver rose to my mind. "It could very well be," I admitted. "But I am attempting to mitigate the risk as much as possible. I have someone very important waiting back home and I intend to return to her."

Nasteho seemed to consider that. "A fair answer, nakhudha." She wiped the baby's mango-covered mouth. "I should like to meet your Marjana someday, God willing."

Dalila joined us, Payasam purring in her arms.

"Do not tell me the useless cat has won you over as well?" I complained. "I woke up to its tail in my *mouth*."

"I remain entranced by its utter inability to provide for itself," Dalila marveled. "Tinbu must hand-feed it so that it does not starve. The only thing it does seek to consume on its own initiative is my black powder. It is such a failure of a cat that I cannot help but be impressed."

"Cat!" The little girl dropped the mango pit and lunged for Payasam with sticky fingers. The feline let out a wheezy rumble, giving Majed's daughter a happy look of blissful incomprehension.

"What about you, Lady Dalila?" Nasteho asked. "Is there anyone back home you are eager to return to?"

Dalila picked at her teeth. "I had to abandon a time-sensitive experiment with extremely promising indications as a new knockout gas."

"For pain relief," I amended quickly. "Dalila is our . . . healer."

Nasteho's brows rose slightly. "Ah, yes. Majed speaks frequently of how you 'healed' him when you first met."

Dalila rolled her eyes. "It was hardly the worst of my poisons. There are some physicians who believe it beneficial to vomit blood every now and then. It balances the humors."

Nasteho blanched, and I pulled Dalila down next to me.

"Eat," I ordered, shoving a sweet roll in my companion's hands. "It will prevent you from talking."

Majed's family ended up spending much of the day on my ship. We ate and chatted while the baby crawled after the cat and Tinbu taught

Ahmad how to catch crabs off the boat's side. I felt a little bad picnicking with Majed's family while he worked on our clues, but my old navigator knew where the *Marawati* was. If he wanted to come by, nothing was stopping him.

Even so, when Nasteho began packing up, I could not help but inquire, "How is your husband today?"

"He has barely left his office since you departed. The man loves a good nautical mystery. Indeed, we should get back. He is liable not to eat unless I remind him."

I picked up the little girl from where she had been climbing a stack of crates, briefly cuddling her to my chest and wondering how my nephew, just as small and snuggly, was doing back home. "Please visit anytime; I've greatly enjoyed your company. And bring Majed. It would be good to see him aboard the *Marawati* again."

A mysterious smile flitted over her lips. "Have no fear, nakhudha. I do not think my husband will be able to keep away much longer."

Nasteho turned out to be correct. We had been in Mogadishu less than a week when my old navigator showed up on the beach unannounced, and as my crew rowed him over in the dunij, I watched Majed's gaze trace the *Marawati* from stern to bow, a thousand emotions warring across his weathered face. It took a bit longer than it used to for him to climb aboard, and as he approached my bench, he ran his hands over the rudder with open nostalgia. Majed looked so much older, a far cry from the man who'd once been the strongest swimmer I'd ever known and would climb the mast to spy new lands at the drop of a cap. A saddlebag hung from one shoulder, and he wore a finely made robe with wide blue stripes and tiraz armbands picked out in silver embroidery. Underneath was a crisp red thawb that might have been new, an equally pristine turban wrapping his head.

"Nakhudha." Majed touched his heart. "Peace be upon you."

"And upon you peace, Father of Maps," I returned.

Tinbu grinned and pulled Majed into a hug, kissing his cheeks. "Hello, old friend."

Dalila emerged from the galley and frowned, her gaze narrowing on his midsection. "You got fat."

"Says the woman squinting like her eyesight is going," Majed replied tartly. He turned to me. "I have what you requested, Amina."

My heart stuttered. For some reason, I did not think Majed would come back, much less with an answer. "You know where Falco took Dunya?"

"I know where the markings on that piece of parchment lead to. And if that is where Dunya told the Frank to go search for the Moon of Saba . . ." Majed motioned to the bench. "You should sit down."

◆

"Socotra?" I repeated. "You are certain?"

"As certain as God allows." Majed gestured to the documents spread before us. Alongside the burned parchment I'd found in Dunya's room were several maps, an early Greek text, a section of al-Mas'udi's geographies, and a star chart. "It's the drawings. I did not wish to raise your hopes, but from the moment I saw them, I could have sworn I knew of something similar. And I found it here"—he jabbed a finger at the Greek text and then at al-Mas'udi's—"and here. Socotra has somewhat fallen out of favor as a destination—"

"For good reason," Tinbu muttered.

"—but in the period between Alexander's conquests through the early centuries of the Abbasids, it was a far more popular entrepôt," Majed explained. "Alexander sent settlers to farm the dragon's blood trees, and centuries later, al-Mas'udi said—"

"Is any of this important?" Dalila cut in.

"*Yes*," Majed replied, in the tone of a long-suffering schoolteacher. "Al-Mas'udi says it was rumored that Socotra was home to an expansive network of caves used as smugglers' points and way stations by ancient seafarers. They would mark the walls to communicate with one another using not only pictographs and words but also drawings of their *hands*."

"'He sleeps beneath a ceiling of stone hands,'" I said, remembering Dunya's verse. "But plenty of islands have caves, Majed. And similar markings."

"Yes, which is why I went back to the original Greek source." Majed opened the slim text to a page marked with a thin ribbon of green silk. "The markings are not just similar. They are exact. Look for yourself."

We all leaned over the book. Majed was correct. The chronicler had painstakingly copied each drawing above a few lines of text. There was the antlered man and the boat, the cruciforms and the hands.

"He explains what the locals believe each mark to have been," Dalila explained. I could speak some Greek but reading it was beyond me. "Oh. Apparently, the antlered man was the lord of the witches, Majed. Did you read that part?"

"Of course, I did. Both al-Mas'udi and the Greek chronicler speak extensively of witches on the island. You will like even less what they wrote about those supposed white snakes . . ." Majed flipped ahead several pages and we recoiled in unison at the sketch of a man being consumed by a serpent ten times his size with a deeply unreasonable number of serrated fangs. "The Greek chronicler never saw such a snake himself, but was apparently warned away by the locals. Centuries after, when al-Mas'udi was writing, he relates that the caves were so feared, their entrances had been purposely hidden. They were believed to be haunted by spirits and guarded by sorcerers. Anyone venturing too close was never seen again."

We all stared at him.

He tossed down the text with a huff. "Forgive me. Next time I sort out your problems, I shall try to make their solution less troublesome for you."

"We are deeply in your debt," Dalila responded. "Indeed, should I find myself being swallowed by a gigantic snake and cursed by a witch, I will be certain who to blame."

Tinbu had unrolled another one of the maps, tracing Socotra's coastline with a finger. "It could fit. I don't know what Socotra was like back then, but it is a hell of a place to travel to now. You can sail there less than half the year; the currents are otherwise too rough."

Majed nodded. "There are definitely times when it fits the description *inaccessible*. And in my opinion, the drawings are damning. I've seen a lot of rock markings in my journeys; none are such a match. The caves would also make for an excellent place to hide something. Whether that something is this supposed Moon of Saba . . ."

"It is," I said softly. I had picked up the Greek text when Majed dropped it, one of the pages he flipped through catching my attention. Among the sketches of the cave's drawings was the outline of a bull's head with stars for eyes. Majed might know his history and his maps, but I knew the sky. "The constellation Taurus," I explained, tapping out the points of the bull's horned head. "And at its left eye, its brightest star: al-Dabaran. The fourth lunar manzil."

I received only baffled stares.

"The fourth lunar manzil. From the stories of Bilqis and the moon she bewitched?" When none of them looked any more enlightened, I asked in exasperation, "Do you not know the story behind the very object we seek?"

"I heard you could use the Moon of Saba to summon storms," Tinbu offered. "And that the pearl is large enough to sink a ship."

"They say licking its surface will cure any ailment," Dalila added. "Even poison."

"And *I* thought the 'object' you were seeking was Dunya," Majed cut in. "Not mythical gems."

"We are seeking Dunya," I assured him. "But she is seeking the Moon of Saba, and al-Dabaran is part of that. At least according to the stories that I know. It was while the moon was in the manzil of al-Dabaran that it was said to have fallen in love with Bilqis."

Tinbu gave me a surprised look. "You're hardly the type to remember romantic folktales."

"It's not the romance I remember. Al-Dabaran is said to rule over ship-wrecks, along with other ill-fated journeys. It's one of the nastier lunar aspects; there are sailors back home so superstitious they will not set foot on a boat for the entire fortnight. It's an old belief, but I remember my grandfather would not sail then."

"Well . . ." Majed said after an ominous pause, "superstition or not, fortunately that lunar manzil doesn't start for months. But it sounds like the pieces fit together even better than I initially believed. Whether or not the Moon of Saba exists, it's reasonable to assume Dunya believes it is hidden in these caves."

"On Socotra," Tinbu said bleakly.

"Indeed." I grimaced. "This job just keeps getting better."

Dalila glanced between us with a frown. "Why do you two look so worried? Is this not good news? 'Large island' could have meant Lanka or Malacca and then we would be traveling for months."

But Tinbu and I had good reason to be concerned.

"Socotra has been a pirates' den since before the time of Suleiman and Bilqis, peace be upon them," I explained. "*Real* pirates. The kind who do not fret about murder charges and travel in convoys strong enough to face down navies. They watch the water like hawks and appear before their victims with less warning than a ghost."

"They are fiercely territorial," Tinbu added. "A number of my people are among them, and when they recruit from our villages, they warn that taking their oaths means renouncing all other bonds. They are allied with the islanders of Socotra; anyone not local would be a fool to think they could sneak around. And someone suspicious? A foreigner searching for treasure or, I don't know . . . *a notorious female smuggler who might be viewed as competition?* We would have kinder fates being tried for brigandry in Aden. If Falco fell into their hands, he and everyone with him might already be dead."

"The situation is not hopeless." Majed tapped his map. "The caves we seek are on the eastern end of the island, where it is far more desolate and less populated. Any pirate with sense sticks to the northern and western ports, where they are closer to the trade routes and have better access to crops and water. It is already out of season to depart from the south, so if you were to approach from that direction and stay east, you could likely do so without being observed. However, the currents are treacherous, the winds whip against the cliffs in a way that makes them terrible for sailing, and the water is littered with reefs."

"So you will *sink*," I said. "But not be observed by pirates when you drown?"

"They would not be the most dangerous waters the *Marawati* has traversed, and you've successfully traveled against the monsoon plenty of times," Majed argued. "Merchant ships would have no reason to make the attempt, but with God's blessing, a skilled nakhudha at the rudders, and a knowledgeable navigator as a guide . . . we could do it."

My head shot up. "*We?*"

Majed met my gaze, his expression resolute. "You would be better served if I were aboard. I have copied out everything I could of the cave locations and surrounding shores, but—"

"Then I will take your notes and pay you handsomely," I interrupted. "I have sailing experience aplenty and cannot take you against this Frank, brother. You have a family."

"*You* have a family," Majed shot back. "What is so different about me that the three of you can risk your lives but I cannot?"

"About fifteen years." Dalila tilted her head, sizing him up. "No . . . more like twenty."

"Woman, if we both jumped overboard, I would still beat you swimming back to shore." Majed crossed his arms over his belly with a challenging air. "What is the score Sayyida Salima offered? *Before* she blackmailed you. It must have been a substantial amount."

Caught out, I confessed. "A million dinars."

"*A million . . .*" Majed swore and then abruptly covered his mouth, as if we had not all heard him say much worse. "By God, no wonder your crew looks so plump."

"I will pay you for the notes," I offered again, more urgently. "Very, *very* handsomely. You need not do this." I reached for the map.

But Majed was faster—rolling the map up and stuffing his notes back in his saddlebag in the blink of an eye.

He gave me a knowing look. "I am not that much older than you. Asif meant as much to me as he did to the three of you, and I am *not* going to watch as other people explore mariners' caves and coastlines not used in centuries. For that reason alone, I would go." He sniffed. "The navigation scholarship demands it."

"You just want to go on an adventure, old man," Dalila teased. She turned to me. "But he has presented a compelling case for his presence making our deaths less likely."

"Let him come." It was Tinbu, his eyes shining. "He is right, you know. We could use him. He reads the stars better than me. Nearly as good as you."

"There you have it," Majed announced. "The three of us have decided."

"The three of you are not the nakhudha!" I scowled. "Does Nasteho know?"

He bristled. "I don't need my wife's permission."

Dalila clucked her tongue. "I bet it was her suggestion."

Majed drew up, indignant. "You owe me this, Amina. I stood by you for years. Trust that I know my heart and my capabilities."

I glared back. But then I remembered the small window in his office that overlooked the sea, where Majed drew maps to places he no longer went. How many years had the two of us spent together, our heads bent over such maps and charts? How many nights had we studied the stars and dreamed of China and a hundred other distant destinations while the *Marawati* drifted through a midnight ocean?

I was not the only one with ambitions deferred.

"Fine." I gave in. "Come die with us. But you will be the one staying aboard the *Marawati* when the three of us search for the cave, understand? *No*—do not argue with me. One of us needs to stay on the ship and you have never wielded a weapon well."

Majed glowered but inclined his head. "Then we are agreed." He patted the bag. "I will need an advance on my share for these notes, you understand."

"That's thievery. I thought you were a man of God now."

The corner of his mouth quirked into a smile. "A family man as well, as you pointed out. Ten dinars for each of my children, Amina, and thirty for my wife. That should set your fears at ease."

I grumbled but agreed. "They will have it."

Tinbu cackled in delight. "Oh, this is wonderful!" He pulled Majed and me into a hug, making an unsuccessful grab for Dalila. "The gang all back together . . . we should *rob* something!"

Dalila's eyes lit up. "That big jahazi headed for Kilwa looked promising."

"*No*," I said firmly. "We are not robbing anyone. We are not smuggling. We are not criminals anymore. Or at least . . . not all of us are. Not on this trip anyway. We sail only to rescue Dunya from this Frank, God willing. And if we get Dunya back safely, we'll all be so rich that none of us will have to steal anything ever again."

Dalila perched on my bench. "I know we're trying to avoid him, but I confess myself intrigued by the prospect of seeing a Frank. They are said to rarely bathe and never remove any of the hair that grows on their bodies. I wonder what sort of lice live amongst such . . . oh, stop gagging, Majed. I know you missed me."

"Not for a single moment in a single day."

"If the two of you keep bickering, I am going to abandon you on Socotra to work out your differences." I stared out at the horizon, the name of our destination squeezing my heart like a vise. "Socotra. God preserve us."

Its Inhabitants Are Christians and Sorcerers

An anecdote from the travels of Ibn al-Mujawir:

In the whole of the ocean, there is no island bigger or better than Socotra. It has date palms, cultivated areas, and fields of sorghum and wheat. There are camels and cattle and thousands upon thousands of sheep. Water flows on the surface of the ground, sweet and fresh, from a large river whose source gushes out, long and wide, from the mountains. More often than not, this river provides an excess of fish for the sea. Aloes and dragon's blood grow, watered by it. On the shores of the island, there is much ambergris.

The inhabitants are Christians and sorcerers. One example of their sorcery is the following. Sayf al-Islam made ready five warships to take the island. When they approached the island, it disappeared from sight. They patrolled up and down, up and down, night and day for several days and nights, but found no sign of the island, nor had any news of it at all. So they returned home in defeat.

◆

A warning from the learned geographer Muhammad ibn Ahmad al-Muqaddasi:

The island of Usqutrah rises like a tower in the dark sea; it is a refuge for pirates, who are the terror of sailing ships in these parts; and not until the island is cleared will they cease to be a cause of fear.

Chapter 14

My old navigator aboard, we departed Mogadishu and followed the Somali coast north for ten days, traversing a distance we likely could have completed in four had we been going in reverse as the winds, common sense, and the accumulated maritime wisdom of centuries advised. And that was *before* we turned east-northeast into the open ocean. We had charted a path intended to avoid the busier routes in the straits between Ras Asir and Socotra's westernmost outer isles, but it was a course that would traverse riskier water, and while I'm an experienced sailor, watching the coast completely vanish on such a route is as unnerving as it is thrilling. The open sea is a dangerous place during favorable conditions, let alone when sailing against the prevailing season. One miscalculation, one storm, and you could be blown completely off course, never to see land again. Indeed, many nawakhidha never risk leaving the coast, and there is little shame in such reluctance—a decent living can be made tramping from port to port, always keeping the shore in sight.

For this reason, among many, I was glad Majed had rejoined us. Not only did it feel as though the last hole in a tattered sail had been patched, but it was also reassuring to have a man aboard who had crossed the deep sea even more times than I. Tinbu was an excellent sailor, but he preferred to stick to the coast. Majed preferred to pick a star and thrust himself into the unknown. The years had lessened his orneriness and I took genuine pleasure in sitting with him to discuss the Quran and his time in Mecca. My crew was mostly Muslim, and many of them appreciated Majed's recitation. More likely welcomed his surety with the *Marawati*. It lightens the heart of a mariner to see another who has grown old doing it, for many do not. When two nights of foul weather clouded the sky, obscuring the stars, I relied on his guidance. When we hit a patch of rogue waves, it was a mercy to have another set of hands to bail out water.

And yet the difficult crossing I had anticipated—the out of season route so dangerous that few nawakhidha would risk it—not only failed to materialize, it turned completely on its head. Ten days at sea, the clouds pulled away from the sun as though yanked, the ocean abruptly gentled, and I was blessed with the most perfect sailing conditions I had ever encountered. There was a steady wind as though an unseen hand tipped us in the direction of Socotra, and though both Majed and Tinbu joined me in checking and rechecking the clear map of stars in the flawless night skies and adjusting the rudders, I suspected they were doing it out of the same routine I was. There were no more rogue waves, no errant currents, no patches of doldrums. We passed through schools of fish so thick they were all but leaping into our firebox, and though there was no rain, the dew gathered so heavily on our catchment cloths that we were able to refill our canteens and water tanks every morning. The oars went untouched, and the heat stayed manageable.

It drove me absolutely mad.

"Amina, stop glaring at the horizon like it has offended you by not brewing up a storm," Tinbu chided as he passed by carrying a bucket of mixed pitch and whale oil—we were taking advantage of the weather to do some routine maintenance. "You are going to bring misfortune upon us."

"It is unnatural," I grumbled while around us the crew sang gaily of dark-eyed beauties; I was the only one bothered by the accommodating sun-dappled sea and wind-filled sails. "We are sailors. The first law of seafaring is that if something can go wrong, it will."

Tinbu rolled his eyes. "You are too much a pessimist. What is wrong with a bit of good luck?"

Because it is not just a bit, and the last time I had luck like this, it cost me a comrade. But I did not say that, of course.

He is dead, I told myself instead. *Dead and buried on the other side of the Indian Ocean. This is not him.*

It can't be.

On dawn of the sixteenth day out of Mogadishu, my lookout gave the cry for land. We had spotted the birds the previous evening. Always seven, one of Socotra's many superstitions. Alone in the sea, a lush island of craggy mountains, fish-crowded rivers, haunted caves, and bizarre plants, Socotra has always attracted such myths. Even from a distance, the island looked magical, jutting out from a corona of brilliant teal water, the sheer top of its rocky plateau swathed in misty clouds.

I took no chances as we neared Socotra, ready to call the order to flee if we were spotted. We were approaching from the most disused side of the island, but I had little doubt Socotra's notorious pirates occasionally patrolled even this desolate stretch of beach. I had archers and oarsmen at the ready; the sharpest-eyed members of my crew in the *Marawati*'s crow's nest and at the bow and stern, calling out when they spotted reefs and coral so we could steer clear. Even so, we anchored a safe distance out.

"I do not like this plan," Majed said for the third time that morning as the dunij was lowered into the water, and Tinbu, Dalila, and I finished packing our bags. "If the Frank is here with armed men, the three of you are hardly a force to be reckoned with."

"That is the point," I reminded him. "Two women and a single man trekking across the hills might be mistaken for locals. A band of armed sailors are more likely to be viewed as a threat. Besides, right now, we are merely scouting." I slung my bag over my shoulder, adjusting my weapons before climbing over the *Marawati*'s side.

"Then I should go *with* you," he insisted, also for the third time. "I have the best sense of direction. And I am not this frail old man you obviously all believe me to be. Why, back home, I still swim the entire length of—"

"I have no doubt you can outswim everyone on the crew, and I know your sense of direction is superior. But I need you on the ship." I began climbing down the rope to the dunij. "One week, brother. That is more than enough time for us to cross the island, seek out the cave, and return. If we do not meet you back here in a week—"

"We will come looking for you."

I gave him an exasperated look. "I was going to say you should return to Mogadishu instead of risking your life."

"Make sure you are here to meet me, and you will not have to worry about such a thing." There was no room for argument in Majed's tone. "I will keep the *Marawati* near enough to see a signal fire from the beach."

Tinbu joined us, his bow freshly polished and the quiver filled with new arrows. Dalila was just behind with her own bags. We had packed as lightly as possible, with a bare number of provisions. This part of the island was mostly scrub. There would be few places to hide, and I suspected the hills would be no pleasure to climb.

We took the dunij to shore, the island looming loftier as we drew close. The tide was out, revealing greenish-blue anemones that covered the enormous black rocks jutting out of the shallows like embroidery upon a hem. We splashed into water as clear as glass, tiny waves chasing and nipping each other across the white sand. The beach was narrow, dwarfed by the towering flat plain that made up the island's heart. Sheer cliffs of limestone rose higher than a multistoried building. Here and there, powdery dunes of pale sand piled against them like failed waves of intruders upon a city's walls.

We bid farewell to the sailors who had rowed us out, then set off, hugging the cliff's shade. Our feet crunched loudly on the sand, seabirds shrieking overhead. The sun's glare upon the water was blinding, and

I fought disorientation as I struggled to regain my footing and sense of space after so many days at sea. Back in al-Mukalla, I'd picked up one of the broad straw hats used by field hands for Dalila to wear over her ribbon cap of poisons, thinking it might help her see better. As the beach curved north, putting us even more at the mercy of the sun, I regretted not getting one for myself.

"Aye." Tinbu whistled. "I suppose not everyone had our luck on the journey."

"What do you . . . *oh*." I shaded my eyes as I realized the dark lumpy shape ahead was not one of the black rocks sticking out of the surf: it was a ship. Well, *half* of a ship. Whatever fate had befallen the vessel had snapped it across the middle and deposited it stern side up, beached among the breaking waves. "No, I fear there were likely few survivors off that."

We approached the shipwreck with caution. The only other visitors were a pair of gulls perched upon the vessel's shattered stern ornament and tiny fish swimming in a tide pool among the broken hull pieces. Judging by its size, the ship had been at least three times bigger than the *Marawati*. The kind of ship with two masts and vast sails; a deep-water vessel meant for carrying horses, royal treasures, and heavy luxury goods.

"I wonder what happened to it?" Dalila pondered aloud as I walked around the wreck. The water lapping at my ankles was cool, shaded by the doomed boat. The wind whistled through the shattered wooden planks, an eerie cry as the broken cords that had once bound the sewn hull shivered in the breeze. There was a strange buzz to the air, like the approach of lightning.

I came around the other side of the hull. My throat caught. "I may have found the cause."

The mystery ship had not sunk because it had hit coral or rocks. It had sunk because it had been *bitten in half*. A semicircle of jagged edges had been torn out of the hull with such violence that two serrated teeth had been left behind in the wood. They were curved like fangs and the color of rust.

Tinbu joined me. "Where did *those* come from?"

I pried one of the teeth loose. It was easily the length of my forearm. "No idea."

Dalila took the tooth from my hands and examined it. "I cannot think of any creature with teeth this size."

"Nor I." Tinbu swallowed loudly and said what I suspected we all feared. "You do not think . . ."

"That this might have been Falco's ship?" Layth had died before he could tell us more about the vessel the Frank had ended up hiring, but Falco sounded like a man who threw his money around, a man who would have wanted the biggest, fanciest ship he could buy. A ship like this. Ocean currents are strong, of course, and I've seen vessels rumored to be wrecked on the other side of the sea wash up on our shores. But they're typically in far worse shape than this one, broken into timbers and weathered and covered in growth by their time in the water.

No . . . this ship was close when it met its doom. Which meant it had likely come here on purpose.

"It might be," I finally admitted, running my fingers over the ripped stitches.

Tinbu made a low sound of distress. "This ship would have sunk quickly, Amina. *Really* quickly, and that's assuming whatever creature struck it wasn't actively pulling it down and attacking its passengers. There might not have been enough time for anyone to escape on its dunij."

When Tinbu couldn't find a way to be hopeful, you really were in trouble. And yet it was difficult to argue with his assessment.

You will never see your daughter again. Would Salima believe me if I brought word of Dunya's death? Grant me mercy for the peace of knowing her granddaughter's fate?

Doubtful. She'd probably find a way to blame me instead.

I turned away from the shipwreck. "We don't know for certain that this was their ship. And staring at it isn't going to help Dunya. Let's go."

The cliffs eventually gentled enough for us to clumsily climb a steep patch of stony sand dunes until we reached the plateau that made up the island's heart. Behind us was the sea, and far to the west, rocky mountains tore at one of the bluest skies I had ever seen. In many ways, the craggy land reminded me of Oman, determined patches of lush green sprouting from the dust and dry rocks, the vibrant color complementing the bright blue water and stunning coast. And yet it was different enough, many of its trees and plants alien, to remind me that I was very far from home.

It was not easy terrain to traverse, particularly for a trio of middle-aged folk who'd spent the last two weeks not walking anything longer than the *Marawati*'s cramped deck. My bad knee was not yet in agony, but there was a pulsing unsteadiness in the joint that promised future retribution with every misstep. The ground was uneven, rising and falling in hills and shallow ravines. The undergrowth was thick and spiky—lovely, yes, with red and purple sea roses climbing to lift their faces to the sun, but thorny vines conspired to snag my shins and bloody my ankles. Fig and frankincense trees grew in abundance, gnarled and twisting old grandfathers whose brief passages of shade were appreciated, but too few to be any true relief. In little time, sweat drenched my body, my garments sticking to my back.

After hiking a damnable number of hills, we emerged in a valley with breathtaking views. Tendrils of mists lingered around distant summits, spiny grasses and prickly bushes spreading everywhere. Here we spotted our first of Socotra's famed dragon's blood trees and stopped to marvel at the specimen. It appeared less like a tree and more like a dome of grassy turf that had been shoved into the sky—an arboreal mushroom. Hundreds of branches snaked out from its trunk, a dense network of bark veins so thick the eye could not pierce them.

"It is as strange as they say," I commented. "It looks like a tree from another realm, like something designed to give shade to angels and djinn."

Tinbu shuddered. "Or demons and ghouls—oh, Dalila, *must* you do that?"

"Yes," she said, twisting one of her knives into the dragon's blood tree's trunk. She yanked it out, pressing a pale cloth to the weeping wound that instantly turned red. "Do you know the properties this sap is rumored to have?"

"You are going to get us eaten by a tree spirit." Tinbu stepped back, as though to put space between Dalila and himself, and then addressed the tree's canopy. "Do not blame me for her offenses!"

"Tinbu, stop yelling at the tree. Dalila, stop *stabbing* the tree." I grabbed them each by an arm as though they were wayward children. "You'll make me regret not bringing Majed."

We continued walking, unmolested by tree spirits and breaking for a rest around midday. Here and there we saw evidence of local people: a tapper's tools left in a frankincense grove, a leather strap caught on a branch, and the hoofprints of sheep in the dust. There was even a path, narrow and full of switchbacks, but still enough of a trail indicating people used it. Though we encountered no one, we tried our best to steer clear, concealing our tracks when we could.

It was difficult to discern how far we had traveled. By the time the sun was setting, staining Socotra's landscape in bloody hues, the sea was far behind us. But there was nothing that hinted at the northern coast being close, and oddly enough . . . there was very little *sound*. No night song of insects, no warbling birds, no rustling as tiny reptiles or rodents skittered about. Rather it felt as though nature itself was holding its breath, prey frozen before a scented predator.

There was a small mercy in such silence, however, for it meant we heard the faint murmuring of a small creek we might have otherwise missed. We reached the brook just as the sun finally slipped beneath the horizon. It was a blessed if eerie sight: bladed palm trees veiled in shadow and the pale humps of boulders rising in the murmuring water like bobbing corpses. The creek cut deeply into the hills, providing a natural place to shelter.

The current was gentle, the water colder than it should have been after a day in the sun. But it was enough to slake our thirst and rinse the dust from our skin. We each of us prayed in our tradition and then, not daring a fire, huddled close as kittens to ward off the night chill. We ate a simple meal of dates, salted fish, and rehydrated biscuits. Another time we would have gossiped and told stories. Now, exhausted by our trek and age, my friends fell asleep easily at my urging.

I wrapped myself up in my cloak to take the first watch and gazed at the sky. It was beautiful—the thick clusters of stars and constellations some of the clearest I had ever seen. I found Taurus and then al-Dabaran, though the moon was not yet in its manzil and would not be for some time. I traced out other constellations, my mind turning to the stories my father would tell me of them. My mother and grandfather had taken care to instill in me practical knowledge: how to read my letters, how to make a meal for one stretch to feed four, how to tell a storm was approaching. But my father had been a dreamer, and he loved the old tales behind the celestial map we relied upon to guide our way. There were spirits said to embody each of the lunar manazil. The beautiful Thurayya who could grant wishes, and al-Na'am, the mighty centaur who watched over hunters. Fearsome al-Dabaran, who wore scaled armor and held aloft a serpent as he rode across the sky on a horse that breathed typhoon winds.

My father's retellings could be dramatic and my mother would often chide him, especially before bedtime when she feared he'd give me nightmares. But his stories never frightened me. I was an overly brash child who delighted in believing every stray cat a djinn, every shadow beneath the waves a mermaid. But it went beyond imaginings. I'd grown up feeling terribly unusual, out of place and never at peace with the fate afforded young girls. In a hidden corner of my heart, I nursed embarrassing dreams. That I was not the child of my parents, but the daughter of a tribe of female warriors who flew upon winged horses. Or I was heir to a hidden sea kingdom below the waves, and the whispered sighs I heard from the water when we sailed and the strange lightning in the distance were not natural weather phenomena but *magic*, my true family calling to me.

Then I grew into an adult. One who learned the hard way that if there was magic in this world, it could be as brutal and cunning as the worst monsters out of a fairy tale.

I wonder, then, what sort of magic is the Moon of Saba?

I struggled to recall what my father had told me. He had liked the story, finding commonality with the lunar aspect so struck with the sight of Bilqis that al-Dabaran took the form of a pearl to join her—this was a man who had nearly fallen off his ship upon spotting my mother, giving up a life of piracy to marry her. If I closed my eyes, I could still see him winking at my mother when he told the story and—to my youthful horror—giving her backside an affectionate squeeze when he thought no one was watching. I wasn't a child who appreciated romance.

But I had a hard time imagining a murderous, power-hungry Frank coming all the way to Socotra on the strength of a love story. So what else had Dunya told him? What did Falco believe the Moon of Saba could *do* that it was worth embarking on such a dangerous quest? I regretted now not taking more of the documents that had been on Dunya's desk. All I remembered was the almanac, left open to the pages discussing the approaching eclipse—now only a few weeks away. In my despair and rage over Salima's threat, I had not been thinking clearly, and the strange words and symbols of the other books had only confounded me further. But if I'd had the wisdom to bring them along, my companions and I might have studied the texts during our voyage, gleaning what we could together.

It matters not, I tried to tell myself. *Worry more about finding Dunya and less about the purpose of magical gems that likely don't exist.* But in my heart, as I stared at the cold stars in the heavens above, I knew it was not going to be that easy . . . neither to spirit her away, nor forget the tales buried deep inside me.

Chapter 15

Sleep clung determinedly to me the next morning, bizarre dreams of locusts sweeping across an eclipsed moon leaving me foggy-headed. Save a solitary vulture circling in the distance, the world still seemed strangely absent of life. We had not awoken to insect bites, and dawn came and went without the sweet twitter of birds. There were no fish in the creek and no spiders in the webs glittering with morning dew. It was as though instead of crossing Socotra, we had slipped into the pages of a storybook, into a realm whose inhabitants had been rendered invisible.

At least until we tried to leave our camp.

Dalila threw out her arms to stop us, her wooden staff nearly smacking me in the chin. "That footprint was not there last night."

The footprint in question, little more than a smudge in the dust, was located on a rise in the winding dirt path from which our small camp would have been visible, even at night. And yet a spot from which the footprint's bearer should have also been visible to *us*. The moon and stars had been bright, neither bushes nor trees obscuring this area.

I frowned. "We would have seen someone. Did either of you fall asleep during your watch?"

When Dalila and Tinbu both gave adamant denials, I drew closer to examine the print. It looked to have been made by a shoe—a sandal or boot, perhaps—around the size of my own. It was a deep impression, and yet bizarrely it was the only one. Now, granted, were I a lone traveler in a notoriously hostile land who came upon strangers at midnight, I might also freeze and silently retreat, sweeping away what I could of my tracks.

But we should have seen them. Heard them.

"Dalila . . ." Tinbu's voice was compassionate. "Do you think the footprint could have been there before we arrived, and you perhaps didn't spot it?"

"It was not there last night," she said firmly. "I look for these things."

I lifted my gaze to the misty horizon. The rising sun was burning away the morning fog, setting it to a sparkling blush of swiftly evaporating dew. This was typically my favorite part of the morning, the peace and the promise of a new day almost magical.

But I did not feel that way now.

Tinbu and Dalila were still arguing.

"You could be getting all riled for nothing," Tinbu said. "I know your eyes—"

"My eyes are *fine*," Dalila snapped.

Rising to my feet, I declared, "We are leaving. I want to put as much distance as possible between us and this camp by nightfall."

We did not get far.

By midday, signs of human habitation, sparse when we set out, had grown impossible to ignore: tufts of sheep hair caught on thistles and a grove of clearly tended olive and fig trees; far more footprints on a widening path and rock cairns indicating directions to unknown destinations.

At first the faint smell of smoke was almost welcome. Cookfires, we assumed, a sign that we were not the only humans in some desolate portal world, though there was no corresponding plume of smoke in the sky. The scent became heavier and ever-present, impossible to avoid no matter which direction we turned. Then it was laced with worse—rot. The sickly sweet aroma of death and decay, of old blood and spilled entrails, grew thick in the hot air, and by the time we came upon a too-quiet village, I think we all knew we were about to discover something dreadful.

We stopped in the shade of neighboring trees. From here, the blackened remains of burnt huts and a broken livestock pen were visible. There were no signs of life. No children shouting, no dogs barking at the approach of strangers. Belongings littered the perimeter, an unlatched door swinging open and shut with a bang.

"What do we do, nakhudha?" Tinbu whispered.

It was an excellent question. No part of me wanted to get any closer to that village, but we were here to scout, to uncover answers even if we didn't like them. The shipwreck on the beach, the odd absence of life in the hills, the footprint we couldn't explain, and now this. None of it was painting a reassuring image of what was to come.

I wanted to turn back. My instincts *told* me to turn back. But every time I thought of climbing aboard the *Marawati* and getting the hell out of here, I saw a knife at Marjana's throat. I saw my home ablaze, my mother assaulted by some vengeful ghost from my past. Mustafa and his little family executed for crimes in which they had no part. My loved ones punished for *my* choices, by *my* enemies before I could save them.

Focus. "Let's take a quick sweep," I decided. "If we are to land more men, it is best we know whether this was pestilence of the natural or human variety. But cover your faces and keep a weapon close." I wrapped the tail of my turban around my nose and my mouth, then freed my sword and a throwing knife.

It was a modest village, no more than a dozen thatch huts and about half that number of small stone homes. But there were signs of abundance in the broken pots, dropped rugs, and shattered furnishings littering the path. The animals were gone, and here and there were trails of grain, indicating carried-off sacks of food. The place had clearly been plundered. But despite the burnt huts, there was little sign of violence. No bodies, no blood.

It made no sense. I have seen the aftermath of raids on villages such as these. They are violent, they are gruesome, and they leave marks. Those cruel enough to steal from and annihilate the lives of the rural poor rarely care about hiding the evidence, and those they attack will fight to the death to defend the homes and livelihoods they've scrabbled together.

"Where is everyone?" Dalila asked under her breath.

"Perhaps whoever attacked this place kidnapped its inhabitants?" I suggested. "I've known slavers to carry off entire populations."

"And *no* one fought back?" Tinbu asked doubtfully. "I don't believe it."

I didn't either. I stopped to peer into one of the huts as Tinbu and Dalila continued. The tattered curtain hanging from its entrance danced in the wind. The interior was dark—darker than seemed possible given the bright sun—though I could spot the lines of a small Christian shrine: a half-melted candle besides an icon of the Prophet Isa and his mother, may they be blessed. I stepped closer and then stilled. Coming from the hut was a very particular odor. Not smoke, not rot.

Lightning. Storm clouds and salt, the brine of decaying maritime creatures, and the heavy moist air of monsoon rains. It was the same stench that had lingered about the ruined ship on the beach.

Then Dalila gasped.

Dalila never gasped. She was my most implacable, enigmatic companion, always ten steps ahead of the rest of us. So when I heard that sound, I tore from the hut and dashed to her side as fast as my feet would take me. She and Tinbu had wandered ahead, beyond a large stone building marked with an unobtrusive bronze cross—a church. Beside it was the largest dragon's blood tree I had seen on Socotra, looming over the small church to provide what must have been a wonderfully shaded central meeting place, the heart of the village.

Three elders—two old women and a gray-haired man dressed in a long black robe—had been speared to the tree's trunk.

My steps slowed, horror stealing over me. My companions were unhurt; it had been the ghastly sight that made Dalila cry out. But ghastly it was. Lances pierced the three elders through the stomach, holding them some distance away from the ground. The corpses were hunched over the weapons, their skin blue and their bodies shriveled. One woman's fingers still clawed around the lance.

It would have been an agonizing death, a *slow* death.

Tinbu covered his mouth. "Gods have mercy, why would anyone hurt old folks like this? Those women are probably *grandmothers*."

"That man is a priest," Dalila said. Her face was expressionless, her eyes locked on the murdered elders, but I did not miss that she was clutching her own cross. "This village is Christian."

"A priest?" Tinbu repeated in surprise. "Does that mean it wasn't the Frank who did this?"

Dalila let out a bitter sound. "The Franks only view the rest of us as Christians when it suits them."

From beyond the village walls, a branch snapped. I spun around, raising my throwing knife. But there was no further sound save the pounding of my own heart. No movement save the rustling garments of the murdered old folks in the tree.

Get out of here. The lightning smell from the burned hut, the footprint, and now three vicious murders. It was all adding up to something I did not like.

"We're leaving," I decided. "Right now."

Dalila ignored me, approaching the bodies. "I want to bury them."

"*Bury* them?"

"Yes," she replied flatly.

"Dalila, do you have any idea how long that will—"

She glared back at me, uncharacteristic anger flashing in her eyes. "You would do it if they were Muslims."

The charge took me completely aback. I had never seen Dalila show such concern for strangers before. And yet . . .

Would I?

If the grandmothers had been veiled in my people's manner and the old man wearing the turban of a sheikh, would my heart have insisted on staying and shrouding them as best I could, offering funeral prayers at their graves? Did Dalila, a friend who had left her home and stood by my side, truly believe that of me?

Was she wrong to? More disconcerted than I would have imagined, I opened my mouth but faltered for a response.

Tinbu beat me to one, touching my wrist. "We'll make the time, Dalila. Why don't you look for a shovel? Amina and I will get their bodies down."

It was grisly work, the sordid details of which I will not relate. The bodies were heartbreakingly frail and light, and I couldn't conceive of a reason these poor people had been slaughtered in such a brutal manner. It was difficult to determine how long ago they had been killed, the wind and dry air having slowed the process of rot.

"Amina, look at this," Tinbu whispered, gesturing to three even puncture marks on the priest's throat, as though the old man had been stabbed by a needle. "I saw a similar wound on one of the women, but thought it might have been an unrelated injury."

I frowned and searched the neck of the woman I had brought down, but her skin was too bruised to see if she had a comparable wound. Even so, there was something about the appearance of the bodies that was unsettling beyond their gruesome manner of death. An odd blue gray cast spread across their skin, their eyes clouded like pale moonstones. There was no sign any of them had been touched by insects or animals.

I shuddered. "Let's dig quickly."

There was no digging quickly, however, not in Socotra's rocky soil, and it was late afternoon by the time we had turned out three shallow graves. Dalila said prayers as Tinbu gently shoveled dirt and stones upon the corpses, and I stalked the perimeter with a weapon in each hand, convinced I could feel eyes upon us. I was drenched in sweat, shivering despite the day's heat and my own exertions.

Another damn stick snapped behind me.

I whirled and threw my knife. It sailed into a thick patch of bushes, and I waited, anticipating an animal's cry, a human's angry bellow. But there was no response.

"Amina?" I jumped at Tinbu's voice and glanced back again to see my friend giving me a wary look of concern. "Everything all right?"

"Thought I heard something." I stalked closer to where I had hurled the knife, gripping my sword. "Are we ready to leave?"

"Aye. Dalila says she has finished."

"Good." I kicked around the bushes, searching for the blade I'd thrown, but the pebbly ground was bare. I pushed deeper into the weeds, swatting away vines and cursing when a thorn snagged my hand.

"Amina, come on!" Dalila called out. "I thought you were in a rush to leave."

"I need to find my knife!" I knelt to search the ground, sweeping my hands through the undergrowth. My fingers brushed something wet and slimy, and I recoiled when I realized it was the remains of a small bird's nest. The eggs were broken and seeping fluid, vines growing out of the skeletal remains of the mother bird.

My heart stuttered at the sight. Maybe I was overreacting; birds died of disease all the time. Plenty of animals hunted eggs. But after what we had witnessed in this village, the particularly maternal death scene sent dread rolling over me in waves. I scrambled back. To hell with my knife. We were getting out of here.

The thorns gave one last tug at my turban, nearly tearing it off. I scrubbed my hands with sand and gave the fresh graves a final look, adding my own prayers for the poor elders. I did not know if their deaths were the Frank's handiwork (I had never seen lances like that, but then again, I had never seen a Frank), but the possibility chilled me to the core. Tinbu and Dalila were already beyond the gate that led out of the village, and I had to hurry to catch up.

But if I'd hoped the sensation of being watched would dissipate when we left the village, I was sorely mistaken. I heard the skittering of hidden beasts in every rustling shrub and felt the weight of watchful eyes in every shadow. I was completely on edge, the hair on the back of my neck sticking straight up.

My companions were not as affected.

"Amina, nothing is following us," Dalila said in exasperation when I decapitated a small palm tree after swearing it had sighed in my ear. "I would hear it."

There was a *laugh* on the breeze, as if in response.

"Tell me you heard *that*!" I spun around, wildly searching the grove of scraggly trees we had entered. After being in Socotra's relentless sun for so long, I found the darkness of the grove disconcerting. Branches entwined and tangled together above our heads, the little sunshine that pierced through the canopy falling in spiky fingers.

"*Amina*." True concern colored Tinbu's voice. He stepped closer to lay his hands on my shoulders. At his side, Dalila remained stone-faced— whatever had passed between us in the village was lingering. "Calm yourself, my friend," he continued. "It has been an awful day. What we saw back there would drive anyone—"

Out of the corner of my eye, a blur of movement.

Seizing Tinbu, I yanked him out of the way just as the knife that would have gone through his throat flew past to thud into a tree. *My* knife, the one I had lost back at the village. It struck the tree so hard that the blade stuck in the trunk, the hilt vibrating madly. I whirled to face the direction from which it had flown.

A smoky figure dropped from the trees with the elegance of a leopard. It was as though the shadows themselves had taken form, a *familiar* form;

shards of premature night twisting together to shape themselves into the worst monster I knew. The creature who offered cruel, cold excuses during the darkest moments of my life and purred my name during the best.

The beast I had left for dead ten years ago. The demon who did worse than murder Asif.

"*Wife*," Raksh drawled. "It has been a long time."

A Regrettable Evening
in the Maldives

—Jamal . . . *Jamal*, stop yelling. Sit down. You're going to knock over your inkpot ranting and pacing like that, and I am not starting the story again.

—I did not mislead you! I just . . . did not offer all information right away. Those were regrettable years and I do not like to recall them. But if you want the whole sordid affair—forgive me, if you want "a rich contextual backdrop," as you called it in fancy scholar-speech—fine.

—Let's talk about the night I accidentally married a demon.

We were in the Maldives, our cargo hold empty after selling off a dozen trunks of filched Gujarati cloth intended for a princess in Lanka and the pearls meant to pay for them (the timing is tricky, but if you rob a business deal in progress, you can nab two prizes for the planning cost of one job). Now, the Maldives are beautiful, one of the most God-blessed places I have ever visited. The beaches are whiter than the moon, the water a stunning tropical blue so vibrant and clear, it is like a hue out of Paradise. The local people are gentle and pragmatically accommodating toward travelers of legal dubiousness, and the food is excellent.

That said, I was not having a merry time in the Maldives. My third husband, Salih, had left me shortly before the job, pulled by the pleading letters of ailing parents to return home to Srivijaya. Our divorce was amicable, the only time I had parted peacefully from a spouse, and yet that made his loss more acute. I had previously selected my husbands more for their ability to raise a sail and their attractiveness while doing so rather than for their personalities. They were companions for a few seasons, nothing more. But Salih had a sweetness I found refreshing and endless stories from a lifetime spent traveling farther east than I had ever gone. I would not call it love, but it was the closest I had come, and though it had been three months, I still missed him terribly.

Which is to say that the night before we were due to depart, I was not feasting on fresh fish with my crew and a band of musical locals. Instead I had taken a very large cask of what the musicians promised was an excellent wine made from native palms to the seashore to drown my sorrows alone.

Now, I have a weakness for wine. Even today, when I have been on the path of righteousness for years and not allowed a drop of that which is forbidden to pass my lips, I still have moments I long for a cup; troubles I know would be eased with its sweetness. But wine was a luxury for people like me, and I never learned to temper my intake. I was not as dependent upon drink as some, but suffice to say that when I drank, I drank too much and usually to disastrous effect.

Which was what I was doing that night, drinking and gazing morosely at the tumbling black waves rushing over the moonlit beach. I cursed the sea, knowing its currents were leading Salih farther away. I cursed myself as well for not following him. The invitation had been there, unspoken between us, and yet I had not taken it. How could I? I had a crew to pay and knew almost nothing of the waters beyond Lanka. Perhaps if I had been free like Salih, free to hire myself out to another ship, I might have dared.

But I was not free. I had a family to feed and a brother starting an expensive apprenticeship. And what law-abiding merchant would hire an unknown female nakhudha to carry their goods? It was absurd, a dream that would always lay just out of touch.

Sighing pathetically, I threw myself back on the damp sand and trailed my fingers through a line of drying seaweed. In the distance, strains of music from the party I had abandoned were barely audible against the crashing surf. The stars spread before me, twinkling and inconceivably vast against the soft velvet night. It was the kind of view that was crushing, that made one feel overwhelmingly small and insignificant. I squeezed my eyes shut. I didn't need the reminder of my place in the cosmos.

"Forgive me . . ." an airy voice interrupted. "But might you be the nakhudha?"

My eyes shot open.

The most beautiful person I had ever seen stood over me.

That should have been alarming—I am not an easy person to sneak up on. But this man had done so, and God forgive me, what a fine specimen of a man. Fine enough to steal my thoughts, my breath, and my good sense. He looked about my height, tall as a reed and lean; lean in a strange way, for his body—well displayed in a short wrap that revealed thick, muscled thighs and a patterned shawl barely clinging to broad shoulders—appeared both solid and insubstantial, as though he were both there and not.

The stunning fellow dropped to an elegant crouch beside me, long fingers sinking into the sand. Bathed in silver moonlight, the curve of his neck was as lovely as a willow in a garden.

"May I join you?" he asked with a flash of white teeth.

I made some sort of garbled noise in response. He had a full handsome face, round dimpled cheeks, and a long nose. His head was uncovered, black hair wound in an uncommonly large knot at the back of his skull. Heavy, graceful brows met over his nose, winging across his eyes like a bird in flight, like a painting of a celestial being. His beard was well trimmed, with a silvery russet hue around his mouth.

Large, liquid black eyes, lovely as a doe's, locked on mine, and then the man smiled, the kind of smile people burrow through a mountain to reclaim. "You are the nakhudha Amina al-Sirafi, yes? Your first mate, Tinbu, said I would find you out here."

With the mention of Tinbu, some of my wits returned. Tinbu had sent this male houri-like creature out to seek me? And then, as the man tilted his head, a few strands of silky hair falling artfully around his face and smelling of musk, the clues fell more neatly into place. Of course Tinbu had sent him to me. He, Asif, and Dalila were probably cackling about it right now.

"Listen," I started regretfully. How did he smell so *good*? "I'm certain you are very talented at your job, but I am neither in the mood nor permitted to engage in such matters." An ill-timed claim, as the drink in my hand was equally impermissible. But one sin at a time.

His lips quirked in amusement. "What job is it you think I was sent to do?"

I gestured a bit unsteadily at his various attributes. "Surely you know."

He burst into delighted peals of laughter. "Why, nakhudha, how blunt! Alas, such a tempting pairing is not the reason I sought you out, though I would not be terribly averse." His impossible eyes twinkled in amusement. "I am here because your first mate told me you were down a man, and I was hoping I might replace him."

My mind went traitorously fast to the ways this gorgeous creature might replace Salih. None of them had anything to do with boats, though he certainly had the thighs for rowing. But there was an otherwise too-polished look to him, his hands manicured and free of calluses. He was no youth, but his skin was smooth, lacking the sun damage that accumulates in my trade.

"You do not have the appearance of a sailor," I remarked.

"Perhaps not, but I have spent time aplenty on ships. I can pull an oar, mend sailcloth, and twist rope well enough." He paused. "But more important, I bring another skill, one far more certain to please you."

From another, this boastful flirtation might have been off-putting. But there was something both unassuming and untouchably confident about the bizarre man before me. "What is your name?" I inquired instead.

Another bemused smile. "You may call me Raksh."

"Raksh?" The name sounded both familiar and foreign, and I struggled to place the way he had pronounced it. Struggled to place *him*. Like many of us descended from those who've spent millennia trekking around the ocean, he looked like he might have hailed from a hundred separate homelands, and his otherwise flawless Arabic was marked by an accent I could not trace. His skin was a lighter brown than mine, touched by a strange, almost blue pallor. A trick of the light, perhaps.

"Is that Gujarati?" I asked.

He laughed. "Not quite."

"Then where are you from?" I pressed, intrigued enough to reveal my own curiosity.

"Here. There. A thousand different places and none."

I snorted. "Pretensions of being a poet, have you? And what skill is it you think would please me more than a sailor being able to sail?"

"Why, Amina al-Sirafi . . ." Raksh's eyes seemed to pin me to the sand. "I can bring you luck."

"*Luck?*"

"Luck. It is what sailors rely on most, is it not?" Raksh leaned closer as he spoke, a few strands of his hair falling upon my shoulder. Their weight and softness reminded me of unspun wool, and I shivered, trying not to reveal how much his presence unbalanced me. But I must have been drunker than I thought, because as he grinned again, I'd swear I caught a glimpse of fangs. This close I could see a dappled pattern of dark spots scattered across his cheeks.

Freckles, I decided and took another swig of my palm wine because I'm an idiot. "I cannot argue with the necessity of luck, but I am hardly fool enough to pay a man who claims he can harness such a slippery thing, Raksh of everywhere and nowhere. Should you be genuinely interested in joining my crew, come see Tinbu tomorrow morning. My ship is the *Marawati*."

"I shall." But Raksh did not leave. "Where are you headed?"

"Calicut and then up the Indian coast. We shall see what sort of jobs are available. It will soon be the season to bring horses over and there is always money in that."

"You do not sound excited."

I shrugged. "It is work."

He cocked his head, seeming to regard me. "And where would you go if you could go anywhere?"

Home. But I did not say that, for the only home I could claim at that time was the *Marawati*. I had not looked upon my mother's face in years, not since the day my father died. How could I? When last we parted, I was a beloved child. Now I was a thief and a murderer, and despite the money I sent home and the pleading letters she relayed back, the prospect of facing her filled me with shame, no matter how much I ached to feel her arms around me once again.

Those were not dreams I'd share with a stranger, no matter how gilded his tongue.

"China," I said softly, echoing the ridiculous promise Majed and I had made to each other. "I would go to China."

Raksh's mesmerizing gaze hadn't left mine. "Why China?"

"I have been no farther east than Lanka." Why had I confessed that? "But I have always wanted to," I gushed, feeling unsteady as I said it, as though the admission had been pulled from me with force.

He leaned closer. "You . . . *radiate* ambition, do you know that?" A strange hunger surged through his voice. "A veritable feast of yearning."

Then—before I could scoff, before I could stop myself from stumbling deeper—Raksh touched my face.

Everything that was not him fell instantly away. The midnight beach, the cold stars, the laughter of my friends in the distance . . . all gone in a moment. Raksh's fingers were featherlight on my jaw, and yet I couldn't move. I couldn't *think*. His eyes were blazing, so bright it hurt to look upon them, but I couldn't drop my gaze. A crimson line blossomed in their ebony depths, illuminating pupils of scorching fire.

"Tell me what you want, Amina al-Sirafi," he purred. "Tell me it all."

"I want to go everywhere. I want to be great." Words poured from my lips, desires and confessions spilling so fast I nearly choked. "I want to look upon my mother again and see pride in her eyes. I want to explore lands I've heard about only in tales and listen to the stories of those who dwell in them. I want . . . I want *so much*."

If I thought I'd spoken too freely before, it was nothing compared to what was happening now. The press of his hand and the burn of his eyes pulled me into a dreamlike haze from which I could not escape. With each desire spoken aloud, I found it harder to stop, until I was scarcely aware of what I was saying at all. At one point, I recall the surf tickling my feet; we must have been sitting on the beach so long that the tide had come in. We were sitting there long enough for me to finish the cask of wine anyway, for when I did, Raksh finally released me and the world cleared, just slightly.

"Do not fear." He tapped my nose and picked up the cask. "I will get more of this. We're just getting started and I find a bit of liquor loosens the tongue."

Indeed, when he returned, it was with two bottles for each of us and a slightly dazzled expression on his face.

"This is *excellent*," he gushed, taking a long drink. "What a marvelous concoction!"

Introducing Raksh to the mysterious Maldivian palm wine was, in retrospect, another mistake.

He drank with a gusto that exceeded mine, and if he did not literally bewitch me again, he hardly needed to—we were genuinely enjoying each other's company now. We drank and we laughed, we swam and we walked along the undulating ribbon of star-splashed beach and dancing surf, tripping and giggling as we held the other one up. At some point we crashed into a grove of swaying palms, splaying onto soft beds of fallen leaves.

"You are *fascinating*," Raksh slurred as we lay with our heads next to each other. "Do you know how long I have been stuck here listening to the stupid, *boring* dreams of fishermen and petty merchants?"

"Sounds dreadful," I agreed fervently, having no idea what he was talking about.

"Worse than that, it is *dull*." He rolled onto his elbows, face hovering over mine. "Save me, nakhudha, and I will make you a legend. People will sing songs of you for centuries."

"People singing songs of me will hardly pay my crew."

"Then I will guide you to treasure. I will scrub the decks, rub your feet . . . *anything*." His hot breath whispered down my neck. "Just take me off this island."

The nearness of Raksh was overwhelming, my body aflame with need. It would be nothing to arch against him, to wrap my legs around his hips and taste the salt drying at the base of his throat.

I played with the hairs at the back of his neck instead, resisting the urge to pull him on top of me. "Do you not have money?" I asked. "Pay me and come as a passenger."

"Regrettably I cannot." Raksh nuzzled my jaw. "But I promise to make myself very, *very* useful."

I was drunk and charmed enough to finally agree. Even if he wasn't a particularly good sailor, I could always find room for someone this captivating and stupidly attractive in the smuggling and swindling part of our operations.

"Fine," I relented. "I will take you off this island."

"Truly?" He pulled back, hope and relief warring in his expression. "You will contract with me?"

"No." I chuckled. "What do you take me for? I am a pirate. I do not sign employment papers for my fellow criminals. We work together on our word and because I pay them well."

My response seem to deflate him.

"That will not be enough." Raksh moved over me again, pressing his hips against mine and stroking my cheek. "Are you sure we cannot lay together? I would make such an experience very worth your time."

My mind was swimming with palm wine, but of the veracity of his offer, I had little doubt. Raksh moved with liquid grace, his long fingers trailing down my arms, my sides. They were hot through the thin material of my garments. The perfume of him, musk and sweetness and earthy wool, filled my nostrils like a drug.

Then he kissed me.

Now, I have kissed many men. More men than I have married (though less in recent years due to the return to the path of righteousness and the realization that very few are worth it). None of those men were like Raksh. There was nothing sweet or romantic about his kiss. It was *urgent* in a way I did not understand until it was too late. His tongue surged into mine, one of his hands carding roughly through my hair with his sharp nails. His teeth grazed my lower lip, and when I gasped, his weight shifted more heavily upon my body, one thigh sliding between mine and his interest becoming *very* apparent.

I groaned, pressing harder against him. I would have stabbed another man for such forwardness, but *oh* . . . I wanted this. I wanted *him*. I did not feel threatened. Did not feel forced. It was hot as hell, honestly, and I have rarely desired a man more than I did at that moment. Enough that when his fingers pulled open the strings of my trousers, I contemplated letting him continue.

But the alcohol had made me both soft and stubborn. I had broken so many other vows, saddling the angels writing my account with a long, sorry list. I would keep this one.

I removed his hand (most reluctantly for it was headed in promising directions) and pushed him away. Doing so felt like resurfacing from a dream, the kind that lingers, making one doubt what is real and what is not.

"I cannot do this," I breathed.

Raksh moaned. "Why not? Is there another? Bring them along. I am not greedy."

"No, there is not. I mean . . . there was, but he is gone now."

His elegant face wrinkled in confusion. "Then what is the problem?"

Swiftly retying my trouser strings, I tried to sit up. Stars danced before my eyes. My head was beginning to pound as well, promising retribution in the morning. "We are not married. And I-I cannot lay with a man who is not my husband."

"Why not?" He sounded genuinely confused.

Why not? Where was this fellow from that he was not familiar with one of the basic rules of every faith I knew? "It is forbidden." I flushed. "I mean . . . many things are forbidden, I suppose." Hypocrisy was another sin frowned upon, and yet here we were. "But I do not—it is my rule," I stammered. "I take but one husband at a time and he is the only man I allow in my bed."

"What a strange custom." Raksh frowned. "But you said your husband was gone. So why not have me in his place?"

I blinked. Surely I was not so drunk to have heard that correctly. "Are you proposing to me?"

"Is that what it is called?" he asked, looking intrigued. "Sure! I propose to you. With the marrying. Now we can lay together?"

"Yes. No. Well . . ." I was flustered. "It is more complicated than that. We would need a cleric to conduct a short ceremony and draft our nikah, our marriage contract," I explained when he appeared even more perplexed. "There are also other stipu . . . stipula . . . laws. Things."

His eyes went wide, crimson flickering in their depths again. "It is a contract . . . a *conjugal* contract. I have not tried something like that in a very long time. It could be quite powerful." Raksh sounded hungry, so hungry. Slightly cautious, but in retrospect, not enough. He drummed his fingers on his knee and then tossed back the rest of his palm wine. "Let us do it!"

I would like to say I hesitated. That I took a moment to think the situation through rather than letting my baser urges and the alcohol running through my blood drive my decision. I can see you wincing already, probably muttering in your head about the importance of a tradition so sacred as marriage in our faith.

I did not hesitate. I drank back the rest of my wine in turn and roared, "To marriage!"

The ready availability of clerics in most port towns willing to find a way to marry two drunken fools at midnight speaks to the ready supply of lovelorn sailors eager to whet their urges while staying narrowly within the boundaries of religion. By the time we stumbled through a few taverns in search of such a person, everything was beginning to take on a blurred happy color, like fragments of stained glass. I remember signing something, saying something, Raksh and I grinning at each other like idiots. He was so very eager; giddy and extremely, almost offensively erotic. I might have signed my name to anything at that point, so focused I was on my desire to lick him.

But then the deed was done. One of them anyway. Raksh found a guesthouse, exchanging money and a whispered word with the proprietor. I remember being confused, vaguely recalling the battered copper coin he had also given me as mahr during our brief ceremony at the urging of the cleric. If Raksh had money, why had he not agreed to my earlier suggestion to book passage on the *Marawati*? But it didn't matter, because then we were going into a room, laughing and tripping over our clothes as we shucked them off.

I pulled at the knot of his hair, and it fell to his knees in shining ebony waves, striping his body and mine. Ripping away his shawl, I discovered a plain leather cord around his neck. From it hung an uncommonly large pendant of rough coral.

"What is this?" I remember asking, running my fingers over the coarse blue surface.

Raksh grinned. "The heart of my enemy." He pulled the pendant from my hands and tugged off his waist wrap in the same motion, leaving his marvelous body bare. "*Now* can we lay together?"

The coral pendant fled my mind at the sight of him. "Now we can lay together," I breathed and promptly wound my fists in his hair.

Now, they recommend that what is intimate between a wife and a husband should stay between them, a concession to modesty and discretion. And though I may be lacking in those attributes, to salvage what little dignity I have, let us simply say the marriage was well consummated. In every way. In ways indeed not even I—who had heard every sort of foulmouthed boast from sailors and pirates—had known was possible. Raksh had promised laying with him would be enjoyable and he had not lied.

Not about that anyway.

I slept through the adhan for fajr—though to be fair, I had fallen asleep only shortly before it, Raksh and I finally exhausted by the comprehensive exploration of our new contract. By the time my throbbing head woke me up, the sun was fully risen, penetrating the tattered curtain covering the guesthouse's narrow window in dusty rays of light. I groaned into a lumpy cushion and pressed my palms against my aching temples. God forgive me, what had possessed me to drink so much? I was supposed to be tempering myself; I had promised Majed the last time he found me in a hungover haze that I was going to try and stay sober.

Searching for water, I rolled onto my back and struck another warm body.

"Sorry, Salih," I croaked, rubbing away a crust of salt from my eyes. "I didn't mean—"

My mouth snapped shut. The man lying naked beside me was not Salih.

Nor was it the raven-haired beauty with large black eyes and a full mouth I had met on the beach last night. No, instead it was a creature who shared that man's lean body and long, capable fingers. But where Raksh's skin had been a sun-scorched brown a few hues lighter than mine, this man—this *beast*—was the green-tinged blue of a murky tropical sky. The lengthy hair I had admired last night now lay as tiger-black stripes of flesh, wild patches of leopard spots falling amongst them as though two great cats had clashed together and been imprinted on his limbs. His fingernails ended in ivory claws, and ruddy silver tusks protruded past wine-stained lips where his beard had been.

And the pendant . . . God have mercy . . . it *was* a heart: pocked like coral, covered in barnacles, and still *actively pulsing*, a long length of gut piercing through one part to hang from Raksh's neck.

"God save me," I choked out.

At my cry, Raksh blinked awake and then squinted in pain as though equally hungover. The ebony eyes I had fallen into last night were gone, replaced by pupil-less pools of scorching fire. He looked briefly confused by the shocked horror in my face. Then he glanced down.

"*Oh.*" Raksh winced at the sight of his body. "I had hoped you would not see this."

Chapter 16

Raksh sauntered closer to us, the little sunlight that broke through the canopy darting away from him. "What . . . no word of greeting from my old friends? No thanks for returning your *knife*?"

I thrust out my arm, keeping a shocked Dalila and Tinbu behind me. "Stay where you are."

"Or what?" Raksh hissed. "Will you lock me in another box? I did not enjoy that, Amina. It was not very romantic of you. It left me weak. Left me *hungry*. Left me so delirious and wanting that I thought I must be going mad to sense your presence last night."

He took another, deliberately provocative step closer, reaching out as though to snatch Dalila by the hair, and I broke. There was no time to go for my blessed iron knife in my belt, so I lunged at him with the sword already in hand, bringing it down on his neck in a move that might have decapitated another man.

It glanced off Raksh like his flesh were stone, leaving barely more than a scratch. Just as it had ten years ago.

And I'd been a fool to move closer. Before I could make another attempt, Raksh ripped the sword from my hands and seized me by the throat. He lifted me clean off my feet and inhaled deeply, a fasting man breathing in the scent of a simmering stew. Color filled his cheeks, the grayish cast giving way to warm brown.

Dalila rushed at him.

Raksh backhanded her across the chest, sending her flying. "Marriage dispute, Mistress of Poisons. One that does not concern you. Nor you, Tinbu. Lower that bow or I will choke the life out of your nakhudha. *Now.*" Raksh turned to me, rage glittering in his black eyes. "You trapped me," he accused. "Undo it."

I did what? Gasping for air, I clawed at his fingers. "I . . ." But I couldn't breathe, let alone answer the charge.

"Let her go!" Tinbu cried. "She cannot say anything being choked like that!"

Raksh made an irritated sound but relaxed his grip. I fell to the ground. Tinbu and Dalila pulled me back, and we cowered together as Raksh paced before us, his long, unbound hair twitching around his knees like a cat's tail. I'd seen lions and tigers locked up in grand mansions move like that—miserable, caged creatures treading back and forth. That's what he reminded me of, and it was freshly shocking I had ever thought him human.

He should be dead. He should be drowned. We had shackled and buried Raksh in a locked chest on a spit of land the ocean rushed to devour with every change of the tides.

"Where is your ship?" Raksh demanded.

"Nowhere that concerns you," I snapped.

"I require it."

This demon could not seriously believe I would ever take him off another island. "I would watch the *Marawati* sink before I see you step foot on it again."

Raksh kicked at the sandy path. "Your ornery mapmaker is not here, so I assume he is either dead or helming it on your behalf. Perhaps burning you three on the beach one by one will persuade him to return."

I was suddenly even gladder I had left Majed behind. "He will not. Majed has your measure, and the moment he spots you, he'll leave. He would not risk returning a fiend like you to our shores. I take it you're the one responsible for those murdered old folks back at the village?"

Raksh pressed his lips into an unhappy line. "Would that I was. There was nothing useful left of them by the time I got there."

He might not have been the one to kill them, but I recoiled at the heartless response. "You're a monster."

"A monster of *your* making! Next time don't leave me in a fucking box to starve. Do you have any idea how long it takes wood to rot and chain to rust?"

"You came after my crew! You—you *fed* on Asif," I managed, rage and grief breaking my voice. "You stole his soul, his very existence!"

"Ah, there you are again," Raksh complained. "Do you know your problem, Amina? You always have to be in charge. Did you ever think that perhaps Asif knew what he was doing and thought our arrangement perfectly acceptable?"

Oh, if I could only hurt this bastard. "No, you snake. I think you manipulated him. I think you toyed with his heart and lied through your teeth."

Raksh stopped in his tracks. "Oh, *I* lied? The absolute gall of you, woman, to say such a thing after bewitching me."

"I did nothing to you!"

"You did! I sign contracts from Sofala to Calicut now and they are like crumbs of a meal." Raksh rubbed his fingers together, tossing his hand like a rich man flinging coins at beggars. "I have not been able to form a proper contract since I married you. I am hungry, I am *famished* all the time. I want to know why. I want you to *fix* it."

I was flabbergasted by the charge. "You think I *wanted* to stay connected to you? Asshole, I left you buried in a locked trunk I was hoping the sea would swallow. I would have been happy to never see you again!"

"Then why do I still feel our connection?" Raksh demanded. "Even now your very touch has left me stronger, and I can sense your desires swimming in my head like some sort of parasite." His eyes narrowed again. "It was that sorcerous marriage contract you insisted on, wasn't it? You snuck some language in there that made me your slave!"

"You're accusing *me* of sorcery? You were the one who wanted to get married! You got me so drunk I could barely see what I was signing!"

"You got *me* drunk. I had never even heard of palm wine!"

Dalila had finally had enough. "For the love of God . . ." she hissed. "Will you both *shut the fuck up*? You're going to bring God only knows who upon our heads with all this shouting."

I flushed, but her warning did little to tamp down my temper. I glared at Raksh again. "What are you even *doing* here? How did you get off that other island? You told me you couldn't cross water without a contract."

A malevolent expression twisted Raksh's pretty face. "I waited until I caught the attention of a ship, of course. Then I begged them to understand that my head . . . it was just so addled from the sun, so please, sir, please—" He shifted his voice. "If you would just put your initials to my hand, God reward you . . ." Raksh smiled sweetly. "Full, healthy crew. I don't often go for human hearts, but after starving for five years . . . you can actually taste the fear, the hope." He licked his lips. "Delicious."

Tinbu recoiled and even Dalila paled. They hadn't seen this side of Raksh. *I* hadn't seen this side of Raksh. He made sure no one did, not when he was enjoying his time as a member of my crew.

I tried not to let it shake me, especially when I realized he'd skirted my first question. "That does not explain why you are *here*."

Raksh shrugged, far too casually. "I heard Socotra was pleasant."

It was a nonsense answer, but his earlier words were already running back through my head. *From Sofala to Calicut* . . . if Raksh had been traveling back and forth across the sea these past years, what was he doing marooning himself on notoriously distant Socotra only to . . .

And then the pieces fell into place. There *had* been another person who knew us all.

"You *bastard*," I said through my teeth. "You're the one who sold us out to the Frank."

I could see several lies flit across Raksh's expression before he gave in. "First of all, 'sold you out' is a very strong charge. If I merely collected and relayed mostly public information—?"

I abruptly lost the fight with my anger, lunging to my feet. "You motherfucking son of a goat, I'm going to kill you!"

Raksh danced back. "Yes, because your earlier attempts went so well." He bared his teeth as Tinbu grabbed my legs. "And you were the first to betray me with your perfidious pact!"

"I already told you: there is nothing that connects us!"

Except there was.

Marjana.

It felt like a bucket of cold water had upended over my head. My daughter. My little love, the dearest person in my life. My heart may have protected me from seeing the similarities at first, but now it was impossible not to notice the shadow of Marjana in the elegant shape of Raksh's lotus eyes and long nose.

"What?" Raksh spun back at me, suspicion sharpening his features. He inhaled like a serpent tasting the air. "You're hiding something. *Tell* me."

I was lost for words. I didn't know how creatures such as Raksh behaved toward their kin. Nightmarish fables of pagan gods who devoured their offspring or drowned them beneath waves to prevent future challenges filled my mind. Raksh was the most opportunistic predator I had ever encountered.

He could not learn of our daughter. So I did what I've always done in a difficult situation.

I gambled. "I know how to dissolve the bind between us," I lied in a rush. "But it is a complicated, delicate process. A spell of sorts, one that may be tricky to navigate."

"How?" Raksh asked, growing breathless. "What is it?"

God guide me. "A divorce."

"Yes, yes, I have heard of that word!" His eyes brightened with hope. "How do we do that? The divorce?" A note of worry snuck into his voice. "You say it is complicated?"

It was a mark of Raksh's arrogance and disinterest in the complexities of his "prey" that he even had to ask such a question. The lying dog could divorce me right now by declaring it three times. But I had wagered on him not knowing, and that seemed to be the case.

"Indeed," I warned. "It is extremely complicated. There are many steps and . . . incantations that can be said only by the wife."

Raksh seemed utterly absorbed. "Then let us start right away."

"Not so fast." It was Dalila. "Amina is correct. To divorce is a difficult process. You would not wish to make an error due to haste and have the marriage become even more permanent, would you?"

God bless and preserve this woman. I did not miss Dalila's stomp on Tinbu's foot when my other friend, looking baffled, opened his mouth. The two of them had lived in Muslim lands long enough to know I was lying through my teeth.

Raksh gave her a cautious look. "No, obviously I do not want that. What are you implying?"

Dalila drew herself up. "Well, you have made it very clear what you want—a divorce and a way off Socotra—but since spilling your tongue to this Frank got us into our own mess, why don't you start being a bit more forthcoming about *that* and we shall see if we can do the same regarding the rituals of divorce?"

He spat like an offended house cat but relented. "What do you wish to know?"

"Is Falco alive?" she asked. "We spotted a ship in the shallows that looked like it came to a violent end."

"You could say that. But yes, Falco lives. He and half of the crew made it to shore."

"Was there a young girl amongst them?" I asked urgently.

"A girl? Do you mean . . . *Oh*." Delayed understanding crossed Raksh's face. "You speak of Dunya. Is she why you are here?"

"Yes, idiot. What can you tell me of her? Is she okay?"

Raksh snorted. "She seems to be regretting her youthful mistakes, but she was alive when I left." He flashed a wicked smile. "Though the yearning in that one, aye. She makes her father seem blissfully content by comparison."

A sick feeling stole through me. "You would not contract with her. You would not dare."

"I would in a heartbeat if I were able; do not be ridiculous. But Falco is no fool, and Dunya is his jewel. He kept her well away."

"What are you even doing with him?" I asked. "You seem too interested in self-preservation to ally with someone so dangerous."

"I did not 'ally' with him," Raksh replied, sounding insulted. "I feed off stupidly ambitious humans. He was a stupidly ambitious human who wanted a captain and a ship to go exploring. As I *also* wanted to track a certain nakhudha down, I figured I could use him to get to you."

"Except you didn't," Dalila noted. "We met his former agent, and it sounds like Falco lost interest in Amina and the *Marawati* when he met Dunya. So why did you follow them to Socotra?"

A brief flush of embarrassment filled Raksh's cheeks. "You have not met him."

I lifted a brow in surprise. "Oh, was it the other sort of 'contract' the two of you brokered, then? Did laying with Falco cast such a spell?"

Raksh sputtered in outrage. "I did not *lay* with that arrogant windbag nor broker a contract. I only went along because . . . well—it's your fault!" he accused, shaking a finger in my face. "Had I not been so hungry, I would have been thinking more clearly. But the prospect of him and Dunya hunting magical artifacts together: I could not walk away from such a prize."

It was a ludicrous stretch to blame me for his mistakes, though I suppose Raksh did look a little worse for wear. His unbound hair was tangled with knots and dead leaves, the lungi wrapping his waist tattered and thin. Very thin. So thin it was impossible not to notice that his backside still looked plump enough to bounce a dinar off.

I lowered my gaze. *Stop ogling a demon's ass. Ogling a demon's ass is what got you into all these troubles in the first place.* I returned to interrogating him. "What sort of magical artifacts?"

Raksh waved a dismissive hand. "The usual nonsense humans believe will grant them power. Dunya told him there was a treasure horde from the days of antiquity hidden in the cave here."

"*Is* there a treasure horde from the days of antiquity hidden in the cave here?" Tinbu asked, speaking for the first time since a knife nearly went through his throat.

"Really?" I asked my friend in exasperation. "*That* is how you find your tongue?"

But Raksh seemed to consider the question. "There could be such a trove. They found a lot of skeletons, and mortals were once very fond of murdering each other to serve as guards in the afterlife."

"And that's what he is after?" I prodded. "Falco came all the way to Socotra on the vague promise of a treasure cave?"

His expression darkened. "I suspect Socotra is only the first of many stops for him. Falco fancies himself some sort of future scholar-king, harnessing all the magic he can to challenge the Divine or some such nonsense. It was all very ridiculous until it became clear Dunya *actually* has the knowledge of such things, if not Falco's ambition. The girl was nattering on about historic interactions between marids and mortals, and next you know, Falco is trying to summon one. At sea!"

I understood less than half of that. "He tried to summon a *what*?"

"A marid," Raksh repeated. "A water elemental in the form of a sea scorpion chimera large enough to eat your *Marawati* for breakfast. Indeed, it ate half the crew before we managed to escape. But Falco was already starting to become suspicious of me, and should either of them figure out I wasn't human, I didn't intend to become their next experiment. So I fled."

Fled. The word took me aback—as did his tale of this monstrous sea beast. Raksh was an overly confident, rash trickster. A demon who devoured souls and drank ambitions like they were bread and water. And Falco had scared him off.

With Dunya's assistance. Don't forget that part. But Dunya was still a child. *Asif's* child and one I had been ordered to return on threat to my own family.

However, there was one thing missing from Raksh's explanation: the Moon of Saba. Did he really not know what *particular* treasure Falco and Dunya were after? Granted, Layth hadn't mentioned anyone else with them on their visit to the al-Hilli residence, and what I knew of the Frank painted a portrait of a cunning man. Perhaps Falco had kept news of the Moon of Saba to himself.

"Is that enough?" Raksh demanded. "I have been talking for a very long time."

"And you will keep talking if you want a divorce," I replied. "Tell us of their situation now. I want to know about this cave."

Raksh let out an exceedingly weary sigh but dropped to a crouch, drawing a map in the sand with one long finger. "The entrance is a half day's walk, but the cave itself is vast and unfathomably deep. The locals say one can wander in there for days and that anyone who ventures too far is never seen again."

"What locals?" Dalila asked. "Do you mean the villagers? What happened to them?"

"Falco and his men rounded them up. Carried off all the food and supplies they could and have been using the survivors for labor."

"So they're still alive?" she pushed.

"Some are. But these are not gentle men you have set yourselves against. They are the nastiest mercenaries Falco could find." Raksh rolled his eyes in disdain. "The *constant* dreams of bloodlust. So uninspired."

Tinbu pinched his brow. "And how many of these bloodlusting mercenaries does the Frank command?"

"When I left, there were about twenty. But they like to get drunk and brawl, so there may be fewer now."

My heart sank. Those were not odds I liked. Most of my crew were sailors, not fighters; we stood no chance if we were forced to battle Falco and his men directly. "What is their camp like?"

Raksh continued his sketch. "Violent as they might be, Falco's men are frightened of the cave. The villagers filled their minds with horror stories and so they make camp at the cave's mouth when the sun sets." He marked the cave's entrance with a slash. "Dunya sleeps farther inside, and Falco stays between them. I would often stay in there as well."

"Then how did you escape?"

"I found another exit." Raksh drew a dizzying number of squiggling paths. "I used to explore the cave when the humans were asleep. There are many branches, but if you follow this one, it takes you to a narrow tunnel that opens into the side of a cliff. It is a very lethal drop if you fall, but if you can *climb*"—he traced a line directly up—"you come out at the top of the plateau, a good distance away from the cave's mouth. I murdered a seagull, doused some of my torn clothing in its blood, and left it in a tunnel they could access, hoping they would think some cave monster ate me."

Dalila appeared dubious. "Do you think the Frank believed that?"

"I planned to be much farther away before Falco got suspicious." Raksh smiled with all his sharp teeth. "What happy news to run into my old friends from the dependable *Marawati*."

I ignored that, studying his sandy map. "How difficult is the climb?"

"It's straight up and as high as the cliffs."

Dalila and I exchanged a glance.

"I should have enough rope to rappel down," she said. "Climbing up will be more difficult. Not impossible, but difficult. I would need to better survey the scene."

Tinbu groaned. "Majed is going to kill us."

"Yes, but only if we survive." I sighed. "I don't see another way. Our crew is not going to be able to outfight the men Raksh has described. But if there's a chance we can sneak in through the back . . ." I paused, realizing my limited possibilities left me with a terrible choice. "But Raksh will need to go with us."

"*What?*" Tinbu and Dalila both whirled on me.

"No!" Raksh sounded terrified. "I just got away!"

"Then you can run around Socotra looking for another ship before Falco catches you," I sniped at him before giving my friends a more beseeching look. "We stand a better chance at succeeding if he is with us. You know it's true. We won't be able to retrace his path through the cave alone."

"There was not supposed to be any succeeding," Dalila reminded me. "Not yet. We came to scout."

"And that's what we are doing," I replied. "Let Raksh show us where Dunya is being kept. We'll see if we can steal her away. If not, then we'll reevaluate."

It was another gamble, yes. But I needed to save Dunya *and* I needed to buy time to find a new way to dispose of Raksh. I didn't trust him—I *despised* him—but for Raksh, self-preservation came before everything, and he clearly wanted off this island.

I prayed that instinct and my lie about divorce were enough.

"My offer stands," I said to him again. "Help me, and I help you. There is no *Marawati* in your future unless Dunya is on it as well."

"You are a fool," Raksh said bluntly. "And no match for Falco. Knowing my luck, he will kill you and I will be tied to your ghost forever."

"Then make sure he doesn't catch me. We are still married, are we not? That bond is supposed to bring me luck."

Raksh swept away the map with an angry dash of his hand. "You better *break* that bond if I help you. I will not be deceived again."

My stomach knotted in apprehension. I had no intention of taking this demon off Socotra, let alone breaking any ties that might make him suspect something else—some*one* else—bound us together.

But one problem at a time. "Does that mean you accept my offer?"

He scowled. "For now, Amina al-Sirafi. For now."

Chapter 17

Raksh marched us out of the grove and along a twisting trail that cut deep into the hillside. It was almost too narrow and thorny for a human to walk, likely a leopard's path, but with an angry demon glaring at me every time I slowed or stopped to readjust the wrapping on my now-throbbing knee, I managed to keep up even as I wondered, desperately, how the hell I was going to get us out of this one.

Dalila and Tinbu snuck occasional glances my way, but we didn't dare converse. Raksh had never struck me as a warrior (he preferred to flee from danger), but he was strong, had access to magics I didn't understand, and already distrusted us. There was no need to make the situation worse by openly conspiring against him. Even if I did briefly entertain notions of shoving him off the cliff. The motherfucker would probably bounce and then climb back up to murder me.

Which I suppose begs the question . . . why hasn't *he murdered me?* It was a rather obvious way of severing a bond, and back in the copse, Raksh had at first seemed furious enough to try. But before I could ponder the delightful topic of my not-murder more deeply there came a sliver of hope on a salty-sweet sea breeze.

We had made it to Socotra's northern coast.

The limestone cliffs were even higher here, but I spotted no cave entrances. However, between the dying light of the setting sun and the eons of salt and mildew covering the cliffs' craggy face, I suspected such an entrance would be easy to miss. The area was desolate—no ships drifted in the blue-green water and no fishermen were dragging in nets. Even so, I was overly conscious of every footfall and snapped twig. When darkness fell, my companions and I took what shelter we could beneath sparse bushes. After seeming surprised and mildly stung that I did not wish to sleep *with* him, Raksh retreated to a nearby tree and climbed into its branches to pass the night.

"I hope you know what you're doing, Amina," Tinbu muttered. "I really do." Dalila said nothing. Whether her silence was due to my decision to work with Raksh again or whatever had passed between us at the Christian village, I didn't know.

Sleep didn't come easily. Every time I closed my eyes, I saw Marjana's sweet little face. Ten years ago I had burned Asif, buried my treacherous husband, and eight months later had an impossibly tiny little girl swaddled and nestled in my arms. Raksh and I hadn't been married long, and we'd never even discussed the possibility of children. Whether it was the sheer labor of ship work, the limited diet of a sailor, or something else, my cycles had always been irregular. Three previous husbands—human husbands—had failed to leave anything in my womb; I never imagined Raksh could.

And once Marjana was born . . . I never thought of her as Raksh's. Never thought of her as anything other than *my* daughter, innocent and kind and wholly, entirely human. My heart would not allow it.

He cannot know of her. By God, he will not.

The oath went through my mind again and again. When I finally did fall asleep, my dreams were full of scorpions that flew like seagulls overhead as I raced after a toddling Marjana along the decks of a *Marawati* that went on forever, screaming her name as she disappeared over the edge. I awoke exhausted and in pain, my head pounding and a pulsing shudder jolting my knee, sharp enough to bring tears to my eyes. I choked down a damp biscuit and we departed, taking advantage of the early morning cool that chilled the salty air.

It was dusk when Raksh finally called out, "Just ahead—do you see that thicket? Stop there."

I reached the stand of trees, peered through the thick leaves, and then jerked back when a warm breeze batted my face. Just beyond the thicket was a sheer, lethal drop to an inlet where a tumbling river poured down from the hills and into the sea, a churning maelstrom of jagged, glistening rocks and crashing water. I immediately threw out a hand to halt my friends and glared daggers at Raksh.

"You might have warned me before I fell to my death!"

He smiled sweetly. "I did tell you to stop. Now, look. Do you see where that sapling emerges from the cliff? The tunnel entrance is just past that."

My stomach dropped. "That is a good deal farther down than I had imagined."

Dalila scrutinized the spot. "My ropes will reach it," she said, giving one of the surrounding trees a tug. "And these are strong enough to serve as an anchor."

I nodded, and as quickly as we had fallen back into our sailing duties, we resumed the usual preparations for a job. Tinbu and I set to cleaning our weapons and readying oil lamps. Dalila tested her ropes, tying the ends of three into strong foot loops. We had run more complicated schemes with worse odds, but they had been against familiar foes: rival smugglers and spoiled nobles, two-timing merchants and kidnapped minor royals. Not against a foreigner with a blood-soaked past and magical tricks who had managed to scare off the *actual* demon I had married. I prayed maghrib with more intention than usual, adding extra raka'at and looping my oft-neglected misbaha around my wrist.

I finished my prayers to find Raksh crouched across from me, the expression on his face incompatible with salah.

"You are different," he declared.

"Of course I'm different," I said, irked at his presence and at myself for how quickly my gaze settled upon his thighs. "It has been over a decade since you last plagued me."

"That is not what I mean." There was a note of curious wonder in his voice. "Your desires, your ambitions; they are not the same. They are—"

"Less impressive, I know. I'm old. That's what happens to humans."

"They're stronger." Raksh's eyes darkened with what might have been lust in another man, but that was not the kind of ardor he favored. Well, not the only kind. "*Sharper.*"

A chill ran down my back. "I don't know what you are talking about."

He didn't seem to register my response, eyeing me like I've seen others hunger after gold. "I sensed you coming, you know. About a week ago. I did not know it was you, of course, but I had a feeling, a premonition things were about to change." He shuddered. "Did you feel it? The magic between us?"

A week ago was when the skies had cleared and I'd been blessed with the best sailing weather of my life. With fish that jumped into our nets, a cistern that never emptied, and winds that pulled us in the direction of Socotra like a leash. I recalled how I had heard Raksh laughing as he stalked us in the grove, long before my companions had noticed anything.

"There is nothing between us," I denied. "Why would you even want there to be? I left you to starve. You greeted me by throwing a knife at Tinbu and then threatening to burn us one by one on the beach."

Raksh shrugged. "Grudges are for humans. Why cling to some petty disagreement from the past when a future prize might be sweeter? And you . . ." A flicker of crimson glowed in his dark eyes. "You have always been promising. But you *are* getting older. Surely your body can't do this sort of thing much longer. What are grudges when you and I might have a few last adventures?"

I knew what Raksh was doing, and his words still struck close. Hadn't that been part of why I'd taken this job, a weakness I'd nearly admitted to my mother? The ache for just one more escapade, one more chance to see the ocean spread before me and shower my loved ones in riches.

I drew back, realizing only as I did that Raksh had crept closer, his knees brushing my own. "I will never forgive you for Asif," I said, hating the tremor in my voice. "And I want *nothing* to do with magic."

Tinbu strode up, seeming to sense trouble. "Stop talking to that ghoul. He's a lying waste of breath."

Raksh cackled. "Oh, people of the *Marawati*, I have missed this! The energy that comes off you when you are excited and terrified . . ." He inhaled. "Delicious."

"Are you ready?" Dalila called.

"Ready as I'll ever be." I took the length of black cloth she handed me and wrapped it around my face. She and Tinbu were already similarly dressed, and Raksh had his own way of blending in when he didn't wish to be seen. "Let's go."

The inlet was more fearsome at dusk, the waves smashing into glittering shards on the black rocks at the bottom of the cliff. I tried hard not to imagine that water tinged with the scarlet of our blood.

"You first," I ordered Raksh, handing him the rope.

He made no move to take it. "I do not need rope." In the blink of an eye, he shape-shifted, his skin turning the color of a storm-tossed sky, and then stepped neatly off the cliff.

Tinbu let out a choked cry of surprise. But Raksh had not jumped to his doom; rather he was climbing down the precipice's sheer face, his clawed hands and feet gripping holds I doubted we could spot, let alone use. The sun's dying light played on his striped skin and the muscles flexing across his bare back. No one who sported tusks should be that attractive, and I wondered again how I could have ever believed he was human.

Palm wine. Palm wine was the reason you believed he was human and why God has wisely forbidden such a thing.

"Is he wearing a *heart* around his neck?" Tinbu asked.

"It appears so." Dalila glanced at me, a hint of suspicion in her eyes. "How did you not realize what he was? You married him. You *slept* with him."

"That is not the man I married." But it was the truth that skirted her question, an evasion I feared Dalila was savvy enough to soon detect.

Below, Raksh reached the tunnel. He flashed a triumphant grin, then slipped inside.

Dalila and Tinbu climbed down next. I grew more and more uneasy as I watched them. I hate heights; I fell from the *Marawati*'s mast as a child, and though I landed in a pile of sailcloth that softened the blow and saved my life, I have never forgotten that gut-wrenching loss of gravity and the sudden awful certainty I was about to die. I trusted Dalila's knot work, but my heart hammered madly in my chest as I put my full weight onto the rope and began descending.

One hand over the other. It was okay until I made the mistake of glancing down, catching a glimpse of the deadly rocks that sent the breath rushing from my body. Cold sweat broke out across my arms, and the rope grew slick in my hands as I gripped it more tightly. But I forced myself to keep going.

Tinbu grabbed my waist when I was close, pulling me into the entrance and helping me find my footing on the stony floor. "Are you all right?" he asked.

I nodded mutely and Tinbu released me. The tunnel's entrance was cramped and dark. But in his natural form, Raksh gave off a blue-gray glow like a puff of extinguished smoke, and it was just enough light to see how narrowly the rest of the tunnel tapered.

"My God . . ." I said. "You came through *that*? How? Crawling on your belly?"

"At times." Raksh sounded no more enthusiastic than I did. "The cave

itself is large, but this tunnel is wretched, like being a worm in a burrow."
He paused. "I should lick you."

I veered away. "Excuse me. You should do what?"

"Lick you. Though I suppose kissing might work as well. I am feeling
weak, and the path ahead is difficult. Perhaps if *someone* had bothered to
sleep with me last night, my magic would be stronger—"

I shoved him forward. "We are not yet that desperate. Go."

But the tunnel was miserable. We were forced to crawl on our hands
and knees and then on our bellies in utter darkness. The rock scraped every patch of exposed skin it could, and the hilts of my sword and khanjar
thrust painfully into my hips. After aching all day, my bad knee had gone
numb, a development I assumed was not good. The close air was hot and
putrid, and more than once I needed to steady my breath to keep from being overwhelmed in the crushingly small space.

After what felt like an eternity, the tunnel finally expanded enough that
we could stand up. Dalila bid us to stop so she could light the lamps with
her flint, and I took one gladly.

"It is just a bit farther," Raksh advised. "You will know when we are
out of the tunnel."

Ducking to avoid a dripping rock formation, I asked, "How will I— *oh.*"

I have seen a great many astonishing sights in my life. Very few com-
pare to my first glimpse of the great cave of Socotra. Our lamps illuminated a space large enough to swallow a dozen *Marawati*s, and I had the
sense that beyond the encompassing blackness it was even larger. The cave
looked like a scene plucked from a dream or brought to life by an art-
ist's paintbrush: lacy lichens, glittering crystals, and mushroom-like stone
growths in every color of the rainbow covering the rocky walls. Writhing
formations in glittering minerals hung from the uneven ceiling, reaching
down to touch their siblings bursting from the floor. Water dripped into
pools and streams both visible and unseen, the pattering of droplets filling

the air with gentle music. Just ahead, a vivid yellow waterfall poured from a break in the rocks to spill through a hole so distant there was no splash. Besides the hush of our breath and pattering water, there was no other sound on the thick, heavy air. Humidity and the aroma of rotten eggs aside, the cave was marked by a silence so profound it felt sacred.

"There's so much water," Tinbu marveled as we walked, holding out his lamp to illuminate a deep pool. It was beautiful in an eerie, alien way, the water bright green against a shockingly white expanse of quartz. "What a miracle this place must have been for the first people who discovered it."

"I doubt any of your people got this far. There's human graffiti on the walls farther ahead but—aye, do not *touch* that." Raksh smacked Tinbu's hand away from the pool. "Half the water in this place can melt your flesh like butter. Follow my footsteps and do not stray."

We did so, walking along skinny edges that loomed over pits that might have gone on forever and ducking under fallen rock formations like the massive statues of deposed tyrants. We crossed silent fields of jutting silver shards that could have been the abandoned swords of a vanished army and climbed steps of such perfect natural geometry that I whispered God's praise. It was a wild place, the darkness just beyond the flickering light of our lamps crushing, but slowly signs of human habitation grew more frequent. Here and there, debris littered the ground, potsherds and crude tools alongside broken clay lamps and dusty glass bottles.

Then around the next bend, as though plucked from Dunya's notes, the markings began.

Sabaean, Ge'ez, Greek, and a half-dozen other letters whose language I couldn't identify. Intricate pictographs and hanging Indian scripts, cuneiform wedges and dash marks. Some were names, some were warnings. More told stories I could not understand, stories in tongues long forgotten. Beyond the ancient messages, there were drawings as well. Boats and handprints, odd cruciforms and antlered creatures.

It was one thing to read about this place in a book, but to *see* the history of travelers and sailors such as me spread before us, their ghosts and the walls they touched, was another experience altogether. I wondered at their lives and their time here. After a long sea journey, a cave offering relief from the sun and plentiful water must have seemed a divinely sent respite or a perfect smuggler's nook. Despite the circumstances, I was feeling a bit whimsical, my storyteller's fancy tickled.

Until we found the path blocked by a massive white snakeskin.

The shed skin was the color of bone, glittering with iridescent discarded slime, and wide enough that we could have walked through the creature's cavity without ducking. Just ahead was a split in the tunnel, the abandoned skin continuing into its leftmost juncture.

"Well . . ." Tinbu swallowed loudly. "I must say: The chroniclers got the size wrong. The snakes are even *bigger* than the books made them out to be."

Raksh gave the forked passage a leery look. "The tunnels are vast, but that skin was not here when I escaped."

Dalila already had her knife out and was cutting and collecting as many shed scales as she could. I watched as she prodded a crevasse with her staff and dragged out a fang the size of a femur. "This is . . . impressive," she remarked. But even Dalila sounded uneasy.

I slashed an opening through the snakeskin with my sword. "Let's go. I would rather not be here if the beast returns."

But the monstrous snakeskin proved to be an ill portent, for the farther we walked, the more alarming our surroundings grew. No longer were there whimsical prints of hands and boats. Instead, bones and decaying shoes littered the path, alongside a rusty knife and a saddlebag torn apart by claws. A complete set of yellowing human teeth jutted out from a rocky lodge, as though its poor former owner had bitten down so hard the teeth had been ripped from his jaw.

Raksh had been leading us along the twists and turns, but shortly after we passed the horrifying teeth, the light of my torch fell upon a direction we were not headed. Cut into the stalactites and carved into the bedrock was a crude staircase.

A staircase? Here? How odd.

Curious, I stepped closer. A warm breath of air seemed to welcome me, smelling sweetly and impossibly of my mother's perfume. The familiar scent upended my heart, stealing my focus, and I had to reach out to brace myself. When I did so, I found I was already standing on the first step. I attempted to regain my bearings, glancing up and peering through the darkness. At the top of the staircase was a large brass door, the bright metal shining like a lighthouse in a foggy harbor.

As though bewitched, I drifted closer. My friends and mission suddenly seemed far away. A strange whooshing, whispers and murmured sighs, pulled me forward, urging me on. Nearer now I could see the door was covered in carved images. Engravings of warriors in braided skirts and kings in splendid headdresses looming over tiny bowed captives stripped of clothes and dignity, their hands and feet shackled together. There were lion hunts and archery contests followed by brutal scenes of warfare and slavery, scattered bodies and broken chariots. I lifted my lamp to illuminate a scene of musicians serenading a banquet. Beside it was a tableau that turned my stomach: broken boats and screaming sailors. A general, or perhaps a king, given his large stature, had his foot on the neck of a captive and was raising a mace over their head.

With a soft breath of warm air, the brass door opened. The opening was not wide, just a sliver of blackness between the shining metal and the stone where there had been none before. It would be nothing to push the door open just a *bit* farther, to glance inside . . .

"*Get down from there.*" It was Raksh, sounding thoroughly and uncharacteristically rattled.

I startled, jerking my hand away from the door: I didn't even recall reaching out. And it was *that* realization—along with the fact that I was at the very top of a long staircase I had no memory of climbing—that made me stumble back, nearly tripping as I retreated down the steps.

Raksh waited until I was about halfway down to dart up the remaining stairs, grab my wrist, and pull me the rest of the way.

"Human fool," he hissed. "I told you not to stray."

I was trembling all over, a sheen of cold sweat erupting across my skin. "What is that place?"

My husband's black gaze skittered to the brass door. "An ill omen." He made what appeared to be some sort of warding motion with his fingers, then glared at me. "This better not be a trap. I will carve out your heart if you think to trick me into that sort of fate."

I yanked my hand free of his. "What sort of fate? What does that even *mean*?"

"Amina?" Tinbu called out. "Is everything all right?"

Before I could open my mouth, Raksh clapped a palm over it.

"Say nothing of that door," he warned. "I'm not unaware you too are holding secrets, wife."

My heart skipped. Whether Raksh had noticed my reticence among my friends or meant something else, now wasn't the time to press. Instead I nodded and he dropped his hand.

"I'm fine," I called back to Tinbu.

We hastened to rejoin them and ventured through another tunnel, its ceiling decorated with swirling constellations. I searched the painted stars for Taurus or al-Dabaran but they marked no night sky I knew, and I finally gave up when staring upward resulted in too many flakes of blue paint dusting my lashes.

"How much farther?" Dalila asked.

"Not much," Raksh said. "You will know we are close when the ground starts to crunch."

"*Crunch?*"

"There are a lot of bones. I told you it was a burial pit."

Indeed it wasn't long before the rocky ground gave way to a carpet of crumbling bone fragments that grew high enough to reach my knees. I prayed for forgiveness as I waded through the shattered skulls and broken ribs flickering in the torchlight. Raksh appeared to have literally hacked a hole through a catacomb of long-decayed corpses; rotten shrouds and remains lay all around us. We clambered over a hill of skeletons, and he held a finger to his lips before pointing up to a grimy marble slab suspended over the packed crypt like the opening of a makeshift hatch.

"Just past that is the treasure chamber," he whispered. "I can move the slab, but we'll need to be quiet. We are getting close to the cave's mouth, where Falco and his men spend the night."

I nodded and he silently edged aside the slab. We slipped through. The so-called treasure chamber was a mess, digging tools and overturned buckets of earth scattered among shattered pottery, inscribed headstones, and tattered clothing. Coins and broken strands of pearls littered the ground, but nothing much else of monetary value was left—perhaps Falco's men had completed their sack. Here and there crudely dug pits revealed more bones, and in the nearest, the remnants of two skeletons were still half buried, seemingly where they died, curled protectively around each other.

Revulsion swept me. I will be honest: I have looted the long dead. Like others of my criminal class, I have traded in baubles and jewelry said to be recovered from the tombs of priests and emperors. I rarely gave doing so much thought; if I had few qualms about stealing from the living rich, I had fewer stealing from the deceased. But there was something about seeing these bodies ripped from their rest, left scattered and discarded, that galled.

Excellent time to gain a conscience about grave-robbing, al-Sirafi. I studied what else I could of the chamber. Just ahead what appeared to be a bricked-over entrance had been reopened.

"Is Dunya that way?" I asked.

"She should be," Raksh replied in a hush. It sounded like he was getting jittery. In the distance, there was faraway laughter, and the air beyond the chamber was fresher, lightly scented by the sea. We followed him into another, more natural opening in the cave. Creeping forward like a roach, Raksh reached for a ragged curtain strung between two stalactites like a poor effort at a door. He carefully pulled it back . . .

To reveal nothing but an empty niche.

Raksh swore and I shoved past his hand, raising my lamp to illuminate a small sleeping space. A small, completely *ransacked* sleeping space. Cushions were slashed apart, their feather stuffing ripped out, and wooden chests smashed open. Clothes and blankets were strewn everywhere, along with ripped pages of parchment and shattered stone icons. Here and there were abandoned personal effects: bits of jewelry, a broken shell comb, and bizarrely, fine embroidered house slippers in bright pink silk.

"Raksh," I said through my teeth, "care to explain?"

My useless spouse seemed taken aback. "Dunya was here when I left," he insisted. "I swear!"

Dalila knelt to examine the torn cushions. "It looks like whoever did this was searching for something. Do you think Dunya might have stolen from the treasure chamber?"

"Perhaps." I rummaged through the abandoned pages littering the ground. A few were in Arabic, but the language was archaic, the seemingly astrological material impossible to comprehend. Beneath one page was a broken clay tablet with the same wedge-like characters as the tablets back in Dunya's library.

"We should leave," Raksh warned in a low voice. "This girl was his prize. If something happened between them . . ."

"We are not leaving. Not yet."

"Amina, you do not know this man. Nothing enrages him like disloyalty."

"*We are not leaving*," I repeated more firmly. "Is there anywhere else Dunya could be?"

Raksh let out an aggravated sigh. "Falco might have locked her up with the villagers. He keeps them closer to the cave entrance. The entrance, you may recall, where twenty armed, violent sellswords with irrational tempers will be waiting."

Tinbu, Dalila, and I looked at one another.

"We could investigate," Dalila suggested. "Get close enough to see if Dunya is among them. It's dark, and most people will likely be sleeping. If we extinguish the lamps, we might pass undetected."

"Since when have you all lost your sense of self-preservation?" Raksh groaned. "I thought you were pirates!"

"We are reformed." I snuffed my lamp and set it down on the ground so we could retrieve it when—if—we left. My companions did the same, leaving us in darkness save Raksh's pale blue glow.

With a contemptuous sneer that was louder than our whispers, Raksh stalked forward. He didn't make it easy to follow him, and more than once we stumbled and crashed into rocky protrusions. Without warning, he shifted back to his human form.

"Hush," he breathed. In the distance was the bare radiance of a bonfire, its light sending wild shadows dancing across the cave's craggy interior. I could hear drunken boasts and smell the aroma of roasting meat.

But from closer, there was soft weeping. The odor of decay, of spilled organs and old blood—the same smells that had clung to the village's murdered elders. Raksh led us in the direction of the weeping, weaving through towering, twisting stone formations. A luminescent stream bubbled underfoot, thick clusters of purple moss covering the limestone walls. The increasingly foul smell made it feel like we were stepping into a fetid wound, the warmly moist brush of the moss against my skin causing me to shudder. Just ahead was a dim glow, as if lamps had been lit and left in the chamber beyond. I stepped inside. And then . . .

And then . . .

—Ah . . . give me a moment if you would, Jamal. I know this is difficult for the both of us. Truthfully, the horror of that night was just beginning, though I could not know it at that moment.

—The chamber, though; what I saw there is seared in my memory. And should I be cursed to live a thousand years, I will never forget it.

The place was a slaughterhouse. A butcher shop of human souls. Vivisected corpses were laid out and decaying on stone slabs, while more hung from the stalactites, their bodies crudely hacked apart and left to drip blood and entrails into collection dishes. Skulls and finger bones had been boiled free of flesh, fat and hair overflowing stinking bowls, and the bones arranged in bizarre shapes surrounding piles of seashells, gull feathers, and lumps of red carnelian. It took several shocking moments of staring for my mind to process that these indeed had been people, that the grisly parts I was looking at had belonged to *humans*, before looking became abominable and I cast my gaze to the ground.

Tinbu fell to his knees and threw up. Dalila—who could steel her reaction like no one I had ever met—let out a low cry before clamping a hand to her mouth and making the sign of the cross.

I was too numb to make a sound. I have seen a great amount of violence in my life. Parents murdered in front of their children, sobbing girls younger than Marjana sold into slavery, elderly divers worked until their brains burst under the water. Things I would never tell my family. People do not take to the seas if the land offers better, and the kind of men lured to a life of smuggling and raiding are not gentle.

But I had never seen anything like this chamber.

"The Frank dies for this." It was Dalila, her whispered voice fierce. "They all do." I could only nod.

A muffled whimper pulled my attention from the ghastly tableau. We were not alone.

A band of about a dozen people were huddled on the other side of the chamber, as far from the bodies as their chains would allow, watching us with open fear. They were filthy and shackled together, dressed in rags and covered in bruises and bleeding wounds. I stepped forward and several of the prisoners cringed back. One woman had her hand clamped over the mouth of a weeping boy, her eyes bright with fear.

"Let me." Dalila swept past, carefully motioning to her cross and then kneeling before the imprisoned villagers. She said something softly that I couldn't make out, and when a man at the front gave a small nod, she gestured for me to join them.

I did so, crouching at her side and trying to block as much of the awful scene behind me as possible. "We mean you no harm," I promised. "Can you understand me?"

The man hesitated but with a glance at the others, replied in accented Arabic, "Yes, I can understand you."

"Is there anyone else here?" I asked. "Other prisoners hidden away?"

"No," the Socotran man choked out, his voice hoarse. "They have killed everyone else."

They have killed everyone else. Dalila swore, and with even greater horror, I stared at the small group before me. Had they been *here* for those murders? Shackled in an abattoir while their loved ones were tortured and killed before their eyes?

I shook my head, trying to keep away the awful buzzing threatening to overwhelm me. Falling apart would not help these people. "We're going to get you out of here, God willing. Dalila, start on their shackles. Tinbu, help me with the ropes."

Raksh groused. "We do not have time for this."

Cutting through the ropes binding the man's legs, I said, "This is the only thing worthy of our time."

The Socotran villager jerked back upon spotting Raksh. "This man belongs to them. He is the servant of their leader."

"I am not his *servant*—"

I shushed them both. "He is with us for now and knows an escape route through the tunnels. The way is arduous, but we will get your people out. I hope you can help me in return."

"How?" the man asked warily.

"I am looking for a young woman who came here from Aden."

The man nodded in recognition. "Their leader's scribe. But she is gone."

Gone. The breath went out of me. All this and Dunya was *gone*? "Where?" I asked urgently. "Where did she go?"

"I am sorry, but I can tell you nothing more. She ran off about two days ago. We only learned when the rest of them did." The Socotran man shuddered, fresh tears rolling down his cheeks. "Their leader . . . he has been in a rage ever since. It is when he began slaughtering my people."

More inebriated laughter rang out from the direction of the cave's mouth, and I made a swift decision.

Get them out of here. I would be trusting the word of a stranger, yes, but the Socotran man's account struck me as the truth. And they were locals; they might be able to help us figure out where Dunya had fled.

We worked swiftly to free the surviving villagers, but it was slow going once we started walking. The Socotrans were frail and sick, many sporting injuries, and it took twice as long to return to the treasure chamber. Raksh lifted the marble slab, setting it on an overturned funerary urn, and Dalila and Tinbu slipped through. We worked to gently lower down the villagers one by one until only Raksh and the man who had spoken were left.

There was a shout in the distance.

"They are gone! The prisoners have escaped!"

I shoved the last man through. "*Go.*"

"Amina, come on." Through the narrow gap in the bone-encrusted burial pit, Tinbu waved me forward. "Hurry!"

But I knew we would not be fast enough. The villagers were injured and weak. It would take hours for them to escape through Raksh's tunnel and that was before they were hoisted up the ropes. They needed more time.

And I needed to know about Dunya.

Coming to a regrettable decision, I freed my grandfather's khanjar and reached through the gap to shove it in Tinbu's belt. "Give me two days."

He looked confused. "Two days?"

"If I am not at the beach where we landed in two days, you signal the *Marawati* and get the hell off this island."

"Amina, no—"

But I was already whirling around. I grabbed Raksh by the collar and shoved him through the gap. "If you abandon them and I live, you lose your ride out," I snarled. "And if you abandon them and I *die*, I will haunt you for the rest of eternity."

Then before I could think better of it, before I could entertain a moment of doubt, I let the marble slab fall.

The block smashed into the ground with a resounding thud, plunging me into darkness, and setting off a new round of cries from Falco's swiftly approaching men. I kicked over a great tower of bones to cover the slab, swinging my sword around to ensure as much chaos and debris as possible, and then I slipped out.

A dozen tunnels snaked away from where I stood, offering hiding spots or the chance to wander until I got lost and was devoured by a giant white snake.

But I didn't flee. Instead, I followed the shouts and ran directly for Falco's men. I found them, arguing and cursing at one another around the next bend.

"Peace be upon you, gentlemen!" I greeted diplomatically, sheathing my sword. "My name is Amina al-Sirafi.

"And I am the nakhudha your boss has been looking for."

An Ill-Fated Decision
Due to Greed

On the morning after my wedding to Raksh, I had no sooner opened my eyes to see my new groom had sprouted tusks then I sprang from the bed, promptly tripped on the sheets, and fell to the floor. However, I was still young then and spry, recovering to fling myself at the door, nakedness be damned. I grabbed the knob.

It turned to cinders in my hand, the rest of door melting away. I gasped, but watching my sole means of escape magically vanish made me only more desperate, and so I quickly resorted to pounding on the wall with my fists.

"*Help!*" I cried. "Dalila! Asif! Maj—"

Raksh grabbed me around the waist, pressing a scalding hand over my mouth.

"Please stop screaming," he implored. "My head is *killing* me."

I writhed in his arms, trying to wake myself from this nightmare, but it was like fighting a man of stone. From beyond the blue fingers pressed over my face, I suddenly spotted our marriage contract. Amongst the wreckage of the room, clothes, palm wine casks, and bedding all tossed about, it was the one thing that had been carefully placed on a wooden table.

At the bottom was my signature.

Raksh let me go, and I crumpled to the floor. For the first time in years, I wept. I had done a great many awful things while nakhudha of the *Marawati*. I had killed and I had stolen. I had gambled, gotten drunk, and stretched the limits of adultery—often doing all three in a single evening—then failed to wake in time for fajr to pray for forgiveness. In short, I had a thousand things for which I already knew I would need to atone.

But this, *this* . . .

"Oh, God . . ." I dropped my head into my hands. I couldn't look at Raksh, the acrid air smelling of future hellfire. "I am doomed. I committed fornication with a demon. I have lost my soul and will burn for a thousand—"

"Was the contract for your soul?" Raksh sounded confused and hungover—if blue beast men could be hungover. I let out another sob and he sighed in irritation. "Will you cease all the crying? It is very loud."

He stepped back, shaking like a dog attempting to dry itself. His devilish appearance vanished, leaving both the man I'd met last night and not. The bluish hue that clung to him might have been a trick of the light; the raven tresses and speckles dotting his skin, both shadows and reality. The silver-dappled red outlining his now-vanished tusks could have passed for a poor henna job.

Raksh shuddered. "I rarely lose my form overnight. Whatever these people put in their palm wine . . . wow. It's been centuries since I've sampled a beverage so fierce."

Centuries? I glanced up through my tears. "What *are* you? Are you some sort of djinn?"

"Not a djinn, no. Though it's a bit hard to explain; your languages no longer have a good word for what I am. Not really." Raksh leaned close as though to confide a secret. "I used to be worshipped as a god."

I made a garbled response.

Twisting at the waist, a grating sound like a blade on a whetstone coming from somewhere in his body, Raksh continued. "Last night was, well . . . my compliments, truly. Rarely can a human keep up with me like that. I might not remember the *details* of our contract, but I do hope it permits further sexual activities."

My entire face went hot. I snatched the sheet and wrapped it around myself like a cocoon as Raksh crossed the small room to pluck up our marriage agreement.

"Hmm . . ." He began to read it. "What an interesting provision—I've never been wedded in your faith's tradition before. Honestly it's been centuries since I tried something like this. The last time I worked a marriage contract, it was with this village that insisted on shutting up spouses in caves when their partner died, and let me tell you, I am *not* interested in doing that again."

My head was spinning, but not enough that I missed the opening in his bizarre words.

"It is invalid!" I burst out. "Our nikah. It is not permissible for me to marry a non-Muslim."

Raksh frowned. "Is that why the man had me say all those words about God and prophets?" He returned to studying the contract. "Trust me, dear wife, I can be a vast number of things."

"But—but you are not a believer."

"Of course I am. Best to know the competition, yes?" Raksh clucked his tongue and rolled the contract back up. "I see nothing in here suggesting you owe me your soul. Truthfully, though I was not exactly clearheaded last night, I doubt I would have agreed to such a deal. Only fools offer their souls, and the pact is so fiendishly complicated I typically prefer other agreements." He shrugged as if any of the words he had just said made sense. "I think you're fine."

I gaped. "I am not *fine*! If I was not headed toward hellfire before, I am now well and truly condemned for marrying a demon while drunk on palm wine!"

"A demon you still intend to save from this horribly dull island, right?" Raksh plucked away the hair falling over my face to peer into my eyes, suddenly looking worried. "Amani, please. I cannot stay here another decade."

"*Amina!*" I snapped. "And no. The only place I am going with you is back to that crooked excuse for a cleric so he can fix this. Then I am getting the hell off this island, and you can return to seducing other fools on the beach."

"But-but that is not fair," he sputtered. "We had an agreement!"

"An agreement you made in bad faith! You did not think to tell me about all *this*"—I gestured at his now-vanished tusks and the coral pendant hiding its foul enchantment—"before I let you in my bed, let alone my boat?"

"To be honest, I was hoping you would never see this side of—no, wait!" Raksh cried as I made to shake free of him. "Amina, you don't understand! I am still the man you met last night. All the things we talked about, that was real. And you . . ." He inhaled as though tasting the air wafting from a fragrant cookpot. "I have been *aching* to contract with someone like you. It has been so long since I found someone interesting, someone *worthy*, with ambitions to savor."

It was impossible to break away from his gaze. In the back of my mind, I knew this was not natural. The way he had mesmerized me last night: I would be willing to bet that hadn't been due only to wine and my poor impulse control around pretty men.

But recognizing such did not break the bonds of his spell completely. "My-my ambitions?"

"*Yes.*" Raksh looped his fingers through my hair like he was placing tapestry threads, marveling at me in a way that felt more assessing than romantic. "I have spent the last three hundred years with boring, selfish men who care for nothing but sleeping with the wives of their neighbors or nonsensical trade rivalries. But you"—he held me out in a twirl—"you are glorious. The tales you told me of your adventures . . ." Raksh shivered with what looked like genuine lust, color rising in his cheeks. "Please, I have no desire other than to stay at your side. To meet your crew and partake of your travels. You will not regret it, I promise."

"I already regret it." I rose to my feet. I needed to put space between us. To get out of this room and breathe fresh air.

But there was no door, and then Raksh was there, standing before me again. He was still naked, and despite my age and experience, I could not help but flush at the sight of him and the memory of how we'd spent the previous evening. I'd never had a lover like that.

"Just one trip," he beseeched. "Take me off this island, and I will show you what I can do. If you remain unconvinced by journey's end, I will leave and pay you for the privilege."

"Pay me for the privilege?" I repeated. And no, I am not proud that was my first response.

His spread his hands, and a shower of gold coins erupted between them. They clattered to the floor, but with another snap of his fingers, the fortune was gone.

I gasped. "Why do you need to contract with anyone if you can do that? You could charter a hundred trips off this island!"

"Because that is not the sort of currency my kind deal in. Nor the kind of currency *you* want, not truly."

I laughed, a savage edge to the sound. "Believe me, demon, if I could summon gold, I would not be risking my life on a rickety boat."

"No . . ." Raksh moved closer, his voice alluring. "If you could summon gold, you would build your mother a castle. Bribe your grandparents to forgive her and set your little brother up with the best education possible." His eyes locked on mine, the impossible depth of them intoxicating. "Then, guilt assuaged, you would buy a *better* ship and sail for the East. You would go see all the places in your stories and have escapades that would make you a legend. Not because you are a woman or a pirate or any of these things people say about you. But because you would be the *best*, period. Because they would be talking about the adventures of

Amina al-Sirafi for centuries. And by the end of it . . . your family might even forgive you. Might welcome you home with open arms."

Well, the spell had finally broken.

"I-I told you nothing of the sort," I said shakily. "And that . . . that is not what I want. I am a pirate. A smuggler. I care for money alone."

Raksh chuckled, his laugh cracking the air like a whip. "You may be a pirate now, nakhudha, but it is neither crime nor gold that makes your heart beat. You are an *explorer*. I bet in another age, another life, you would be one of those traveling men of letters, seeing the world on the wealth and connections you do not possess in this one." He raised a palm at my protest. "And no, you did not confess any of this last night. Perhaps you have yet to even confess it to yourself. It matters not. While our contract binds us, I can read your ambitions like an open book. And I can *assist* them. In ways you could never imagine."

I felt stripped bare, Raksh dragging from the bottom of my soul desires I had not dared let take root; the sand falling away to reveal wants that seemed naïve and raw in the bright light of the sun, squirming creatures that belonged hidden beneath the seabed.

"Why?" I asked hoarsely. "Why would you help me?"

He twined a finger around one of my disheveled braids again. "So that I *can* summon gold. There is power in human ambition. Sustenance in desire. At least . . . for beings such as myself."

Sustenance. "It sounds like we are your prey."

Raksh grinned. "Well sated prey, I assure you."

"Ah, am I to be well sated when I am finally devoured?"

"Who says I intend to devour you?" There was a note of surprise in his voice. "Why would I?"

I stared at him in disbelief. "Maybe because you are a lying demon who referred to my Creator as competition?"

"Not a demon," Raksh corrected. "That is your word. I have no desire to harm you, Amina al-Sirafi. For one, I am rather enjoying you, but more important, I would only be hurting myself. You need not fear our bond. I am a . . . how do you say it? Like a streak of good luck. While I am contracted with you—*married*," he added with a lascivious wiggle of his hips, "you will always have that favorable wind you need. Your nets will stay full, and your enemy's arrows fall short. If you get ten tips on a mark, I will sense that which is correct. I know sailors: your lives run on luck.

"I am the blessing that makes all the difference."

I wish I could say I was not tempted, but he'd spoken truthfully. Our lives *did* run on luck. Mariners' careers are short and hard, and on the off chance you survive the sea—every crossing its own risk—you often end up blind and crippled by the labor of doing so. My family had already struggled so much. Everyone in my crew had. We weren't wealthy. We weren't *poor*, not like I had been as a child, but we had to keep chasing jobs. To be hounded and hunted, and prey on others in the same bloody way we were preyed upon.

What if it could be different?

"Just one trip," Raksh whispered, his words curling around me. "Let me show you what I can do."

This was madness . . . but God, I wanted it. I wanted everything he said. With my ship blessed, I could go anywhere. See the world past India. Build my mother and my little brother a palace.

I breathed in and out, my heart pounding. "What about my crew?"

"What about them?"

"Do you mean *them* any harm?"

Raksh appeared genuinely baffled by the question. "Why should I? My contract is not with them, and your desires are feast enough. I suspect theirs are terribly dull in comparison."

I should have said no. I will regret to the end of my days that I did not—well, no, I suppose that is not true, for if I had turned Raksh away I would not have Marjana. Maybe that makes me a monster, but are not all mothers capable of being monsters when it comes to their children?

However, that wasn't the choice put to me that morning. And whether it was my wicked heart or Raksh's magic, I couldn't get the images he'd painted out of my mind. Sailing into Khanfu and seeing China like I had promised Majed. Exploring forgotten islands and wandering cities on the other side of the world with my companions. Setting down my adventures, my stories, and getting acclaim not as a thief but as a *traveler*. An explorer like the great chroniclers of our age. Someone honorable and venerated.

I imagined returning to my mother in such a way. As a daughter of whom she could be proud. A daughter who could pay her back in a comfortable life. Had she not endured so much on my account?

I was already damned. Surely for that, I could go home.

"Show me what you can do," I whispered.

Chapter 18

In the dancing light of their torches, Falco's men appeared almost comically loutish. There was a glassy red hue to their eyes and a wild filth to their bodies that spoke of a breakdown of mores to which even most criminals cling. They were ridiculously over-armed, not only with normal weapons, but with hammers, pickaxes, and hastily constructed contraptions of broken glass, metal shavings, and rocks. Pieces of treasure and bones from the burial pit hung against their chests and around their wrists in a twisted interpretation of protective amulets. Strung pearls, rotting silk scarves, and gold chains with rubies, emeralds, and carved lapis beads looped their necks; gilded belts and gauntlets gleamed from bloody sweat-streaked skin.

Such a spectacle did not seem promising for me, and yet at the word "nakhudha," the fearsome group seemed to exhale as one, wonder widening their too-bright eyes. The men fanned around me, and my heart skipped. The way they moved—low to the ground, their shoulders hunched as though they feared being seized by a spectral beast—was thoroughly unsettling. It felt more like being surveyed by a pack of wary starving hyenas than people I might have once called kindred: fellow sailors who spoke my tongue, many who likely once prayed in my faith. What had the Frank *done* to them?

"A nakhudha," a man wearing a crown of teeth and moonstones whispered, his voice breathy as though he had screamed himself hoarse.

"It has worked," another intoned. A crudely sewn panel of rib bones was bound across his chest. "It is as he said it would be."

"We bring her?"

"We bring her."

Before I had time to question *any* of that, I was roughly grabbed and disarmed all at once.

Rib-Bone Man motioned to a pair of mercenaries. "Keep searching for the villagers. They can't have gotten far."

The chosen two did not look pleased to be sent deeper into the cave with only a single torch. I could only pray they found nothing and be grateful I was deemed enough of a threat (a mystery? a foretold arrival?) to have the bulk of the men accompany me.

I dawdled, loitered, stumbled, and generally made as much a nuisance of myself as possible while being bodily escorted out of the cavern. The cave's mouth came up quicker than I expected, and I blinked in the bright light of the enormous firepit dug into the rocky soil. A dozen or so men were clustered in small groups, some drinking and eating, a few sparring. Their camp was a mess; I suppose the Frank had little time between murder and torture to appreciate the benefits of a neatly maintained base. They had no tents, and their supplies were disorganized: filthy blankets piled in a heap and the food they'd stolen from the Socotran villagers spilling out of baskets. Plundered grave goods were everywhere: burial masks and treasure chests littering the sand, ceremonial silver weapons and painted redware urns tossed in a pile.

My captors dragged me toward the bonfire. A single man stood there, tending the roaring flames with his back to us.

Rib-Bone Man shoved me to my knees. "We are *saved*, my lord." Hope and fear commingled in his voice, like a hunting dog returning a prize to an abusive master. "Your magic worked. We've been granted a way off the island."

The other man didn't bother turning around, instead continuing to root through the smoldering logs with a long iron poker. "You found a way off Socotra *inside* the cave?" he asked with weary doubt.

"*Yes*," Rib-Bone Man said, more frantic this time. "We found the na-khudha you wanted! The nakhudha Amina al-Sirafi."

When the man tending the fire first spoke, his stilted Arabic unlike any accent I had ever heard, I suspected. When he dropped the poker and spun around at my name, I knew.

Falco Palamenestra and I had found each other.

◆

Our stories always want to make villains larger than life. They should be snarling or scarred, hunchbacked or otherwise marred in a way society doesn't like. It makes them easier to demonize.

But life is not nearly so simple, and if you were expecting a cruel Frankish sorcerer to be looming and freakish, with pale watery eyes and parchment-colored skin, I fear I will disappoint. Much of what was to come that night is mercifully blurred in my memory, but my first glimpse of Falco Palamenestra remains inscribed upon my mind's eye. There was no robe with warded spells stitched into the fabric, nor even a tunic with a bloody cross. Instead, Falco was dressed in the custom of our men, down to his sandals and jubba. Unsurprisingly for someone who'd made his living killing for others, he was largely built: my height at least and with shoulders that could easily wield the heavy broadswords the Franks are said to favor. He had keen brown eyes under a thick brow, a strong nose, and a cleanly shaved square jaw, his wavy brown hair streaked with sil-ver. He must have been at least a decade older than me, but he otherwise appeared healthy and strong if a bit pale.

But as he stared me up and down with open, curious appraisal, I could not help but notice there was something wrong, something *missing* in his otherwise warm eyes. The gentle quizzical expression on his face didn't fit the man responsible for the horrific scene in the cave.

Because it's a mask. Of a type I had seen before. Most criminals are driven by desperation and poverty, by circumstances they would change if they could. But occasionally you come across someone who simply enjoys the violence of it. Someone who kills when he could injure, who injures when he need not do any harm. The kind of man who could have consigned three elders to a grisly, lingering death and slaughtered people like cattle as their loved ones watched and wailed.

Falco spoke again. "Show me her left arm."

The men holding me complied, twisting my wrist and shoving up my sleeve to reveal the scarred flesh.

"It is as they say," he murmured. "And her teeth?"

"If any fingers come near my mouth, I'm going to bite them off," I warned. "Please don't test me."

A small smile played over Falco's mouth in response. His gaze had yet to leave my body. I've been looked at any number of ways by men: with desire and rage, bemusement and condescension. This was different. There was . . . happy delight in his twinkling eyes, a weirdly childish reaction—if that child was the type to pull the wings off flies and drown kittens.

I strongly suspected it did not bode well for me.

"She certainly sounds like the nakhudha I've heard so much about. And at just the right time." Falco tilted his head. "Fascinating."

"My lord, the villagers . . ." Rib-Bone Man wrung his hands. "Forgive me, but they are gone. They must have fled deeper into the cave."

"Then I suppose they will get lost in the darkness and starve. They have served their purpose; if we are to find our wayward scribe, the nakhudha may be all I require." Falco briefly turned back to the fire, picking up the iron poker to retrieve a covered cauldron from beneath the glowing embers. Then he walked off, beckoning me to follow. "Come, Amina al-Sirafi! We have much to discuss."

We do? I wasn't sure how I had anticipated my first encounter with

Falco Palamenestra going, mostly because I had hoped to find a way to avoid ever meeting the sorcerer who made Layth choke to death on a purse of dirhams. But being treated like I was his expected passage off Socotra was not it. Then again, it was better than being murdered outright, especially when I was trying to learn more about Dunya and buy my companions time. Besides, I had made small talk with worse people, right?

The slaughter in the cave flashed before my eyes. Well, no. Falco would probably be the worst.

"Do you care for wine?" he asked, nodding for me to sit on a rug spread before the bonfire. He dipped a cup into a half-buried clay amphora. "Something to eat? I know how important guest right is to your people, and I would not wish to start our relationship on poor footing."

He had carried the cauldron over with the iron poker and opened it now, releasing a noxious greasy stench. There was a crackling sound like splattering animal fat, and within the caldron's molten crimson depths I would swear something writhed.

My stomach churned. "I do not drink. And my dietary restrictions are . . . comprehensive," I decided, hoping that would encompass whatever was wriggling in his pot.

"Alas." Falco took a seat across from me. God forgive my old weakness, but as he drank from his cup, I ached for some wine. I was giving my best effort at bravado, but I had walked into the camp of my enemy, even if Falco did not seem to consider me that, with no plan other than stalling, and there was clearly something terribly wrong with these people.

Swallowing back as much fear as I could, I nodded at the amphora. "I found what was left of your ship. Odd you had the presence of mind to save that."

"A good wine is worth the risk." He took another sip, appearing to savor it. "One I doubted the creature who attacked us would appreciate."

With little desire for the Frank to learn Raksh and I had crossed paths, I feigned ignorance. "You were *attacked*? By what?"

"By something less picky than you in its food preferences. But you need not fear. The creature is now well sated and under control. It would pose no risk to your *Marawati* unless I commanded it so." Falco smiled, an expression that didn't touch his eyes. "So where is your ship?"

It was my turn to be evasive. "She goes where she likes."

"And the rest of your compatriots? Surely they are with you. Your Indian first mate and the female assassin? There is the navigator as well, yes? The African they call Majed? I could not find him, but I hear he is brilliant."

So the Frank had looked for Majed. I cursed Raksh anew in my head. "You went to a lot of effort to learn about me and my crew."

"What can I say? I like to collect extraordinary things." Falco regarded me over his cup. "Though I will confess I was not sure what to believe from the stories. Some say you are a heinous sea witch, others a siren who uses her beauty to lure honorable men into sin. You certainly don't look like what I expected of a woman of your creed, hidden behind walls and veils and sharing a husband with a dozen others."

"I must admit I find myself equally surprised. I assumed most Franks covered in their own body filth and tattered animal hides." I smiled. "I can trade caricatures too."

He bowed his head. "Point made, nakhudha. I must admit I am glad to find you what you obviously are."

"And what's that?"

"A warrior. Warriors of your creed I know very, very well."

Considering his background, I wasn't sure that was more promising than if he thought me a harlot. "I've heard," I replied carefully. "Was killing people in Palestine and Syria not engrossing enough for you anymore?"

"Now who is trading caricatures? Do you imagine I left my natal home merely to murder Muslims?"

"No. I imagine Muslim plunder was more likely a draw."

He chuckled. "The riches of these lands are appealing. The first time I gazed upon the walls of Constantinople, saw the fountains in Jerusalem, and the ways people irrigate the fields in Egypt . . ." Genuine wistfulness entered his tone. "There is a great deal to admire."

"You have traveled more widely than I would have expected," I noted, attempting a conciliatory response. I was supposed to be drawing this man in, and he was clearly the type who liked to talk about himself. "So you came to admire us?"

"Oh, no. I came to kill you," he said conversationally. "Our bishops said we needed to. They claimed Saracens and heathens had sullied the ground our Savior walked, torn down our churches, and robbed and raped our pilgrims. They said it was our duty as Christian men to put a stop to it all; that to fail to answer the call would damn our souls." Falco met my gaze, and for the first time, I would swear his mask briefly shifted, revealing a flash of true anger. "So my father sold off our possessions, bankrupted our family, and mortgaged our lands to the very Church that ordered us to fight, in order to pay for the horses, weapons, and means to do so."

I took all that in. "And then?"

"Why then, we conquered Jerusalem." Falco drank from his cup again. "And nothing changed."

Every appalling tale I'd heard of the carnage in the north played across my memory. "*Nothing?*"

Falco wiped his mouth. "Oh, I'm aware of the masses who died. Then again, by now I've seen so many different cities fall—at *everyone's* hands, mind you—that the massacres are starting to blend together. But have we built a new city for Christendom? Hastened the arrival of a more just world? Hardly. We no sooner took Jerusalem than the bickering started again, the princes and nobles of the Latin West dividing up the spoils and

warring over territory. My father, the man who sold my birthright because he believed it was what God desired, died in a drunken brawl over
a stolen gold tabernacle."

I looked Falco over again. "You would have been very young." But I
didn't pity him. He hadn't been young when he'd tortured and murdered
the Socotrans.

"I was. Tried to go home too, only to learn that my homeland had *also*
been ripped apart and sold. By Normans in my case. Foreign barbarians,"
he added, with a knowing lift of his brow. "Leave your land to invade
another and what do you know . . ."

"A shame," I said dryly. "And yet you came back."

"I did. I tried to stay away. Tried to find *something* . . ." Falco loosened
the neck of his shirt, pulling free a dark sash heavy with dozens of glittering ornaments. Small decorated buttons and pins in a variety of materials:
copper, brass, tin, and bone. Flaming hearts and dragons, swords and
unfamiliar symbols.

"What are those?" I asked.

"Pilgrim badges," he explained. "Took me most of my life to earn
these. Decades spent fighting for whoever would have me and spending
those profits seeking out the places and objects people said God once visited. I prayed that in some tucked-away shrine heavy with the gilded relics
of saints, I would finally see Him. *Hear* Him. Feel *something* that would
give what happened in Jerusalem meaning."

By now, I was past the point of politeness. There were a *lot* of badges.
"Did you never stop to think, after the first dozen failures, that maybe
God was less than pleased with your murdering innocents?"

"A somewhat hypocritical response from a pirate, no?"

"I take what is my due as a denizen of these shores," I said flatly. "I do
not kill unless my hand is forced, and I've yet to participate in the slaughter of tens of thousands."

"To be fair . . . I *did* try and leave." He drank back the rest of his wine.

"Holy missions and plunder, they are such pretty distractions. Truth be told, the Frankish kings in your lands are there as much to compete politically as they are for riches. God just provides an awfully tempting cover, does He not?"

"I have never been arrogant enough to assume God would approve of my actions."

Falco leaned closer. "And what if you stopped concerning yourself with what God thought altogether?"

I paused, uncertain whether it was the wine or his own bizarre inclinations speaking. "That sounds like a strange prospect for a supposed holy warrior to entertain."

"If I am a warrior anymore, it is for myself. For knowledge." Falco dropped his sash, the pilgrim badges tinkling together. "These wars have become such corrupt conflicts. Fought for mortal treasures, patches of dirt, and fleeting promises of salvation—and fought so crudely. By *your* people as well as mine. Surely you are not so ignorant as to believe Muslim kings and generals any better? Most are more concerned with using the wars to conquer their neighbors, settle petty feuds, and get rich off Christian trade." Falco gave me a pointed look. "I would imagine a woman pressured into piracy is all too familiar with the hypocrisy and cruelties of the ruling class?"

I doubted the Frank genuinely cared about those being crushed by the ruling class, but I could not otherwise find much fault in his words. For I *had* lost kin in those petty wars, the uncle I would never meet killed in the service of a greedy prince. I lived in a world where one could never forget their place, where everyone I knew had been scarred and shaped by poverty—in some of the wealthiest cities around. Indeed, I was only sitting here now because a rich woman was forcing me to save the child *she* loved if I did not wish mine to pay the ultimate price.

But I refused to let the barb land. "You assume I was forced into banditry. Maybe I like being a pirate."

"Do you? For you certainly do not speak like a self-serving criminal, defending the dead of a distant land. A true pirate might be trying to strike a deal with me."

I met his gaze. "You do not know me."

"No, but I would like to. I would like that very much." Falco tilted his head. "I met a man who claimed to know you, and *he* said you were an adventurer, an explorer—the most extraordinary person he had met in a very long time. And I wonder, nakhudha, if you might like to embark on something extraordinary with me."

I genuinely could not tell if Falco wanted to seduce me, hire me, or cut my throat and hang me in the cave to perform nefarious magic with my blood. "And what is that?" I asked, hoping it wasn't the first option almost as much as I hoped it wasn't the last.

"Help me end these wars forever and set things right in a new world. Or rather . . . an older one."

"An *older* one?"

Falco waved a hand around. "Surely you have seen the treasures of this cave? The tombs and remnants of grand palisades and arenas and citadels? Grown up listening to legends of Hercules and Jupiter, Alexander and Pharaoh, King Solomon and his consort, the queen your people call Bilqis?"

The inclusion of Bilqis struck a bit too closely to the reason he had supposedly traveled here. Did Falco suspect I knew about Dunya? He seemed bizarrely uninterested in what had brought me here—how I had ended up in the cave but hadn't come through the entrance—as though he simply assumed the world orbited around his needs.

"I have seen and know of such places and people," I said cautiously.

"Then do you not wonder why they had access to powers beyond ours? Why they could perform miracles of strength and speak with the Divine?" He shook his sash of badges more fiercely. "Why do these *exist*? What made these people so special that they could fly across the world and raise the dead? Command legions with magical talismans?"

I hesitated. As I've told you, I boasted an active imagination as a child. It was easy to believe such fantastic tales, growing up on fables and in places where ancient legends did linger, relics and stories with roots we modern believers had yet to shed entirely.

"My people say such an age is over," I finally replied. "Though a great many would be happy to sell you items and texts promising otherwise."

"Ah, but they are mostly charlatans. And I would know, for I have spent a lifetime searching for such items to little avail. But in *your* part of the world . . ." Falco's eyes gleamed. "You have so much more. More of *everything*. You have the texts and knowledge of the ancients. Your scholars read and translate their work, preserving and expanding upon their thoughts. But they dare not go further when there are things in this world that, if mastered, could give you powers to rival God."

Aye, no wonder Raksh had been drawn to this monster; his ambitions were beyond delusional.

"You truly believe that in the handful of years you've spent in my world, you have stumbled upon powers and secrets our greatest scholars haven't the temerity to attempt in lifetimes?" I asked. "You will forgive me, but that is a staggering level of arrogance."

"Confidence is not the same as arrogance. Your scholars are too passive. You'll bow and praise God your entire lives, never challenging His cruel abandonment. Do you think the innocents of Jerusalem would have been lost if they had had a Hercules to fight back?"

A great violence scorched through me. Were there injustices in my world? Yes. The young girl in Aden sold into slavery, the shadows in Tinbu's eyes when he spoke of his past, the children who starved while others feasted. But those sufferings were at the hands of other people, and from the gleam in his eyes, I knew it wasn't a more just world Falco wanted. He wanted *power*. He wanted a talented nakhudha to ferry him around the ocean and snatch up every glittering thing he could.

"The innocents of Jerusalem were not *lost*," I snapped, glaring at the Frank. "They were *murdered* by foreign barbarians who will burn in hellfire for their crimes. It has nothing to do with God's wishes."

"No, it has to do with petty kings and power-hungry generals," Falco said fervently, as though he did not have that blood on his hands. As if he did not have Socotran blood on his hands. As if it was not becoming abundantly clear I wished to have *his* blood on *my* hands. "And yet there is a way. A way to be united again. To build a new Rome, to seize the magic of the celestial beings with whom our ancestors once communed." His face was alight with wonder. "We could do it together, traveling the seas and collecting an arsenal to strike fear into any pope or caliph."

God save me, Salima had been right to call him a madman. What sort of small talk was I meant to continue with someone like this? I hesitated, struggling to respond.

"You do not believe me," Falco assessed plainly. "I fear my words sound too astonishing. So I will prove it. Surely you must wonder why such hardened men remain loyal to me?"

I glanced at his mercenaries. They were hunkered in groups of two and three, doing a poor job of pretending they weren't watching us. There was a mix of hunger and fear in their expressions, firelight glinting on their bone ornaments and makeshift weapons. I wondered how often they thought of the other half of the crew, the ones eaten alive by some ghastly sea beast, the "marid" of Raksh's tale. Were these survivors truly loyal or had they gotten themselves trapped with this foreigner on a faraway island and had no choice but to follow through?

"Perhaps they have no other option," I suggested mildly.

Falco straightened up as if my words had been sharper. "Yazid, come here. Our nakhudha requires a demonstration."

Rib-Bone Man—Yazid—approached, and Falco tossed him the iron poker he had used to retrieve the cauldron from the fire.

Yazid caught it with a single hand as though it were a reed, and I flew to my feet, anticipating an attack. But Yazid made no move toward me. Instead, before my disbelieving eyes, he *bent* the poker. Not once, not twice, but multiple times, manipulating and tying the iron bar into a sailor's knot and pulling it tight as if it were string. When he was done, he tossed it to my feet, and it landed with a heavy thud in the dust.

My mouth fell open in shock. Raksh had said *nothing* about this.

"A trick." I denied it. But when I prodded the iron knot with my foot, it was as heavy and solid as anything one might find in a blacksmith's shop.

Falco gestured at the tree nearest us. It was an old, gnarled specimen twice my height and with a girth that would take several men to encircle. Its roots sprawled, sunk deep into the earth. "Another display, Yazid."

Yazid stepped up to the tree. Grasping the trunk, he ripped the entire thing out of the ground with his bare hands. With a grunt, he hurled the tree into the dark night. Far in the distance, I heard it crash.

"That's not possible," I whispered.

Falco shot me a triumphant look. "Some of them have gained strength, others the ability to see in the dark or swim without fear of drowning. Abilities they would not have without serving me. *That* is why they are loyal."

"I see," I said, trying to hide the trembling in my voice. Apparently it was not enough to be outnumbered by vicious mercenaries. I had to be outnumbered by *supernaturally empowered* vicious mercenaries.

"Good," Falco replied. "Then we can begin our partnership with you telling me where your ship is."

Our partnership. Right. At this point, I would let Yazid bend my own bones before letting Falco anywhere near the *Marawati*. "There is another matter I need resolved before I consider such a union," I cautioned.

Impatience flickered in his eyes. "And that is?"

"Dunya al-Hilli."

Falco sat back, his entire demeanor changing. "You did not come because I summoned you."

No shit, asshole. But truthfully, it was more frightening that he *did* believe such a thing. That this man who could speak knowledgeably of religious and political deception also believed he could summon random nawakhidha with vicious blood sacrifices.

Because he can do worse. *He can murder those who betray his oaths from across the sea and grant his followers magical strength.* Cold fear swirled in my belly.

"No, I'm afraid it was not you who brought me to Socotra. Though I do remain impressed by your passion and your man's skills," I added quickly, hoping to delay the bending of my bones for as long as possible. "However, you must understand your offer of partnership is complicated by your kidnapping the daughter of one of my crewmen."

Falco pursed his lips. "The grandmother hired you, I take it? Is she the one who called it an abduction?"

"That is what she charged."

"And you believe her?"

"Despite your earlier objection, I *am* a pirate. My opinions tend to be flexible."

He rose to his feet. "The girl was as willing as they come. She's a smart thing with a talent for languages. A talent that might have seen her rise very far had she not betrayed me. Unfortunately, you see, your timing could be better. I am afraid Miss al-Hilli has run off."

So the villagers had been telling the truth. "When?" I demanded.

"Two days ago. She fled after begging to bathe in the sea, stealing our only means of transportation in the process." His voice was strained for the first time, rage simmering just below the surface. "She is as much of a liar as her grandmother."

"What sort of boat did she take?" I pressed. "Was it supplied?"

"Not in the slightest. It was our longboat, already left barely seaworthy after the attack. What good fortune that a nakhudha has arrived to help me find her."

Falco said the words with such a poor effort at a smile that it chilled me, like a man pretending to be human. "I strongly suspect she would not do well to fall into your hands," I replied.

"On the contrary, I understand the rashness of youth. If she was willing to beg forgiveness and serve me again, I might prove quite accommodating. Which brings us back to my earlier question, nakhudha . . . *Where is your ship?*"

"Away." I kept stalling. "Let me ask you something else: How would you have left the island to go after Dunya had I not fallen into your lap?"

He eyed me, irritation entering his gaze. "Attacked the pirate clans sheltering in the west and taken one of their ships."

"A foolish choice. Your man may bend metal, but those clans can take on navies. They would have annihilated you. Such a decision reflects poorly upon you as a business partner."

Falco exhaled. "I know your people have a penchant for rambling small talk, but the more time you waste, the farther away Dunya could be getting. How long do you imagine she'll survive in the open sea on a small boat with no food and water?"

"Perhaps you should let me go and recover her."

"You'll forgive my doubt you'd return." Falco was not smiling anymore. "No more dallying, al-Sirafi. Tell me where to find your ship."

I pressed my trembling hands against my knees, trying to cling to as much courage as I could. In Falco's eyes, I suspected, I was about to cross the line between "prospective ally" and "intransigent problem."

"I fear I cannot help you. When we spotted your shipwreck, I sent the *Marawati* away, staying behind to scout the area myself. She will not return for two weeks."

"I do not believe you."

"Whether or not you believe me means nothing. I cannot alter the course of time."

"You must have a way to signal her in case you need help," he insisted.

"Fortunately, I do not require help."

Falco had risen to pace but halted in his tracks now. "And if I were to let my men take you? One by one, again and again until you submit. Do you think you would 'require help' then?"

The swiftness with which he disregarded his polite façade to reach for such a crude threat: here was the man who had left three elders pinned to a tree and carved up the innocents in the cave like a butcher. I attempted to let the threat slide away, as though it had not been there, a blade at my throat since I let the funeral slab fall in the treasure chamber. I am not ignorant of the ways violent men exercise power.

Instead I held his gaze, refusing to back down. "As long as we are speaking so bluntly, you will never step foot on my ship. You and your men can rot here for all I care."

Falco sighed. "It doesn't need to be this difficult. You strike me as an eminently pragmatic woman. Ruthless even, if some of the stories are to be believed. I have no doubt if I could make you *see* the potential . . ." He trailed off, as if caught by an idea, and spun back on me. His face was shining again, like when he'd rambled about building a new Rome and confronting God. "Yes, perhaps that is it. For the men, I insisted their participation be voluntary. I would not trust their loyalty elsewhere. But you and your ship are too valuable to leave to chance. Yazid!" he called. "Bind her!"

I was lunging for the knotted iron poker at my feet, swinging it up before his men even moved on me. I managed to smash one of them across the face, but then Yazid ripped the poker from my hands, and the mob shoved me to the ground. I kicked and writhed like a rabid animal, spitting in their eyes and roaring with anger. I kneed one man so hard in the groin that he shrieked and rolled away, and scratched another across the face so ruthlessly, his cheek was left in bloody tatters.

But in the end, there were too many of them and they were too strong. They seized my hands, binding my wrists with rope as Yazid sat on my legs. They went no further. Falco had a different fate in mind for me, and fully immobilized, I could only watch in horror as the Frank returned to his cauldron with the copper ladle he had been using to bring up wine.

He stirred its wiggling contents. "Find something to open her mouth. I do believe that threat about biting off fingers."

True terror surged through me. I clamped my jaw shut as tightly as I could, but with multiple hands prying at my lips with their unnatural strength, trying to shove sticks into my mouth and pinching my nose so I had no other recourse to breath, they finally succeeded in shoving the hilt of a blade between my teeth. I tasted metal and blood.

Falco's expression was condescendingly soothing as he approached with the ladle. I wanted to claw his fucking eyes out and soothe the pain with salt. Whatever he intended to feed me was the frothy gray blue of a storm-tossed ocean, seething and *moving*, shuddering and shifting like a dozen maggots squirmed beneath the surface. I fought best as I could, swearing vengeance through my gagged mouth, but then it was too late, and the ladle was touching my lips.

If there was mercy, it was that it was quick. There was the awful, gut-churning horror of movement on my tongue, and then ice poured down my throat. The hilt was pulled from my teeth and a meaty hand clamped across my mouth as the urge to vomit nearly overcame me. I trembled madly, cold perspiration bursting all over my skin. My head was dizzy, spots dancing before my eyes. The spots swirled and swirled and swirled, becoming typhoons and roiling waves. My limbs were going weak, my body distant . . .

"Do not fear, nakhudha," Falco whispered as unconsciousness stole over me. "It will all be better soon."

◆

It was so very, very cold.

That was my first thought upon waking. I lay on a chilly beach, damp sand soaking through my garments, and I was freezing, shivering more violently than I ever had in my life. Shivering so violently that I'd rubbed the skin under my rope binds raw while unconscious.

And my *head* . . . I might have drunken a dozen casks of Maldivian palm wine. Groaning, I tried to sit up.

A hand clasped my shoulder. "Take care. The potion left the others quite sluggish."

Falco.

The memory of what he had done ripped through my mind, hatred searing in its wake. I wrenched away from his touch and tried to strike him but wildly missed, sprawling face-first in the sand. I turned back . . .

I cried out. The Frank's men were not right.

They loomed over and about me, their eyes glazed over in the same frothy gray blue as the foul concoction I'd been forced to drink. A pattern of scales and tentacles traced over their limbs and burst from their cheeks. When Yazid stepped closer, I would swear his arms had been replaced by giant scorpion claws, his skull capped like the blunt shell of a horseshoe crab.

I tried to scramble away, but Falco grabbed my bound wrists. He alone appeared unchanged.

"Do not fear, nakhudha," he said again, the same words as before, in the soothing tone one might use with a spooked horse. "This is only the first step. We offer you a taste of her, but she—she must accept you." He straightened up. "Bring al-Sirafi to the pit! We shall call our great ally!"

They picked me up, dragging me closer to the water's edge. Dazed, delirious, and desperately attempting to recover my addled wits, I could offer little fight. I didn't know what Falco had done to me, didn't know how long I'd been unconscious. It was still night . . . had my companions and the villagers gotten away?

Think, Amina, think! But I couldn't think. It was like being trapped in a nightmare where no matter how desperately you need to run away, you can't move your legs. The black water crashing against the beach pounded in my head, the foul smoke of unnatural torches making me nauseous. Some of the men had built another bonfire from gathered driftwood; their bodies seemed to undulate and skitter before the dancing flames, the horrifying spectacle plucked from a wine-soaked hallucination. Others were digging. Digging with hands and shovels, wet sloshy sand flinging back and landing with heavy plops as they clawed a pit at the tide line. Falco was chanting in a foreign tongue, a language that did not sound human.

Still they pulled me toward the sea, a place I loved, but had always respected and often feared. Now my terror was beyond simply that of drowning—drowning might be a blessing at this point. In the scattered starlight ribboning over the roiling surf, hundreds of small forms were scuttling out of the waves, claws clacking and stingers held aloft.

Scorpions. Some sort of *sea* scorpions. Though only about the size of my hand, their number seemed endless, poison glinting at the end of their tails. The scorpions poured into the pit, filling it with their wriggling bodies.

The pit *I* was being dragged to. With great horror, I realized the men meant to toss me in with that horde of creatures. And though I could scarcely see straight, though I felt half drunk and my earlier struggles had been for naught, I resumed them with great ferocity, punching and biting and lunging at anyone I could as we passed the driftwood fire. I was suddenly sure that if I fell into that pit, I would not emerge the same. Falco meant to make me like the rest of them. A monstrous thrall, a transfigured pawn for a vicious foreign sorcerer. I snaked my ankle around that of one of my captors, seizing another's collar as they tried to shove me in the scorpion-filled grave. The sand began to give way beneath my feet—

A whistling sound spilt the air, and an arrow dashed across my line of sight.

It plunged into the bonfire, and I had just a moment to spot Tinbu's familiar fletching through the blaze. The arrow's shaft was oddly thick. *Swollen*, like something had been strapped to—

The entire contraption exploded.

It did so with far, *far* more force than Dalila's earlier experiment with the black powder, erupting in a fireball that rushed to consume the men closest to it. They screamed, running away as flames licked down their clothes. In the chaos, the hands holding me briefly loosened, and I threw myself backward, shoving away from my captors with such force that two of them tumbled into the pit in my stead.

They shrieked, their cries adding to the mad cacophony. Another arrow flew into the fire and a second explosion ripped across the sand. My hands bound, I clambered awkwardly to my feet. Still delirious, I spotted Falco among the burning debris about ten paces away, looking equally stunned. A sword lay discarded near his feet, perhaps belonging to one of the burning men running into the sea.

Were I brave, I might have made a grab for it. Might have taken the chance to send the Frank to the hellfire he so richly deserved. But I have not survived this long by confusing courage with foolishness. People may call my kind sea rats, but let me tell you, rats know when to fucking run.

So I did, fleeing into the darkness of the hills, away from the ocean and in the direction from which Tinbu's arrows had flown. I stumbled and tripped, my usual grace gone as I staggered across the rocky ground, desperate for the cover of trees and thorny scrub. Anything that would put distance between myself and the horror on the beach.

Hands caught me. I tried to wrench free before realizing they belonged to Dalila. Just past her shoulder, Tinbu was raining arrows down at the beach, his movements dancing shadows in the darkness. I burst into tears. Another time I would have berated my friends for disobeying my orders and risking their lives, but God be praised, I was just so relieved to be rescued.

"Great plan," Dalila muttered as she cut the ropes binding my wrists and looped one of my arms over her shoulder. More gently, she added, "I have you, nakhudha. Tinbu, let's—"

A grating howl roared from the sea, louder than thunder. The high-pitched shriek ripped across the air, shaking the entire beach, and sending a knife of pain through my chest. I stumbled and cried out. It was as though claws had grasped my heart, squeezing tight.

"Amina!"

I fell to my knees, gasping for breath. "My chest . . . it—" The creature roared again, even louder, and a fresh wave of agony scorched through me. "Oh, God!"

"Amina." Raksh had emerged from the darkness to grab my face. "Did you drink anything? Did Falco make you eat or consume anything at all?" I managed a nod, and he swore. "That fucking idiot. Leave it to a human to try something so dangerous." He groaned, sounding more annoyed than anything. "Lay her down."

Dalila protested. "We don't have time!"

"Time won't matter if I don't get this out of her." Raksh straddled my waist. Racked with pain, I was only vaguely aware of the improbable things happening before my eyes. Raksh's hands shifting to claws, the ripping sound of torn fabric.

My estranged husband slicing open my sternum, reaching his demonic hand inside my chest and *grasping* . . .

A glistening stinger, the same gray blue as the concoction Falco had forced down my throat, surfaced from my skin. It sizzled and spat where Raksh's fingers met its wet surface, like fire and water fighting for dominance. He flung it aside with a shudder.

The world cleared, my body and mind mine yet again. I glanced wildly down at my chest, expecting to see my torso ripped open, but there was nothing but smooth skin.

A final roar rent the air. In the distance, I would swear I saw a vast form rising from the ocean, an enormous armor-plated body surging forward like a mighty wave. But then Raksh grabbed me again and threw me over his shoulder, obscuring my sight.

"Run!" he shouted.

This time no one argued with him.

Chapter 19

We fled through the night as fast as we could, following the villagers along a dizzying trail of hills and groves, wadis and beaches they said the Frank and his men would not be able to trace. After some time, Raksh dropped me to the ground without warning, complaining of my weight. My knee was in active agony, but I staggered on, wanting nothing more than to get off Socotra.

Day was breaking when we stopped at a quiet lagoon, the still water painted with the colors of sunrise and surrounded by spiky black shadows of rustling trees and shrubs. Through a narrow break in the cliffs, I could see where the lagoon trickled out in a tidal creek to meet the ocean.

"This is where we part," the village man I'd originally spoken to announced after exchanging some quiet words with Dalila. He had not given his name and I had not asked—judging from the cautious yet empathetic looks his people had been casting, I suspected they knew some of what happened to me at Falco's hands. "We will go to the pirate clans in the west, for they owe us protection, but they are wary of strangers and will be more so when they learn what happened here. I could not assure your safety."

"Then perhaps it's best not to mention us at all," I cautioned. "Do you think they will be able to protect you? The Frank mentioned trying to steal a ship from them."

He scoffed. "I should like to see him try. The clans are more than capable of defending themselves."

"And your village?" I hesitated, thinking of the burned huts and three fresh graves. "Will you go back?"

"When God wills it," the man said, with conviction. "That fiend was not the first to invade our lives with violence and he will not be the last. But this is our land, our island, and we will not leave it for foreign greed." Grief twisted his face. "Though should the clan decide swifter vengeance is needed, I will not argue."

Nor would I. The prospect of Socotran pirates mopping up whatever remained of Falco and his men was about the only thing that gave me comfort right now. "Then God bless and preserve you," I said, touching my heart. The place where Raksh had pulled the stinger from my chest was still cold through my garments.

"And you as well, nakhudha." The man's gaze flickered to mine. "Will you go after their scribe? The girl you were seeking?"

My heart sank. "We will try."

"I wish you luck, then." He led his people away from the cove.

My companions and I delayed only long enough to eat and pray. I was weary to the bone, my soul drained, and yet I would have walked for days straight if it got us to the *Marawati* faster. We had to cross the damnable island again, and Dalila and Tinbu prodded me for plans, clearly troubled by my distressed manner and sparse, faltering explanation for what had happened with Falco.

But I had energy only to go forward. Not dwell on the disgusting thing that had been forced upon me, or my panic at being at the mercy of those men. I woke screaming at night and saw blurred visions of enormous snakes and scorpions twining over the landscape. When I was awake, I felt little better. Whether it was the brush with death or nearly being turned into something monstrous, I was sick with how close I had come to leaving Marjana motherless. What had I been *thinking* taking this job—

before Salima had given me no choice? And how could I have left Marjana without a single word—a single word!—about her origins?

For Raksh's return had brought forth a cruel truth: If I died out here, there would be no one who could tell Marjana who her father was. *What* he was. No one to aid her if eventually her supernatural heritage did manifest. I'd been an ignorant, arrogant fool to convince myself I would never need to face this part of my girl's life, to let my hatred of magic blind me to the fact that Raksh's blood *did* flow through our daughter. Now if I failed to return home, she would have no warning at all.

On his part, however, Raksh behaved, becoming astonishingly helpful. He found springs to refill our waterskins, caught a hare for a meal, and even offered to massage my legs. Twice. (I took him up on it the second time, aching muscles winning out over pride, and the bastard promptly did something to my knee that reduced the pain by half, giving me a smirk so smug the relief was almost not worth it. Almost.) I was no fool—the demon was only briefly being good in hopes of being permitted on the *Marawati*. But it didn't matter. I'd made my decision when he explained how he'd known to pull the stinger from my chest.

"I did warn you Falco had been trying to possess a marid," he'd said nonchalantly as he set the spiked hare over a small fire. "But that kind of magic takes more than the blood he spilled in the cave—it needs hosts. Or pawns, rather. People whose life force he can slowly feed to the marid in exchange for control over all of them."

"What?" I had asked, helplessly lost.

Raksh had rolled his eyes. "It's beyond your understanding, but suffice to say Falco would have been able to track and control you to some degree if that stinger had remained." He popped the hare's raw heart into his mouth and gave me a bloody smile. "Good thing your husband was around to save the day."

My "husband" was right, as much as I was loath to admit it. We were desperate and outmatched. Dunya had left days ago and could have floated in any direction. There was no time to waste searching, not when I had a creature who could point us in the right direction.

Dalila was the first to call me out on it.

I was building a signal fire for the *Marawati* when she approached, silently as always, and touched my shoulder. I nearly jumped out of my skin, thrown back into the nightmare of Falco's men shoving me to the sand.

"Sorry," I muttered, flushing in embarrassment.

"You need not apologize." Dalila crouched beside me. "Did they touch you?" she asked after another moment.

My mouth went dry. We both knew what she was really asking. "No. Not like that," I replied. "He threatened it . . . but had other plans in the end."

Dalila's lip curled in disgust. "I wish we could have watched them burn."

I didn't disagree, but Raksh chose that unfortunate moment to cross our line of sight, and my companion's gaze sharpened.

"You're letting that demon come with us, aren't you?" she said flatly.

Breaking another branch, I tossed it on the pile. "I have no choice."

"And why is that?" There was no judgment in her voice, which itself was suspicious. It felt like Dalila was leaving room for me to explain, something for which she did not typically have patience.

I chose my words with caution. "For one, he would throw a fit worthy of a toddler if we tried to leave him behind and then undoubtedly find a violent way to force the issue. Second, I truly believe we shall have better luck searching for Dunya if he is with us. And third . . ." I exhaled. "Dalila, I don't know how to fight this Frank if he comes for us again. He has access to powers I can scarcely imagine."

"*If* he comes for us," she pointed out. "Falco has no way off Socotra right now, if he's even alive. And Raksh might be less help than you think. I would pray that it was *exceedingly* obvious he holds loyalty to none but himself."

If only she knew. "I do not trust him one whit. But for the time being, he is more useful on our side than set against us."

Dalila stared at me. "You are keeping secrets from him. Why do I feel as though you are doing the same with Tinbu and me?"

Because I am. Because I knew what Raksh was when I let him join us and everything that happened after is my fault. I hesitated. Dalila was the one member of my crew who might understand, who might not rush to condemn me. A woman who had spent years acting in her own self-interest and never apologized for it.

But my shame was still too great. "This is enough wood," I said, changing the subject. "Let us . . . let us just return to the *Marawati*. Find Dunya. Then we will deal with Raksh." I lit the signal fire. "Thank you, by the way."

Dalila sighed, clearly aware I was avoiding her prying. "Thank me for what?"

"For saving my life with the black powder I told you that you couldn't have and then for being so magnanimous as to not throw it in my face."

She let out a barking laugh and some of the tension between us melted away. "Oh, nakhudha, I am merely waiting for the most profitable moment."

"I figured as much." But as I recalled what had originally led to our spat, I could not help but venture, "Can I ask you something ridiculous?"

"Amuse me."

"Are you from here?" When the humor vanished from Dalila's face like a door had been slammed, I quickly added, "The way you reacted at the village. I thought that-that maybe this was home."

Dalila pressed her lips in a thin line, gazing at the fire as the kindling caught. Finally she answered. "No. I am not from Socotra. I am from a Christian village like it." She paused. "But the people who burned it weren't Franks. Or Christians."

Messy guilt snarled through me; I could read her carefully selected words well enough. "I'm sorry," I said softly. "I didn't know. I mean, I figured *something* must have happened to lead to your joining the Banu Sasan, but—"

"I don't want to talk about that. It's not—looking backward serves no purpose," she said more fiercely as a few spots of color blossomed in her cheeks. "And you don't need to apologize for things you had nothing to do with. But if you want to make it up to me . . . don't go another decade without corresponding. I have very few friends, you know."

Oh, Dalila. My heart panged as I looked at her, really looked at her. I *had* assumed there was some sort of early tragedy in her life, but Dalila had always seemed so unshakably capable, frighteningly so, at times, given her profession. Her past—her very identity—was a subject strictly off-limits, and I wondered now how much of that studied indifference and inscrutable secrecy was a front, the way she'd learned to survive in a world that made viciously clear what parts of your identity could doom you.

Wordlessly, I reached out to squeeze her hand. When she didn't pull away, I spoke. "I won't, I promise. I should have reached out sooner, and for that, I *do* apologize. But I am sorry for what happened at the village. I would never want you to think I would make such a distinction between our peoples, and if I've acted in a manner that suggests so . . . I need to change that."

"All right." We both sat there in a moment of mutual discomfort and weird warmth before Dalila added, "You must have really feared meeting God to have just admitted you were wrong in multiple situations."

"And you must have really feared losing me to confess that we're friends." When she grimaced, I let out a small sound of triumph. "You did!"

Dalila rolled her eyes. "Do not let a moment of emotional weakness delude you further."

"You would have mourned me for a thousand years." I tilted my head. "Can I ask you something else, since you have declared our undying bonds of sisterhood and amity?"

"I am going to hit you with my staff."

"Will you at least tell me your name?" I asked more gently, ignoring the threat. "Your real one. Not your Banu Sasan one, Crafty Dalila."

She laughed and rose to her feet. "You shall not have that, Amina al-Sirafi. Names are for tombstones. And us? We are not yet dead."

We weren't, and yet by the time the *Marawati* returned, I wondered if dying might have been easier than telling Majed that Raksh was alive and we needed to take him with us.

My navigator had his old sword in his hand and was standing at the prow of the dunij by the time the small boat neared the beach, the *Marawati* bobbing in the distance.

"That," he hissed, pointing to my estranged husband with the blade, "is not Asif's daughter."

"No, it is not," I agreed. "Asif's daughter is floating out to sea with a limited amount of time until she dies of thirst, and Raksh is our only line of knowledgeable defense against the Frank—who now conjures sea monsters and has granted his men the strength of djinn. We will discuss it once this damnable island is away, God willing."

"Dunya is where? The Frank does *what*?" Majed shook his head and called for the oarsmen to stop rowing. "No matter. That demon is not getting on this boat. Not if you want me to stay on it."

"Majed . . ." I was exhausted, my entire body aching. "We can fight about this later."

"And we will." Majed glared at Raksh. "But he stays."

"Ah, but you are as unpleasant as I remember," Raksh tutted. "Though a good bit grayer and rounder. Really, Father of Maps, you should take better care of yourself."

"Oh, shut up," I snapped at Raksh. "You're not doing yourself any favors." I turned back to my navigator. "Majed, we are not having this discussion from across the surf. Bring me the boat."

With a look that promised future argument, Majed relented enough to lead the dunij to the beach, and we all headed back to my ship. I could have kissed the *Marawati* as I clambered aboard but settled for collapsing into my captain's bench, watching suspiciously as Raksh strolled onto the deck like he owned it. The men's gazes followed him, a mix of curiosity and the intense longing he tended to cultivate.

"Leave them be," I said harshly. "And come up here."

Raksh snorted, but as though puppet strings had been cut, several men blinked and returned to their work, looking vaguely puzzled by their distraction. Raksh plopped beside me on my bench, close enough that his hip grazed my own.

"Ah, the *Marawati* . . ." he mused, patting my leg. "How I have missed you and all your adventures."

"If your hand does not leave my thigh, I am going to put a knife through it."

"Still so hostile. I suppose that means a reconciliatory bout of sexual intercourse is out of the—*ow!*" Raksh's black eyes went wide with surprise (not pain, unfortunately) as the point of my dagger pressed into his hand. "Fine," he muttered snippily. "But you're only punishing yourself."

Before I could adamantly and angrily—if not entirely truthfully—deny such a thing, my companions joined us.

"You two seem to be getting on well," Tinbu greeted, Dalila and Majed behind him. "Do we have a direction?"

I pulled the knife from Raksh's hand. "We were getting to that. Bring me the map."

With obvious reluctance, Majed spread out one of his precious maps. "Tinbu said the villagers told you Dunya departed from the northern shore. Considering what we know of the tides and currents . . ." Majed traced his fingers eastward toward the open ocean. "I suspect she was pulled in this direction."

"No." Raksh's eyes had fluttered shut. "Give me your hand, Amina.

Preferably without stabbing me. Focus on Dunya. Long to find her as if she were your own daughter."

Your own daughter. I credit fatigue that by the time my body was capable of reacting, I'd already shut down the impulse. I would not dare let my thoughts linger in Marjana's direction when Raksh was trying to read me.

Instead I thought of what I owed Asif. Of Salima's threats and a young girl possibly dying of thirst right now. I thought of how desperately I ached to return to my family, to retrieve Dunya and put this all behind me.

Raksh's hand dragged mine straight north. "That way," he murmured, spellbound. "I will need to sit at the rudders as we proceed, but she went north."

Majed looked skeptical. "So you trust the hunch of a demon over the science of our ancestors now, Amina?"

I thought back to the malice glittering in Falco's eyes and the easy might of his men, scales and stingers laid over their shifting bodies. There was nothing in my rahmani—in any text of human navigation—that dealt with things like that.

"In this case, yes," I said. "Set a course."

Chapter 20

—Are you sure you wish me to relate this part? It is understandable if you desire to skip it.

—Why am I asking this? Are you serious, you irascible scribe? We both know why. And God knows the madness that ended up happening afterward is enough to fill plenty of pages. We need not—

—Oh, by the *Most High*, Jamal, I am not insulting your ability to remain impartial in "constructing a narrative of both disport and verisimilitude." *What does that even mean?* You do realize that if you want to be a proper storyteller, your words need to flow like warm honey, not choke like the stones of a dry academic. So let me be more direct: Do you wish me to relate what is to come—*who* is to come—as I knew them at the time?

—Yes? Then if that is your choice, I shall continue . . .

◆

On the second day at sea, in the humid haze of a late afternoon, we spotted a small boat bobbing along the northern horizon.

It was a sizable dunij, of the kind I associated with larger vessels. Whoever was aboard had fashioned a miserable tent from an oar and a cloak, and the remaining paddles were positioned at the least useful angles imaginable. The dunij's hull was badly scorched, a jagged piece of the edge broken away. Indeed, it was a miracle the boat was even afloat. Had there been an inkling of bad weather, it would have capsized.

We shouted as we approached in our own dunij, but there was no response. No sign of life or movement from amongst the scattered debris. Dunya had been at sea nearly a week with only the few provisions she would have been able to hide under her clothes. Could I even hope for anything more than a body her grandmother could bury?

Firoz called out. "I think I see something. Yes . . . yes, there is someone under the cloak."

"Bring us aside." I carefully jumped to the other boat. "The rest of you stay back."

My heart in my throat, I approached the small form curled beneath the makeshift tent. Her garments were frayed and torn, sunburnt, blistered skin showing through. There was no response as I lifted the cloak covering her upper body. Her face was turned toward the hull, flies buzzing over dirty, sweat-soaked hair that had been crudely chopped just past her ears.

I touched a scorching hot shoulder. *God, please* . . . "Dunya?" I whispered.

She stirred.

I breathed out a ragged sigh of relief. "She is alive, God be praised!" At my feet, Dunya let out a hoarse little sound, and I gestured impatiently at my comrades. "Hand me some water!"

Dalila tossed me a skin, and I carefully eased Dunya's head up enough that I could dribble some water into her mouth. "It is all right, little one," I said soothingly. "You are safe."

Her eyes blinked blearily open; the same light brown as Asif's but terribly bloodshot and yellowed. "Who-who are . . ." she tried to croak out.

I tipped a bit more water into her mouth. "My name is Amina."

Dunya started to cough, and I quickly sat her up, fearing she had taken too much water. But it had been a sob, not a cough, and if she had not been entirely dehydrated, I suspect she would have started to cry.

"Baba's nakhudha?" she asked, relief flooding her sweaty, sunburnt face.

"Yes," I replied, shame sweeping through me. "I was your baba's na-khudha." I smoothed back the hair plastered across her face. "I am going to take you to my ship."

She flailed a hand toward a bundle of cloth. "My tablets . . ."

"I will retrieve your things." Dunya felt as light and insubstantial as a leaf as I cradled her to my chest, and no matter what things I had seen in her library, no matter what accusations of forbidden sorcery and collaboration Raksh had flung her way, a protective surge coursed over me for this shattered teenager on a broken boat. I was a grown woman and a former pirate, and my brief time with Falco had scarred me. God only knew what Dunya had been through.

He will never set a hand on her again, I swore to myself. To Dunya, I said, "Just breathe, child. You're safe now. I promise."

◆

Dunya had lapsed back into unconsciousness by the time I carried her aboard the *Marawati*, and it was a state in which she spent much of the next two days. When she was awake, we got as much food and liquid into her as possible: Hamid cooking her a fishy broth with soft rice and Dalila brewing a tisane with dried citron peel and vinegar for the girl's frail stomach. I kept Dunya in the private shade of the galley cabin, and Dalila and I bathed and tended her wounds, applying salve to the blistered burns covering her skin. Tinbu brought fresh clothing and blankets the crew had donated, and Majed stayed by her side, softly reciting Quran and the adventure poems he no doubt related to his own children. With her large, haunted eyes and skinny frame, Dunya looked closer to twelve, not anything like the bright, confident sixteen-year-old runaway Falco had painted her to be.

"Do you think she knew?" I asked Majed the third day after we found her. She was fast asleep, my navigator reciting at her side. I had not missed that he was selecting the gentlest verses, reminders of God's compassion and incomparable mercy. They were the same teachings I clung to.

Majed looked as though he'd aged another decade. "I don't know how involved she was, Amina. She is clearly traumatized. She screams and weeps in her sleep and looks like a ghost when she's awake. I have not dared ask her anything."

No, that would be my job. "She recognized Raksh at one point," I remarked. "She didn't say anything, but she looked terrified at the sight of him."

"An understandable reaction." Majed leaned against the galley wall. "Any plan on how to get rid of him before we reach the mainland?"

"Still working on that." I picked up the cloth bundle that Dunya had escaped with. I had already examined it, finding nothing but two palm-sized clay tablets with more of the bizarre wedge-shaped cuneiform writing on it. "Any idea what these are?"

"Presumably something best tossed in the sea if it came from that infernal cave."

I was inclined to agree but didn't think tossing Dunya's belongings overboard would make for a good impression. "Go get some fresh air, brother. I will sit with her."

It was a hot day, the atmosphere heavy with a stillness I didn't like though we had spotted no thunderheads. I brought an inkpot and a wooden lap board into the galley, and sat on the floor besides Dunya, resting my bad knee on a cushion and writing in my rahmani about Socotra. The *Marawati* gently rose and fell with the sea, the water knocking pleasantly against the hull and nearly lulling me into a late afternoon nap.

But I was not so unaware that I did not realize when I was being watched. Dunya had awakened without moving, her haunted gaze locked on my profile.

Finally she spoke. "My father used to write about you."

I set down the rahmani and turned to face her. At some point, Dunya had used what little strength she had to bind away her hair, wrapping a cloth around her head. It made her look like the boy Asif had once been, a specter returned to trouble me.

"Yes, I have heard of those letters," I said wryly. "Though you must have been very young when he sent them."

"My grandmother hid his letters away. I only found them a few years ago." Grief, guilt, admiration . . . the mix of emotions churning across Dunya's face was gut-wrenching. "I used to dream about meeting you. My father said you were the bravest and cleverest person he'd ever met, an adventurer like Sindbad the Sailor—" Her voice cracked. "I wish I were not meeting my childhood hero under such shameful circumstances."

"I am no hero," I tried to assure her, the word sticking in my throat. Would Asif have written so warmly of his nakhudha if he'd known I'd let Raksh into our lives aware of what he was? But I pushed the past away for now, handing Dunya a cup of water. "Do you feel strong enough to talk?"

Dunya hesitated, but then nodded and slowly sat up, wincing as she did so. "Did my grandmother hire you to find me?"

"I'm not quite sure I'd use the word 'hire,' but something like that. She and Falco have very different accounts of your leaving."

"You *met* Falco?"

"Most regrettably, yes. We caught up with him in Socotra after you escaped. And God willing, we left him there." She opened her mouth to speak again, and I held up a hand. "My questions first. Tell me what happened from the beginning. Your grandmother said Falco kidnapped you when she refused to sell him family talismans. Is that true?"

She bit her lip, visibly nervous. "No . . . not quite," she admitted. "My grandmother threw him out, but I followed him and his man. I said I might have items they were interested in."

"Why? Forgive me, child, but it seems a rash move to offer family secrets to a foreign stranger. What did you need the money for so badly?"

"I needed it to escape before the wedding."

"The *wedding*?"

Dunya glanced up, a hint of bitterness in her face. "No, I suppose my grandmother would not tell you that part. She would not wish to cause scandal. But I am to wed the governor of Aden."

The governor of Aden? I blinked in surprise. Damn. No wonder Salima had been so angry about the chaos I'd wreaked there. That was a hell of a rise in status for the al-Hilli family. The governor of Aden was one of the most powerful men in the region, ruling over its richest city. And not just its richest city. Its most *fortified* city, despite what I'd done to its fledgling navy and woebegone police prefect. There would be armies and sturdy walls, garrisons and trained guards between Dunya and Falco should the Frank still be alive and seeking vengeance.

"Oh." I let out a relieved sigh. "Well, that is not so bad. Your husband can protect you. And you will want for nothing."

Dunya's eyes lit in teenaged outrage. "I will want for *everything*. He is more than twice my age and already has wives and heirs. My grandmother says he chose me because I am reputed to be clever, because he desires a wife with whom he can discuss history and science without leaving his bedchamber. Never mind that I will lose everything I *am* once I step foot in his house." She met my gaze. "Would you have agreed to that at my age?"

"Dunya, when I was your age, I had just lost my father and my family was a week from starving. Our circumstances could not have been more different. But regardless . . . how did meeting with Falco turn into running off with him to look for the Moon of Saba? I saw your library. You could have offered any number of objects you had on hand, gotten your money, and been done."

"That was the original plan. But when we got to talking, he . . . he *listened* to me, nakhudha." She blushed in embarrassment. "It was the first time anyone listened to me like that. I tried for years to get my grandmother interested in our family's legacy, but all she wanted to do was sell it off, piece by piece."

I frowned. "What legacy? Your grandmother mentioned your ancestors collecting some occult items as curiosities but nothing further."

"*Curiosities*? Is that what she called them?" Dunya sounded even more incensed at that word than at the prospect of marriage. "We were not mere collectors, nakhudha. We were *guardians*. Stories of my ancestors date back to before the birth of the Prophet, peace and blessings upon him. We were priests and exorcists in the old world, the binders of demons and the protectors of childbirth."

Her words made my skin prickle, the mention of "the old world" reminding me far too much of Falco's rantings. "Perhaps your grandmother wished to keep you from that which is forbidden, child. There is a reason we call those centuries the jahiliyyah."

"It was an age of knowledge as well as ignorance," Dunya said fiercely. "My ancestors sought to safeguard people from demons and from the harm that evil magic could do. They were scholars, not power-seeking murderers like Falco."

"All right." I pinched my brow, unwilling to fight about this with a traumatized teenager. I didn't know if Dunya's forebears were the magic-working scholar-warriors she believed—though it would certainly explain that library—but it didn't speak well of her grasp on reality if she believed no one with access to that kind of power would abuse it. "Getting back to your meeting with Falco . . ."

"As I said, he complimented my work. Said how clever I was, said someone of my intellect could not be shut away as a rich man's wife." Dunya dropped her gaze to her lap. "He claimed he needed me at his side and that together we would travel the world and make all sorts of wondrous discoveries. So I offered the most impressive thing I knew."

"The Moon of Saba."

"The Moon of Saba," she confirmed, still staring at her hands. "Falco promised that I would be rewarded, that I would be free. I-I know how ridiculous that sounds now. But when he was offering these things . . . it felt like I was under a spell."

She probably all but was. Dunya had been rash in meeting with Falco, but an ambitious girl dreaming of scholarly adventure and about to be pressured into an unwanted marriage would have been clay in his hands. "I take it that's when you ran away?"

She nodded. "When we first departed, it was like a dream to be on the open ocean, searching for places out of legend. Falco had so many texts and artifacts he had collected, items he was eager to let me study and translate. I shared everything I learned—I felt like I owed him that."

"You owed him nothing," I said intensely, my desire to keelhaul Falco increasing with every wave we crested. "Men such as him will prey on your kindness like a parasite."

"I know . . . or rather, I discovered who he really was when the ship was approaching Socotra." Dunya squeezed her eyes shut. "It's all my fault. I thought he was just after treasure. I didn't realize he actually wanted to *use* the kind of spells I read about. I didn't think anyone would be so foolish."

"What happened?"

"I did not have a clear view; Falco kept me in the cabin most of the time, claimed it was for my safety. He was ranting to the men about loyalty, about which ones would be willing to bind their souls to his in a new world. Whatever he was asking them to do . . . it must have been heinous, because a number of the crew refused." She swallowed loudly. "So he summoned a sea beast to devour them. To devour half the ship."

"Yes, we found that ship. What remained of it anyway," I added grimly, recalling as well the shrieking I'd heard on the beach, the crashing black water and starry night implying a leviathan of monstrous size. I could only pray again that it and Falco were gone. I did not want to imagine going up against such a threat. "What happened after it attacked?"

"The rest of us got to the dunij, but we barely escaped with our lives. When we landed on the beach, some fishermen from a local village came to help and Falco . . ." Dunya began to weep. "I thought he was just a scholar. I thought I was just translating poems."

"Poems that said *what*?"

Her teary gaze met mine. "There was a spell for knowledge. Knowledge that could be obtained by siphoning the lifeblood of an elder."

I jerked back. "*You* were behind what happened at the village?"

"I didn't know!" she choked out. "I know that doesn't make it any better. I know God will judge me for what happened, but I never imagined someone would kill people because of things I read on a tablet!"

"Oh, Dunya . . ." I forced myself to check my tongue. The girl was sixteen. She had grown up the pampered, sheltered orphan of an overprotective noble grandmother. She likely knew little of the world outside her books, little of the evil that lurked in men's hearts. Hell, *I* had run afoul of the magical world myself.

But her ignorance had gotten people killed. Far more people than she likely realized, in horrible, brutal ways. I had little doubt it was her translations that led to the ghastly scene in the cave after she fled.

She is going back to Aden. It was no love match, but better a rich husband with tall walls and plenty of guards than her library of lethal magic and a head that had gotten her caught in the misdeeds of a monster.

Dunya was still staring at me, shame flaming her cheeks. "I know you must be cursing me. You are right to. I wish to God I had not told Falco the things I knew. I wish I had thrown myself from the ship before it landed."

"And yet you stayed with him," I pointed out with a bit more force than necessary. "You must have been excavating at the cave for weeks."

"I had little choice. I feared I had already told him too much about the Moon of Saba, and I did not want to risk him discovering it."

Considering that in the past week I'd seen evidence of a snake large enough to swallow ten men and had the foul potion of a possessed sea scorpion shoved through my lips, perhaps I should not have balked at the nonchalance with which Dunya spoke of the possibility of Falco discovering the Moon of Saba.

But I did, stammering out, "Wait—the Moon of Saba is *real*?"

Dunya nodded with a scholar's grave air. "Oh, yes. Or at least . . . that is what my research indicates. But on that I have some good news. A breakthrough that makes it unlikely Falco would recognize the Moon even if it were dangled before his eyes."

"Which is . . ." When she hesitated, I snapped my fingers. "Out with it, girl."

Her shoulders rose and fell dramatically. "Sorry . . . it is just . . . I fear I will sound ridiculous. But in truth, the Moon of Saba is not a pearl."

"Then what the hell is it?"

Dunya's eyes were shining with wonder. "A *washbasin*."

The Second Tale of the Moon of Saba

Yes, I do apologize, dear reader, though in my defense, would you not share the disappointment about to befall Amina if I told you the magical, legendary gem of beauty and power she had left her family and crossed a sea to hunt was little more than a glorified bucket? That is no way to begin a story.

You will remember where last I left you in the grand romance of the queen Bilqis and her lunar admirer, the manzil al-Dabaran. For it is true al-Dabaran longed for her, aching to spend more than a fortnight a year in her presence (we shall return later to his affection, which may have not been . . . *entirely* returned). He did wish to gift her an, ah, "manifestation" of himself. So he waited until the moon was at its peak in his house and his power at its highest. Then when Bilqis went to tend to her ablutions, al-Dabaran blessed the basin with his reflection. The moon filled it completely in its silver loveliness, the water trembling like quickened loins. It is related that the basin was incomparably lovely, carved with hoopoe birds and flowering jasmine. A perfect sphere to hold the reflection of a silvery round moon.

It would have *resembled* a pearl, which I'll admit is a far better object for lore than a washbasin. Perhaps another storyteller long ago decided this was best, just as I briefly held back the truth from you. Or maybe it was an honest mistranslation. We will likely never know.

Either way the scene ends the same: with Queen Bilqis of Saba. One of the most powerful women of antiquity. The chosen companion of the prophet who subdued the djinn. A queen who bound troublesome demons, flew upon the winds, and constructed great masterpieces of castles and forts, holding in her hands a manifestation of al-Dabaran. The soul of the manzil of discord trapped—no, forgive me again, we have not gotten to that part yet. Why should she wish to trap him!—*nestled most voluntarily* in an object that could be easily carried. Traded. Gifted.

Stolen. An awful possibility, no? For Bilqis may have been wise and generous, but let us be honest . . . The vast majority of mortals who seek power do so for far more craven reasons. Generals who order a besieged population starved and their wells poisoned, kings who command the sack of distant cities—the slaughter of tens of thousands—because a petty chieftain has displeased them. By God, the destruction such people might wreak with even a taste of the powers al-Dabaran was rumored to possess makes hearts quake.

Would there be anyone to stop them? Anyone with the knowledge of how to undo an enchantment or hide such a magical object away from the most prying of eyes? Such a feat would seem to require sorcery itself, something we have started to shy away from in our good and righteous age. Thank God, then, that there were once such guardians, a family skilled in the disposal of dangerous talismans.

But alas, I get ahead of myself yet again.

Chapter 21

"Awashbasin," I repeated after listening to Dunya ramble about the unreliability of literary sources and dialectical differences in early South Arabian. "You are telling me that one of the most legendary gems in all of history is a glorified lota? Because of a *mistranslation?*"

"I wouldn't call it a *lota* . . ." Dunya wrung her hands. "I understand why you are disappointed. Though in truth, the idea of the moon's reflection is more poetic, is it not? The washbasin is reputed to be lovely."

I swore profusely enough to make Dunya blanch. "So, no gem at all? Just a washbasin?" When she nodded, I asked, "Then why go through so much effort to hide it? I'm sure it's lovely, but silver washbasins are not exactly rare. I have probably stolen at least a dozen."

"And washbasins imbued with celestial spirits? Basins with the power to grant Sight? How many of those have you encountered?"

I let out an aggravated groan. "Please stop talking like a back-alley soothsayer and speak plainly."

Dunya took a deep breath, perhaps trying to figure out the best way to explain ancient occult practices to an elderly ignoramus. "Al-Dabaran wanted to *manifest* before Bilqis so the bowl grants one Sight—and not just to gaze upon an aspect of the moon. The moon's reflection gave Bilqis the Sight to see *everything* in al-ghayb, the hidden realm. All manner of djinn and spirits. Demons and angels, the unknown Holy Names and mysteries of the Divine. More than most human minds are capable of comprehending. I mean . . . that is what my notes suggested. Apparently a great number of people who came into contact with the basin ended up going mad and killing themselves to stop the visions."

I tried to take that all in. "If you believed such, why trick Falco? You might have guided him to the Moon, let him catch a glimpse of his own foul reflection, and waited until he threw himself in the sea."

"I was not trying to *murder* him." Dunya sounded shocked that I would suggest something so awful as ridding the world of a fanatical sorcerer who had slaughtered dozens. "Besides, some of the stories I read of what happened when the Moon fell into the wrong hands . . . My ancestors would not have gone to such lengths to hide the Moon of Saba if they believed it would simply kill any unworthy person who sought to possess it. It is not merely hidden, it is inaccessible. Those tablets I found—" She nodded to the cloth bundle she'd escaped with. "They are instructions for additional rituals in another location in the cave. A portal where the boundaries between the realms are said to be more porous."

"A brass door, by any chance?"

She gasped. "You've seen it?"

"Just before we came through the treasure chamber looking for you." I shuddered at the memory of the shining door and its grisly carvings. "So Falco needs those tablets to retrieve the Moon?"

"Yes. Well, them *and* me, to decipher and lead the ritual. The tablets are the only artifacts I've discovered that give the incantations necessary to possess al-Dabaran's power."

"All right." I snatched up the bundle and rose to my feet. "Let's throw them overboard."

Dunya flung herself in front of me. "You cannot! Those are the only instructions to retrieving the Moon of Saba, and they are powerful spells! You could anger the lunar aspects and be hurled into a storm. You could risk a sea djinn gaining its power!"

"Oh, for the love of God . . ." I tossed the bundle back on her blanket.

"This is why this sort of magic is forbidden! So what were *you* planning to do with the tablets besides launching yourself into the ocean with no boating skills and limited supplies?"

Fresh disgrace colored her face. "I do not know. Not yet. But I . . . I will find a way to safely dispose of them, I swear. For now, no one but you and I know the true form of the Moon of Saba. And there are likely time constraints on al-Dabaran's return, such as certain cosmological occasions or his particular manzil, which is not for months. I have distant family back in Iraq, some who keep the old ways. They may be able to—"

"Dunya . . ."

"What happened in Socotra was *my* fault, nakhudha!" she said, sounding more distressed. "Which means ensuring Falco cannot do worse is my responsibility."

"Then go back to your grandmother! Back to your library! Surely there is something there that would help."

"If I return to my grandmother, I will never get away. She will marry me off and I . . ." Dunya exhaled, and a pleading note entered her voice. "I cannot marry that man."

"Why not? Because he is old? So what? Put in a few years and you will be a rich widow. You'll be able to buy as many foul spell books as you want!"

"Because I cannot marry *any* man. I cannot . . ." Her face went red, and she averted her gaze. "I know women do it. But when I think of being touched like that . . . of being made up as a bride . . . I-I cannot. I cannot do it."

There was something in her words, and even more in her *utterly* panic-stricken expression, that gave me pause. Because such a marriage was exactly what a noble-born girl from a fading family *would* have been raised to expect. To make peace with, even if it wasn't what their heart desired. For the clever ones—and Dunya was certainly that—to learn how to turn to their advantage.

But as I took a moment to regard Dunya standing there before me, I suddenly wondered if her reservations ran far deeper, recalling the well-worn pamphlet in her room lyrically relating the giddy delight the caliph al-Amin's companions took in imitating the hairstyles and garments of the opposite gender. Though Dalila had offered a dress that would have fit more comfortably, Dunya had chosen men's clothing.

"Is this how you see yourself?" I asked, nodding to her outfit. When Dunya's eyes skittered nervously at me, I tried to reassure her. "A life at sea often attracts those who don't fit in, Dunya. You would hardly be the first soul I've met to prefer the effects of another gender. Or none at all."

She dropped her gaze, visibly struggling to compose herself. Gone was the eager scholar; I had clearly touched upon something more personal. "My grandmother would say you were lying. Would say those you met were merely misguided souls. I should know, for that was her response every time I read of such a person in one of my books and tried to share with her my feelings." Bitterness crept into her voice. "Falco said the same."

"You spoke of this to him?"

Dunya shook her head. "Not truly. I wanted to cut my hair while we were at sea, give up some of my more feminine aspects. See how it felt. When he asked why, I lied and suggested it might be better, safer if I did not look so girlish." Dunya pressed her lips into an unhappy line. "He told me not to, claimed it would be too confusing for his men."

"Oh, fuck his men. And him." I sat on the cushion opposite of her. "*Is this how you see yourself? How you wish to be addressed?*"

Letting out a broken laugh that sounded like it belonged to someone far older, Dunya met my gaze. "I do not know, nakhudha. Nothing has ever felt quite right. I had hoped to find out, but for now I suppose I am still Dunya." A hint of grief entered her brown eyes. "I *do* know, however, that if you insist on returning me to my grandmother, I will be made into a governor's wife and nothing else."

"You would be *safe*," I argued weakly, but the fire had left my voice as the true weight of her situation became more apparent. "That's not nothing. If Falco lives, he might come for you again, and you and your grandmother would do well to be behind a governor's walls. There is *power* behind those walls. You are from Yemen; think of Queen Arwa and Queen Asma! Being tied to a powerful man is not the worst fate."

Dunya blinked away tears. "I don't want power. I just want my books. And even they would not be worth the future awaiting me back home."

Staring at the pleading young person before me, I could not help but waver. It is not permissible, of course, to force someone to wed against their will, though it happens, especially among powerful families who rely on such ties. And while Sayyida Salima didn't strike me as the type to force her grandchild into a wedding bed, she was an ornery old woman set on a course Dunya had already endangered.

You would not have stood for such a fate, a voice in my head chided. *Nor would you consign your own daughter to such unhappiness.* And yet . . . if my child were dabbling in forbidden magics, making enemies out of Frankish sorcerers, and such a husband offered her the best means of protection and safety . . . I might be tempted. There was also the harsh truth that Dunya was not the only one with no choice. Salima had made it clear that if I didn't return her grandchild, my family would pay the price.

But I didn't want to tell Dunya that. She wasn't responsible for her grandmother's actions and was already dealing with enough.

Instead, I sighed. "You have admirable scholarly skills, aye. But you have no connections, no money. No papers from the right school, no letters of recommendation with the right names. The world is not kind to women—to those *raised* as women," I amended, "particularly those who reject what society deems respectable."

Her bottom lip quivered. "You did it."

"Did I?" It was everything I could do not to laugh. How rich the irony that the woman Dunya saw as a hero for blazing her own path was now being blackmailed because of that path by Dunya's own kin. "Is this what you think I wish to be doing? No—don't answer that. It matters not." I rose to my feet. "You can war with your grandmother over all this when we return to Aden; neither your fate nor your wedding are written."

"But—"

"But I am taking you home."

◆

My heart was a tangled mess when I stepped out of the galley, but not so tangled that I didn't immediately go still when I noticed how abruptly the weather had changed. The sky had darkened far more than it should have in the time I'd spent inside, and though there had been only a few wispy clouds when I went to check on Dunya, a greenish haze now limned the entire horizon.

Whether cloud cover or some trick of the light, I could not discern. I had never seen anything like it before—which is not something you want to say on a boat in the middle of the ocean. The wind had picked up as well, in a bizarre choppy way, little drunken breezes dipping here and there. I glanced down to study the sea, for such a wind should have been stirring ripples into the surface. But the water, a deep and fathomless blue, was nigh mercurial.

I didn't like it. There is little that unsettles a nakhudha's heart more than a rapid shift in weather, and I was irked that none of my crew had thought to inform me *and* that my supposed streak of luck—Raksh— seemed to be asleep at the job. I turned, intending to head to my captain's bench.

Instead I ran into my companions, Dalila, Tinbu, and Majed, circling me like impatient crows.

"We heard Dunya's voice," Tinbu said by way of greeting. "It sounded like you were arguing."

I gave another glance at the soupy horizon, then beckoned for them to follow me away from the galley in case Dunya was inspired to press her ear to the door. I would handle this matter first.

"You heard correctly," I said, wiping the sweat from my brow with the end of my turban. "We spoke at length and doing so was enough to convince me of our original course. We head for Aden as quickly as possible. It won't be easy to sail north this time of year, but we shall make the best of it."

There was silence for a long moment before Majed asked, "Does Dunya wish to go?"

My conservative old navigator—a parent like me—was the last person I expected to ask that question. And frankly, I had no idea how to respond. Dunya's entire demeanor had changed when I asked her how she saw herself; I did not imagine she would want that part of our conversation shared.

I settled for bluster, perhaps hoping that speaking so confidently would shut down my own misgivings. "Her wishes do not concern me," I lied. "Her safety does. And the sooner Dunya is reunited with her grandmother and behind the walls of a rich husband, the better."

"A *husband*?" Tinbu repeated. "Is that why she ran away from home?"

"Part of the reason. From what she tells me, I take it she is not . . . well, not the marrying type," I replied evasively. "Her bridegroom is the governor of Aden."

Majed let out a soft sound of surprise. "The governor of Aden . . . oh."

"Oh, indeed. I am normally not one to deliver teenagers to unwanted marriages, but if Falco is alive and comes for her?" I grimaced. "She will be far safer as a governor's wife than with an old lady pirate. Truthfully I cannot imagine a better shelter for her. Aden's navy might have been fledging, but the governor's mansion is more secure than a fort."

"And that is the fate you would visit upon Asif's daughter?" Tinbu challenged. "Locked up as a rich man's wife? A girl who is *not the marry-ing type?*"

A girl who is perhaps not a girl at all. "I'm trying my best, Tinbu, all right?" I shot back. "You didn't hear the things Dunya confessed to. She ran away with a Frank and taught him the magic he worked to murder dozens because *she didn't believe people would use it for evil.* She jumped in a boat and ran off with a set of magical tablets in the vague hope of finding a way to dispose of them. She needs to go home and have an adult put some sense in her head."

"Magical tablets?" Dalila sounded baffled. "Do you mean those clay slabs?"

Still bitter, I was in little mood to give a recounting of Dunya's entire diatribe. "Ask her yourself. She was rambling about lunar spirits and the divine Sight and the Moon of Saba being a bucket."

Tinbu blinked, briefly startled out of his anger. "The Moon of Saba is a bucket?"

"A fancy one. Yes. According to some tablets. Suffice to say, we have been conned yet again. Which is another reason not to delay. Without the pearl, without any of the treasures we were hoping for, I am going to need payment from Salima immediately. I know the men are expecting riches."

"I would pray riches didn't matter," Majed said hotly. "Surely you are not *disappointed?*"

But I was. I was disappointed and the shame of it cut deep. Was that who I was? A selfish woman who had left her child to chase adventure, convincing herself it was for some greater good? A selfish woman whose ambitions had gotten her trapped yet again and was now dragging some-one else into a future I would have fled?

Some hero I turned out to be.

It's for the best, I tried to tell myself. The world was not a fair place, and Dunya al-Hilli's lot in life could be far worse. It *would* be far worse if she had her way, at least when it came to the supernatural; I had watched the shame in her eyes turn into determination when she spoke of it being her duty to thwart Falco. There were almost certainly more harebrained schemes brewing in her head.

"I have made my decision," I declared, ignoring Majed's accusation. "I'm not going to let some youth run off with naught but the clothes on their back, delusions of grandeur, and the enmity of a Frankish sorcerer."

"You were her age when you stole the *Marawati*," Tinbu reminded me. "Majed was not much older when he left his cartography apprenticeship, I was even *younger* when I was sold into slavery, and Dalila spent her entire childhood in the Banu Sasan."

"None of us are examples of good decision-making!"

"Is this because of the money?" Majed demanded again, clearly spotting my evasion and deciding to twist the knife. "Tell me you're not turning a girl over to an unwanted groom because of money."

"I'm *returning* a teenager to her *family* because I don't have a choice!" I snapped. "Salima is not threatening your children, and none of you saw the things I did back in Socotra. None of you saw what happened to Asif when we left him to burn. That kid is fatherless because of me and—"

"*For the thousandth time*, Amina!" Tinbu exclaimed. "What happened to Asif was not your fault!"

"Yes, it was!"

Tinbu jerked back in surprise. "What?" His eyes searched my face, and whatever he saw there must have made it clear I was holding back. "Why-why do you say it like that?"

Maybe I should have lied, should have continued to guard the secret I had held for so long. But I was tired. If I was going to lose their friendship when I dragged Dunya kicking and screaming over Salima's threshold, if Majed was ready to believe I would do such a thing for money alone, what was one more fault in their eyes?

"I *knew*, all right?" I pressed my palms against my brow, running my fingers down my face. "I knew what Raksh was when I brought him on the *Marawati*."

There was a long moment of silence.

Too long. My heart skipping, I forced myself to look at my companions. The vile truth of my deception was *there*, finally laid bare, and yet . . .

None of them were reacting?

Were they too shocked to speak? Tinbu was staring at me with very wide, rather panicked eyes. Majed appeared to be swallowing multiple responses, his throat bobbing up and down. Dalila . . . well, her expression was slightly more inscrutable than usual.

"I-I understand if this means you would no longer like to crew with me," I added awkwardly, their reticence agonizing. "Trust that I will see you properly paid out in Aden and compensate your passage home. But my decision regarding Dunya is final." I stepped back, meaning to return to my captain's bench.

A strangled voice stopped me.

"*No*," Tinbu choked out. "It was me. I am the reason Raksh got to Asif."

I spun around and stared at Tinbu in bewilderment. "*What?*"

Tinbu hung his head. "Back in the Maldives . . . I met Raksh during a card game. I don't normally gamble so much, but it was like I had lost all my wits. I got in over my head with another player. His friends were threatening to take the money out of my hide and—"

"Why did you not come to us?" Dalila demanded. "I would have killed them for you!"

"*Or* paid off your debt," Majed offered, with an exasperated glance at Dalila.

"I was embarrassed," Tinbu confessed. "And *confused*. I remember feeling so addled, like I'd been drinking, though I hadn't touched a drop that night—I don't go near Maldivian palm wine; it'll knock out an elephant. But then Raksh offered to pay the men. He said it was no trouble;

that in return, I could refer him to the lady sea captain he'd been hearing so much about. We needed another sailor, and I didn't see the harm in telling him where to find you. Honestly . . . he seemed your type and I thought you might appreciate the distraction after Salih. I'm so sorry. I should have informed you. But then he turned out to be a decent sailor—"

"No." It was Majed, sounding haunted. "Raksh was a terrible sailor. If he seemed adequate, it was because I was covering for him. I . . . we made a deal too."

"*You?*" I repeated in astonishment. "What could Raksh possibly have to offer you?"

Majed's face fell. "He said he had a cousin in Calicut who was looking to charter a ship for a scientific exploration beyond Malacca. It sounded so exciting; I planned to surprise you all when we landed the contract. But then . . ."

"But then Asif." I faced Dalila. "What about you?"

She bristled. "What about me?"

"Admit it," Tinbu prodded. "I can see the truth in your expression. You made a deal with him too. What was it, Mistress of Poisons? A concoction to melt flesh? The pickled heads of the rogues who ran you out of Basrah?"

Dalila drew up, dignity clasped close. "We were in *discussions*. Nothing more."

"He tricked us all," I whispered, the realization stunning me. "Oh, God, you are all so stupid. We were all *so stupid* together." I felt both terribly relieved and completely embarrassed, like I wanted to hug and smack each of my friends. "But wait . . . did any of you have to sign a contract?" My face went slightly hot. "Or, er, do anything else with him?"

Tinbu and Majed adamantly shook their heads.

"Perhaps it was a lesser kind of pact," Dalila suggested. "Did Raksh not say something about being bound to you?"

"He did." But Raksh had *also* sworn in all feigned innocence the morning after we consummated our marriage that he had no interest in my companions. Relief and embarrassment gave way to a new desire scorching through me:

Murder.

"That lying motherfucker . . ." I gripped the hilt of my dagger. "Dalila, do you have any more of that black powder?"

"Why?"

"Because I'm going to blow his demon ass off my ship!" I spun sharply on my heel, heading in the direction I had last seen Raksh being useless and challenging the ship's carpenter to a poetry competition.

"Amina, wait!"

I was already stomping away. But the *Marawati* was not large, and I quickly spotted Raksh. He wasn't devising lyrical odes to his beauty nor reclining in a bed of ropes while he convinced others to fetch him refreshments. Instead, I spied him standing alone at the *Marawati*'s bow. Payasam was cradled in his arms, the oblivious cat clueless to the many jokes Raksh made about eating it.

However, Raksh didn't look like he was about to crack a joke. Every line of his body was tense. And the expression on his face . . . I'd seen my husband hungry; I'd seen him angry. Worried.

But not even when he was about to be buried alive had I seen the expression of terror in his face as he gazed at the southern horizon.

"Nakhudha!" Firoz cried out from the crow's nest, pointing in the direction Raksh was staring. "There is something in the water!"

Chapter 22

I n the time I had spent with my new ship's boy, I'd learned Firoz had a vibrant imagination. Incredibly sharp eyes—he was in the crow's nest for a reason—but an unfortunate propensity to both overreact and put his foot in his mouth. He saw mermaids in every dolphin and heard djinn in every breeze, a tendency I hoped would lessen with age and experience.

But I had a terrible premonition this was not one of his exaggerations.

I was at the mast the next moment. "What do you mean, 'something'?"

"I-I do not know," Firoz stammered, his wide eyes darting between my face and the southern horizon. "At first I thought it might be a whale, but its color is strange and the way the water moves around it . . . it looks like it could be a ship, the spray splashing out from a bow. But there's no vessel; there's nothing but a smudge of pink upon the horizon."

What in God's name? "Tinbu!"

"On it." After Firoz, Tinbu had the clearest vision of anyone I knew and far better marine sense. He was climbing up before Firoz had even left the crow's nest, and I watched him ascend, shading his face to examine the horizon.

Tinbu frowned. "Whatever it is, it isn't a ship—the shape would be visible above the surface and Firoz is right, all I can discern is a pinkish dome. It's moving pretty erratically, like an animal might. Like a very, very *large* animal might. But"—he stiffened—"it's changed direction."

I was halfway up the mast, fear of heights be damned. *"Meaning?"*

Tinbu glanced down with ill-concealed panic. "It's coming toward us. *Fast*."

Clutching the rope ladder, I peered into the southern distance. It was difficult to distinguish anything from the murky, soupy sky that lay heavy upon the horizon. The sun was no longer visible, the smell of approaching rain thick in the air. But then—*there*, a rapidly enlarging speck at the center of a patch of rough surf.

I was not the only one to notice it. Some of my men had stopped what they were doing, pointing and talking excitedly amongst each other. As if in warning, a swell swept under the *Marawati*, my ship rising and falling in a sea that had been calm only moments earlier. I held tight to the rope, swaying with its movement as the yard creaked overhead, and then I quickly climbed down, jumping to the deck.

I nearly landed on Raksh. He had dashed over and now grabbed me by the shoulders. His face was pale, a ghostly blue hue flooding his cheeks.

"Get rid of Dunya," he hissed, his voice a low purr of warning. "*Now*."

I jerked back—or rather tried to; his grip on my arms was too strong. "What?"

"Throw her overboard," he said even more urgently. "And do it quickly. We are being pursued."

"Yes, I noticed that," I said acidly, finally wrenching away. A misty rain began to patter against my skin. "Do you know what's chasing us?"

"Don't you?" Raksh tapped my chest, the same place from where he'd yanked out the spectral stinger.

"Surely you don't mean . . . Falco's *beast*?" I whispered, going cold all over when he nodded. And not only because I was frightened—but because the very air itself had chilled. Clouds the color of molten iron were chasing across the sky from the direction of the approaching creature. The *Marawati* began rolling on the increasingly choppy water, forcing me to steady my feet. "Are you certain?"

Raksh gave a grim look to the south. The creature had gone from a speck to a spot the size of an orange, an unfathomable speed. "Yes. I warned you Falco would not let Dunya escape. Get rid of her, Amina. In the dunij, if that will ease your conscience, but do it now. Hopefully it will buy us time to flee."

Dunya's pleading face played before my eyes. The prospect of sacrificing her to some monstrous leviathan was reprehensible. "I will not," I said defiantly. "There must be *something* else we can do. What happened to you bringing me luck!"

"Do you have a spare oar I could use? Because while my presence might give you an edge of fortune, I suspect speed will be more useful. A creature like that is beyond me."

By God, if the demon was willing to row, we were in direr straits than I realized.

I thought fast. "Back in Socotra, you said Falco was a fool to try and control a creature like that. Do you think . . . there's a way to *dissuade* it? To convince the creature to give up the chase?"

Raksh licked his lips, looking fretful. "I don't know. The marid are old, incomparably bizarre and tempestuous beasts. I have met some that can be reasoned with, some that deal in bargains and pacts with mortals, but this one . . ." He shuddered. "It was like a wild animal when we first encountered it. And Falco was not interested in a pact. He wanted to *own* it. The marid would probably gobble him up if it could."

"So you're telling me there's a chance?"

"No, that's not what I'm telling you at all! I'm telling you Falco's magic *defeated* it." My husband lowered his voice. "Amina, I warned you once that the Frank had powers beyond your comprehension. You did not listen and nearly ended up his thrall. We are earthen creatures; there is nothing between us and a watery grave right now except a few lashed-together logs. You cannot challenge Falco at sea, not while he possesses a creature of the ocean's domain."

"What's going on?" It was Dalila, her voice sharp. She was joined by

Tinbu; Majed had rushed to the captain's bench to secure the rahmani and his maps when a swell rocked the boat.

"Raksh wants to throw Dunya overboard," I snarled under my breath. I wasn't keeping secrets from my friends any longer, not on Raksh's behalf, but I spoke quietly, not wanting the rest of the crew to overhear. "Says it's Falco's beast pursuing us."

Raksh looked imploringly at Dalila. "Your nakhudha is being a sentimental fool, but you've always had a clearer head. Dunya is the one they want."

"Then they will have to take her from us," Dalila said firmly.

Another wave knocked across the *Marawati*, this one far more drenching.

I caught my balance and picked up a bucket, shoving it into Raksh's arms. "Go make yourself useful," I ordered, gesturing to the men bailing water. When Raksh stomped off, I turned to Tinbu. "Speed up. We will try to flee."

"It's moving too quickly," Tinbu said, sounding sick. The creature was now the size of a melon, but obscured by fog and its own frothy, crashing wake, its exact shape could not be seen, like an amorphous ghost stalking forth. "We can't outrun something like that, Amina. Where would we even go?"

Tinbu had a point. We were nowhere near land, near the kinds of hidden creeks and mangrove swamps we typically disappeared into while hunting prey. To be caught and forced to battle in the open ocean was an entirely different situation, one at which my kind of ship did not excel. And that was against another vessel, not a sea monster. If we could last until the sun set, we might be able to douse the lights and flee into the darkness. Had another ship caught us out, we would likely do just that.

But we were not facing another ship. We were being pursued by something beyond our understanding. A foul breeze blew from the direction of the distant creature, the sea surrounding it churning with yellowed froth.

Majed had joined us and was silently listening, his expression grave. Now he spoke. "If we tack east there is a chance we'll hit the monsoon current. It might take us wildly off course, but we could lose the creature."

I doubted any monsoon current was strong enough to help us now but didn't say so. "Then we try that," I decided. "We run and pray it gets bored or, more ideally, breaks free of Falco's influence and eats him. Tinbu, I want your best men on the sails. Firoz, make sure the deck is clear. Anything that cannot get tied down gets thrown overboard or stashed in the cargo hold. Ideally thrown overboard. The rest of you to the oars!" I shouted and then cursed as Payasam darted between my legs, meowing loudly and threading my ankles like a besotted drunk.

Dalila's expression was steely. "I will check the remaining spheres of naft and put together more tubes of black powder for arrows. But I have very little left."

"Use what you have, but do me a favor." I stepped closer, lowering my voice. "Stay near Dunya. I don't trust Raksh not to try and get rid of her himself."

Dalila hefted her wooden staff. I doubted it could genuinely harm Raksh; we'd had no luck fighting him thus far, but Dalila made for a fearsome sight and my husband was nothing if not a coward. "Understood."

I picked up Payasam, who was still trying to trip me, and carried the little cat to the galley. Inside, Dunya was sitting straight up on her cushion, clutching her tablets to her chest.

"Is something going on?" she asked, sounding frightened.

"Nothing to worry you." It was a lie, but Dunya had been through enough, and there was nothing she could do to help. I folded Payasam in her arms. "Keep this wretched thing safe for me, yes? And stay in here."

She nodded. "I promise."

By the time I returned to my captain's bench and took up the rudder ropes, the creature had tripled in size on the horizon. It was darker than dusk, unnatural clouds casting an eerie green light to everything. The beast was still moving too fast to see its body clearly, tearing through the water with such violence that it looked like an explosion of waves was coming our way. The smell of marine rot was thick on the fetid air and rain lashed my face, the crashing ocean loud as a drum.

You cannot outrun this one, al-Sirafi.

With Tinbu at the sails and as many men rowing as we had oars, the *Marawati* flew across the rough sea. But we were hopelessly outmatched, and the weather was only getting worse. Majed joined me on the bench. Neither of us spoke for a long moment, our gazes locked on the beast.

"We should stop," he finally said. "Give the men a few minutes to recover before they fight. A few minutes for prayer or to collect themselves just in case . . ."

He didn't finish his sentence. He didn't have to. This wasn't the first time the two of us had faced down the likelihood of an imminent death at sea; no mariner with as many years between them as we had avoided such experiences. We'd weathered cyclones and rogue waves, doldrums and broken sails. Many a time, we chucked everything overboard, tied ourselves to the ship, and prayed, expecting the watery grave that takes so many of us.

But I had a daughter to return to now. And we weren't facing a storm that couldn't be avoided, couldn't be outwitted. "We might still make it, God willing," I said stubbornly, nodding at the thunderheads in the distance. "Night approaches and the weather is turning fouler. We could lose the creature in the darkness."

"We are more likely to lose *ourselves* in the darkness than any creature that lives in the sea. And if we are to have any hope of surviving a storm, we should be bringing the sails in."

I took a deep breath, considering my fleeting options. "We will go on a bit longer. We cannot know the mind of this creature, nor the depths of the Frank's control over it."

Majed met my gaze. "You are the only one of us who met this man.

What sort of control do you *think* he exercises? What sort of vengeance on the girl who betrayed him and the pirates who tried to blow him up?"

"Careful, Majed. You would not wish to risk your reputation for cynicism." But my poor effort at a joke only made him flinch. I spoke again, more intent. "If the creature catches up and we are forced to fight, you will flee in the dunij. Take the four youngest sailors," I added, begging forgiveness from Asif in my heart. I hated to leave Dunya out of such a calculation but feared Raksh had likely spoken the truth. They would have a better chance of escaping without her.

Majed was already shaking his head. "I will not leave you."

"I am the nakhudha; I was always going to be the last to leave. But you are a navigator, not a fighter, and those kids don't stand a chance of finding land without you. *Please*, brother," I said more urgently when Majed's expression turned mutinous. "Go to my family. Warn them. If Marjana—"

A strong gust ripped through the air. The *Marawati* jerked heavily to port, provoking a few startled cries. I gripped the edge of my bench, fighting for balance as the ship rolled back, startled by how abruptly the storm had strengthened.

Because this is no storm, not truly. It was magic beyond my understanding. And I feared it was shortly to be beyond my ability to fight as well. "Take down the sails!" I shouted.

From beyond the curtain of driving rain, a screeching roar rent the sky.

It was the same unnatural sound I had heard on the beach in Socotra, the cry so high-pitched it sounded like a rusted celestial-sized blade on an unpolished, craggy whetstone. It made the thunder seem meek in comparison.

And it sounded *way* too close. But I was the nakhudha, and I didn't get to panic. "Archers along the port side! The rest of you, keep rowing." I rose to my feet and turned to Majed. "Brother, go."

"Not yet," he pleaded.

A wave smashed into the *Marawati*, nearly sending us sideways. Water rushed across the decks with enough force to knock two men down and rip the oars from another. Grasping for the rudder rope to steady myself, I quickly climbed back to my feet, searching the ranks to make sure no one had gone overboard. The rain was coming down slanted and the wind was relentless, whipping any bit of exposed skin. The creature roared again even louder, even closer, but still invisible in the fog.

"You bastard, no!" Tinbu cried from the other side of the ship, hidden behind the billowing sails. "Amina, it's Raksh! He stole the dunij!"

Cursing, I jumped down from the captain's deck. But I hadn't gone two steps when a blistering purple tentacle burst out of the sea.

I screeched to a halt on the wet deck. The tentacle rose straight in the air as though searching for the sun, wiggling and squirming, covered in razor-edged suckers the size of my face. It was thick as a tree trunk, long as a city street, and—in the space of a heartbeat—was joined by two more massive appendages. The second tentacle slapped the *Marawati*, shaking the entire ship. The third slithered across the cargo hold, rushing up the mast and wrapping itself around the wooden beam like a vine. Men were screaming, fleeing their posts and ducking flying debris.

I seized the railing, fighting not to be chucked off the wave-tossed *Marawati*. "Grab something sturdy!" I shouted. "Tie yourselves to the ship!"

The still mostly unseen creature shrieked. One of the tentacles swept out wide, nearly knocking a cowering Hamid overboard, and at the sight of the creature attacking my crew, I abruptly discarded my own advice. Letting go of the railing, I drew my sword and rushed the tentacle gripping the mast.

I slashed down with my blade. A spray of acidic silver blood splashed across my arms and face, stinging like salt upon a wound. I hissed in pain but didn't stop my attack, striking again and again and then *again* as the beast howled. The fourth hack finally severed the damn thing, and the tentacle crashed to the deck, unspooling like a dropped spindle.

Breathing hard and barely able to see past the blinding rain and crashing waves, I stumbled back, searching for my next target.

But my success was short-lived.

A dozen tentacles exploded out of the raging sea. They surrounded us like the fingers of a vile, grasping hand, lunging for the mast, twining around the stern and bow points, and winding through the railings. For a second, the *Marawati* went completely still, the waves unable to batter us in the marid's firm grip.

Then the creature thrust the ship straight up into the air.

Sailors screamed, sobbing for their mothers and praying in every tongue as we flew skyward. I fell hard, still yelling for my crew to grab something, anything, yet somehow managing to keep a grip on my sword and hooking my other arm through one of the joints bolting the cistern to the railing. I shoved my sword in my belt, lunging to catch Firoz before he rolled off the ship.

The boy buried his head in my neck. "I don't want to look."

I could do nothing *but* look as flashes of lightning revealed storm-churned waves far, *far* below, indicating a beast of impossible size and conception. The marid had an insect-like abdomen large enough to pass as an island and a wicked stinger curving out of the water to drip bright blue poison. Dozens of squid-like tentacles shuddered from its body, and six flat bloodred eyes stared up from an armored plate of a head. Perched like a crown on its skull was a corona of broken timbers.

But the marid, a monstrous beast of whom a single glimpse might paralyze the bravest man with fear . . . even *it* paled in comparison with how high my ship was suspended.

"Oh, God," I whispered, suddenly aware that to fall from this height would be instant death. Suddenly aware that my last adventure was likely about to be abruptly ended.

The marid shook us.

It was a single firm shake, like one might give a disobeying child.

Firoz screamed in my ear, clasping me tighter. We didn't fall: my arm was too firmly hooked into the cistern's joint, and though the motion nearly wrenched my shoulder out of its socket, we didn't plummet to our deaths.

Which, judging from the fading shrieks of my men, was not a mercy granted to everyone. But I had not a second to grieve, to rage or cry warning before the creature pulled us back down.

We fell heavily into the sea, the *Marawati* all but inundated by the resulting wave. I clutched the cistern and Firoz, holding my breath as black water rushed over our heads. Debris surged around us, pounding my limbs. We were only underwater for a few moments before the ship bobbed back up. I gasped, choking for air. Everything hurt. My ears were ringing, and I could taste blood in my mouth, more streaming from lacerations all over my body.

But I was alive. Which I feared was far more than I could say for everyone who had been on the *Marawati*.

There was nothing but silence for a long, awful moment. The creature's tentacles held fast, but it did not roar, did not attack further. Maybe it was contemplating the best way to eat us. With a groan, I pulled my pummeled arm from the cistern joint and untangled Firoz. "Stay here," I ordered.

Rising to my feet, I tried to survey what I could. The sail had ripped free of its bindings, the massive cloth billowing up as we fell and then catching on the yard and rigging so that it tented part of the *Marawati*. Between that and the fog, I could see almost nothing; what *was* visible of my wrecked ship and weeping, bloodied crew filled my heart with grief.

"Amina!"

Dalila. I staggered in the direction of my friend's voice, climbing over wreckage and checking on the men I passed.

"Over here!" she cried. Dalila had left the galley and was crouched over the broken starboard rudder. The massive wooden beam had snapped, one half lying heavily across the deck.

Pinned beneath was Tinbu.

I ran over. My first mate was unconscious, blood crusting his face. "Oh, God. Is he . . ."

"He's alive," Dalila said quickly. "He took a blow to the head and his leg is likely broken. It's stuck under the beam, but it's too heavy for me to lift."

"Let me help." It was Tiny, the massive sailor from Sumatra, followed by Majed, bleeding badly but alive.

"Take this end," I urged. "If we get a couple more men to lift—"

"Oh, nakhudha!" The voice that sang out from beyond the fog was horribly, immediately familiar—indeed, Falco sounded almost cheerful as he continued. "I do believe you have something of mine."

◆

Over Tinbu's body, my and my friend's gazes caught.

I grabbed Dalila's wrist when she reached for one of the poison tablets dangling from her ribbon cap.

"No, Dalila," I said firmly, my heart sinking. "Nor you, Majed—drop your hand away from that knife." I gave them both the fiercest look I could. "Tinbu is the only one who could possibly patch this ship up. And if it is *not* patched up, everyone on it will die. You will stay here and save him. *Promise me you will save him.* If I can't outwit Falco, do whatever is necessary to keep yourselves and the crew alive."

Dalila opened and closed her mouth, looking more emotional than I had ever seen her. "I swore to return you to your daughter."

Her words were a knife to my heart. "We are not yet dead, Dalila."

Majed grabbed my wrist as I stood, anguish and fear in his face. "Do not be proud. The Frank may let you live."

"I don't intend to be proud," I said, trying to sound brave. "I'm a pirate, not an idiot knight."

But I was a pirate who trembled as I crossed the *Marawati*, the eyes of my crew heavy upon me. The weight of their *lives* heavy upon me. The state of my ship and the faces I saw missing tearing at my soul. A clever trickster knows when she has lost, knows when to surrender to fight another day. And yet I still freed my blades, my sword in one hand and my grandfather's khanjar in the other as I slipped past the fallen sailcloth and got my first good look at the Frank's enslaved marid.

"God save me," I said hoarsely.

Even half submerged, the tentacled sea scorpion towered over the *Marawati*. Its crown of broken timbers were the remains of Falco's ship, bonded to its massive skull with craggy blossoms of dead coral, rotting seaweed, and jagged broken shells like some twisted interpretation of a palanquin. Cracks traced out across the marid's head like an infected wound, weeping silvery ichor. Pustules and blisters covered other parts of the beast's body, disease-ridden and foul-smelling. Its bladed tail arched out of sight, melting into the gloom, though I could feel it hanging overhead like an executioner's axe.

"There you are," Falco drawled from a perch in his ruined ship. "I feared you might have perished in the attack." He made as though to move toward the *Marawati*.

"That's close enough," I snapped, raising my sword. Several of my men followed suit, even as the Frank's mercenaries—many sporting burns and injuries from the explosion in Socotra—flanked him.

Falco snorted. "I know your people have fierce hearts and a great love of martyrdom, but look around you. You do realize with a snap of my fingers, I could have all of you drowned and devoured."

He had no sooner said the words than the tentacles around the *Marawati* abruptly dragged the ship lower. Water surged over the deck, twining around my ankles.

"Enough!" I made no move to lower my weapon, but Falco lifted a hand and his marid relented, the *Marawati* bobbing back upward. He had made his point and I feared my ship could not take much more— God knew if the *Marawati* was even seaworthy at this point. I counted only twelve men with Falco now, but I'd learned the hard way what they were physically capable of and feared our superior numbers would not be enough.

"What do you want?" I asked, the words bitter in my mouth.

Falco jumped from his perch, landing on a boil on the creature's skull. The marid let out a high-pitched squeal of pain, but the Frank seemed unbothered. He was armed this time, a broadsword at his side.

He kicked one of the marid's tentacles, and it whimpered. "This creature may have served in capturing you, but it is an animal, unreliable and hungry. Therefore, I am still in need of a good vessel and talented crew. Join me, hand Dunya over, and I will let you and your shipmates live."

"Dunya is not here."

Falco strode closer, his sinister half smile unwavering. "If I begin feeding your crew one by one to my beast, how many will it take before you stop lying?"

"You will recall the last time you tried to force my hand, we blew up your men."

"That you did." Falco hopped from the creature's skull onto the *Marawati*, and the moment his feet touched my boat, I felt dirty. "I did not like that, al-Sirafi. I offered you a gift, an incomparable opportunity, and you threw it in my face. I hoped you might be cleverer than those of your faith I have killed in the north. But your people only understand violence, don't they?"

He unsheathed his sword. It slipped silently from its scabbard, glittering as the rain misted against steel. Dread crawled through me. I had been sparring with Tinbu and the other men when we had time, but I hadn't been in a true sword fight in nearly a decade, and I'd never battled a Frank. I'd never even *seen* a Frank fight. I knew neither their style nor its strengths and weaknesses.

But I did know my *Marawati*.

"Now, listen," I started, lowering my scimitar. "There is no reason we cannot—" I lunged forward, sliding on the wet deck as I dodged past and slashed the backs of his knees. I got his left leg good, blood staining my blade, but that was not my primary target.

The ropes holding the yard were.

I ducked as it came swinging for both of us, but the Frank was not as swift. The yard smashed into his chest, sending him stumbling. I ran up a stack of crates, meaning to cut him down from above, but one of the creature's tentacles seized my ankle. It tossed me to the deck, and I rolled just in time to avoid Falco's sword cleaving me in two. I was on my feet the next moment, breathing fast, but I'd landed badly on my weak knee, and it jostled unreliably as we clashed again. Several of my men moved to assist, but I waved them off. The Frank was clearly the vengeful type, and if he struck me down, they didn't need to follow me into death when he'd made his need for sailors plain.

Our styles were as mismatched as our blades. Falco fought well, his training and comfort with his weapon evident in every move. But he was not the best man I'd fought, and a decade ago I wouldn't have been barely missing the strikes that came hammering my way. Now my arms were shaking and sweat poured from my brow as I narrowly dodged back, forced to defend myself instead of being on the offensive. I was a shadow of my former glory, the sparring I'd done be damned.

It must have been obvious. Falco smirked. "I'd heard you were a more accomplished fighter. I suppose retirement had its downsides."

I gritted my teeth. "It was nice while it lasted."

His sword bore down against mine, nearing my throat. "Your life would be better spent in my service than ended before your people. I can see the panic in your eyes, al-Sirafi. This need not continue."

"Oh, *fuck off*, you fish-brained wizard." Grabbing for the pile of turned-over carpenter's tools, I dropped a hand from my sword, picked up a hammer, and smashed it into Falco's wrist.

He yelped in genuine pain, a glorious sound, and jerked back, removing the broadsword from where it had been bearing down upon my neck and foolishly offering a clean path to smash him in the face with the most excellent hammer. I moved to do so . . .

Then he was gone, retreating with unnatural speed.

Well, shit. I suppose Falco's men were not the only ones who had been transformed.

I didn't let my surprise linger, taking advantage of the moment he was briefly on the defensive by charging forward and slashing down again with my scimitar. He blocked my blade with his own, shoving me back so hard I slipped on the wet deck. I cursed as my knee nearly gave way, and Falco grinned, seeming to spot the weakness. He lunged—

"Stop!" a wavering voice cried.

Dunya.

The young scholar looked terribly vulnerable and small, standing in the open galley door as the wind and rain whipped at her oversized robe. Majed made a wild grab to pull her back, but it was too late.

Falco had spotted her.

"Dunya," he greeted coldly. "Good to see your recklessness did not kill you."

"Do not pretend to care for me," she said, trembling. "You are a monster who cares only for yourself."

"On the contrary, I care very much for the rarity of your knowledge. It will make you a leading light in the new world, if you are wise enough to offer amends." His eyes narrowed. "Do you think me a fool not to have noticed what you took? Those tablets lead to the Moon, don't they?"

"These tablets?" Dunya pulled them from her robe. "Why, yes. Yes, they do."

She dashed them against the deck.

I gasped as the ancient clay slabs shattered into dust. Falco snarled, but Dunya only drew up, looking more defiant.

"And now that knowledge only exists here," she warned, tapping her head. "If you want the Moon of Saba, you will let the *Marawati* and its people go."

"That was not my offer," Falco snapped. "And I'm half inclined to drown them for your insolence."

Oh, great, now I had to be the sensible one between the sorcerous fanatic and the dramatic teenager. "You still need a ship," I reminded him. "And a crew. We will take your offer. Leave Dunya alone."

He glared at me. "The *Marawati* and its crew will see me to Socotra. *You*," he said to Dunya. "You will get me the Moon, or I will harvest each of these people before your eyes. Understand?"

A doomed expression I didn't like flickered in Dunya's gaze. "I will get you to the Moon of Saba. I swear on God and my ancestors."

"And he won't *touch* my people," I added sharply. "Nor force his foul potion upon them."

"Agreed," Dunya said, turning back to the Frank. "I will get you the Moon, but when the time comes that we enter that cave, you will release the *Marawati*'s crew unharmed."

Falco gave me a long, cold look. It must have been obvious we were desperate and bluffing; I had little doubt he could come up with a nasty variety of ways to force Dunya's hand.

"Perhaps by the time the Moon of Saba is mine, your crew will have decided to serve a better captain," he said coolly. "But I am agreed. Throw your weapons over and tell your men to disarm."

It killed me to toss down my sword and motion for my people to do the same, but my pride was a small price to pay. Falco's fighters came from the beast's head, collecting our weapons and rounding up my crew. They bound the men in rope, and I was briefly relieved to spot Tiny carrying Tinbu. My friend was still unconscious, but at least they'd freed him from the fallen rudder. Dalila was at his side, her ribbon cap gone and iron shackles around her wrists and feet. Falco had obviously been warned about the Mistress of Poisons.

"Bring the nakhudha here," he ordered.

His men dragged me forward, holding my arms painfully behind my back. The Frank bent to pick up my weapons, examining my scimitar before tossing it to Yazid.

"More your kind of blade, I believe. But this . . ." Falco retrieved the khanjar I had dropped among the tangle of carpentry tools, and my blood boiled as he ran his fingers over the hilt of my grandfather's dagger. "A leopard? Ah, yes, I think I remember. They used to call your grandfather 'the Sea Leopard,' no?"

"Your obsession with me is embarrassing."

"I suppose it was an obsession, yes. I'm disappointed; I had hoped to find in you a kindred spirit." Falco closed the distance between us, continuing to caress the khanjar as his men tightened their grip on my arms. "The Sea Leopard," he mused. "A fearsome pirate, he must have been. A true adventurer. Whereas you, well . . .

"You're nothing."

He struck me so hard across the face with the khanjar's hilt that my vision briefly went black. A great shock of pain spasmed across my cheek, blood bursting in my mouth. Before I could even think to react, he aimed a savage kick at my bad knee.

The world went white. His men let me go and I collapsed to the deck in agony, my leg crumpling beneath me.

"Stop!" Dunya cried. "You swore not to hurt her!"

At the edge of my starry vision, I saw my men lunge at Falco's, but already disarmed and bound, they were swiftly pushed back.

"No, I said I would let the crew live." Falco's clammy fingers wrapped around my neck as he lifted me in the air with unnatural strength. "I'm a man of my word, if nothing else."

I scrabbled at the iron grip on my throat, an echo of my encounter with Raksh. I could not breathe, could not fight, my sandals slipping on the wet deck as the Frank dragged me to the *Marawati*'s edge.

"I wished we could have worked something out back in Socotra, na-khudha," he continued. "But you see . . . I have your navigator and your first mate. Your poisoner, your crew, *and* your ship. And you strike me as a distrustful rat. Why, then, would I risk keeping you around?"

Gasping for air, I writhed in his hands. The storm raged around us, the ship rising and falling in crashing waves as rain blasted my face. I was aware of Majed's angry bellow. Of Dalila yelling my name and Dunya pleading.

Falco raised the khanjar. "I suppose I have taken enough from you. Here. Have this back."

He shoved the dagger at my chest.

I tried to twist away, but pain sliced through my shoulder, hot blood spilling across my already drenched robe. My vision was going blurry, Falco was thrusting me over the railing. There were screams, so many screams . . .

Marjana, I'm sorry. I'm so sorry.

Falco let go.

I crashed into the hard, cold water, and everything went black.

Chapter 23

ere's the thing about getting thrown off a battered ship in the middle of a raging storm: there tends to be a lot of debris floating around. And should one strike such debris, yes, it will likely be hard enough to knock you senseless. But by the grace of God, you may also get snagged on a piece of bobbing rubbish instead of slipping below the waves. You may drift away unseen in the sideways rain, impenetrable mist, and roaring waves, past the arrows your enemies shoot into the water after you.

And you may wake with the worst headache of your life just in time to see the unmistakable fin of a shark slicing in your direction.

A lifetime at sea had me hauling my body out of the water and onto the broken wooden platform that had caught my cloak before I could even think straight. Pain scorched through my shoulder, the platform nearly toppling over with my weight. It was little more than a few roughly lashed planks, barely large enough to sit on and small enough to offer an excellent look at the unfathomable deep below.

Sick with fear, I watched as the shark swam directly beneath the crossed timbers, so close I could have touched it. My shoulder and knee pounded again, reminding me that if I was going to be eaten alive, I would do it hurting in a variety of exciting ways. A red cloud of blood stained the water, more soaking my clothes. Startled, I glanced down to see the leopard-headed hilt of my khanjar sticking out of my cloak.

Oh, right.

I was stabbed.

But I didn't *feel* stabbed, mostly because I was still alive and not actively bleeding to death. I touched the handle with trembling fingers, terrified to jostle the blade in case the wound was worse than I feared. But the dagger was caught in the fabric of my cloak, not buried in my body. Falco had cut deep, but it had been an ugly slash across the top of my shoulder rather than a fatal puncture wound.

However, not being stabbed to death with my own khanjar was of little relief. For a glance revealed no *Marawati*. No ships of any kind. No *land*. Nothing but ocean stretching to the horizon in every direction I looked. A few odds and ends bobbed about: broken railings, a wooden cup, a sandal.

"No," I whispered, desperately turning here and there, praying I was wrong, praying there was *something*. A smudge of beach in the distance. The hint of a boat. A *bird*. "No. Oh, God . . . *no*."

But there was nothing. Nothing but a sailor's worst nightmare come to life around me. It's one thing to drown in a sinking ship or be dashed upon rocks. But to be *lost*, adrift in the middle of the ocean and doomed to a long grueling death of thirst and starvation while you are baked alive by the sun?

"Oh, God," I said again, for who else could I call upon? I choked back a sob. "What do I do?" Shock was setting in and I shivered madly. "Oh, Marjana. My little love . . ."

But it wasn't only Marjana who needed me. Falco had my *crew*. Majed, Dalila, and Tinbu. Dunya and the men who had joined me only so recently. They were now all under the thumb of a monstrous Frankish wizard who might feed them to his marid or force them into the same foul servitude he had tried to foist upon me, Dunya's deal be damned.

I had failed them. I had failed *everyone*.

In the distance, the shark turned around for another pass.

Say the shahada and slip into the water, you coward. One last prayer for mercy I didn't deserve and an end that would be faster than dying of exposure. Hell, it wouldn't even be a useless end—I'd feed something.

But as the shark neared, a fierce madness stole through me.

I picked up one of the broken railings drifting in the water. "We are not yet dead," I whispered, repeating Dalila's words. "We are not yet— *AHH!*" I smashed the broken railing into the shark's face, striking it as hard and fast as I could. After the second hit, it reeled back, quickly swimming away from the crazy human.

I was alone . . . at least for now.

First I looked to my injury. It was a nasty gash and in an ideal world, could have used stitching, but at least the wound was well washed due to me being in the fucking sea all night. Cutting a strip from my cloak, I bound the injury best I could, praying the blood would cease leading a trail for any curious maritime predator.

Next I turned my attention to the sky. Directions were easy enough to pick out with the sun's position. They were also useless. God only knew where the storm had taken us. I might be in the middle of the Indian Ocean or a few days from the coast. Unless I saw birds or fishing boats, I would have no clue which way to head. But I needed to go somewhere.

Northwest, I decided. I was likely still closer to the familiar shores of Africa and Arabia. To the east, but weeks away, was India, and to the south nothing but water. I snagged the cup and the lost sandal and then, positioning myself awkwardly upon the wooden planks, I set my course.

"God, please have mercy on me once more," I begged, using the broken railing as an oar. The sun scorched overhead, the white glare off the ocean blinding. "Get me out of this and I am done with these adventures. I shall repent and never again venture upon the sea."

It did not take long for time to blur, thirst and the sweltering heat pushing me toward madness. To distract myself, I counted to one thousand in all the languages I knew and made dua for everyone I had ever held a passing fondness. I recited Quran, sang bedtime rhymes from Marjana's childhood, chanted dhikr to the beat of my paddle, and invented increasingly elaborate fantasies of revenge and murder toward Falco and Raksh (and yes, I am aware some of these methods clashed most ardently in spirit). When my mouth dried up, I did this all silently in my head. I set out the cup each night to catch condensation, and on the third day caught and killed a turtle; imploring forgiveness as I drank its blood.

With my cup, I was able to gather a bit of water from two achingly brief rain showers. With the cord of the sandal and a couple of bites of turtle meat, I caught a few fish. But there was nothing to ease the blisters erupting across my sunburnt skin and the pounding feeling of nails being driven into my skull. My strength faded, my bouts of confusion increasing. I paddled less and less as days slipped into dreamless nights.

And then, as though creatures out of a mirage, the birds began to arrive.

Loud squawking gulls and tiny pipers. Elegant long-necked cranes and sharp-taloned raptors. They came in pairs and alone, in great flocks and bobbing parties that swiftly learned to keep their distance after I killed and ate a bright-beaked booby.

I do not recall if I remember finding strange their bizarre colors. Purple and orange feathers in hues I had never seen, glittering ruby eyes and fringed heads. I may have chalked up any oddities to my own sunbaked skull. All were headed firmly east and so with some hesitation I changed direction to follow them.

On the fifth day after sighting the birds, a green-brown smear of land appeared on the hazy horizon.

My remaining wits vanished the moment I spotted it, so desperate I was to get ashore before the sun vanished and I lost sight of land forever. I paddled myself to exhaustion, my arms going numb and the platform breaking apart. I did not care, I kept pulling my makeshift oar through the water, my eyes pinned on the sliver of distant beach. I swam, I kicked, the sea closed more and more frequently over my head . . .

Please, God, don't let me die. Not now, not like this. In a cruel goad to myself, I conjured Marjana's voice, heard my daughter urging me forward. Begging me to come home as the sun splashed into the mighty ocean and its last vestiges of light faded away.

Mama, please. Please! Her earnest, little face and trusting eyes. Her small fingers winding through my hair and the warmth of her breath as she slept in my arms.

Come home.

Then, finally—*finally*—there was sand beneath my toes. Sand beneath my knees and hands. Waves crashed around my shoulders, and I burst into dry sobs of relief as I crawled forward onto a midnight shore and collapsed in a pile of seaweed, my body completely spent.

"God be praised," I croaked and promptly passed out.

◆

I woke under the light of a silver sun.

The tide was lapping at my lips. I sputtered and groaned, every muscle, joint, and bone in my starved, sore body protesting as I spat a mouthful of blood and salt water. Attempting to peel myself off the wet sand, I succeeded only in throwing up black bile.

Breathe, Amina.

My head was pounding and the world was spinning in shattered fragments of teal water, amber shores, and indigo forest. The colors were wrong, overly vibrant and mismatched. I took a couple of deep breaths and then sat up more slowly, the sand that clung to my fingers dripping like honey.

It was like no beach I'd ever seen. The tide line was marked by stringy bubbles of bloodred waterweeds and needle-sharp blue sea stars. Ahead was a jungle so dense its interior was black, soft, and dangerously inviting. There were palm trees at the edge, their cinnamon-colored trunks gleaming as though the bark were jeweled, the razor-edged fronds shaking in the windless air with the crash of clashing sabers. Birds in unnatural hues dove and careened overhead, emitting grumbly roars.

Where in God's name am I? But then—a gleam of wetness that banished all other thoughts.

Water.

I lurched to my feet. I was dimly aware of odd blurs in my vision, objects that refused to resolve themselves. Floating in the bizarrely frothy shallows were the broken remnants of the platform that had carried me. The wooden planks were being roughly tossed about as though an unseen figure was poking through them. I barely noticed, staggering with single-minded focus toward the shining beacon of liquid I had spotted.

It was coming from a *tree*. Though none of the surrounding plants showed even a drop of dew, this tree was so soaked with moisture that the dark wood had grown spongy orange moss covering it in thick patches. Large ivory blossoms and broad cup-shaped leaves curled toward the sky, perfectly positioned to capture rain and all brimming with water.

I did not hesitate. Weeping in gratitude, I whispered the name of my Lord and drank my fill. The water was deliciously cool, sweet and *restorative*, racing through my body with the ease and happy delight wine had once done. Indeed, the relief was so immediate that it made me dizzy. I reached out to steady myself against the tree trunk, inhaling deeply and closing my eyes.

When I opened them again, the world had changed.

It was as though the sun had broken through the clouds, though of course it had not—the sky was already clear. All the vibrant colors were even more vivid, and yet now they didn't seem so strange. It felt like they fit, like *I* fit, as though I'd previously been witnessing the island through the wrong eyes.

"Lack of water has made you a deranged poet," I muttered, drinking from a second leaf. I plucked up a third and turned back toward the beach. It really would be foolish not to salvage what I could of the broken platform before the tide went . . .

I froze. Rooting through the wooden planks was a purple cowlike creature. I say cow*like* because it was twice the size of a cow, covered in cheerful yellow spots, and had spiny, webbed fins protruding from its humped back and broad sides. And the mysterious beach cow was not the only oddity—oh, no. The bright blue sea stars I had spotted earlier were now . . . *marching*? They cartwheeled across the sand in neat lines, shrieking as they raised minuscule spears of driftwood at a seagull in their midst—no, not a seagull. What I had earlier thought was merely an odd-colored gull was now a flying lizard, squawking and diving at the warring starfish.

I rubbed my eyes, but the bizarre scene did not change. Was I dreaming? Hallucinating? Dead?

"*Waqwaq!*"

I jumped at the cry coming from somewhere deep in the jungle. It sounded like a child's hiccupping sob and was followed by a loud thud, as though something heavy had fallen to the earth.

A bead of cold sweat—or possibly blood, considering my state—rolled down my spine. The sea cow was still rummaging through the wreckage as though searching for treats. It let out a doleful moo and glanced up, gazing at me morosely. The water lapping around its feet had turned choppy and opaque, a pink, jellyfish-like film floating on the surface.

I was still staring at the sea cow when the water attacked it.

The pink film surged upward, teeth and claws erupting from the surf to rip into the sea cow. The beast screamed, buckling to its knees as blood and skin went flying. In seconds, the creature was nothing but guts and bits of bone, the watery pink film still hanging in the air. It shifted, turning in my direction . . .

The floating jellyfish mooed, exactly like the creature it had turned to bloody mist.

I fled.

Heedless of whatever was waqwaq-ing in the jungle, I bolted into its depths, desperate to put distance between myself and the horror on the beach. I ran *fast*, faster than I ever had before, faster than I should have been capable, the forest floor zipping beneath my feet. Branches and vines lashed at my face. I swung out an arm to knock one away, sending a sapling flying.

The jungle was so dense that in moments, every sign of the beach was gone. The sky as well, obscured by a leafy green canopy. I stumbled into a dark glen and clutched my thighs, fighting for breath.

"*Waqwaq!*"

"Ahhh!" Recalling I had a weapon, I grabbed my khanjar and dropped into a fighting stance.

But there was no one there. A massive tree towered over me, its distant branches melting into an emerald gloom so dark it looked like the night sky, its fruit twinkling as if they were stars. The tree was taller than any I had ever seen. Taller than the mightiest minaret, taller than the mysterious pyramids outside Cairo. Its enormous trunk would have taken a hundred men to encircle, a single one of its broad leaves providing cover for a human house.

Its size and magnificence were not what drew the eye and held it, however. What held it were the hundreds, nay *thousands* of humanoid creatures hanging from its leafy confines. They grew like blossoms, their heads tapered to sprout from unfurling buds.

"*Waqwaq!*"

No sooner had the cry come a third time than one of the tree people fell, like overripe fruit giving away to gravity's pull. I cried out as it hurtled toward the ground, a distance surely nothing could survive. The undergrowth exploded in a burst of dead leaves.

I froze, uncertain. But after some rustling, the tree person emerged unscathed. It was half my height and bald, its skin that of moss-shrouded bark. It shook itself and seemed to catch sight of me. A mouth opened in what might have been a small, surprised smile, revealing knobby teeth. It toddled forth, waving merrily.

Before I could decide whether to bolt again, the canopy broke open. A shaft of bright sunlight fell upon the newly fallen tree creature, illuminating it just in time for an enormous crimson bird to dive through and snatch up the little bark person in glittering talons.

I did not scream. I think I was too shocked to make a sound. You see one magical creature devoured by another, that is dreadful enough. Two of them in a row and one must be in a nightmare. Yes, that was right. A nightmare. I had passed out while drifting in the sea and none of this was real.

But nightmare or not, you better believe that when that bird shrieked again, I ran the fuck away.

Through the trees, leaping over broken logs spilling with maggots that sang like doves. Butterflies the size of platters and hissing winged snakes lit as though fire flushed beneath their scales. A rush of wind briefly seized me, carding through my hair with murmured sighs before flinging me into a bush with berries that burst and stung my skin. I picked myself up and ran faster. Splinters of blue and amber were visible through the trees. Another section of beach was just ahead, hopefully free of monstrous tidal creatures.

I burst out of the jungle and could have wept with gratitude. Not just a beach—a *boat* was drifting in the shallows, anchored by a golden filament. It was unlike any vessel I was familiar with, perfectly round and constructed with shimmering reeds, bound like a basket. Fine silk pillows and woven rugs draped the interior and a great sail of muslin floated like a cloud from a carved rosewood mast.

And *people*. Oh, God be praised! Two sailors reclined in the boat's shade, one leaning over the side to chat with a maiden swimming in the water. I staggered toward them.

The trio did not seem to notice. Judging from the smiles and tittering laughs, I was interrupting some sort of flirtation. All three were well-formed and uncommonly beautiful. One man might have been East African, dark-skinned and elegantly dressed in voluminous teal robes, fanning himself with the edge of his turban as he drank from a large silver seashell. The second man was the same brown as myself . . . although his exposed skin seemed to *gleam* as though gilded, and his hair, pulled into a topknot, was a fiery orange-streaked black. The maiden was even stranger. Beautiful, if pale. She moved with a willowy grace in the water, seaweed-green hair streaming around delicate shoulders.

But they were people—with a ship!—and that was all that mattered.

"Please," I implored as I stumbled forward. "Help me!"

The trio started, the maiden leaping back with a splash, the sailor whirling around, and his fellow dropping his shell cup.

My mouth fell open. They were not people.

At least not as *I* knew people. The men's eyes were bright gold and copper, their ears twisting away into points. The splashing girl had a *tail*, mirror bright and shaped like a whale's.

I dropped to my knees, which in retrospect should have hurt like hell yet didn't.

"What *are* you?" I cried in despair. "*WHERE AM I?*"

With a dolphin yelp, the mermaiden vanished beneath the glittering waves. The fire-haired man yelled after her in an incomprehensible, musical language before turning back to me, aggravation clear in his metal-toned eyes.

But if I feared being punished for interrupting the amorous activities of magical beings, I need not have worried. The sailor had no sooner sparked a flame in his hands (yes, in his very hands!) than he halted. He and his fellow's otherworldly gazes widened with fear at something beyond my shoulder. In a flash, they too were gone, their boat catching not a wave, but the very wind, sailing into the air.

"No, wait!" I begged, splashing into the shallows after the ship. "Please!"

"Amina?" Raksh's horribly familiar voice spoke up from behind me. "Is that *you*?"

Chapter 24

My supernatural spouse appeared to be thoroughly enjoying his island adventure. He'd reverted to his magical form, his skin blue and wildly striped, and the foul heart pulsing from the cord around his neck. The patterned yellow tubban he'd stolen from one of my sailors looked clean and fresh wrapped around his waist, and he was in the middle of eating a plump red bass, its blood running down his tusks.

Raksh took another bite of his fish, then cocked his head. "What are you doing here? I thought you were back on the *Mara*—"

With a bellow like an enraged elephant, I charged him.

Propelled by nothing but spite, I somehow managed to hurl my exhausted body at my traitorous husband hard enough to knock us both off our feet. I landed on his chest, straddling his waist. Though I knew it would do nothing but irritate him, a fly buzzing around his head, I punched him square in the face.

There was a solid *smack* when my fist struck his cheek. Raksh cried out in pain, and I glanced in astonishment at my knuckles.

They were covered in blue blood. *Raksh's* blood. The two of us both stared at my hand in mutual shock for a long moment.

His eyes went wide with panic. "Now, wait just a—"

I punched him again. This time his nose crunched under my fist. God, it felt wonderful. So wonderful I did it again. And then a fourth time. I had no idea what strength had blessed me, and I didn't care.

Raksh snarled and spat, trying unsuccessfully to grab my wrists. "Stop hitting me!" he cried. "What did you expect me to do? Falco was going to kill us!"

"You motherfucking traitorous son of Iblis, *I* am going to kill you!" I went for his eyes, intending to claw them out. "You abandoned us! You stole the dunij!"

"You were going to be defeated!" Raksh protested, ducking to avoid my overgrown fingernails. "Why should I have had to die as well?"

"Because maybe we wouldn't have been defeated if you stayed! What happened to you bringing me *luck*?" I moved for his throat. I was going to choke the life out of this lying, manipulative bastard once and for all.

"To be fair . . ." he wheezed out, "luck does not always work as neatly as—argh!" He gagged as I tightened my grip, repaying the favor both he and Falco had granted me earlier.

But the physical contact and fury that let me strangle Raksh gave him strength as well. My overwhelming desire for vengeance suddenly spiked and partially leached away as he consumed it. The wild rush left me unbalanced, and Raksh took advantage of my faltering to shove me away. He gasped for air, spitting and cursing.

I was already on my feet and stalking back toward him. So furious I couldn't think straight, I picked up his fish and flung it at his face. "You fucking bastard. I should have thrown you overboard the moment we found Dunya. If you didn't steal the dunij, I could have gotten some of my people away!"

"Yes. Because the oceanic leviathan who blotted out the sun wouldn't have been able to pursue two boats at once." Raksh touched his broken nose, looking offended when his claws came away bloodstained. "I told you Falco wasn't going to let her escape."

"Where is the dunij now?" I demanded.

"Gone."

"*Gone?*"

"Smashed to pieces. It broke up in the surf when I arrived. You should have invested in a better one."

I closed my eyes, counting to ten. I might be capable of tearing out his tongue now, but then I wouldn't learn anything. "Where are the *pieces*?"

"I assume they were washed out to sea." Raksh frowned in confusion "Why?"

"Because I could have tried to fix them! God almighty . . ." I paced away, pressing my hands against my head. "Where are we? Those people—" I waved in the direction the boat and its bizarre inhabitants had flown. "They didn't look human."

"Oh, those weren't humans. Those were daevas."

"What in God's name is a *daeva*?"

He held up a hand. "You don't want to know, trust me. More overdramatic creatures have never existed. And they're not even the worst ones here. Everyone likes to complain about humans, but let me tell you . . . spend a couple centuries with the inhabitants of the unseen realms, and you'll be *aching* to haunt a mortal latrine."

God save me; among Falco's ramblings around challenging the Divine, Dunya's enthusiastic translation about magical chamber pots, and whatever the fuck Raksh had just tried to explain, all I wanted to do was go back to my house with its leaking roof and never hear a whisper of the supernatural again.

"So we're stuck on an island of demons?" I asked, despondent.

"You keep calling everything a demon and one of those beings is eventually going to smite you for the offense. *Especially* the creatures who rule this place." Raksh rolled his eyes. "Bunch of bores. I should have known when I followed those birds that *this* is where they were going."

"This is madness," I muttered. "I need to return to Socotra."

"Socotra? You want to go *back* to Falco?"

"I want to go back for my crew! For Dunya! To make sure Falco doesn't commit any more atrocities! What *else* am I supposed to do?"

He pulled at one of his tusks, seeming to genuinely contemplate the question. "Well. The fish is good. And you might as well enjoy what time you have left before the island's court learns of your presence and kills you. We could have sexual intercourse," he suggested. "That's always a pleasant way to pass the time." Raksh paused, seeming to take in my haggard appearance. "You know . . . if you washed up."

"Raksh . . ." I clenched and unclenched my fists. "There is no earthly power that would convince me to have sex with you again. And definitely *not* when my crew is at the mercy of some lunatic obsessed with a God-damned magical bowl!"

Raksh spun back around. For the first time since I arrived at the island, I saw true fear in his fire-bright eyes.

"*What* magical bowl?" he demanded.

There seemed little point in keeping him in the dark. "The Moon of Saba," I explained. "That was what Falco and Dunya were truly after in the cave. It's apparently not the pearl of legend, but a wash—"

"Basin," Raksh finished. He sounded like he was going to throw up. "Please tell me Falco does not know the truth about it. Tell me that vile idiot has not managed to take possession of the Moon of Saba the week before an *eclipse*."

I blinked in surprise—I would not have thought Raksh one for astrological awareness. But if the eclipse was in a week, that meant I had been at sea a fortnight.

A fortnight. What terrible things might Falco have done to my crew in all that time? But there was no saving my friends if I didn't know what was going on, so I forced myself to return to Raksh's bizarre question.

"I have no idea if the Frank has taken possession of the Moon," I replied. "Dunya believes she's the only one who knows how to retrieve it, but Falco *has* Dunya, because you left us in such straits that she was forced to bargain that knowledge to save our lives!"

"The Moon of Saba . . ." Raksh pulled at his hair in despair, the long black strands drifting around his knees like unspun flax. "Of all damnable things!"

I threw up my hands. "Are you telling me you had no idea what they were truly after? Were you not *concerned*?"

"No!" Raksh went to rub his brow and cursed when he touched a rising bruise. "They said they were after treasure," he offered weakly. "Socotra is lousy with it. But the *Moon of Saba* . . ." He groaned and then whirled on me again, accusation flashing in his eyes. "This is all your fault! You should have mentioned the Moon to me earlier. We could have let Dunya die with her knowledge!"

"Letting Dunya die with her knowledge was never an option. And my God . . . what about this damn bowl has all of you so worked up?" I asked, thinking back to how fervently Dunya had flung herself before the "instruction" tablets when I mentioned tossing them overboard. "I thought al-Dabaran was just some moon phase that fell in love with Bilqis!"

"*Fell in love?*" Raksh burst into vicious laughter. "Don't tell me *you* fell for that ludicrous tale? I would have thought you wiser."

If this man insulted me one more time while ignoring my questions, I was going to lose the battle against not tearing out his tongue. "It's the only story I've heard," I said through my teeth. "If you believe you know better, why don't you try *explaining* something instead of ranting at the sky?"

"Fine. You want to know the truth about the Moon of Saba?" Raksh challenged. "Then listen."

The Third Tale of the Moon of Saba

Yes, dear listener, I do apologize. For it is time to puncture the final myth about the Moon of Saba. There was no grand romance, no great star-crossed love. Al-Dabaran, the mighty, the fearsome, he who rides upon a black stallion with his snake staff striking discord and strife into the hearts of men and djinn alike . . .

Well, he was a bit of a lecher.

Now, in what defense I can muster, he apparently was truly smitten with Bilqis. She was an impressive woman! There are whispers that al-Dabaran did approach Bilqis on a beam of celestial light in hopes of seducing her, but the queen was decidedly not impressed. She rejected him.

Ah, dear sisters, I can see from the looks in your eyes that some of you know where this is going. There are certain men, even lunar aspects, who do not handle rejection with grace. So in a fit of stung male feelings, al-Dabaran decided to bewitch Bilqis's washbasin, hoping to spy upon her bathing.

It did not go according to plan.

The lusty lunar fool had no sooner manifested in the glimmering water than Bilqis trapped him. This woman had been the companion of a great prophet, a queen who ruled with djinn servants over a splendid and blessed land. Al-Dabaran thought he could sneak into *her* bathroom unawares? Hardly. He had barely caught a glimpse before he was snapped up.

Which I suppose worked out well for the queen. Bilqis kept al-Dabaran in her washbasin, drawing on his aspects when she needed them. A rival dynasty was conspiring against her? She'd set al-Dabaran on them, causing her enemies to fall into inner turmoil. People were going hungry? Then here was al-Dabaran to make the fields and terraces grow lush and fertile.

He was indeed the "jewel" in her crown. But not the way storytellers spin it.

Now, of course, what is it they say about great power? Bilqis may have been wise, but not all her descendants inherited such prudence. The Moon soon fell into chaotic hands, the stories growing convoluted. If Bilqis set down her thoughts on what to do with the Moon, we have never discovered a record in her own hand. Instead, we have half-baked tales of would-be despots trying to lay claim to the Moon and going mad when they gazed upon their reflection. Or worse—some who held their sanity long enough to use the Moon of Saba to enact great violence across the land, causing bloodshed and discord beyond even the manzil's wildest dreams.

It was pandemonium. So eventually a group of people—a family trained for this very purpose—stepped in.

They tracked down the Moon of Saba, stealing it from the smoking wreckage of a kingdom it had brought to ruin. They scried for ways to dispose of it, places to bind its power and hide it away when destroying the artifact was deemed too dangerous to attempt. A place where the boundary between the realms was narrow and porous. Where one would have to be a member of the family who knew the rituals or a suicidal fool to enter. In a cave whose innermost depths humans rarely delved on an isolated island.

There, indeed, al-Dabaran slept beneath a ceiling of stone hands, separated from his lunar kin by a veil of water, for untold centuries.

Until a violent man from a foreign land heard whispers of his potential by a desperate scholar. Until they crossed paths with a female nakhudha whose legend would dwarf them all.

But I am getting ahead of myself.

Chapter 25

I stared at Raksh for a very long time after he had finished speaking, trying to formulate a coherent response.

"You've got to be kidding me," I finally replied. "This man could manifest as a beam of celestial light, and he chose to use that power to spy on a naked woman?"

"Are you surprised?"

Honestly, no. The details might have been fantastical, but strangely I bought this lunar aspect being a pervert. Men . . . useless, the vast lot of them, celestial and mortal.

"No," I confessed. "Just disappointed." I paced across the sand, avoiding a driftwood log covered in bubbling yellow barnacles—I trusted nothing on this cursed island. "But the rest of what you're saying about people being able to control the Moon of Saba and use al-Dabaran to unleash all this violence . . . this is *true*?"

Raksh looked like he might vomit with genuine fear—if creatures such as him could vomit. "It is rare, but yes," he replied. "And with the eclipse coming, there could hardly be a worse time."

"Why? What does the eclipse have to do with any of this?"

"It has always been easier to access the lunar spirits during such events. The unseen realm is heavily influenced by celestial happenings, and an eclipse is a momentous occasion, one that can bring great calamity." Raksh touched his heart. "I can feel this one approaching like a hungry wave. Falco is an idiot, but if there was ever a time even *he* could blunder into this—" My husband abruptly dropped to the sand, his head falling into his hands. "I can't go through that again. I won't."

I exhaled. What Raksh was saying sounded ludicrous. But Falco had chased me on a beast out of legend. His magic had brutally killed the agent who'd betrayed him from across the sea. The war against God of which the Frank had spoken, the scorching of the old world to build a new—if Falco got access to even a fraction of the power Raksh was implying . . .

"Surely there is a way to stop him," I urged. "Eclipses do not last long. If we return to Socotra . . ."

Raksh didn't look up from his storm of self-pity. "We would never catch up in time. We don't even have a way off the island."

"We'll never catch up if you sit here wasting time feeling sorry for yourself! You think you are the only one affected? He has my crew! He wants to burn down my world!"

"*My crew, my world.*" Raksh glanced up and rolled his eyes. "Please, I am sure your little friends will do fine as slaves. They only have what, a couple decades left in them?"

It was everything I had not to put my dagger through whatever burnt piece of charcoal passed for his heart. "You'll forgive the impulse to save my people from a horrific fate. I know you care about none save yourself, so it's impossible to—" Then I paused, taking in Raksh's palpable despair. "Wait, you *do* care only about yourself. So why are you so upset about the possibility of Falco gaining control of al-Dabaran?"

Raksh hesitated. "It's complicated."

"How?" When he didn't respond, I kicked him in the shin, and he hissed in pain. "*How?*" I demanded again. "Asshole, it's only you and me right now. I need to know all the angles."

Raksh sniffed in disdain. "I do not see what *you* could do to solve anything, but I am technically one of them."

"One of what?"

"A being of discord."

I blinked. That both explained nothing and made perfect sense. "You are a 'being of discord'?"

"Yes."

"And that *means* . . ."

Raksh spat, clearly annoyed to be pulled from his spiral of doom. "It *means* that discord is the purpose of my existence. When al-Dabaran used to be in ascendance, it was like being drunk. But everything changed when that lunar idiot got himself trapped. Most of the time, he is asleep and I feel nothing. But when the rare human takes control of the Moon . . ." Raksh shuddered. "It is like having my soul and body ripped apart and fed to flames. We are like a power source, understand? Like oil for a lamp. So we burn. We burn and we burn and we burn. You fear your hellfire? I fear this. It is constant torment until whoever is possessing the Moon of Saba dies."

We burn and we burn and we burn. All too well I saw Asif in my mind, heard him screaming as fire consumed him. I gazed at my husband, at this demon who had known me intimately, who had known things about my desires and ambitions not even I had been willing to admit, and then utterly betrayed me.

"You once called my people prey," I reminded him coldly. "What's wrong, Raksh? Do you not like being hunted? Will you not be *well sated* on Falco's ambitions when you are devoured?"

I rarely got through to Raksh; his soul was too alien, too incomprehensibly selfish to truly hurt his feelings. But from the flash of anger in his face, it was clear my words had struck.

"And the rest of us, Amina?" he challenged. "You worship a God you call the Most Merciful? Will He be proud to hear you cheering the burning of innocents?"

I refused to flinch. "What *innocents*?"

"Not all spirits of discord are like me. *Love* causes discord, the birth of a child causes discord, the sudden discovery of some new cure for a deadly disease causes discord." Raksh glared at me. "There are those among my cousins who have far, *far* less blood on their hands than you. And not all of us merely burn when the Moon of Saba is possessed. The weakest succumb."

Everything inside me went still. Not because I was moved by his rather poetic, evocative discussion of love and newness and strife, nor hurt by the jab about my violent history. Only one word was ringing in my head.

No. He could not possibly be implying . . . "What do you mean by *cousins*?"

The question came out in a growl, and Raksh frowned, looking baffled. "What do you not understand about it? The other spirits of discord are my kin—*aye!*"

I didn't recall drawing my khanjar. Didn't recall crossing the distance between Raksh and myself. But I was suddenly there, my blade at his throat. "You have a *family*?"

His eyes were bright with shock. "Not quite in the human sense but—yes! Okay, yes!" he yelled when I pressed the dagger harder.

"And if Falco gets control of the Moon . . ." Oh, God, I could scarcely say this. "He will be able to enslave all of you? All of your kin?"

"*Yes*. Why are you being so inquisitive?" Suspicion twisted Raksh's expression. "Are *you* planning to seize control of the Moon?"

I barely heard the accusation, rocking back on my heels. The insinuation of what he was saying punctured me like a spear. All of his kin . . . did that mean *Marjana*?

My Marjana?

My sweet child, the daughter I had left safe and hidden away from all this, believing her secure with my family. Except no matter how much I hated it, we weren't her only family. She had ties—blood ties, *kin* ties—Raksh was suggesting might enslave her. Might turn her into the tool of a man who wanted to war against God. For a moment, I saw Marjana whisked from our home under a spell she didn't understand. I saw her sobbing, heard her screaming my name as she burned and burned . . .

The weakest succumb. I felt as though I'd been hurled back into the churning sea, like a brick wall had collapsed over my head.

But I was not the only one affected.

Raksh exhaled noisily, looking overwhelmed, drunk, on the emotions he must have felt coursing through my blood.

"What is this?" he whispered. Heedless of the khanjar still at his neck, he reached out to touch my cheek and the crimson line in his pupils brightened. "No . . . you do not want the Moon of Saba for yourself. It is something different. Some*one* different—"

I wrenched his hand away. "You will get me to Falco."

Raksh swayed at the abrupt severance of physical contact, like a man attempting to shake off one of Dalila's knockout gases. "I-I cannot," he said clumsily. "It is beyond me."

Wary of touching his skin with my bare hands, I thrust the khanjar harder against his throat, drawing Raksh's blood with a weapon for the first time since he had crossed my path.

"*You will get me to Falco.* We will stop him, or I swear to my Creator what you suffer during the Moon of Saba's possession is nothing compared to what I will do to you." I shoved him back, breathing hard. "We are on a magical island full of magical beasts. I watched a ship fly away like a kite! There must be a way off."

Raksh snarled. "Do you think I want to be enslaved, Amina? I know all too well the agony that awaits me if the Moon is possessed, and it's enough to make me almost wish I had been eaten by the marid instead."

"Then help me!"

"*I don't know how!*" Raksh aimed a frustrated kick at the barnacle-covered driftwood log, and the log *got up* on centipede-like feet to scramble off. "I am no hero out of your human stories; I cannot summon a ship to sail us away nor wrestle a rukh into submission. I am a spirit of discord on an island whose very court despises anything that disrupts their precious balance."

"There must be *something* we can do!" I turned his words over in my head, desperate to find a way out of this. It was bad enough the Frank had my crew and my friends; on top of that my fear for Marjana was like an arrow to my heart.

Balance. I spun around. "What sort of balance?"

My husband flapped a dismissive hand. "The supposed 'balance of power' between the elemental races. They believe in keeping magic away from humans and guarding the boundaries between our realms. The feathery bastards think interaction between the different worlds brings chaos and disorder, and there is nothing they loathe more."

I took that all in. "It doesn't sound like they would be pleased to see a human get their hands on something as magically disruptive as the Moon of Saba."

Raksh was already shaking his head. "They don't interfere. It is their strictest law. Unless it suits them, of course," he said sarcastically. "*Then* they manage to find a loophole."

"A loophole like putting *us* in a position to stop Falco?"

We stared at each other.

"That . . . is a terrible idea," Raksh marveled. "They might execute us simply for being on their island. And yet—"

"And yet what choice do we have? I'm not particularly inclined to throw my lot in with more magical creatures, but we won't make it to Socotra in a week without supernatural assistance. Surely if you explained—"

"Not me." Raksh appeared to be thinking fast. "I am an anathema to them. It would have to be you."

"*Me?*"

"Yes, you are weaker than them. They may be reluctant to murder you without cause."

It was a judgment on our current circumstances that a reluctance to murder me without cause sounded promising. "All right. How do we do that?"

"We petition the court." Raksh's gaze turned brutally appraising, and his mouth puckered as though he'd sucked on a lemon. "But not looking like you do now. They already think poorly of mortals, and you appear barely capable of standing, let alone facing the Frank."

"You'll have to forgive me," I said acidly. "I was stranded at sea for two weeks. If only I'd had my dunij." Raksh gave me a quizzical look, and I sighed. "What do you suggest?"

He drew up like he had accepted some sort of challenge. "Grant me a day, wife. We shall get you ready to impress."

Chapter 26

The first step in getting me ready to impress a court of feathery bastards apparently required having my clothes yanked off and then being dragged to a freshwater creek, where my estranged husband forcibly bathed me. I resisted at first, but soon gave in. Raksh had already seen everything, we were still technically married, and it felt heavenly to be scrubbed and massaged.

It was only when he loosened the grimy remains of my turban and began to wash my hair that I stopped him.

"You-you don't have to do that," I said, flustered at the unexpected intimacy of the act.

Raksh's exasperated huff was hot against the back of my neck, a not entirely unpleasant contrast to the cool water. "There's a sea snail living in your hair, Amina." He returned to unsnarling the knots. "I'm fairly certain I do."

God, but I hated how good his touch felt. Hated the memories it drew from where I had buried them: stolen moments in the *Marawati*'s galley and hot, languid nights on lonely stretches of beach. It was exceedingly unjust that the backstabbing motherfucker should be so skilled at this.

"I know but—" My protest died as his fingers kneaded my scalp, a sigh slipping my lips. All right. Maybe I'd let him continue. Just this once because of all the troubles he'd caused me.

After the completely platonic bathing experience during which I never contemplated ripping off his briefs and letting him *really* make things up to me, Raksh vanished for several hours. When he reappeared, it was with a bundle of astonishing garments.

"Where did you *get* these?" I asked, marveling at a hooded cloak constructed from what seemed to be porcupine quills—if that porcupine had been made of diamonds. A tunic of woven, brilliantly violet leaves was folded underneath a gossamer sea silk sarong.

"I stole them." At my wary glance, Raksh shrugged. "Don't worry. The court will almost certainly help us off Socotra or execute us themselves before the owners of these clothes track us down."

"You are a deeply unreassuring person, do you know that?" But I dressed in the filched clothing anyway.

I was not eager to delay, but Raksh seemed convinced I would present a better case if I was stronger, and so I forced myself to rest, moving only to stretch my limbs and take a walk in the cool dusk. I ate and drank as much as possible. The water was sweet and the food bizarre if nourishing—the bright orange coconuts were meaty, heavy things; the plump fish with mirrorlike scales had flesh that made me jittery; and the midnight-hued berries crackled in my mouth. Raksh made some sort of salve from a plant with wriggling, serrated fronds and applied it to my skin. In a single afternoon, my sunburns were gone, and my wounds scabbed over. Even my bad knee felt . . . well, not good as new, but as though a decade of hardship had been removed from the troublesome joint.

"I could be a miracle worker in the human world with a plant like this," I mused while we sat beside a fire that evening.

"You better make sure the court doesn't hear you speaking so. That's the exact sort of scenario they seek to avoid."

"Humans thriving due to magical means?"

"Precisely." Raksh handed over a coconut shell of mashed gourd. "Eat."

It smelled awful and tasted metallic, but I ate without complaint. After my days at sea, I would likely eat without complaint for the rest of my life. "Is there any more?"

"No. And if you keep eating at this rate, you'll starve the entire island."

I scarfed down the mash and set it aside. I suppose I *was* eating a lot, my stomach feeling like the bottomless pit of a youth undergoing the world's most severe growth spurt.

"Have you seen any of those water trees?" I asked. "The one with the white blossoms and cuplike leaves?"

"I have not, though that means little. Things tend to move around here on their own, including the plants."

Of course they did. I stretched out my legs, studying the familiar scars and fading bruises beneath the coarse black hairs. I'd always been strong, my well-muscled limbs attesting to a life of labor. But not like this. Not capable of breaking a demon's nose or accidentally knocking over a tree. This strength had not erased my physical sufferings and yet it had lessoned them. I felt like a feverish bull calf, sick and yet capable of destruction, my body feeling bizarrely unfamiliar.

"And you've never heard of such a thing? Of a plant whose water—"

"A plant whose water gives an already violent human woman the ability to be more effectively violent? No, I told you a dozen times. I don't know what has happened to you. It might have been the plant or it might have been the very act of washing up on these shores." Raksh retrieved a pair of birds roasting over the fire. "Either way, I'd think you'd be pleased. Being more effectively violent makes it more likely you'll be able to stop Falco from enslaving me. And, you know, doing bad stuff to your crew or whatever," he added without much conviction when I glared at him.

I took the birds he handed me and tore into them with my teeth. I suppose he did have a point: I would welcome nearly any development that helped me save my crew and keep Falco from making my daughter his thrall. But since I *could* now hurt Raksh . . .

"Why didn't you kill me?" I asked, finally voicing the question I'd wondered weeks ago. "Back in Socotra, when you were so determined to 'sever our bond'?"

"I do not like the sight of blood."

"Oh, fuck off. That's not even a good lie."

Raksh rolled his eyes. "*Fine*. I once tried a pact similar to your marriage contract, all right? Many, many eons ago though it was less about paper contracts and more about exchanging looms and walking around a vat of warm beer."

"It was about *what*?"

"That part isn't important," he said flippantly. "Like you and me, we were akin to spouses and the bond made me quite powerful. But I was also young and not always the most . . . attentive when it came to completing tasks. Point is, there *might* have been a brewing incident at my hands that fatally poisoned the entire village, including my spouse, and accidentally killing them nearly wiped me out. No magic for centuries." Raksh shuddered. "I had to eat *so* many hearts before I stopped feeling like a ghost of myself. It was really very troubling."

I opened and closed my mouth. "Just to be clear . . . the only reason you didn't kill me—the only reason I am currently *alive*—is because you accidentally murdered your last spouse with a batch of bad beer and it left *you* weak?"

"Yes." Raksh picked up a hairy purple melon he'd gathered from the forest, broke it in half, and slurped out the still-quivering insides. "Though I suppose it worked out in the end."

"And how's that?" I asked, feeling slightly faint.

"Because I'm glad I didn't kill you. Because as much as I hate to admit it, I still mean what I said the night we first met: your ambitions are a feast, Amina al-Sirafi, and I would enjoy nothing more than making you a legend." He twirled a lock of unbound hair around his finger like a spinner twisting thread. "It is what I was made to do, and I have not had such an opportunity for a very long time."

There was no guile in his voice. Raksh had yet to shift to his human form since we'd been here and it was unnerving to see him such as he now was: the moonlight gleaming on his tusks, the beating heart around his neck. With the waves crashing on the beach and the smell of the sea air, it suddenly did feel like the night I'd met him, the night before everything had gone wrong.

But gone wrong it had.

"So why did you *betray* me?" I asked, barely concealing the hurt in my voice. "You could have stayed at my side, we could have had those legendary adventures! You were the one to ruin it by going after Asif."

He let out a disgruntled sound. "It is more complicated than that."

"How is it *compli*—"

Raksh held up a hand to interrupt me. "Not that you will understand any of this, but if it will put the topic to rest, let us try. First, I was always going to be preying on you. That was part of the deal, a part I made clear before I set foot on your boat. I granted you luck, and in exchange, I fed on your ambition, which would have only grown as my presence made you more successful, to the benefit of us both. And though our time together was short, I did enjoy it. I would have been happy to voyage around the sea with you and your crew for decades."

"The crew you swore you had no interest in," I reminded him. "I know you ended up striking deals with all of them."

"What can I say? Your companions were more fascinating than I had imagined. But they were not *deals*. Not properly. Not like what I had with you. Not like what I was in the process of making with Asif."

"So you did go after him."

Raksh tutted. "You have it wrong. Dunya isn't the only al-Hilli who knows her family's history. Asif may not have had his spawn's scholarly urges, but he did have her ambition. And enough familiarity with the unseen to spot that I wasn't exactly the aspiring sailor I pretended to be. *He* approached *me*. Told me his parents had unreasonable expectations and that he feared the wife he barely knew would never forgive him for abandoning her and their child. So he wanted to return to them in style. Wanted to be responsible for leading you all to a life-changing score, a discovery that *mattered*, and go home to his family richer than a sultan and more admired than a saint."

Oh, Asif . . . I wish I could have denied Raksh's words, but I could so easily envision my dreamy, naïve friend speaking such. Asif had been so young, so eager to impress. "What did you say?"

"Amina, do you think you would have found me in the Maldives begging to be taken aboard a ship if I had that kind of power? I laughed at him. Said, 'Sure, I shall find you a gilded cave of kingly treasure and forgotten magical cure-alls. All it will cost is your soul.' It was a jest." Raksh shrugged. "Then he said yes."

A jest. Asif had condemned himself because of a demon's joke. If I had ever seen a starker power disparity between the human and magical realms . . .

"You could have turned him down," I snapped, unable to check my anger. "You could have told him it *was* a joke!"

Raksh shook his head. "There are some hungers I cannot deny. It's what I am. The moment he said yes sealed us both. If I regret anything, it is that I did not act with more haste in completing our pact. Doing so might have preserved his life, and even if it had not, I could have taken his soul properly when he died rather than see it be wasted." Raksh took a sip from his cup. "It was . . . a messy end."

A messy end. Is that what you call it? I remembered Asif wailing for his mother and God's forgiveness as his soul was blotted out of existence, consumed by a void I will never unsee. "So you truly have no remorse over hurting the humans you partner with?"

"I neither seek harm nor take pleasure in it. But I am a creature of ambition, and it is rarely bloodless."

"Then you are a demon."

Raksh put his cup down. "That is your word. You do not—"

"Yes, yes, so I've been told. My people don't have a word for you. But from where I'm sitting, *demon* fits well enough."

He stared at me for a long moment, his eerie eyes going black and impenetrable as a shark's. "What would you call yourself to a person who had no concept of water?"

Baffled by the question, I drew up. "What do you mean?"

"Imagine for a moment a people who have no concept of water. No understanding of liquid or rain, let alone vast oceans. How would you begin to describe your profession? How you sail? The currents you travel? The way that the ocean created an entire world of trade and transportation, stories and diasporas that made you *you*? Would you spend centuries trotting out useless comparisons? Or would you finally give up when they keep calling you a 'cow' and say, 'Yes, that works.'"

It was a strange analogy, an imperfect one, I suppose, but one that hinted at a far wider gulf between myself and the creature beside me.

"There must have been a word for you once," I countered. "A name. Something *we* called you."

"There was. In a tongue forgotten before your race built even the most primitive of rafts." Raksh suddenly sounded weary. "Leave it alone, Amina. Yours is not the mind that is going to break through in comprehension after all these centuries."

It was a conversation that in typical Raksh fashion explained nothing and left me only more aware of how different we were.

Except there *was* a bridge between us, one beloved to me and unknown to him. It had once been easier to deny Marjana's heritage, yet I now feared such avoidance had only put my daughter at risk. What else didn't I know about these so-called spirits of discord?

"Then tell me of your kin," I urged. "In our time together, you never mentioned having a family."

Raksh let out a harsh laugh. "*Family* is a human concept."

"But you called them cousins," I pressed. "Kin. And surely baby spirits of discord come from somewhere. You must have had parents or—"

"I know what you're doing." Raksh threw me a glare so suspicious it briefly stopped my heart. "You're prodding for weaknesses in case you need to trap me again. Save your breath; my kin are nothing to me."

The brusque response sent ice flooding into my veins. "Nothing to me" did not necessarily translate to "wish harm upon," but it sounded closer to that sentiment than anything that could be interpreted as beneficial to Marjana.

You are stuck with this creature as your only ally right now. No need to make things worse. I swiftly changed the topic. "Then tell me of this island court we need to petition. Do *they* have a name?"

Raksh gave me one more wary frown but answered. "It would do better to let them tell you. The less you know about the magical world in their mind, the better."

"I am literally wedded to a primordial chaos spirit with a name so old it's forgotten."

"And there is no reason the court needs to know that. Our story will be that Falco tricked us into helping him and all we want is to go back and stop him." Raksh gestured to the sloping emerald peak at the island's heart. A sheer stone plateau, like a pillar draped with lacy weeds, jutted straight up from the jungle, so tall it melted into the clouds. "They are creatures of air, so we will go to them, as high as we can."

My stomach dropped at the sight of the lethally elevated formation. Of course it had to be someplace high. "I cannot climb that."

"You won't need to. Once we catch their attention, they will come to us." Despite his confident words, Raksh showed a trace of fear. "Sleep well, wife. We have quite the adventure ahead of us."

Chapter 27

We woke early the next day and set out after dawn. I prayed fajr with more intention than usual, though I was not sure which dua to choose for "successful petition of judgmental supernatural creatures." I felt strange and slightly ridiculous garbed in the stolen magical raiment, my own ruined clothes reduced to foot wrappings, and my only weapons my khanjar and a rough spear I had carved. But I was no longer throwing up blood and limping all over the sand, so at least I had that going for me.

It was a humid day, but the air was cool in the forest, growing dryer as we ventured deeper into the island's heart. The trees were so thick here that their canopy blotted out the sky, the only light an occasional dusty shaft that pierced the gloom. The ground was soft and loamy underfoot, smelling richly of life. More than once I thought I caught a glimpse of the ivory-blossomed water tree nestled amongst the platter-sized poppies and fanged ferns, but every time I turned to look, it was gone.

Unlike my first flight through the jungle, it was astonishingly quiet. A great cacophony of birdsong had originally greeted us but quickly petered out to silence; a troupe of flying foxes with multiple tails that had been trilling about and grooming their little ones dashed away. I felt the weight of eyes, caught their occasional gleam from the dark undergrowth and gnarled branches, and yet nothing approached, the air heavy with fraught tension, like the drawn-out moments before an execution.

"Where is everything?" I asked as I clambered over a moss-encrusted boulder. The ground had started to slope upward.

"Probably hiding. We do not belong here, and anything that does knows well what happens when the court senses strangers." Raksh slashed through a thick vine with his claws. "Do not fret. I'm certain it will not be long before . . ."

He trailed off as his breath clouded the air. A cold wind rushed over my shoulder, setting my skin to gooseflesh. Lines of frost were spiraling across the emerald ferns surrounding us, glazing them as their swaying in the breeze abruptly froze.

"Is it them?" I whispered, pulling up my quilled hood to cover my hair. The diamond spines rustled in the wind, and a thin layer of ice raced to drape over the mossy rocks, silvering the damp black tree trunks as though everything were covered in a fine piece of sheer muslin.

"Yes." Raksh gulped. "Honored ones!" he called, sounding more polite than I thought him capable. "Solitude and harmony upon you. We seek—"

But Raksh did not get to say what we sought. Because he had no sooner attempted to explain than the very air seized us.

It whipped from the trees, from the ground, from the suddenly silver-gray sky, howling and swirling into a vortex that yanked me off my feet and spun me around as if it were a potter's wheel. Blinded by the swirling ice, dirt, and debris from the forest floor, I could barely see Raksh, though his wail of outrage seemed to indicate that he'd been trapped as well. There was movement—the vortex seeming to race through the jungle. I caught glimpses of distant trees and a stony plain. Blue fragments of sea and a ground that was way, *way* too far below my feet.

And then it was over. The funnel cloud vanished in an explosion of dead leaves and twigs, dumping me onto a cold stone floor. I heard angry squawking and could have sworn I glimpsed a blurry lime-green creature getting chased away, but because I am cursed, I had landed on my bad knee and the jolt of pain was distracting. I swore profusely, rolling into the fetal position only to crash into Raksh, who had landed facedown in a pool of mist.

"Ow!" He pushed me away with a groan. "Do you *mind*?"

Still dizzy, I moved to sit, trying hard not to throw up. The floor beneath me, rock hard when I landed, abruptly softened and shifted, making me feel as though I sat upon a suspended net. I looked around, trying to get my bearings straight with little luck. The jungle was gone, replaced by icy mists that drifted about us, delicate white flakes falling lightly upon my skin.

Snow, I realized, staring at the melting slivers in my palms. I had seen snow only once in my life, on a childhood trip through the mountains of Jabal Shams. And yet this snow didn't seem right. It melted without leaving any water behind, and the air was too dry, too . . . animated to be natural. The wind blew from multiple shifting directions as though it were dancing, sending jewel-hued leaves and snowflakes cartwheeling. Though the misty chamber was vast, enormous branches towered overhead, gleaming ebony and mahogany, as though we had fallen into the heart of some tree out of a creation tale.

I glanced up, snow tickling my eyelashes, to see movement. Shadowy lithe bodies climbing through the tangled branches and soaring through the air. It was like gazing at the night sky, more stars appearing the longer you looked. The creatures did not appear much larger than me, occasionally flashing by with a glimmer of scaled skin and dazzling wings.

"Raksh," I whispered. "Are those—"

A chittering from high above interrupted my question, a hair-raising noise that sounded like a cross between a swarm of buzzing locusts and a flock of squawking birds. The creatures were landing, perching and hopping along the branches as though settling in for a better view. There were easily hundreds flittering about, staring down at us with glittering pale eyes. Between the weight of their gazes and a clearer view of just how high the canopy extended, I felt like an insect about to be devoured.

"This is the court you mentioned?" I asked under my breath as Raksh and I slowly rose to our feet. The creatures all appeared capable of flight but were otherwise diverse. Some had the wings and glittering proboscises of enormous dragonflies, while others were mostly parrot save bright blue-and-yellow humanoid faces.

"It is." Raksh made a small choking noise. "May I recommend not looking at the floor?"

I immediately peeked down to discover that there *was* no floor, not truly. There was nothing but diaphanous fog and the extremely distant ground, and I no sooner realized this than the illusion weakened. Whatever was beneath my feet grew spongy and I sank to my ankles with an alarmed cry.

"Eyes up *here*," a new, very weary voice announced in Arabic crisper than a Mecca-trained cleric's. "Name?"

I glanced wildly up. One of the bird people had dropped to perch on a cinnamon-hued branch just above my head. Though she had some human features, she reminded me instantly of a palm dove; her round head was rosy white and a spotted plumage of feathers circled her neck. Large, rather unsympathetic, pupilless eyes sat on the sides of her face, framing a beak-like nose.

"Wh-what?" I stammered.

She let out a sigh, if bird people could sigh. I suppose why not . . . they already spoke Arabic. "*Your name*. What is it?" She shook out a pair of blue-gray winged arms and picked up a scroll and writing stylus. "We need it for our records."

They had records? "I . . . Amina," I managed.

"Birthplace and elemental composition?"

What? "I was born in Sur, but—"

"She is human," Raksh cut in. "*Obviously*."

"Your testimony has been deemed unnecessary," the bird woman said curtly. "No peri has time for a creature such as yourself."

A peri? Is that what they were? I took in their avian forms again, the sight before me clashing with fables I'd heard of gentle winged maidens of uncommon beauty. "He speaks truly," I said quickly. "I am human."

The peri tilted her head in doubt. "Are you certain? I did not think humans came in your height. Are there by any chance giants in your heritage? Nephilim maybe?"

By God, even here my size was being judged? And what the fuck was a Nephilim? "I'm certain," I said acidly.

She made a notation. "Excellent. Had you a trace of either, your case might have been complicated. As you are entirely human, it is much more straightforward: Humans are not permitted here. Nor are they allowed to leave alive. Your method of removal will be—"

"Wait!" I pleaded. "Before you . . . remove me, I beg that you listen. My companion spoke of you as a noble, honorable race tasked with keeping balance between the magical world and mine. Should that be your true intent, trust you will want to hear what I say."

"She is allowed to bring a petition, is she not?" Raksh challenged, clearly not caring he'd been told to shut up. "I know enough of your arcane rules that you cannot simply remove yourselves of a lesser being without hearing her case."

The peri exhaled noisily as though we were keeping her from more pressing matters. "Go on, then."

I wasted no time. "I came to your island neither of my own free will nor with ill intent toward your people. My companion and I were kidnapped and forced into the service of another human, a vicious criminal who hopes to gain access to magic and bring destruction to my people. To *all* people. He speaks of challenging God the Almighty!"

The peri did not look impressed. "A great number of humans have had similar delusions. He will fail as the rest have."

"But not many of those humans succeeded in subduing a marid," Raksh pressed. "This man bound one with blood magic."

"The Creator cannot be challenged by a mortal," the peri replied bluntly. "And whatever this human does in the earthly realm does not concern us. We do not interfere."

"And if he uses *unearthly* means?" I asked. "He is in the process of obtaining the Moon of Saba. Surely the possession of a powerful lunar aspect is closer to your realm of worries."

The peri frowned in confusion. "The Moon of Saba?" She glanced at her fellows arrayed above. "Why does that sound familiar?"

A parrot-red peri with glittering wasp eyes dropped to the branch beside her. "Because the Moon of Saba is one of our listed Transgressions. It can be used to bestow kingship."

"No," a third peri squawked from the shadows. "You speak of the Golden Fleece. The Moon of Saba is the Transgression that takes form as a pearl. Humans lick it to heal maladies."

"Do not be a fool," a fourth peri corrected. "Mortals are savages. They do not eat pearls, they wear them. *You* are describing the Apple of Samarkand."

"You are *all* wrong," Raksh said, exasperated. "The Moon of Saba is the basin in which Bilqis trapped the lunar spirit al-Dabaran. When the moon is in his manzil or during other lunar deviations—like, say, the eclipse due to occur *next week*—anyone who gazes upon their reflection in the basin's water can gain control of all the aspects of discord. Sound familiar?"

The two peris on the branch above my head were flipping through a stack of pearlescent scrolls that had appeared out of nowhere, shimmered like rainbows, and vanished as soon as they were set aside.

"Ah, yes, here it is," the dove peri said. "The Moon of Saba. It is a newer Transgression, one classified as low to insignificant risk."

"*Low to insignificant risk?*" I repeated in disbelief.

"Indeed." The peri scanned the scroll, her thin lips pursed. "The Moon of Saba does have the capacity to provoke a great amount of turmoil among mortals, but it says here the bloodshed typically falls into the standard parameters of human violence."

"*Oh.*" The other peri chittered in excitement. "If this human they fear is truly so volatile, does it not stand to reason his chaos might be enough to finally break the bond between al-Dabaran and the vessel trapping him? That would be ideal."

"We can only hope," the other peri said gravely. "It would restore things to their natural order."

I gasped. "And if scores of innocents are killed 'restoring things to their natural order'?"

"As I said, we believe the violence would be within the standard parameters." The peri finally glanced up from her scrolls to peer down at me. "Your request for our interference is denied."

My mouth fell open in shock. "So that's it?"

"No, of course not," she said with officious dispassion. "There is still the question of your removal. *Yours*"—she cut her eyes at Raksh—"is more complicated, but the human's remains a straightforward case. As I said, mortals are neither permitted to know about, dwell upon, or leave this island alive. Therefore . . ." She lifted a taloned hand.

The floor beneath me vanished.

Chapter 28

It happened so fast I didn't even have time to scream. One moment I was arguing to a bunch of stuck-up winged people that my species had the right not to be murdered, the next moment the floor beneath me opened and I was plummeting to my death.

I tumbled wildly through the air. The ground was so far away I could see the entire island: the misty stone mountains and verdant jungle surrounded by white sand and teal ocean. I was higher than a flock of birds, higher than a human had any right being. And it would have been extraordinary and beautiful had I, you might recall, not been falling to my very imminent and no doubt painful death. I did scream now, quite loudly.

There was a green blur in the corner of my eye and something large slammed into me.

No, not slammed into me—*caught* me. For a moment, we were both falling, feathered arms holding me tight. Then I was briefly tossed in the air before being seized again, this time by a pair of powerful taloned feet.

"Hold on!" the creature—another peri—cried.

The peri flew me back to an enormous tree, dropping me on a terrace of woven branches and vines heavy with—of all things—eggplant. I immediately went for my knife, spinning on the creature when he landed beside me.

"Oh!" The peri hopped back, ruffling his wings. "Forgive me! I assumed you did not wish to be falling to your death."

"Of course I did not wish to be falling to my death!" I shouted, my entire body shaking.

The peri gave me a quizzical look. He was as strange as the rest, a mix of bird and insect. His wings were a dazzling lime green, more striking when compared with the gray hue of his pale skin and oddly colorless eyes. Silver scales traced over a ridged, hairless scalp, feathers growing around his long, tapered ears like a crest.

"Then why are you waving a weapon at me?" He frowned. "Are you . . . are you offering it to me? I require no recompense, though I would not want to offend human custom."

"I'm waving it at you because a bunch of your feathered cousins just tried to murder me! Oh, sorry—*remove* me." Perhaps lumping the peri who had just saved my life in with the ones who had tried to end it wasn't fair, but I was too worked up to be polite.

"Remove you?" he repeated, sounding horrified. "It was the court that did this? Why?"

I shivered, barely hearing the question as the recognition of just how close I'd come to death—*again*—washed over me. By God, I wanted to go home. I wanted this to be nothing more than an awful nightmare. My teeth were chattering so violently it hurt, and I squeezed my eyes shut, trying to breathe.

"Child, why don't you sit?" The peri laid a cool hand on my wrist, and I jumped at his touch. "You have had a great shock."

I opened my eyes, realizing as I did so that the peri had stopped me from pacing off the terrace. "Yes," I mumbled. "Sitting sounds good."

The peri guided me to a moss-covered perch and I collapsed, knocking down half the vines with a clumsy kick of my foot.

"Do you take tea?" he asked politely, ignoring the falling leaves.

"Do I take *what*?"

"Tea?"

I blinked. "What is tea?"

The peri wrinkled a beak-like nose. "Ah, I forget how far I am from home sometimes. Tea is a drink, a wondrous one. It will undoubtedly make its way to this part of the world in another century or two, but I shall give you an early taste."

He snapped his fingers, and a slender copper ewer and two glass cups appeared from thin air. The peri poured a steaming liquid rich with the aroma of peppercorns, mace, and some sort of grassy substance into the cups, turning the glass globes a pale golden green. He gently untangled one of my hands from where it had been wrapped around my knees as I rocked back and forth in distress, placing the warm cup in my palm.

Whatever tea was smelled delicious, but I made no move to drink. "None of this can be real," I whispered, half marveling, half despairing.

"I feel that way myself sometimes," the peri said conversationally, taking a sip from his cup. "Now. Would you tell me what led to you getting tossed into the sky?"

I grew instantly more guarded. "Why?"

"Mayhap I can help you further."

My previous experience with peris did not leave me optimistic, but I took a chance. "You could fly me away from here. There's this island . . . Socotra. Really lovely place."

But his eyes dimmed. "I fear I cannot. If I directly counteracted their decision to remove you, we would both be dead before we were out of sight."

"They would kill you? Just for helping me leave?" Regardless of the peris' bizarre rules, that seemed a ridiculous overreaction. "But *why*? Why are your people so worked up about the briefest human contact?"

He sighed. "My people . . . they mean well. But we have witnessed terrible violence when the realms get entangled with each other: great wars between the elemental races and destruction across all our worlds. Their response has been to restore balance, believing that if everyone and everything is kept in their place—*firmly* in their place and away from each other—it will bring peace and pleasure to the Maker."

Wars between elemental races and destruction across multiple worlds? I had no idea what any of that meant; indeed, I felt so hopelessly human and small that I scarcely knew what to question first.

The part that involves you, idiot. "And you . . . do not believe this?" I asked, inferring from his tone. "That these realms—the human and magical worlds—should stay separate?"

"If believing that means the death of an innocent, absolutely not." The peri's expression grew fierce as a Friday preacher's. "I believe our Maker prioritizes justice and the preservation of lives before order. If that puts me at odds with my people, so be it."

I stared at him, wishing I could trust that earnest reply, then took a sip of the tea—it was indeed delicious. "Who are you?"

"I am called Khayzur. And you?"

God, please do not let this be a mistake. "Amina al-Sirafi."

Khayzur bobbed his head in a birdlike bow. "The Maker's justice upon you, Amina al-Sirafi. Now . . . would you tell me what happened?"

I took a deep breath, but figuring I had little left to lose, I did just that, telling Khayzur what I knew of Falco and the Moon of Saba. What had led to Raksh and me being shipwrecked on the island and our hopes the peri court would return us to Socotra so we could prevent Falco's taking possession of al-Dabaran before the lunar eclipse.

The peri tutted when I finished speaking. "The Transgressions are a sensitive subject, but in my opinion, your request was reasonable."

"What are they?" I asked. "These Transgressions?"

"Objects that bridge the realms, mostly between that of the human world and various magical ones. Your people are the cleverest when it comes to devising such talismans—and the riskiest. Other races were granted magic because they did not have human ingenuity, but their power is not meant to be wielded by human hands."

I tried to take that all in. "And the Moon of Saba is one of these talismans, these Transgressions?"

"I had not heard of a Moon of Saba previously, but it sounds like it."

"How could you *not* have heard of it?" I asked, disbelieving. "It sounds incredibly powerful!"

Khayzur let out a disillusioned warble. "Because there are now more Transgressions than *any* one person could remember: enslaved souls in rings and more bound for eternal torment on distant mountains; capes of invisibility and goblets that transform any liquid into poison; portal keys and flying cauldrons. It's all really quite impressive. And intimidating when you think upon their possibility of chaos."

My mind was spinning. "*How?* How were humans able to create such things?"

"The barriers between our worlds were once more permeable," Khayzur explained, sounding almost nostalgic. "There was more interaction between our peoples, between all the elemental races. Though it is admittedly the rare human capable of creating such a talisman—usually because they are either uncommonly saintly or uncommonly evil. As you can imagine, either way such Transgressions are order-destroying abominations in the eyes of most peris."

"Then why wouldn't the peri court return me to Socotra? I could help your people get *rid* of a Transgression!"

"Because we are having this conversation." When I frowned in confusion, Khayzur clarified, "Because you can *see* me, Amina al-Sirafi. Because you can hear me and have a chat with a being of air over a cup of tea. You have eaten and drunk of this island, have you not?"

I hesitated, but Khayzur had spoken knowingly, and I saw little benefit in lying to the one peri who had shown me sympathy. "I have."

"Then you are changed. You likely began that transformation the moment you stepped on these shores. In ways that might not be clear until you leave. In ways that cannot be undone. You are now in your own way . . ."

"A Transgression," I finished when Khayzur trailed off, clearly reluctant to say the word I just realized condemned me.

His expression was somber. "Yes."

Oh. I set down my tea with trembling fingers and rose to my feet, needing to move, needing to make space for all that to settle. Khayzur said nothing, but I could feel the weight of his gaze as I crossed to the edge of the terrace. The island's impossible sky and silver sun beat down upon me, a pair of long-necked geese with spiny protrusions soaring past. One of the eggplants nearest my elbow wiggled, giving off a citrusy aroma, as I gazed down upon a realm I should not have been able to see.

Only a few months ago, I had stood in my fishing boat, fending off a bat-winged demon and haranguing the young men from Aden about the dangers of the magical world. Now I was trapped on an island of air elementals, reunited with the supernatural spouse I'd tried to kill, and having tea with a man who had wings for arms while my crew was being held prisoner by a sorcerer. That was all terrible enough.

But what Khayzur was saying went deeper. I *myself* had been transformed. Changed by magic—that slippery, despised thing in my heart—in ways that could not be undone. In ways that might not become clear until all this was over, if I even survived.

What did that *make* me?

The word "Transgression" didn't inspire hope. Had I somehow stained my soul? Violated a law of Creation I hadn't known existed? Being able to punch Raksh in the face was indeed agreeable, and my new strength might aid me in fighting Falco. And yet . . .

You are as God made you. You are the nakhudha. You are a mother and a friend. And right now your people need you to stop fretting and deal with this. Save them—with any blessing you are granted.

A bit more determined if not entirely at peace, I turned back to Khayzur. "How do I convince the court to let me go?"

"Do you have a plan for defeating the human named Falco?"

No. "I am . . . letting some options brew in my mind."

"Then I may be able to convince them that the opportunity to get rid of the Moon of Saba is worth letting a lesser Transgression, namely you, slip away. I was already preparing to depart; carrying you along can hardly be called interfering." He nodded at my cup. "Would you like some more tea?"

I diplomatically demurred; I was not consuming another damn thing on this island. "No, but thank you . . . and thank you for saving my life earlier," I added with an embarrassed flush. "I apologize for the knife."

"You need not apologize." Khayzur snapped his fingers and the tea supplies disappeared. "My only hope is that I can do so again."

He led me through an opening in the branches, along snaking tunnels of gleaming hardwood and beneath canopies of icy clouds. The air was fresher than the sweetest breeze, the wind whistling like music and darting about my waist as though it were an eager, happy pet. I tried to find some wonder in it, reminding myself to appreciate God's marvels, even if my heart was heavy with apprehension.

Raksh's arguing voice could be heard long before we reached the court.

"You have no right to decide anything for me!" he roared as we entered the chamber. My husband was leaping around like a frantic gazelle, bouncing from misty patch to misty patch as they dissolved beneath his feet, and angry peris squawked and dived overhead. "Your concept of order is a *lie*! I was created to be chaos! To disrupt and inspire and spin and weave such legends you could never—"

Khayzur loudly cleared his throat.

A thousand pairs of eyes turned to regard us.

"Oh, for fuck's sake." It was the dove peri who said that. All right, she did not say those exact words, but trust that whatever came warbling out of her mouth at the sight of Khayzur and me was the peri equivalent—I can recognize such a tone in any language. "Khayzur," she continued in Arabic (Why? How? One of the many mysteries I've yet to unravel).

"I believe we made clear you were no longer welcome. Why in the Creator's Judgment are you not only *still* here but in the company of a human meant to be removed?"

Holding my arm in a courtly manner, though probably more to catch me should the floor vanish again, Khayzur strolled before the assembled peris. "I would think you glad for my tardiness. Should I not have delayed, I wouldn't have been able to stop such a grave crime! Really, murdering an innocent human in front of your own court? Before hundreds of witnesses?"

"It was not murder," the dove peri snapped. "The magic that governs our realm can be unpredictable, as is the floor. If she had not been here, she would not have fallen."

The audacity, truly. "You dragged me here in a cyclone!" I accused.

The dove peri ignored me, glaring at Khayzur with her beady eyes. "This mortal's fate is *not* your concern, Khayzur." The dispassion she had shown me earlier was gone, replaced by true fury. "You should have never interfered by saving her in the first place!"

The rest of the winged creatures grew silent, uncertain tension filling the air.

Khayzur was just as firm. "Is it interfering if the Maker has placed us where we're needed? Are we not told to look for signs and act accordingly?" When the dove peri clacked her beak like she wanted to bite his head off, he swiftly clarified. "You have made your opinions on our differing beliefs clear. I will not press my 'radicalism' in your court any further. But this is no grand theological debate, it's a single human life. Let me take Amina to Socotra on my way home. I will not interfere beyond that, I swear."

The dove peri was already squawking her disagreement. "It is too late. The human has dwelled here long enough for the island's magic to change her. She is a Transgression herself."

"But not of her own accord!" Khayzur persisted. "A few days in our realm aren't enough to transform her into a threat anywhere *near* that presented by a human criminal obtaining control of the Moon of Saba. She may be just the person to destroy it! We've been fretting about these Transgressions for centuries. Why not allow Amina to deal with one?"

"*Deal* with it? Is that what you think she would do, a human who's attracted a spirit of discord to her side? She is just as likely to take the Moon of Saba for herself!"

"I will not," I said resolutely. "I swear upon God, would place my hand on the Holy Quran. Indeed, I promise to destroy it before Khayzur's eyes if that would put your worries at ease."

My offer was met with a shuffling of taloned feet, the audience of peris appearing disquieted.

The peri elder pursed her thin lips. "There is no precedent. It would be one thing if the human used her new abilities only to dispose of the Moon of Saba, but we cannot undo what has been done to her."

I was weary of being spoken over. "Then I shall *retire*. Believe me, if I manage to defeat Falco and hand over this cursed chamber pot, I would be content to spend the rest of my days fishing and puttering at home with my family." I even meant it. Yes, I had hungered for adventure, for riches, but such desires had led me utterly astray and risked everyone I loved. All I wanted to do was save my crew, rescue Dunya, absolutely *murder* Falco, and return to Marjana.

The dove peri looked at me without emotion. "We do not work on trust."

Her condemnation hung in the air for a long moment—until Raksh let out the most obnoxious, world-exhausted sigh I had ever heard.

"My God . . ." he complained, his voice dripping with contempt. "Do you hear yourselves? Is it not *obvious* the solution to your petty haranguing?"

We all turned to look at him.

I was *immediately* suspicious. There was an expression of pure boredom on Raksh's face—but not in his eyes. No, his eyes had brightened, the fire in their depths mesmerizing. Or at least it would have been mesmerizing had I not known exactly what that look meant.

That was the look Raksh got when scenting ambition.

But the peris must not have had much experience with beings like him, for they didn't seem to notice. "Speak clearly, fiend," the dove peri sniffed instead.

"Send the human after *more* of them," Raksh urged. "You have been given a tool. Why wouldn't you use it to your fullest advantage?"

"Excuse me," I cut in, affronted. "A *tool*?"

Raksh ignored my protest, strolling closer to the peris. "You wish to hunt down and destroy Transgressions? Then this woman was qualified to help you even before your island wrought these so-called transformations upon her. She is one of the most talented sea captains in her world and has a crew equally talented at sussing out treasures and stealing them away. She is *exactly* the human to assist you. But why stop at the Moon of Saba when you could send her after more?"

Khayzur appeared to consider Raksh's suggestion, a fleeting glimpse of hope in his colorless eyes. "That is an idea." But then he glanced at me and whatever he saw in my face must have struck him. "Though what it would imply for Amina . . ."

Yes, what would it imply for Amina? I glared at Raksh. "You suggest because I passed two nights on their island, I spend the rest of my life in service to creatures who tried to kill me?"

Raksh shrugged. "Can you see another solution?"

I had offered another solution! I destroy the Moon of Saba and we'd be even. And if Raksh hadn't opened his damn mouth, I might have continued trying to convince the dove peri of the validity of my word.

But no, it was at *Raksh's* proposal that several other peris joined the dove one. They huddled together in a feathery cluster, chirping in fervent whispers. Khayzur was watching me with a mixture of worry and uncertainty. Raksh was examining a fingernail like this was barely of interest to him.

I swayed on my feet. This was all happening too fast. I was desperate enough to do almost anything to stop Falco, but what sort of fate was I dooming myself to? I had accidentally gotten involved with the supernatural once, the drunken wedding that tied me to Raksh and cost Asif his soul. Now I was to sign my life over to a bunch of squabbling bird-people who referred to mass human slaughter as within acceptable parameters of violence? Would I even be allowed to see my family again?

The dove peri and her cronies abruptly unhuddled. "We have spoken amongst ourselves. The human will be permitted to leave for a lifetime of—"

"No," I said shakily.

Raksh whirled on me. "Have you lost your mind?" he hissed. "This is how we stop Falco. You promised to save me!"

I had certainly *not* promised the latter, but nevertheless. "I will not enslave myself to these creatures," I said, trying to sound more confident than I felt. "They desire my service? Then our deal will be on my terms."

The dove peri let out a chittering, condescending sound. "This is no *deal*. We are simply discussing the various possibilities that you yourself may choose of your own free will—"

"Yes, my free will not to be dropped to my death," I said bitterly. "Some choice."

Khayzur stepped in. "What are your conditions, Amina?"

I glared at the court, eyeing not only the dove peri but the others watching and flying around. "First, I will not belong to your people. I will search for these talismans, Transgressions, whatever you call them, but I will do so at my pace and in my fashion. When I am not working, my life is my own."

"As long as you're not using magical gifts to wreak chaos, we hardly care what mortal affairs you get up to," the dove peri said snobbishly. "But how are we to judge whether you are dedicating an appropriate amount of time to the hunt?"

I took a deep breath, choosing my next words carefully. "Because I will have an incentive. I don't know how long your people live, but I am not young," I warned. "And I won't spend my final years hunting magic on the other side of the world from my family. I will retrieve three items for you. Then you let me retire in peace."

There was a vanished hint of displeasure in Raksh's carefully composed face, there and gone in the blink of an eye. Khayzur nodded as though what I said was reasonable—as if *any* of this was reasonable—giving my arm a reassuring pat as the other peris huddled together again.

The dove one glanced up from their discussion. "Three hundred."

"Not in the realm of possibility. Three."

"One hundred."

Negotiating numbers was apparently not a common experience. "Four."

She glowered. "*Five*. No less."

Five. The number settled in my soul, snares winding around my ankles. "Five items," I agreed. "Of which the Moon of Saba is the first. Then you leave me in peace, no matter how changed I may be."

The dove peri nodded. "You will be permitted to leave this island and dwell in the mortal world on the condition you live as discreetly as possible with your gifts and retrieve five Transgressions of our choosing. You will not keep or attempt to use them in any way. Once you have them, they are to be given to us for disposal immediately."

There had to be at least a dozen loopholes in those words, a hundred ways this could all go terribly wrong. And yet what choice did I have?

My family, my crew. I swallowed hard, praying I wasn't making a terrible decision. "Understood."

The dove peri was still looking at me, her feathers bristling as the wasp peri leaned close to whisper in her ear. She cooed low in her throat in what sounded more like a growl than birdsong. "Then in light of our conversation, should you desire to accompany Khayzur when he leaves, we will not stop you. He will be your . . . *liaison* moving forth."

"Excellent." Khayzur took my arm more firmly and stepped back. "Then we shall not delay your court any—"

"*We are not finished.*" The dove peri's beady gaze narrowed on my savior. "Khayzur, you have a predilection to share your misunderstandings about our people's role in ways that endanger social harmony and lead soft-minded peris astray. You have been warned by more than one court, seemingly to little avail."

His fingers trembled ever so slightly on my arm, but Khayzur stared calmly at the assembly, replying, "As I believe our Maker wishes for justice over order, I also believe our people are better for having different opinions discussed freely."

"We disagree," the other peri said loftily. "And have decided to formally charge you with interfering."

He instantly stiffened. "Is that truly necessary?"

"It seems to be." Her voice grew harsh, her gaze merciless. "Take care, Khayzur. It would be a great pity if your affection for mortals got you killed one day."

She didn't sound like it would be a great pity, but Khayzur bowed his head. Before I could open my mouth and interject with something rude, he looped his other arm through Raksh's and dragged us out.

"We go," he whispered under his breath. "Before they change their minds."

"Wait . . . what just happened?" I demanded. "What did they do to you?"

"It matters not."

"It certainly seemed to!"

Khayzur turned to face me. "It is not always easy to do the right thing, Amina al-Sirafi. More often than not, it is a lonely, thankless ordeal. That does not mean it is not worth doing."

Raksh scoffed. "You, of all people, would find a peri political radical, Amina."

"A peri political radical who just helped save your worthless life," I shot back as Khayzur hustled us out of the enormous tree. "You and I, *husband*, are going to have a long talk about what happened back there after all this is over."

He rolled his eyes. "The slim chance of surviving Falco is worth some haranguing from you."

Ah, yes; we were at that part now, weren't we? Forget Raksh attempting to sell me out to the peri court, the "not-deal" I'd struck was moot if we didn't stop Falco in the first place.

But despite what I'd told Khayzur, I had very little idea of how to accomplish that. My crew was being held prisoner and I had no allies on Socotra. I didn't even *know* anyone on Socotra save the few remaining villagers Falco had tortured. And they were already gone, on their way to shelter with the fearsome pirate clans they claimed owed them protection.

Khayzur led us out to a flat stretch of branch as I mulled over my options—which weren't many. No matter what strengths this island had blessed me with, I could not take on Falco, his supernaturally empowered men, *and* the marid alone. Raksh was a terrible fighter and could barely be trusted. Where did that leave me? Did I have any hope of secretly freeing my most capable fighters and happening upon a convenient weapons cache we could use to defeat our enemies?

The memory of Dalila in shackles played across my mind. No, I didn't think so. Falco no doubt kept them bound and well guarded. If I had a single advantage, it was that he also likely believed me dead. Falco wouldn't be expecting me, much less a magically blessed version of me. I tapped my fingers against the leopard's head on my khanjar's hilt in contemplation. So how else could I surprise him?

But the unconscious movement offered its own rude reminder of how thoroughly I'd already been beaten: thrown off my ship with this very dagger plunged into my shoulder, Falco's humiliating words ringing in my ears.

They used to call your grandfather "the Sea Leopard," yes? A fear-some pirate, he must have been. A true adventurer. Whereas you, well . . . you're nothing.

I stopped tapping my fingers.

A fearsome pirate.

Khayzur leapt in the air, hovering over us with great gusty flaps of his wings. "So it is to be Socotra, then?" he asked. "I know of the island; the magical world has its own history there. But this cave you mentioned—"

"We're not going to the cave," I decided.

Raksh spun on me. "What? Says *who*? In mere days, Falco is going to be able to take possession of the Moon of Saba and enslave me! We don't have time to go traipsing about—"

"No traipsing either." I flipped the khanjar in my hand and caught it neatly. "Falco wanted to meet a real pirate, did he not?

"Let's bring him some."

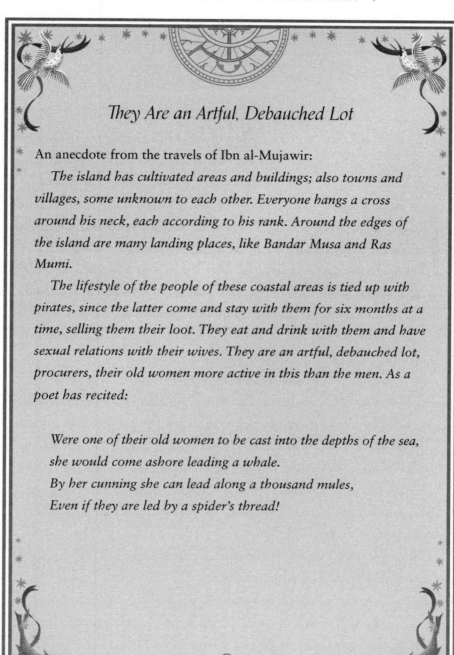

They Are an Artful, Debauched Lot

An anecdote from the travels of Ibn al-Mujawir:

The island has cultivated areas and buildings; also towns and villages, some unknown to each other. Everyone hangs a cross around his neck, each according to his rank. Around the edges of the island are many landing places, like Bandar Musa and Ras Mumi.

The lifestyle of the people of these coastal areas is tied up with pirates, since the latter come and stay with them for six months at a time, selling them their loot. They eat and drink with them and have sexual relations with their wives. They are an artful, debauched lot, procurers, their old women more active in this than the men. As a poet has recited:

Were one of their old women to be cast into the depths of the sea, she would come ashore leading a whale.
By her cunning she can lead along a thousand mules,
Even if they are led by a spider's thread!

Chapter 29

It took Khayzur three days to fly us from the accursed peri island to the western coast of Socotra where the pirate clans dwelled. I'd had a fear of heights *before* getting hoisted into the sky by a sea monster and nearly dropped to my death by avian bureaucrats, so you can probably imagine how I felt clutching one of Khayzur's talons as he soared over endless stretches of ocean and Raksh screamed in my ear. So please, continue to imagine it. Because I am not recounting it.

We broke for occasional respite on a series of tiny islands Khayzur seemed to know like the back of his hand. My peri "liaison" was otherwise quiet on the journey, subdued even, but I didn't know if his silence was due to the exertion of travel or the charges the court had laid upon him. In truth, I didn't know Khayzur at all. All I knew was that we seemed to believe in the same God, he was a political radical among his people, and a combination of those principles had led him to help me and then get sanctioned for doing so.

I hoped he didn't regret it. But after catching him watch me pray upon a tiny atoll, I pressed my luck once more.

"Have you any advice for me on how to fight Falco and his marid?" I asked hopefully. "I don't think I'll be much use to your people if I wind up dead, but I don't wish to get you in trouble for further 'interference.'"

Khayzur winced. "I have been trying to heed my tongue."

"I had noticed."

"Yes. You seem the perceptive type." The peri paused. "Though in a general form of advice that could not possibly be construed as interference . . . you were right to object to being forced into service. There is no living thing that doesn't desire freedom. And the marid are incredibly proud creatures. They have long memories and strongly held beliefs about . . . about f-f . . ."—Khayzur seemed to literally be fighting his tongue—"*favors*," he finally squawked out. He ruffled his feathers, his pale face sweating silver scales. "If you will excuse me . . ."

Living things did not enjoy being enslaved. That seemed more like a truism along the lines of "the sky is blue" rather than advice on combating the supernatural, but the peri had already saved my life at risk to his own, so I guess I couldn't complain.

Favors. That had seemed key, the word he'd fought to say. But how did one do a favor for a massive sea monster tasked to kill you?

By the next day, we'd arrived. Geographically, the northwestern coast of Socotra is similar to the quiet shores and soaring limestone caves of the more desolate east. But the beaches here were wider, the craggy cliffs gentler, and facing the Somali peninsula and the Gulf of Aden—the well-traveled waters between them plied by ships carrying some of the richest cargoes in the world—I suspected this part of the island was an easier place to make a living.

However, with wealthy trade ships comes their constant shadow, and if my first glimpse of the pirate fleet of Socotra was anything to judge by, these waters were *very* rich. There were nearly as many vessels here as I'd seen in Aden, at least a dozen anchored in the glittering shallows and more dragged up on the sand for repairs. Khayzur had taken us to a hidden overpass tucked away in the cliffs, and yet the nakhudha in me could not help but peek out to admire the impressive armada below. The deep-water qaraqir with ornate stern carvings and the best sails one could buy. The sleek galleys with room for a hundred oarsmen that were twice as fast as any vessel I'd ever been on. The much-feared barija with its naft-spewing bellows and battering rams. Even the smaller bandit skiffs, the kind of boats that float so close to the waterline they're all but invisible until their fighting men are throwing grappling hooks over your rails, were glossy and striking, drifting on the clear blue water like clouds on a beautiful day.

"I leave you two here," Khayzur said softly, a low coo of distress in his voice. "The Maker be with you, Amina al-Sirafi. I pray we see one another on the other side of this."

"God willing," I agreed, tearing myself away from the sight of the fearsomely gorgeous pirate fleet so I could bid farewell to my peri savior. "And thank you, Khayzur, for—"

But Khayzur was already gone, vanished into the cobalt sky like he had never been there, leaving Raksh and me alone. My treacherous husband had shifted back into his human guise and the effect was disconcerting. Though he was more visually pleasing without the tusks and the beating heart around his neck, it sometimes felt easier to remember that Raksh was a monster when he looked like one.

He stepped closer to the cliff's edge, stretching his long fingers toward the distant beach. "*Oh.*" Raksh swayed like a spellbound drunk. "There are some *interesting* personalities down there."

"Anyone with ambitions to fight a Frankish sorcerer?"

"My abilities are not that precise." Raksh shivered, the crimson line blossoming in his eyes. "But I'm eager to find out. Shall we go introduce ourselves?"

◆

Introducing ourselves did not go well.

After we had been greeted by waves of javelins on the beach and forced to take cover behind an exceedingly small boulder, shouting my name and swearing I'd come in peace had finally resulted in something of a ceasefire. If by cease-fire, I meant being divested of my weapons and marched to face the judgment of yet another court of hostile strangers, this time the pirate council of Socotra.

Let me first say this on behalf of the much-dreaded pirates of Socotra: they were not the idle, filthy, debauched murderers out of legend (well, perhaps they were debauched, but if so, they were doing it discreetly and in style). Raksh and I had been led to a splendid tent perched upon a bluff overlooking the sea. Fine rugs from Persia and the Maghreb made the rocky ground inside as soft as a cushion, and ornate Egyptian glass lanterns were strung overhead (hopefully among their painted holy verses was an admonition against killing guests). The air was scented with frankincense, rose, and musk, along with the smell of ink from the other side of the tent, where a dozen scribes sat with writing boards, taking inventory from piles of loot and speaking with the most patiently queued group I had ever encountered.

It was a scene of such wealth and organization to make a sultan weep in envy, and I felt a great lout sitting before them—my own criminal days had never been so officious. Then again I never had to oversee multi-ship convoys, fend off navies, or snarl an entire seaway, so perhaps this was the usual practice. The pirate representatives themselves were even more magnificently intimidating. Six nawakhidha and an elderly local woman, all arrayed in fine jewels and embellished garments, sat on plump silk cushions, each with handsome personal retainers and servants to stir the hot air with palm-frond fans. At hand was iced sherbet (yes, iced!), wine so tempting I couldn't even look at it, and cut fruit.

If *I* found it all overwhelming, it turned out the extraordinary display of fortune and criminality was quite literally intoxicating for Raksh. My estranged spouse had taken one look at the most ambitious, cunning, and accomplished sea raiders of the Indian Ocean, let out a deeply inappropriate gasp of pleasure, and been promptly stupefied into speechlessness. Helpful, I know.

However, we were not the only ones in the tent who had heard legends of the other.

"Amina al-Sirafi . . ." the youngest nakhudha drawled after I finished relating my tale, with several key parts missing. The nakhudha was a Malabar man like Tinbu, though better dressed in orange-and-purple-patterned silk. "The Sea Witch of Sur, the Harlot of Horse Thieves . . . so you do exist."

"Of course she exists," a far more elderly pirate opined. Henna colored his beard, gold ringed his wrists, and I heard Mombasa in his accent. "If there were any man to spawn a girl-child in his fashion, it would have been the Sea Leopard."

My hopes rose. "Were you and my grandfather companions?"

His gaze turned severe. "It was not a compliment, al-Sirafi. Your grandfather stole a very valuable cargo of tortoiseshells from me, and I am disinclined to believe anything you say, let alone some nonsensical tale about pursuing a Frank to Socotra to rescue the daughter of a comrade."

"And yet her tale matches the rumors we heard of a foreign killer in the east." It was the lone woman of the bunch. She had a Socotran inflection not too dissimilar from that of the villagers I'd met and wore an ornate iron cross around her neck. "The news about that slaughtered village, news the group of *you* did not believe bore investigating," she added pointedly to the pirate council.

"*Yes*," I said. "That sounds like the village we encountered. Are the survivors safe? They intended to ask your clan for aid."

A grim expression crossed the old woman's face. "They have not yet made it here. There are apparently wounded amongst them, and another village invited them to rest and recover before continuing onward. A messenger was sent to apprise us of the situation, but the things they were saying—"

"They claimed they were attacked by a foreign sorcerer," the young nakhudha interjected. "They spoke of their people being harvested like cattle and of a great leviathan that could be summoned from the sea." His dark eyes narrowed on me. "Interesting that *you* left those parts out of your story, and the villagers said nothing of being saved by a female nakhudha."

I cringed. "I asked them not to mention me," I explained, hating how suspicious the response must sound. "It was suggested you might not look kindly on my presence in Socotra. But the rest of their story is true, I swear."

"Sure it is." The Mombasa man let loose a scornful harrumph. "You know what I think, al-Sirafi? I think you came here with this Frankish sorcerer. I think you planned to plunder the tombs, but things went poorly and he betrayed you. And now you'd like *us* to clean up your mess."

It was absolutely a strategy I might have considered a decade ago, which made it slightly more difficult to deny. Slightly. "God forbid!" I cried, with great affront.

At my side, Raksh took a shaky breath and attempted to stop being useless.

"I have been to the cave," he said softly, and even muted, his voice was laced with magic and suggestion, impossible to ignore. "They are glorious. There are sapphires and rubies larger than melons and polished to such perfection that their dazzle could blind a man. Automatons whose clever construction has yet to be surpassed and enough gold coins to swim in. The treasure chambers are deep within the cave and thus you would need us as guides, but you would be amply rewarded. Think on it!" he urged. "You are fearsome, well-sourced warriors. This would be an easy victory for you, an easy victory followed by an empire's ransom in plunder."

Raksh's exaggerated description was ludicrous, but the enchantment he painted was difficult even for me to shake free. I watched wonder blossom in their eyes, a shadow of the dreamy haze Raksh had once used to lure me and countless mortals into his deals.

But then the young nakhudha shivered and shook free. "I don't trust any of this. Those caves are cursed for a reason. And I suspect the Frank these two have set themselves against is far more powerful than they are letting on."

"If that Frank is the one who attacked the village, it doesn't matter who you trust." The old woman's response cracked like a whip. "That is the covenant between our communities, one *we've* held for centuries. Socotra offers shelter to the pirate clans, and in return, you protect our people."

"Yes, we protect you from foreign navies and would-be slavers," said a third nakhudha, with a distractingly handsome face and full black beard. He was missing his left leg beyond the knee, the baggy cut of his kameez that of a Balochi man. "Not from foreign witches and the machinations of notorious smugglers. Granted, I am not averse to obtaining the riches of a treasure cave, but it is wiser to first learn what we can of this Frank and his possible magic." He cut a glance my way. "Al-Sirafi, you and your man will stay here while we send a scout."

"There's no time for a scout!" I argued, trying to curb the desperation in my voice; the Moon of Saba was another part of the story I had left out, but getting to it before the eclipse was paramount. "Falco is only getting more powerful. If we delay further—"

A new voice boomed from behind me. "My, what a *curious* discussion."

Startled, I spun around to see a great barrel of a man standing at the entrance of the tent who could have single-handedly inspired every fearsome tale of the sea brigands of Socotra. He was even taller than me, with the craggy face only decades upon the ocean can carve. Arms thicker than Raksh's thighs were covered in tattoos of horses and female warriors, his biceps bound with sheathed knives. A savage scar traced from his chin to his belly as though someone had once tried to hack him in two, an ostentatiously large yellow turban splattered with boat pitch wrapped his head, and a cord of shark's teeth hung from around his neck.

He strolled farther into the tent, tossing and catching a heavy wooden mallet in his hand, and every member of the pirate council went visibly tense.

"I was unpleasantly surprised to hear a meeting was called without me," the new arrival drawled in a heavy Egyptian accent. "Particularly when I was told what was being said in our tent. Frankish villains, treasure caves, entrancing female rogues . . ." His glittering eyes filled with delight as they took me in, and he grinned, revealing three gold teeth to my one. "Peace be upon you, nakhudha. I am called Magnun. For I have been driven mad by love into the wilds of the sea, where I thirst forevermore."

"Oh, is that what they call getting thrown out of the Fatimid navy?" the Malabar captain muttered under his breath. Magnun whirled on him, spinning the hammer, and the younger man abruptly shut his mouth.

"Magnun . . ." the Balochi nakhudha said more diplomatically. "You seemed busy with repairs. We did not wish to trouble you."

"Hamza, you lie very sweetly, but I always recognize the taste of sugar. And now I am quite troubled," Magnun declared, his already loud voice rising in incredulity. "Troubled to learn my comrades are nothing but cowards!"

That earned him glares from the other pirates.

"What you call cowardice, we call wisdom, you rash fool," the Mombasa man snapped. "There is a reason our clans have thrived here for so long, and it is because we do *not* go chasing after foreign wizards on the word of one extremely untrustworthy woman."

Magnun rolled his eyes. "And you call yourselves pirates . . . Where is your sense of adventure!" He turned to me. "Forget these yellow-bellied infants, Lady Sea Leopard. *I* will fight this Frank and his beasts with you. I will crack open his skull and see his brain dashed before your feet. In return, you will lead me and my crew to this treasure cave the rest of these cowards are too small-balled to seize."

His challenging words landed with a thunderous air. As you might imagine, it is incredibly easy to provoke a group of combative old sea dogs. Let alone by calling them "small-balled cowards." I expected blades to be drawn, blood to be shed.

Instead, a cunning expression slid into the eyes of the Balochi nakhudha. He glanced at the Socotran woman. "I do believe that would fulfill our covenant."

The old woman regarded Magnun, Raksh, and me with open skepticism. "You would send only the three of them? To fight off a sorcerer?"

"Why not?" the Mombasa elder asked sarcastically. "Magnun is very confident in his abilities, and we were already planning to send a scout. Let him go instead. If he deals with this Frank on his own, he will have earned any riches he recovers." He smiled at Magnun with all his teeth. "And if they are devoured by a sea monster, we will better know the scope of the threat."

"Sounds good to me," grumbled the young Malabar man in his own tongue—which I knew decently. "Let the brash idiot learn a lesson the hard way."

Any relief I might have enjoyed upon the Socotran pirate council offering assistance was doused by how eager the rest were to see Magnun chastened.

I tried again, looking more desperately at the other captains. "Surely some of the rest of you are intrigued . . . the cave truly is an extraordinary prize." I elbowed Raksh. "Raksh, tell them again about the treasure."

"No need." At my side, Raksh was glowing with excitement, gazing upon Magnun like a child expecting Eid money. "He's *perfect*."

"Then it is settled!" Magnun beckoned me to follow. "Come! I will show you my ship."

Despite my apprehension, Magnun ended up possessing one of the terrifying bawarij I had admired, a genuine pirate ship with fighting platforms, archer galleys, and oars for sixty men. Its hull and sails were painted to blend in with the colors of a midnight ocean, there were battering rams on each side, hoses for naft, and some sort of catapult system. I spotted at least a dozen fireboxes, barrels of spears, and a false half mast studded with throwing knives and axes. For all his eccentricities, I could tell Magnun ran a tight ship. He had sprung for extremely high-quality cloth for his sails, and the rudders moved with a whisper. No wonder the other captains had put up with his brazenness; in a fight, this seemed like a good boat to have.

"She is a beauty," I said appreciatively. "I suspect you have had many adventures with her."

"Aye, though it can be a lonely life. Not many women want to live at sea. You, though . . ." Magnun clucked his tongue. "Bet you could bear strong sons with those legs."

"I could snap a man's bones with these legs," I replied pointedly, with a grin at Raksh he did not return. "And can provide a demonstration anytime."

Magnun cackled. "Understood, nakhudha. You cannot blame a man for trying." He gave me a more critical look. "While the cloak of—quills, is it?—is rather fetching, I take it you would prefer proper armor?"

"I would." I yanked free a spear from the practice mast with the ease of snapping my fingers. It was featherlight in my hand. "And weapons if you can spare them. When is the soonest we can leave?"

"I need only call my crew; I prefer haste as well." Magnun jerked a thumb in the direction of the tent. "I would not put it past those craven fools to realize they might be letting a fortune slip through their hands and rush to show up after the fight to claim some for themselves. But for now?" He grinned. "Let's get you outfitted."

◆

"Well . . ." Raksh said when I reemerged from the ship's galley. "You certainly look like you belong with your new friend."

He spoke the truth. Magnun clearly had a penchant for robbing nobles and leaving them in their underthings, for his cargo hold had been filled with some of the finest fabrics I had ever touched, each more colorful and expensive than the last. A great number were too delicate for the task at hand: painted silks and muslins so sheer they were more likely to sweat apart than buffer chain mail.

But there was still plenty for me to choose from. I might have originally taken this job with the aim of being discreet, of burying my brash, flamboyant younger self away, but to hell with all that now. I would fight in the manner truest to my soul. Accordingly, the old Amina al-Sirafi had been unearthed in an emerald tunic embroidered with fire-yellow sunbursts, butter-soft bloodred leather boots, and billowy trousers the exact blue of a dusk sea. A layer of finely made chain mail went over it all, followed by the sharpest green and black jacket I had ever seen, picked through with silver thread. I wrapped my hair in an ebony block-print turban, then donned a domed helmet inscribed with protective verses.

For weapons, I had gone well and thoroughly overboard. If I'd bargained away part of my life to leave the peris' island with my new strength, then by God, such strength would be wielded. My khanjar was now tucked besides a pair of throwing knives, and on my back I bore two good Toledo swords. Dwarfing all was a battle-axe heavy and large enough to fell a celestial grove, yet one that now felt barely heavier than a carpenter's mallet in my hand.

Magnun roared in approval when he caught a glimpse. "I bet the pope in Rome just shat himself."

Indeed, the Latin leader might have if he'd gotten a look at the assembled crew, and I suspect many a caliph, sultan, and admiral would have lost their bowels in similar fashion. Magnun had pulled his people from fights and drinking huts, from hunts and naps, and they appeared as wild and formidable as him. A handful were women, many as broadly built as me. They bristled with weapons and laughter, some wearing talismanic shirts and others, necklaces of shark's teeth in emulation of their nakhudha.

Raksh was bouncing in excitement, feeding on ambitions I could scarcely imagine as he tossed a steel mace with a wickedly spiked end from hand to hand. "Oh, this is brilliant. Truly brilliant. I might genuinely be saved!"

"I hope that inspires you not to turn tail and run away again," I warned. "Remember *you* stand to benefit from Falco's downfall as much as anyone else."

But just saying Falco's name was enough to dim my mood. We might have assembled a fearsome offense, but I wasn't certain any of the new weapons at my disposal could even cut the Frank down. What if he was protected by his sorcery? I might be able to draw Raksh's blood, but for all I knew Falco was guarded by something stronger.

Magnun passed by, carrying an armful of lances, and an idea struck me.

"Nakhudha," I called out. "May I request another favor?"

He gave an admiring look down my person before responding. "Speak it."

"Do you have any talismanic weapons, anything engraved with holy verses?" I asked, thinking back to my blessed blade. I had been divested of it along with most of my weapons when Falco took the *Marawati*. It might not have worked on Raksh, but it *had* dispatched the creature in the lagoon all those weeks ago. "Or any iron knives?"

The mouthy pirate leader went strangely still.

"An iron knife?" Magnun gave me a curious look. "Have you been talking to my crew, then?"

When I shook my head, he motioned for me to follow him into the ship's shadowy hold. I held open the hatch to let in a few rays of dusty sunlight, watching as Magnun shifted crates of plunder, jostling bottles of precious oils, sacks of grain, and parcels of embroidered brocade.

"It is odd you should ask me about an iron knife, al-Sirafi," he said over his shoulder. "Very odd indeed." Magnun extracted a gorgeous silver-worked box. "For I stole *this* just before I was kicked out of my country."

He opened the box. Nestled inside amongst linen batting was a long flat dagger with a dark iron blade. About the length of my forearm, the knife gleamed as though lit from within. The handle was gold and engraved with a pattern of stylized waterlilies and rising suns, small lapis and carnelian gems set in spiraling designs.

"What sort of weapon is that?" I breathed, entranced by its glow.

"A celestial one," Magnun replied, sounding just as awed. When I gave him a skeptical glance, he chuckled. "Well, it's carved from an iron meteor that fell from the stars anyway. They find blades like this on occasion in the underground tombs of the great sun kings in my land. It was meant as a gift for the caliph but"—he tilted the box, and the dagger caught a ray of light, its reflection dazzling—"I decided I could find a better use for it."

"Such as giving it to a random female nakhudha?"

"*Lending* it to a fascinating female nakhudha," Magnun clarified. "I heard what you were saying to the council about the Frank having access to magic. This seems a worthy counter-weapon."

"Then wouldn't you rather wield it yourself?"

"If this Frank had my crew, I would fight through fire to save them. I suspect it will be most effective in your hands." He held out the box. "Take it."

The dagger seemed to sing when I touched it. The handle warmed to my hand, and green and purple crystals glimmered in the murky iron depths like the scales of fish rising below the water's surface. I caught my breath, but Magnun did not seem to notice anything unusual.

Transgression, the voice of the dove peri whispered in my ear as I raised the dagger, sunlight blazing like a torch as it danced down the sharp blade. Was that what this was? What *I* was?

And yet as the faces of my crew and my daughter flashed through my mind, I found I did not quite care.

I am coming for you, I promised. *And I will fight through fire.*

Chapter 30

I will come out and confess that it is a very strange experience to plot the theft of one's beloved ship. Yet after two days of furious, speedy travel along Socotra's northern coast, two days of arguing and scheming with Raksh, Magnun, and his top commanders, two days of praying my people were still alive and Dunya's deal had kept the crew safe, we approached Falco's camp outside the cave where the Moon of Saba resided, on a dark night whose moon was about to be swallowed in an eclipse with a scheme only pirates could concoct.

What we decided on was a diversion: we were going to pretend to steal the *Marawati*. Which meant even now, Magnun's magnificent ship—its sails and hulls painted black and gray, its lights doused, its expert oarsmen pulling with a grace and discretion that made me want to weep in envy—was coursing through the dark water, nigh invisible, toward *my* beloved ship, with Magnun, a proper pirate if I had ever met one, in command.

However, I was not on Magnun's attacking ship. Instead, I stalked across the cliffs overlooking the cave's mouth, staying low to the ground. Raksh was at my side, ten of the fiercest pirates behind us. Magnun had dropped us off in the inlet with ropes and climbing equipment, and I would be lying if I said I had no misgivings about the Egyptian nakhudha possibly having ulterior motives.

But it turns out I hadn't told the truth to Dalila back in Aden: my people *were* more important than the *Marawati*, and if I had to risk my ship to free them, so be it.

We settled into a vantage point hidden by scrubby bushes from which we could spy the bonfire blazing at the heart of Falco's camp. The moon was bright and round as a silver coin, no sign of the eclipse yet. Creeping forward, I tried to make out what I could of the dark flitting figures below. My vision was no longer great at night, but what I could see of the dancing flames was enough to turn my stomach, memories of nearly being made Falco's thrall flooding over me. *Hands shoving me to the sand and the foul potion wriggling down my throat. The skittering army of scorpions pouring into the pit . . .*

Focus. Steadying myself, I pressed the strange meteor blade sheathed at my waist, and it instantly warmed, tingling beneath my fingers. A few weeks ago, a celestial weapon activating at my touch would have been deeply unsettling. Now it was reassuring. I had indeed been changed. But not at the Frank's behest.

Closer to the beach, a breeze must have blown in off the ocean. The bonfire flared, its flames briefly illuminating a small knot of people whose faces filled my heart with joy.

My crew. Not all of them, but relief coursed through me as I recognized Tinbu, Hamid, Tiny, the ship's carpenter, and a few more of the talented boatwrights. They were the group you would want to do repairs on a wounded vessel; indeed, I could now make out my *Marawati* bobbing not too far from the shore, moonlight rippling and breaking on the rolling swells surrounding her. It was too dark to assess my ship's state, but at least she was floating. I rocked up onto my toes, searching for the rest of my people.

Instead I spotted something far less promising. What I'd taken to be part of the landscape—a rocky outcropping jutting out of the shallows beside a sandy dune—suddenly moved, an undulating shudder followed by the waft of infection on the salty air. It was Falco's *marid*, the enormous creature half beached on the shore.

I stilled, fearing it had somehow caught sight of us, but the monster merely flopped a few tentacles before slowly opening and closing one enormous claw.

Was it dying? Sleeping? Its behavior seemed sluggish, though I'm not sure how much that meant when you were a leviathan the size of a building. A jumble of broken timbers and glimmering boils were still fused to its skull, all that was left of Falco's wrecked ship.

One of Magnun's warriors joined me.

"I assume that is the creature?" he whispered. I had filled them in as best I could on the journey, describing the camp, its fighters, the cave, and my people to Magnun and his crew and trying to take some assurance in the fact that they apparently conducted successful midnight raids on supposedly larger, more lethal targets all the time (and I should know, for they spent the trip boasting, Magnun's men in particular making sure I knew how skilled, virile, and successful their nakhudha was).

"Aye." I glanced his way, hoping the sight wasn't enough to scare him off, but the man's eyes were shining.

"It will be a glorious fight," he murmured, sounding like his boss. "Do you see your crew?"

"Only a few." I pointed out Tinbu and the rest, peering through the darkness a second time in hopes of spotting more faces to little success. "But I don't see the others, nor the Frank himself. They may be in the cave." At least, I *prayed* they were in the cave; Dalila, Majed, and Dunya were among the missing faces.

"Then we await my nakhudha's signal."

We withdrew to join the others. Raksh was breathing fast and holding his mace the wrong way.

I plucked the mace from his hands, turning it right side up and handing it back. "Please watch where you swing that. I don't need you attacking our side."

He wet his lips, his eyes bright with fear. "I have mentioned the not-being-a-warrior thing, yes?"

"At least a dozen times. Just keep reminding yourself of the alternative."

"Believe me, I am," he muttered, pulling a sour face. "Fucking lunar idiot had to go and screw us all over."

Before Raksh could fall deeper into self-pity, Magnun's signal came: at sea, his rowers picked up speed, intentionally splashing enough to make visible the large pirate vessel heading directly for the *Marawati*. We watched in tense silence, waiting, but it wasn't more than another minute before Falco's mercenaries noticed, one of them shouting:

"There is a ship approaching!"

Still aboard his vessel, Magnun's archers lit their arrows, fire flickering to life from the bows of a dozen men in perfect symmetry (my God, had his fellow pirates underestimated the Egyptian; I was half ready to sign on with him myself), and then true panic seemed to set in at Falco's camp.

A large man shot to his feet—Yazid, I recognized, mostly from the sight of my own scimitar hanging at his waist. "Go tell our master!" I heard him cry.

Perhaps awakened by all the commotion, the marid let out a sickly roar. It sounded far weaker than it had before, but it was still very capable of heaving its vast body up onto its many legs. It returned to the water, the entire beach trembling with its mighty steps, and I whispered a prayer for Magnun and his crew as the creature swam directly toward his ship.

Time for the second part of our plan.

"*Go!*" I hissed to the fighters accompanying me.

We poured down upon the beach. Magnun's warriors were clearly more skilled hunters of men than I, perhaps even more so than Falco's loutish brutes, used to daring raids and split-second decisions. They were deadly quiet, fast as a javelin as they pierced the camp. I had barely spotted the Frank's lookout before one of the pirates seized him from behind, slit his throat, cradled his fall to the ground so it would be silent, and moved on.

The ease of it both stunned and slightly intimidated me—these were some salty killers. But then the sight of the dead scout stopped me cold. Not only did the man appear as monstrous as he had when the Frank forced his foul potion upon me, with four clouded gray eyes on stalks that erupted from his brow and fish scales covering his skin, there was something even more bizarre: a thick cord of what looked like braided seaweed sprouting straight from his chest. It was glowing silver but rapidly disintegrating, the light within fading.

What in God's name is that? Disgusted and yet strangely compelled, I gave the cord a slight tug and nearly fell flat back on my ass as the seaweed cord—and the *gray-blue stinger* it was attached to—erupted from the man's sternum with a repulsive wet splotching sound.

It looked exactly like the stinger Raksh had pulled from me.

Raksh himself ran up just then. "What are you *doing?*"

"What is this?" I asked, keeping my voice below the crash of the surf. I gestured to the remains of the seaweed chain, now so decayed it was hard to pick out. The stinger had already crumbled away, leaving nothing more than a curved pile of broken shells.

His gaze darted between my face and the ground. "What is what?"

"This *cord*," I explained. "It was attached to a stinger like the one you cut out of my chest. And it stretches—" But I couldn't see where it ended, the tether no longer glowing in the dark night. "Somewhere over there."

Raksh visibly startled. "You can see a *cord?* Coming from a stinger like the one that was in your chest?" When I nodded, Raksh gave me a wild look. "That sounds like the oath he made to Falco made manifest; magical bonds exist in some realms as physical forms. But you should not be able to see that. *I* cannot see that."

Now also wasn't the time to discuss it, pandemonium erupting around us. Offshore, Magnun let out a burst of naft toward the marid, which shrieked in response. In the scattered moonlight and flickers of burning naft reflecting off the midnight ocean, it was difficult to see anything save grappling limbs and gleaming weapons as Magnun's fighters threw themselves upon Falco's.

These were the sort of battles I'd spent my career avoiding—a smuggler who wants to live to retirement relies on tricks and thievery rather than open, bloody fighting. I'd been in plenty of skirmishes. Killed my first man at eighteen. But I'd never savored violence.

However, as I left the scout's body and rushed to join the fight, something came over me, energy singing through my blood. I lunged for a man with a score of eyes clustered across a pink spiderlike face. He dropped the cup he had been about to drink from, grabbing a double-ended hatchet.

I decapitated him with a single blow.

Another time the feat would have shocked, perhaps even horrified me. Not tonight. I cut through the men who had attacked my ship, threatened my people, and signed their souls over to a foreign butcher with all the supernatural strength I had.

Perhaps if I'd had more time, more mercy, I might have tried to reason with them. But I was out of time and so were they. They had chosen to join this monster, to remain at his side as he tortured and murdered a score of innocent villagers. I would do what needed to be done to put a stop to it.

I sent one man flying with a blow to his chest, whipping around lightning fast to rip open the belly of another attempting to sneak up on me, but then I stumbled, thrown off-balance by the ease of the strike. My strength, my speed . . . both vastly improved, yes, but my strike was an adjustment probably *not* best made in the heat of battle. Around me, Magnun's men were grappling with Falco's, doing their best against the magically enhanced warriors. Across the camp, I briefly spotted the small group of my crew. Bound in ropes and almost certainly unarmed, they were throwing themselves against their guards with shouts and curses.

I tried to reach them, only to be blocked by another of Falco's warriors— a far more hulking specimen than the ones I had dispatched. He came rushing my way, sporting six crab arms and a mouth full of shark's teeth. I barely ducked an enormous pair of his pincers, whirling around to swing my axe at his head before he blocked that with another arm.

"Raksh!" I shouted, spotting my husband hiding behind a rock. "A little help!"

In response, Raksh threw his mace at the both of us, nearly taking my head off and missing my opponent entirely.

That useless motherfucker. I gritted my teeth, shoving the handle of my axe between serrated claws that had been about to rip my face off. The claws jerked back but took my axe with them. I grabbed for one of my swords, slashing down across the man's chest.

It was a blow that would have ripped open a human. But my foe was no longer that, and all the sword did was slide along the crab-shell-like carapace glistening beneath his torn shirt. My blade didn't even leave a scratch, though there was something clearly capable of piercing it: a spectral seaweed tether just like the one that had been in the scout's chest.

The man misinterpreted the shock on my face, smirking with all his shark's teeth (do not attempt to envision this—it is a deeply cursed sight) and running an admiring claw down the rock-hard carapace protecting his chest. "Even better than armor if I do say so myself."

"You look like a fucking prawn." Acting on instinct, I reached for my meteor blade.

He snorted. "Is it a spider you plan to kill with that puny thing?"

"Not quite." I lunged forward and sliced through his spectral chain. The meteor blade cut through the seaweed tether with a sizzling flash of light.

The effect was instantaneous. Falco's fighter sucked for breath like a fish on land, lurching back as though he'd lost control of his limbs. His armored carapace vanished, melting into all-too-human skin. The man didn't even have a chance to scream before his extra limbs also fell away, the pincer claws reduced to the size of small crabs by the time they landed in the sand. With a low cry of disbelief, he clutched his chest, grasping the bony gray-blue stinger emerging from his sternum.

Diminished, he fell to his knees. "You freed me," he said hoarsely, touching his human teeth and bare belly with palpable despair. "Falco . . . I cannot feel him."

"Where is he?" I demanded. "Help me and I'll spare you."

"*Help you?*" He laughed, the sound hollow. "Do you know the price I paid for this? I stood by while my cousin was eaten alive." He gazed up, hate scorching in his eyes. "Bitch, I *wanted* it."

He sprang at me, but it was a desperate move and it was nothing to shove the dagger into his heart. I yanked it out and his body crumpled back to the sand. Breathing fast, I stared in astonishment at the meteor blade, reflected firelight dancing in its depth.

Raksh peeked out from behind his rock. "What did you *do*?"

I think I figured out how to strip Falco's men of their magic. But there was no way I was telling my cowardly, could-swap-sides-at-any-time spouse that.

Instead I glared at him. "Right. New plan since you seem more likely to hurt me than the person I'm fighting. Free my men, then get to the cave."

He gave me a nervous look. "Falco might be in the cave."

"Yes, idiot, and hopefully so are the rest of my crew. You're the trickster, aren't you? Find a way to free them so they can fight and possibly delay Falco. And save *you*," I added, putting it in terms he could understand. "Go!"

Raksh swore but ran off, and I turned back toward Magnun's warriors. If I could cut the spectral tethers from Falco's remaining fighters, defeating them would be child's play for the Socotran pirates.

But I'd barely taken two steps when a heavy blow rang out against my helmet, knocking me nearly senseless.

I staggered, my ears ringing, and the helmet was ripped off entirely. Falco's beast of a man—Yazid, the mercenary who had twisted and tied up an iron bar like it was a piece of rope—stood behind me.

Surprise lit his blood-streaked face. "Al-Sirafi," he exhaled. In one of his hands was my scimitar.

Oh, God, my head hurt. "Came back for my blade," I said, trying to wish away the stars dancing merrily before my vision. "You mind?"

Yazid licked his lips. "Come and get it."

Now, past experience has taught me that those kinds of challenges typically speak poorly of their boasters—efforts to boost their own ineptitude or low confidence.

Regrettably, it took less than a minute of action with Yazid to learn he had earned every bit of his mocking arrogance.

He moved faster than I could blink. Forget the meteor blade, I barely had enough time to raise my sword before his blows were hammering down on me like those of a furious carpenter venting their frustration on a broken nail. My strength might have been improved, but it was nowhere close to Yazid's. As we parried back and forth, he pressed me farther into the shadows, away from my allies.

"You were a fool not to join us when Falco invited you, al-Sirafi," Yazid said, his eyes glittering. "He would have given you the world."

I grunted in frustration, fending off another of Yazid's blows. There was a weird mix of bitterness and jealousy in his voice; maybe someone was feeling insecure in his relationship with the Frankish sorcerer. "Is that what he told your shipmates before feeding half of them to a sea monster?"

Yazid swung down hard—*with my own sword*—and I stumbled, barely avoiding the steel as it swept over my face. Closer now, I could see his spectral leash, glowing healthy and bright as it draped from his chest to the ground. Severing it seemed my only hope, but Yazid had me completely on my toes. Needing to wield my sword with both hands, I'd shoved the iron dagger in my belt early in our fight, nearly dropping it in my haste.

Growing desperate, I fled backward, hoping to buy myself even the briefest of openings to snatch the knife. But I'd badly miscalculated. Yazid was as swift as he was strong, and he made use of the distance between us to slash down wide and fast with the sword. I twisted away, the blade sliding on my chain mail instead of ripping open my abdomen, but the blow was still hard enough that I would swear I felt a rib crack.

Yazid took advantage of his strike, kicking me in the same spot. I gasped in pain, the wind knocked from my lungs, and he swept my feet out from under me.

I fell to the sand. Abandoning my sword, I made a wild grab for the meteor blade, but my fingers had barely closed on its hilt when he knocked it out of my hand, returning to press a booted foot on my ribs, pinning me in place. I cried out in equal parts pain and frustrated rage as he stood over my body. Yazid raised his sword—*my* sword—over my heart, murderous triumph blazing in his expression.

A familiar scream ripped through the air. Familiar enough that despite my likely imminent death, I glanced to my left . . . to see *Tinbu.*

Looking like a possessed rabbit, my friend hopped madly in our direction, his bandaged leg held at an awkward angle, some sort of crutch under one arm and a flaming piece of driftwood in his other hand. It was such a bizarre apparition that even Yazid briefly paused my murder, glancing wildly at Tinbu just before my first mate flung himself at Yazid—broken leg, crutch, flaming driftwood, and all.

Under most circumstances, I suspect Tinbu would have made for little more than a fly pestering Yazid, but even villainous warriors get surprised when a torch-bearing, hopping man screams and throws himself at your face. Yazid staggered back, swatting and cursing as Tinbu thrust the flaming driftwood at his eyes. Finally with a solid smack, Yazid knocked my friend away, and Tinbu fell hard to the ground, landing on his bad leg and letting out an anguished shriek. But still he clawed in my direction, using the crutch to drag himself across the sand, his face pale as parchment.

"Amina," he choked out, his voice thick with grief and pain. "*Cover your face.*"

Cover my . . .

Then I realized it wasn't a crutch Tinbu was using.

It was Dalila's staff.

A shadow fell across us, a petite form in a billowing tattered gown standing before the roaring bonfire. Bruises and bloodstains ringed her wrists from where she'd been bound, her hair wild and blowing everywhere. Her ribbon cap was clenched in one hand, the lower half of her face already covered. One might have thought her broken, but her expression as she glared at Yazid, hatred and vengeance scorching in her eyes, showed how very alive she was.

"For the villagers," Dalila snarled. Then she ripped her fingers through the ribbons of her cap, breaking away the glass vials—*all* of the vials, what must have been a decade of work—and flung the contents at his face.

I was already clamping the end of my turban over my nose and mouth, turning away before the fumes hit me. Even through the cloth, the vapors were so acidic and foul I wanted to vomit. Yazid was screaming, shrieking and howling in pain.

He fell to his knees beside me, and I scrambled back in horror. His eyes were *gone*, the melting flesh of his cheeks bubbling and dripping away. Dalila—standing behind him like some sort of avenging angel—picked up my stolen sword from where Yazid had dropped it.

"Dalila," I gasped out, the air still burning. "I can—"

With a heartbreaking cry, she shoved the sword into Yazid's throat. She had to throw her whole weight into the blade before it finally pierced through and she let go, stumbling away.

Yazid collapsed with a thud.

There was a long moment of shocked silence. Dalila was trembling and breathing so fast I was surprised she didn't collapse herself. Her hands were bleeding badly and the ribbon cap lay discarded at her feet in a heap of broken glass and torn cloth. But she didn't drop the sword, not even as she turned to me. If anything, the wildness in her dark eyes blazed higher, grief and sick fear twisting across her expression.

"Falco killed you," Dalila said hoarsely. "Are you . . . is this like Asif?"

Tears burned in my eyes. "No, my friend. I am different. But not like—"

I didn't have to finish my explanation. Dalila dropped the sword and flung her arms around me. Tinbu was there the next moment, the three of us hugging and crying.

"We thought you were dead," Tinbu wept. "They said he stabbed you and threw your body overboard."

"I thought I was dead too," I whispered, stroking his hair and pressing my brow against Dalila's. "I'm sorry. I'm so sorry I couldn't protect you. I'm sorry it took me so long to get back."

"*Amina!*" It was Majed, staggering across the sand, a wary Raksh behind him. My navigator threw himself around us, his long arms wrapping our group in an even tighter hug.

"Please, not so hard," Tinbu croaked out. "I am fairly certain I rebroke my leg."

I immediately let him go, relief flooding over me as I spotted the rest of my crew emerging from the cave. Magnun's fighters were mopping up the few of Falco's men who remained—with one critical exception.

"Where's the Frank?" I demanded. "Where's *Dunya*?"

"Gone," Majed said, sounding sick. "As soon as the scout told Falco someone was attacking, the rat grabbed her and ran off deeper into the cave."

"I need to go after them," I said urgently. "Right now. Before—"

The land gave a great tremble.

It was followed by more shudders, like an earthquake warming up.

With an ill feeling of premonition, I turned toward the water. I had been too busy not being murdered by Yazid to keep an eye on the sea battle, but I was now partly relieved to see Magnun's ship was still afloat. But only *partly* relieved, because even though they were still shooting arrows and aiming naft at the marid, the creature—perhaps at Falco's magical command—was rushing in our direction, its skittering steps causing the quakes.

"God preserve me," I whispered as it approached. If I thought the marid looked intimidating earlier, that was nothing to how it compared now, surging through the breaking waves. Its titanic bulk and lethal tail blotted out half the stars in the sky, the foul air from its festering wounds noxious and thick, competing with Dalila's concoction. This close, I could see something else as well: spectral bonds similar to the tethers that Falco's men had sported.

But not one, oh, no. That would be too easy. Instead, *scores* of glittering seaweed bonds held tight to the marid. They clung from its skull and its tentacles, wrapping its mighty stinger and hanging from its broad abdomen. They were even brighter and thicker than the chains I had severed, so vibrant I could follow where the great mass of them led—all trailing across the beach and vanishing into the depths of the cave where Falco had fled. Not just tethers, then.

Leashes. With revulsion, I looked upon the shackles tying the mighty creature to the diabolical sorcerer. How did it feel to be forced to obey the whims of something so much smaller?

However, my empathy was tried when the marid scuttled onto the beach, going entirely, eerily still. The only movement was the seawater streaming from its raised pincers, falling from such a height, they might have been waterfalls. Its segmented tail was raised and ready to strike, the bladed stinger twice the length of my body. All of us froze. My companions, Magnun's warriors, even what was left of Falco's men.

The whoosh of air was the only warning.

I shoved my friends away and dove to the side. The stinger plunged into the ground where we had been standing with enough force to send rocks and clumps of dirt flying.

"Get to the cave!" I cried. "All of you! The tunnel narrows quickly. It will not be able to follow."

"We're not leaving you!" Dalila shouted. The marid skittered forward, enormous pincers clacking.

There was nothing my friends could do here other than potentially die, though. Me, however . . .

Living things liked being free. That's what Khayzur had said, and I could only pray the marid felt that way as well.

"I'll be right behind you, promise!" I shouted and then grabbed Raksh by the back of his cloak before he could flee. "Oh, no. You're with me. *Distract it.*"

"Do *what*?"

I pushed him down the rocky slope. "You heard me!" I'd shoved him a bit too hard though, sending my husband rolling like a runaway barrel to land directly beneath the marid's body. It screeched in triumph, its attention briefly diverted.

Perhaps not entirely what I'd intended, but it would serve.

Meteor blade in hand, I raced for the nearest cord of glowing oath bonds. My heart rose into my throat, but the blade cut through them as easily as it had sliced through the tether on Falco's man. However, unlike the mercenary's cord, these bonds writhed and wriggled like snakes, twisting away from my hands. I kept at it, furiously severing as many as I could. Beyond, Raksh screamed and cursed my existence, racing to avoid the marid's pincers.

BAM.

An enormous insect leg slammed into the sand, nearly crushing me. I flew to my feet, dashing away, but the marid was blocking my access to the remaining bonds now—as well as the cave. About a dozen chains remained, three around its legs and the others hooked about its head.

Great plan, al-Sirafi. I ran down the beach, ducking its stinger and weaving through the sea scorpion's dancing limbs as I slashed out at the bonds around its legs. But there was no way to sever the ones near its head unless I got closer. *Much* closer.

"To hell with this job," I swore, bracing my feet and waiting for the right moment. "To hell with Falco and Salima and that lewd fucking moon!"

One of the severed bonds hanging from the marid's neck swept past. Before I could think better of things, before I could allow a moment's fear or hesitation to change my mind, I seized the bond.

And began to climb.

I shall like to go on the record in saying that ascending a magical seaweed rope no one else can see—and that may or may not disintegrate at any moment—up the moving body of a warship-sized scorpion as it shrieks and tries to stab you with its stinger remains, hands down, one of the worst fucking experiences of a career that involved having Falco's foul maggot potion shoved down my throat. I clung for dear life to the spectral tether as it swung wildly, narrowly avoiding being dashed on the cliffs twice.

The marid did *not* like being climbed. Not at all. Its tentacles flailed and darted about, trying to seize the impertinent mortal who dared to do so, but I was swinging too erratically to catch. Even so, it hit me in the back once so hard that I nearly let go of the cord, gasping in pain.

Finally, *finally*, the top of the creature was in reach. I gripped the barnacles and coral growing from its slippery shell and hauled myself up, breathing hard and thanking God when I could finally stand on its armored back, the terrible ascent complete.

Which is when a tentacle, a skinny little baby one, snaked around my ankle and yanked me off.

I went flying through the air, but as though by a miracle, I ended up tangled in the oath bonds, swinging around the creature's moving legs yet again.

"You ungrateful oversized bug," I cried, "*I am trying to free you!*"

There was no way to tell if the marid understood any of that, but it did seem like the tentacles were slightly less determined to murder me as I climbed a second time. When I made it to the top, I kept one hand on a tether, quickly scrambling into the remains of Falco's ship. I was fascinated by the merging of lumber and beast, yet didn't hesitate as I raced for the shining bonds connecting the wreckage to the marid. The last two cords were located on the other side of the marid's skull. I darted across, grabbed the chains, and severed them.

The meteor blade had no sooner finished slicing through the final one than the tether crumbled in my hands, all the severed oath chains turning to dust that blew instantly away on the ocean's breeze.

The marid wailed, a heartrending cry of pain and what sounded like confusion (or what I believe was confusion—God knows best the inner life of leviathan-esque monsters).

But not out loud . . . in my *head*. A rush of images—memories, sounds, even tastes—ran through my mind. The heaviness of a pitch-black seabed and the different, subtle flavors of salt. The song of whales and clicks of dolphins. Chomping through a wooden hull and being summoned—*trapped*—by a net of blood. I clamped my hands over my ears, but it did nothing to stop the cacophony of noise, underwater visions flashing before my eyes as a shining spectral ribbon of bright yellow scales, like a rope covered in fish skin, blossomed between me and the marid.

"Oh, absolutely the fuck not," I said, staggering to my feet. The ribbon flickered in and out of sight like a sunbeam crossed by a cloud, but now I could also *feel* it, a hook in my heart. "I do not wish to be connected to you!" I slashed at the ribbon with the meteor blade, but it did nothing, passing through the ribbon as if it weren't even there.

The marid seemed to share my feelings. It roared and swayed, skittering about like an angry drunk. With a crackling sound and a rush of acerbic air, its giant blisters began healing over. The crust of jagged barnacles and dead coral that had fused the ship pieces to its head broke off, falling to the beach. It cried out again, then clearly fed up with all our human nonsense, it rushed toward the sea.

The movement flung me backward. I slid madly down the slippery wet shell like leaves rushing along a swollen river. Desperate, I lashed out for anything to break my fall, but there was nothing. Not even my blade would stick in its shell as the ocean came up faster and faster . . .

I crashed through the water hard enough for my vision to flash black, part of my body probably wondering if we might just give up and go into the void this time. Still wearing my armor and several heavy weapons, I submerged instantly and sank fast.

Swim, you idiot! After all this, drowning would be an almost embarrassing way to go. I tried to fight for the surface, but I was too dazed to coordinate my limbs—to even figure out which direction was *up* in the crashing midnight water. My lungs burning, I kicked and I kicked but a wave caught me, dashing me into the sandy bottom. It refused to let go, spinning me around and around—

A pair of arms grabbed me.

I could offer no fight and little assistance as I was hauled to the surface, but then *air*, precious and sweet. I gasped, coughing and choking.

"I've got you, sister," Majed panted, treading water at my side. "I've got you." He cut the straps holding my armor in place, dragging the jacket and chain mail over my head.

"I thought you were lying," I wheezed. "About still being able to swim like that."

"See what happens when you underestimate me?" he asked, breathing fast, though his voice was tart as usual. "Should have taken me ashore in the first place. We might have never gotten to this point at all."

I was too tired to argue. Dalila and my shipmates helped us through the surf. I could still sense the marid in the back of my mind, feel the tug in my heart as I crawled onto the beach to find the rest of my crew. Literally none of them had fled into the cave as I had commanded. Terrible pirates, they were. No sense of self-preservation.

And speaking of no sense of self-preservation. "I need to go after Falco," I said hoarsely.

"It is too late," Raksh replied, his voice somber. "They will be beyond the door by now. And even if what dwells there, in the place between realms, doesn't kill them, it has already started." He jerked his head toward the sky.

I followed his gaze. At the very edge of the full moon, a delicate shadowy bite had been taken.

The eclipse had begun.

"Amina, what is he talking about?" Dalila demanded.

I stared at the moon, swallowing the lump in my throat. I wanted to lie down in the wet sand and sleep for a hundred years. New strength be damned, I was exhausted and battered. I'd lost most of my borrowed weapons, all of my armor, and a lot of my strength. I was fighting magic I did not understand on half information about lunar patterns, *and* my blasted knee was beginning to pulse yet again.

More, I had already saved my crew, had I not? Maybe Raksh was right, maybe whatever was beyond that door would kill Falco before he possessed the Moon and used it to wreak God only knew what horrors on my people. Maybe this *wasn't* magic that risked my daughter, who had always seemed so preciously mortal.

But I could not take that gamble. And if I was being honest with myself, I could not leave Dunya to such a fate.

I rose shakily to my feet. "I need to try."

Tinbu grabbed my ankle—or rather attempted to from where he was lying on the sand, having Dalila tend his broken leg for the second time. "We will go with you."

I gently shook free. "Forgive me, my friends, but you cannot follow me into this."

"Nor can I," Raksh warned sharply. "No threats this time, Amina.

What dwells beyond that door is a prison for beings such as myself, a trap that can never be unsprung. I would rather be enslaved by Falco than damned for eternity."

"Then I go alone." I raised my hand to stop my friends' brewing protests and crossed to retrieve my sword from Yazid's body. I would take that and the meteor dagger, praying they were enough. "I'm sorry, but I'll be faster without you. I'll explain everything later, I promise . . . but Falco is no longer the only one touched by the supernatural."

Majed gasped, but before any of them could stop me, I ran. My body protested, but as I had on the peris' island, I flew upon the sand and into the cave, sprinting faster than any human had the right to.

The door called to me like the ghost of a lover, a haunting I did not want and yet couldn't deny. I had planned on taking one of the lamps from inside the cave but did not need it. Whatever magic ruled this place glowed brightly in my new Sight, illuminating the twisting tunnel. The door tugged at my heart like an invisible grappling hook, pulling me deeper and deeper until I once again stood before the bronze entrance with its grisly scenes.

It had been left wide open.

A faintly cool breeze whispered past, laced with murmurs that seemed to fade the more I tried to parse them out. With a prayer, I stepped through and the world turned over.

The dank air of the cave, the brass door, and dripping water . . . all gone, replaced by a black void darker than space emptied of its stars. There was an unearthly screech in my ear, and I yelped, stumbling back.

By all rights, I should have stepped back through the bronze doors onto stone steps. Instead, I stepped onto creaking wood, the darkness giving way to shadows and a smoke-choked night sky as though one by one veils were plucked from my eyes. I was outside, the moon a bare sickle, the cold stars hidden. I instinctively steadied my feet as whatever I was standing on rose and fell, like the chest of a sleeping beast—after my encounter with the marid, this was not a feeling I was keen to experience again. But it wasn't a monster: there was the knocking of the ocean against a hull and the crackle of burning sailcloth.

A boat, I realized, for there is no world I know more intimately than the deck of a ship. But not just any boat. With rising horror, I realized that I *recognized* this ship.

I recognized this night.

And there, chained to the ship's mast where I had burned him so many years ago, I recognized Asif.

"Amina," he wept. "Please help me."

Chapter 31

I scrambled back only to crash into the ship's railing.

"God forgive me," I breathed. "This cannot be real."

Asif lunged against his chains, panting like a rabid animal. "No, don't leave me!"

"*This cannot be real*," I whispered again. I scrubbed my eyes, desperate for whatever hallucination or nightmare this was to vanish, but there was no sign of the brass door or the cave. Only dark water and smoke surrounded us—the worst night of my life conjured into reality.

"Nakhudha . . ." Asif begged. "Please just look at me."

However, I was looking everywhere *but* at him. I had already lived this night once—to gaze upon Asif as he suffered and shrieked a second time would destroy me. With a choked sob, I tried to turn away, but my body was slow to respond, as though trapped in a dream.

"*LOOK AT ME.*"

My head snapped around like a spectral hand had seized me by the chin, forcing me to gaze upon the friend I had condemned.

It was Asif as I had seen him last, blood staining his lips and fingers. A shroud soiled with grave dirt hung from his wasted body—his thin wrists and visible ribs evidence of the fever that had taken him, the sickness that had started as a cough and plagued him with such whiplashes of fever and chills, bleeding and vomiting, that in five days, he was gone. Asif hadn't been the only one to die that summer; a vicious wave of disease had swept through the ports of the Persian Gulf, taking nearly a fourth of my crew.

But Asif had been the only one to *rise* from the dead. To climb out of his shallow grave, ravenous and bewildered. To rip through a band of innocent merchants, sucking down their flesh like a ghoul out of a monstrous fireside tale.

"Better," he murmured, his yellowed eyes pinning me in place. His voice sounded briefly unfamiliar, breathy and high-pitched. A heavy weight seemed to shift on my chest. "Much better. Just keep looking. Now . . ." A wave of dizziness swept over me, the night coming even more alive with the acrid aroma of the burning sails and the gentle rock of the tide. Thoughts of the cave, of Dunya and my mission were suddenly far away, as if that was all a dream and this was my true present.

Maybe it was. Maybe I had really condemned myself that night, the past ten years a hallucination.

"Nakhudha, please." Asif's voice was his own again, sounding exactly like it did in my memories and pulling me deeper into whatever delusion or twisted reality had trapped me. "I won't do it again, I swear! Amina, I was so hungry. I was just so hungry. I couldn't think straight."

He will *do it again.* Raksh's stammering explanation rose to my mind: a confession we only got when Asif, painted with the lifeblood of the men he had slaughtered, begged Raksh to save him.

You promised to make me a legend! Asif had cried. *We had a deal!*

Raksh had turned away from him, looking to me. *Fire*, he'd said grimly. *It's the only way to prevent him from doing this again. His soul is gone, and he will not stop hungering without it.*

"You killed a dozen men," I choked out. "I had no choice."

Asif fell to his knees, writhing as his chains grew hotter, the flames licking closer to his tattered shroud.

"Please don't do this. I heard what Raksh said about my soul . . . I will be *gone* if you burn me. I will have no hope of redemption." Asif's desperate gaze met mine. "How can you condemn me to that?"

"Because I didn't know what else to do!" The words ripped from me. It felt impossible to speak past the grief and pressure in my chest, as though a vise were crushing my body. "I am sorry, my friend. I am so sorry. But I couldn't let you hurt anyone else."

Asif stared mournfully at me, his mouth twisted in regret. "I just wanted to dream for a bit. To live a life greater than the one that had been written. I thought I would have time to make up the cost. Was that so wrong?"

"No." I was lost, unmoored within the memory and my own purpose. There was a stinging sensation at my throat, followed by wetness. I tried to touch it, but my arm would not move. "I know how that feels."

"Then how can you sentence me to *this*?" Asif held out his arms. It wasn't only flames ripping at him now, but wriggling worms of utter nothingness that winked pieces of his body out of existence as if his body were a ragged sail. "You were my nakhudha!" he shrieked. "I trusted you!"

My chest hurt so much, the weight upon it growing heavier. I could barely gasp out a reply. "He swore he wouldn't hurt any of you. I didn't know—"

Asif's face snapped up. His eyes were gone, nothing but voids. "You *did* know. You knew what he was and still you let him dwell among us."

"I—" The merchant's ship was burning fiercely now all around me, rope snapping and pitch-soaked wood sizzling. If I did not escape soon, I would burn to death alongside him. Dunya and Falco . . .

Something hit me then.

This is not how it happened.

For Asif had not raged, had not blamed me. He had wept. He had sobbed for his mother, for God, for a few more moments. He was *terrified*, not angry, and he'd begged me to stay not so I'd burn alongside him, but so he wouldn't face his end alone. I had done so shamefaced, holding my tongue when he said he knew I was not to blame, knowing the lie in that.

"You're the one who deserves to die," Asif hissed. The burden on my chest was pressing me into a floor that was cold stone, not sizzling wood.

My arms and legs were tingling as though the limbs had fallen asleep and were slowly regaining sensation. There were blurry spots before my eyes, like two clashing visions of the world . . .

Because this is not real. Asif is long dead or gone or whatever happened to him. And you can never undo it.

But I could still save others.

"Asif, brother . . ." I was weeping. "I cannot stay with you this time. But I swear on our Lord—I will save your child."

He opened his mouth—to protest or scream or try to bite me, I do not know. I slammed my head forward.

The illusion shattered. Pinned over me was a humanoid creature that appeared to have been ripped in half lengthwise. One large orange eye leered at me, one gray arm pressed against my collar, and one fang dripped with the blood it had been drinking from my neck. Earthworms wriggled from its absent left half and its spongy flesh was soft enough that my head had left an imprint in its severed brow.

Its eye widened with what appeared to be surprise. "You should not be able to see me," it said in a slithering voice, hopping back on its single foot. "This is a trick!"

I seized it by the wormy throat before it could flee farther. "Trust that I would rather not see you," I snarled. "What is this place? Where am I?"

"Nasnas do not answer to food," it snapped, trying to wiggle away.

I tightened my grip on its mess of a neck, gagging as worms slithered between my fingers. With my other hand, I freed my sword and pressed it to the so-called nasnas's throat. "You answer to *this* food. Where am I?"

The nasnas glowered resentfully. "The place between realms."

The same nonsensical explanation Raksh had given. "Another pair of humans should have recently come this way. Did you hurt them?"

"No," the creature spat. "The small one knew spells. Spells to ward away nasnas and other folk of the between realms."

"Where did they go?"

It jerked its head to a section of cave that snaked toward the left. "To the eternal waters of chaos."

Was there a rule by which the magical world could not speak plainly? I released the nasnas. "The food thanks you."

The creature gave me a look of hateful, wounded pride. "I will not forget this," it warned. "I will come for you in your dreams of despair and make you relive them again and again until you are nothing but a mad husk."

So the nasnas was the one who put that memory in my head? "Do you promise?"

"Yes! You will not know a single night of peace!"

With a single strike of my sword, I lopped off its head.

"Idiot." I wiped the blade but kept the weapon handy. This seemed like the sort of place where I was going to need it. Then I took a deep breath, wiping my eyes and realizing as I did so that tears were running down my cheeks. I could still hear Asif weeping, see his doomed, pleading expression. He might have been a nasnas hallucination, but that didn't make his final torment—or the charges he'd rightfully laid at my feet—any less real.

Then keep your promise and save Dunya. I forced myself to focus, studying what I could of my surroundings. The air was warm and suffocating, smelling of a sickly sweetness I couldn't identify. The craggy walls were the color of dead flesh, with veins of smoky gray quartz, and stalactites dripping with slimy weeds. Though there was no hint of sky, the stone ceiling seemed to glow like an enclosed lamp.

There was a decent chance the nasnas was leading me to a trap, but I had nowhere else to start.

"To the eternal waters of chaos we go," I muttered and set off.

The sides of the corridor soon pressed even tighter, the rocky ceiling swooping low. The weeds hanging from the stalactites were joined by feathery fronds that reached out from the walls to brush my arms and legs. Occasionally they clung, thorned claws erupting from their tips. I sliced them away, never losing sight of the path ahead. Not even when the ceiling started whispering, buzzing words and soft susurrations, nor when the stone beneath my feet flooded with foul-smelling water thick with unnatural vermin and drowned insects. Nothing would distract me. Not until Falco was dead at my hand and Dunya was safe.

Without warning, the corridor abruptly veered left, then right, doing so again several times before opening into a vast chamber of astonishing wonders. Stone columns carved with the likenesses of beasts and strange symbols held up an intricately sculpted ceiling. A garden of gemstones decorated the walls, ruby roses glittering amongst emerald leaves and diamond thorns. From each corner, water poured out of the chiseled mouths of dragons and bull-headed men to meet in channels that should have overflowed but somehow only churned and churned, like a monsoon sea. The tiled floor, big enough to serve as a city's plaza, was a deep black with silver constellations blinking like true stars.

It would have made for an extraordinarily beautiful sight, a vision out of Paradise . . . were it not entirely crawling with monsters.

A green-skinned woman carrying her own decapitated head by its hissing snake locks wailed and wandered. Dogs with smoldering skin and four flashing eyes prowled the narrow exit on the other side of the chamber, while winged shadows wheeled around the lofty columns. There were scorpion men and lions with dragon heads and tails of barbed quills. Way, *way* more nasnas than I ever wanted to see again and a nightmarish flying bat that reminded me of the creature in the lagoon. Sobbing ghastly wraiths were trapped in the stone walls, their grasping hands reaching out to drag any passerby into their tombs, and a demon with fiery orange skin and a wickedly sharp bronze mace stalked the floor.

Raksh had said this place was meant to imprison beings such as himself, and he hadn't lied. Not technically. He had, however, *vastly* understated just how terrifying and monstrous those beings were. I would take a thousand selfish chaos spirits over just one of the creatures prowling the chamber before me.

Then a familiar scream sounded in the distance, pulling my attention to an archway on the other side of the vast chamber.

Dunya.

Wonderful. I'd found her. There was just a prison's worth of monsters separating us. I took an experimental step forward . . .

And the floor evaporated.

Again.

I cried out in shock, nearly tumbling from the vanishingly small patch of shimmering yellow-gold light that remained under my boots. The rest of the floor had been transformed into the night sky it resembled, as if the world had turned over and had gravity reversed. Demons fell screaming into the stellar abyss, while others sprouted wings covered in festering sores, flapping away to save themselves. But my shout must have drawn their attention, for more than a handful hissed, wheeling around in the air to fly in my direction.

Desperate, I glanced back the way I had come. A small bank of black sky separated me from the stone passage, but I could probably jump to it. Ahead, a terrifyingly slender, barely visible beam of the same golden shimmer that was beneath my feet seemed to stretch to the archway. But the beam could have equally been a trick of the light, of my own misplaced hopes.

Run, you fool, a voice in my mind urged. *Back to your family, back to your friends.* Surely this place was dangerous enough to take care of Falco. Surely it was not all up to *me.*

"I cannot do this," I choked out. It suddenly seemed madness to think I could, arrogant to believe the fate of the world relied on *me*—a criminal, a sinner, a foul-mouthed middle-aged woman with a bad knee. Did it not seem far more likely I would be devoured by these monsters or fall forever, doomed and forgotten? Had I been so naïve to see *purpose* in the incidents that had led to me being here, rather than quirks of an uncaring universe? What madness to gaze upon the violent chaos and cruelty of this world and have *faith*!

Tears ran down my cheeks. I took a steadying breath, fixing my gaze on the golden shimmer I prayed was truly there. This was going to be either the bravest or the stupidest thing I had ever done.

"God is greatest," I whispered, sheathing my sword. Then I took off across the hall.

There was a moment—terrifying, heart-stopping—when I seemed to plummet, but then my foot landed on the narrow beam of sunlight made physical. I let out a garbled sound that could have been a prayer, a curse, or just a scream—but I did not stop running. I drew no weapons, not even as creatures swooped and snarled at my head.

I knew in my heart that they were not my test.

The hall and its narrow bridge seemed to last forever, but then I was stumbling through the archway and collapsing onto solid rock once again. I might have kissed it had my entire body not been shaking so badly that any additional movement seemed beyond me. I crawled around a stony pass, eager to put myself beyond the reach of the devils in the hall, my heart still racing.

But the creatures in the chamber weren't the only monsters here.

"Do not move, whoever you are," Falco's cold, curt voice greeted from some distance away. "Interrupt and we die."

◆

Falco had no sooner warned me *not* to move than I immediately sat up, both because my disposition tends toward contrariness and because he could go jump off a cliff. But then I did freeze and not because of the Frank's warning.

But because Dunya was *levitating*.

Not particularly high, mind you, but she was still very much floating before a tall stone column that stretched to the ceiling and was covered in cuneiform characters similar to those on her shattered tablets. This chamber was larger than the last but looked like a natural part of the cave, illuminated by torches and the reflections of cleverly placed copper mirrors. Wisps of light twirled around Dunya's limbs, her garments fluttering in an invisible wind. A blindfold had been tied around her face, and in her outstretched hands, she held a lump of salt and a stylus. Blindfolded or not, she was writing, using the stylus to carve characters into the stone column as easily as one might inscribe warm wax.

"*Al-Sirafi?*" Falco drew closer, stepping out of the shadows with his sword dangling from his hand. Dunya seemed oblivious to my arrival, lost in whatever magic she was doing, but the Frank looked shocked, his wide astonished eyes tracing over me. "It *is* you. But how?"

In the back of my mind, the marid suddenly screamed.

I fought a gasp as my entire body shook, cold sweat breaking across my skin. It sounded exactly like a ghostly relic of the marid's wail. A warning in a language that was not words but still clearly told me to beware, to retreat. To flee from the man before me and dive into the depths of the seabed, where I could not be pursued.

The Frank inhaled as though he'd heard it as well. "You are changed."

The knowing in his voice unnerved me nearly as much as the marid having a toehold in my mind. Did whatever powers Falco possessed enable him to sense such magic?

And yet . . . I rose to my feet, cracking my neck and drawing my weapons with all the unnatural grace I now possessed. Let this fucker see me. Because he would definitely not be beating me in swordplay again. "Indeed," I replied evenly.

A hint of trepidation flickered in his face. "All the bleating you did about my arrogance and yet you made your own deal with the supernatural to survive." Hunger filled his voice. "With what? How did you summon them? What did they offer?"

"If I could send you their way, trust me, I would." The prospect of the obnoxious peri court having to deal with the power-hungry Frank was genuinely tempting. But more worried about Dunya, I ignored Falco's questions to draw closer to the young scholar. She was still engraving characters in the stone column, working as though bewitched. Beads of water rose and dripped from the silvery rock like sweat.

"Dunya?" I called softly. "Are you—"

Falco hissed at me to shush. "Need you be told *twice*? She is calling forth the Moon of Saba and warned that if the spell was disturbed, it might bring down the entire chamber."

She's doing what? I spun back to Dunya. But neither the spellbound youth nor the weeping veneer of text I wasn't able to read could tell me. I hesitated, uncertain what to do next. I was here to make sure Falco could not take possession of the Moon and was admittedly a little reluctant to believe Dunya had a sound plan for thwarting him. But bringing down the cave upon all our heads because I interrupted some sorcery I didn't understand was not an agreeable end.

Deciding to leave Dunya alone for now, I returned my attention to Falco. Him, I would deal with. "Frightened of a child, are you?" I mocked, taking a purposeful step in his direction.

He lifted his chin. "I recognize talent when I see it," he said with obnoxious conceit. "Dunya is a clever, curious person. She's going to do wonderful things."

"As long as she does them in your service."

"I was the one who saved her from her family, no?" Falco gave me a plaintive look. "You could still join us, nakhudha. Indeed, I cannot help but feel you are *meant* to. Do you not see fate in arriving at this very moment? We could bring our peoples together! Build a new world!"

Oh, I saw fate in my timely arrival. Just not the way Falco did.

I stalked closer to the Frank. "Did fate tell you to throw me off my ship? Because I took that personally, Palamenestra," I said, finally hissing every syllable correctly. "And spare me this self-aggrandizing nattering about building a better world. You're not doing this to improve the occult sciences or bring people together. You didn't *save* Dunya—*you* needed *her*. You're just a craven little man who wants power and is looking for any excuse to believe yourself a hero. But you know what?" I raised my sword. "I *am* going to give you a taste of the magic that changed me."

I was across the chamber the next moment.

Falco wasted a precious second looking displeased and unhappy—this man was genuinely disappointed the woman he'd tried to kill didn't wish to serve him—but seeming to realize I was indeed intent on murder, he ducked behind a sulfur-yellow stalagmite that smelled of rotting eggs before I could separate his head from his body.

My arm smashed through the stalagmite, sulfur exploding in messy, fetid crumbles. I kicked at the base, sending a spray into the Frank's face as he backpedaled and lifted his weapon, attempting an offensive strike.

But *I* was the faster one now. The stronger one. I brought my sword down again and again on his, Falco struggling to defend himself. He shouted in pain as one of my strikes ripped through his chain mail, opening a nasty, bloody gash across his torso. I slashed down at his neck and while he jerked away to avoid the killing blow, he caught the hilt in his face, blood spurting from his nose.

"Wait!" he cried, spitting out a tooth and staggering back. His eyes were wild in his bloody face. "You *plague* of a woman, if you would just listen to reason!"

The only thing I wanted to listen to was this man's last gurgling breath. I circled closer, contemplating the best approach to end this. Falco had lowered his sword, but I did not trust his seemingly vulnerable position.

Dunya suddenly shrieked.

It was an unnatural yelp, as though something old and inhuman had briefly stolen her voice. I whirled back to see the lump of salt in her hand vanish in a burst of mist. And then the entire stone *column* exploded, great geysers of water tearing through the rock as if it were nothing but pebbles, lashing the air with drenching sprays of liquid gravel.

"Dunya!" Shielding my face, I ran for the scholar.

When I got to her, she was crumpled on the wet ground, whatever magic had made her float vanishing. She'd taken a nasty bump to the head, and blood was streaming down her brow and arms from a dozen small lacerations. I dropped to her side. Dunya's damp face was pale as parchment and cold to the touch. Her eyes were closed but her lips were still moving, murmuring breathy chants I couldn't understand.

"Dunya," I said urgently, gently shaking her shoulder. To hell with this not-interrupting-the-spell rubbish. "Dunya, can you hear me? Are you all right?"

She stopped her nonsensical rambling and, God be praised, a little color reappeared in her cheeks. Her eyes slowly blinked open, her bleary gaze struggling to focus on my face.

"Nakhudha . . ." she whispered. "Is it really you?"

"Aye." I cradled her head, trying to examine the bruise already swelling on her brow. "Take care. You are bleeding."

But Dunya was already trying to sit up, wincing in pain. "Did it work?"

From the other side of the cave came a giddy chuckle.

Falco. I'd been so concerned with Dunya that I'd briefly paused my mission to murder the Frank, but I glanced up now to see him sitting on the ground, happy delight in his expression. He was gazing at his lap like he didn't have a care in the world.

No, not at his lap. At the *silver basin* nestled in his hands.

The Moon of Saba.

Its glimmer entranced me, *snared* me, and all other thoughts vanished. The silver-worked basin that had once belonged to Queen Bilqis, that had trapped a lunar admirer, that had launched wars and destroyed kingdoms, was magnificent. I suppose that should have been obvious—it had belonged to a queen. It was not overly large, about the size of a winter melon, and yet I could see the scenes carved on its curving sides as though the basin were right before my eyes. A garden with date palms and a lute player, an ibex with scrolled horns peeking mischievously from behind a screen of leaves, and a pair of hoopoe birds with their beaks opened in mid-song. The silver gleamed as though freshly polished, as though it had not already been ancient a millennium ago.

And staring upon it . . . I felt *silly*, my cares gone and my heart loosened. Falco's and my gaze caught, briefly sharing a moment of happy, drunken commune before the disgust of doing so with the murderous sorcerer broke whatever spell the Moon of Saba had cast upon me. I shivered and blinked rapidly—then realized the basin's gleam wasn't only coming from the polished silver.

It was coming from the water glistening in the basin's depths.

Water.

The stories rushed back to me, the lies and truths mixing together. One had to see their reflection to possess al-Dabaran and now Falco was—

"No!" I shot to my feet, but not even my new speed would get me across the chamber in time. However, I *did* have time to rip off my boot and hurl it at the Moon of Saba with enough force to send the lovely, priceless historical artifact spinning out of Falco's hands and toppling to the dirty floor.

But it was too late.

Falco kept laughing, a light airy sound. He met my gaze again, and I gasped. His brown eyes were filling with celestial light.

"Behold!" he cried. "I have accomplished what no man has since Solomon! I have mastered the spirits of discord and the hidden sciences!" He raised his hands, and from around the chamber there was hissing and the papery brush of wings and chitin as moths, snakes, centipedes, and a whole host of foul creatures emerged from every dark crevasse. "Let God Himself tremble at the world I will build!"

Chapter 32

I stared at Falco in disbelieving horror as moonlight shone out of his eyes and insects flew around his shoulders like great schools of fish. It seemed impossible that after everything, *everything*—my life-altering deal with the peris, the battle on the beach, climbing up a fucking marid *twice*, the celestial hall of monsters—this man had still beat me.

He has not won yet, I tried to tell myself. *Not truly*. With raw power swirling around him like an eager wave and the legendary Moon of Saba lying in the dust near his feet, Falco certainly looked triumphant. But Raksh and Dunya had both made clear that a human possessing the power of al-Dabaran was still just that: human. *Mortal*. But as I drew the meteor blade, suddenly its glimmer didn't seem so ethereal.

Dunya grabbed my sleeve. "Don't go near him. Not yet." She was watching Falco as he threw his head back and laughed in merry delight, his hair and garments fluttering madly in an invisible wind—but not with shock. Rather with anticipation. She coughed out a bit of dust. "There's something I should tell you—"

Every torch in the cave abruptly flickered, the insects all shrilled as one, and Falco began to shriek.

"No, *stop!*" he screamed, clawing at his eyes. They had filled completely with a silver glow, resembling miniature moons. "You cannot! *YOU ARE MINE!*" He cried out again, this time in what must have been his native language, and frantically jerked about, like he was fighting for control of his body.

Then he went entirely, utterly still. His eyes were no longer full glowing lunar spheres. A pale gray haze had slipped over part of them. Just like . . .

"Is that . . . is that the eclipse?" I stammered in a hush.

"Yes," Dunya whispered. "It worked."

It worked? What did that mean? I stared again at Falco. His pompous bravado was gone, and his posture ramrod straight, straight in a way that did not look comfortable to any creature with a spine. He gazed about the cave, an eerie, unnatural assessment in his face as though he were surveying an army about to be crushed, snakes, lizards, and insects all still rushing to his feet. Tilting his head in an expression that was not quite human, his unearthly gaze fell upon the Moon of Saba.

His lips drew back in a snarl.

"Dunya . . ." I breathed. "What did you do?"

She gave me a frightened look. "I had to stop him, nakhudha, and I knew no other way. Falco was determined to get his hands on the Moon of Saba."

"*What did you do?*"

"Well, I suspected the eclipse might offer a rare opportunity. With the exchange of lunar and solar houses of power and the ascendance of the Aries—"

"Dunya, stop talking like a court astrologer on hashish and tell me plainly what you did!"

"I reversed the incantation!" she spluttered. "I think. I . . . hope. God willing."

"*Meaning?*"

"Meaning when Falco saw his reflection, it was not he who gained control of al-Dabaran, rather—"

"It was al-Dabaran who gained control of Falco. Oh," I choked, "how creative." And it was. Part of me was proud of Dunya and inordinately pleased Falco had been done in by his own arrogance in assuming our scholars were not as clever as he. "And when the eclipse ends?"

"I did not work that part out yet," she confessed. "I thought we might speak to al-Dabaran and ask him how to break the enchantment."

"Break the enchantment?" I repeated, a bit of, well, not hope—I wasn't that deluded—but a feeling that was not dread briefly blossoming in my heart. That *was* what the peris wanted, after all, what *I* wanted: the Transgression that might endanger my child destroyed. "Can we do that?"

"Yes and no." Dunya wrung her hands. "There should be ways to free al-Dabaran, but apparently in order to return to the moon, he must *see* the moon."

"And we're underground. Wonderful." I racked my brain, but I didn't know how to bring moonlight to an underground cave. I also wasn't sure we had the time or knowledge to return to the surface if we could even convince al-Dabaran to accompany us.

"Why don't we try talking to him?" Dunya suggested as al-Dabaran picked up the silver basin, lifting it in the air as though it were a fragile offering. "He's a powerful spirit. He must know some magic."

Falco—al-Dabaran—abruptly smashed the silver basin upon the stone floor, and we both jumped. The Moon of Saba didn't so much as crack, instead bouncing on the ground in a way that might have been comical if a clearly irate al-Dabaran hadn't thrown back his head, screeched a sound like shattering glass, and sent a gush of crickets pouring from his mouth.

Dunya and I ducked but the crickets simply flew overhead; disgusting as the display was, al-Dabaran was clearly more focused on attempting to destroy his silver prison than harass two humans. The rest of the insects flocked to al-Dabaran's side, forming a fluttering cloak of locusts, cicadas, and moths.

Dunya loudly cleared her throat. "Right. Well. I shall try to talk to him. But this is not your responsibility, nakhudha. In case things go wrong, you should escape while—"

"Oh, shut up." Al-Dabaran had picked up Falco's sword, and the weapon doubled in size, gleaming like a bone-white moon. Its razor-sharp edges were now serrated, pocked like craters, and yet the entire thing *wiggled and hissed*—transformed into a horrifying combination of a sword, a snake, and a staff. Magical sword snake staffs were not a Dunya-level problem. "You're bleeding like a sieve, and this isn't the first supernatural entity I've had to bargain with this week." I pointed to a protected niche below a rocky outcropping. "Can you make it over there?"

She gave me an alarmed look. "Why?"

I watched in wary apprehension as al-Dabaran returned to the Moon of Saba and began bashing it with the weaponized snake staff, trying to break the ensorcelled basin to no avail. "In case he doesn't like chatting. *Go*," I insisted, shooing her off.

Foreboding curdling in my belly, I waited until Dunya was gone before cautiously approaching the angry lunar spirit.

"Dear manzil al-Dabaran!" I greeted, raising my hands in what I hoped was a motion of peace. "Blessings upon you!"

Al-Dabaran stopped attacking the basin and spun to regard me. His eerie eyes were expressionless, the snake staff wriggling in his hand. He did the creepy head tilt again, seeming to size me up. For a moment, I briefly entertained hopes of this plan working.

Then he *howled*, sending a far angrier flock of insects—locusts this time!—from his mouth my way, and I realized centuries of captivity might not have done his mind well.

I ducked behind a stalagmite, slapping insects away. "We might need another plan!"

Dunya peeked out from her position. "Can you get me the bowl? If there are incantations on it, I might be able to reverse the spell!"

"I'll try!" And because I tend toward violence when nothing else works, I picked up a rock, charged al-Dabaran, and hurled it at his head.

Perhaps the manzil had some aggressions to work out or maybe he just didn't like interfering humans throwing rocks at him because he was only too happy to turn his attentions from the basin and rage after me. I dashed past the Moon of Saba, pausing only to kick it in Dunya's direction like a child's ball. Then I ducked as al-Dabaran's serpentine staff went whooshing over my head, close enough to feel the chill of his bewitched blade. I recovered quickly, whirling around to strike out with my own sword.

The serpentine staff hardened like steel when it met my weapon. For a moment, we stayed locked together, neither of us gaining ground until the tip of his sword staff *turned into a snake's head* and reached back to snap at my hands.

And people ask me why I don't like magic.

I jumped away before the snake sword could bite me and ran. Al-Dabaran gave chase as I sprinted to the other side of the cave, leaping back and forth across a twisting stream that emptied into a steaming pool of milky-blue water. Over the manzil's insect-cloaked shoulder, I could see Dunya turning the Moon of Saba over in her hands, her panic-stricken expression deeply uninspiring.

The momentary distraction nearly got me stabbed in the stomach. I jerked back, springing along a path of boulders nosing out of the no-doubt-poisonous pool, leading al-Dabaran farther from Dunya.

"And here I thought you liked your women fierce," I challenged, dodging a stream of hissing roaches. "Or is that only when you can spy on them in the bath, you petty, perverted excuse for a planet?"

It was honestly among my weakest of insults—you try insulting a demi-god while they're attempting to kill you!—but al-Dabaran didn't take it well. Not well at all. So badly in fact that he briefly drew back from attempting to decapitate me with his snake staff and brought his palms together with a terrific cracking sound. The water in the pond instantly drained, great clouds of steam scalding the air and leaving a pit large enough to swallow a fishing boat. The ground shook with great force and I scrambled away, eager to avoid tumbling into that forbidding maw.

But al-Dabaran now had me cornered. I stepped back, only to collide with the cave's clammy wall and become instantly drenched. Saltwater springs were running freely down the lichen-covered rock. I inhaled, the familiar scent of the ocean filling my lungs as the trickling rivulets of water curled around my fingers.

The marid's ghostly presence reached out to touch me.

Not *physically*. Rather I felt it stir again in the back corner of my mind. And not just stir; our tether—the bond I'd accidently forged when I freed the creature—flashed into sight, its sunny scales shining bright before vanishing again.

Is it close? Is this some sort of message? But I had little time to ponder the doings of an oversized monster because al-Dabaran had apparently summoned his own when he shattered the ground.

From the ruined pit lunged an enormous white serpent.

I had barely registered this last horror of Socotran folktales coming to life before the snake hurled itself at me. I threw myself out of the way, rolling to hide in the emptied creek bed as the serpent smashed into the spot where I had been standing hard enough to split the rock. I covered my head, stone shards flying everywhere.

But now the smell of sea air wasn't faint—it was palpable. It was on a *breeze*, an undeniable whisper of ocean air teasing my face.

Dunya said that al-Dabaran had to see the Moon. God, could that mean . . .

Foolishly hopeful, I glanced up to see what sort of damage the snake had done. It had shattered part of the rock, but not enough to break through the cave entirely. The serpent was coiling around, seeming to have trouble with its vast bulk in the confined space.

Taking advantage of its struggle, I raced for the rift in the cave wall. I could feel the breeze more strongly now, through a gap barely the size of my fist. With no better options, I slashed at the gap with my sword. But new strength or not, the weapon was not meant to break through rocks.

The steel cracked and then shattered as I struck out again and again, leaving me with only the hilt.

"Nakhudha, the eclipse is going to end!"

At Dunya's cry, the snake hissed and perhaps realizing it had an easier target, it darted in her direction.

"Dunya, run!" I shouted. I could do nothing else for her; al-Dabaran had called the snake and the only way we were going to defeat *it* was if we defeated *him*. I threw myself into trying to widen the gap, bashing at the stone with the broken sword hilt, crying out in frustration as my hands grew bloody, and all I had to show for it was a few flying splinters of rock. If I had weeks, I might make a hole big enough for me to crawl out of it. As it was, we had mere minutes, if that.

From beyond the cave, I heard the muffled screech of the scorpion marid. Not only in my head this time—it was out there, swimming in the sea nearby. In my mind, its presence had grown more insistent and *needy*, pounding like the world's worst hangover. I swore. Did the creature truly need to harass me *now*? I had already freed it!

I had already freed it.

They have strongly held beliefs about favors. That last word, the one Khayzur had struggled to spit out. Dunya screamed again, sounding far more terrified.

Desperate, I did what I never wanted to do. I closed my eyes, pulled as hard as I could on the presence in my head, and threw myself at the mercy of a magical creature.

The marid's presence poured through my mind, my blood running cold as my eyes were snapped back open without me controlling the motion. The world was eerily gray, the marid seeming to survey the scene through my gaze. The snake chasing Dunya. Al-Dabaran wailing and spewing spiders. The salty-sweet ocean breeze whistling through the narrow gap in the cave wall . . .

The water trickling beneath my feet abruptly transformed. It wound around my ankle like a liquid rope and tossed me clear across the cave. I crashed into Dunya, the two of us rolling in the protected niche as if we were a part of some grand monster ball game. Pain ripped through my body, but I barely noticed.

Because a gargantuan stinger came slicing through the cave wall.

A second strike sent seawater surging in. A third and a fourth. I could feel the marid's power and frustration, and I was starting to fear nothing could break through the cave before a fifth blow of the marid's mighty tail ripped apart the rock.

A shaft of moonlight spilled inside.

Al-Dabaran rushed to the illuminated spot. He ran his fingers over the moonlight, wailing in grief and despair. It was a sound that cut through any differences between us.

For I too wanted to go home.

Acting on instinct, I grabbed the Moon of Saba out of Dunya's hands and threw the silver basin to the feet of the lunar being it had trapped for so long. Al-Dabaran gave me one last wild look—madness and thanks and relief—the eclipse vanishing from Falco's transformed eyes. Then he slammed his staff into the silver basin.

This time the Moon of Saba did a lot more than crack.

The moonlight brightened so explosively I had to turn away. The serpent was hissing, wind was ripping around us, sending insects and debris everywhere. With a final howl, a *presence* ripped from Falco's body with enough force to send a wave of pressure ricocheting across the cave. I scrambled back beneath the outcropping, sheltering Dunya as best I could while rocks, broken bronze mirrors, and shattered stalactites rained down around us.

It was probably only a few moments but it felt like forever, waiting to be crushed by a boulder or pierced by wreckage. Finally the cave stopped quaking. I waited until the only sound was Dunya's and my ragged breathing. Then I lifted my head.

The entire half of the chamber facing the sea was destroyed. The ocean had poured in to flood the lower part, but mercifully, there was a clear way to climb out, a shard of midnight beach just visible. But our path to freedom wasn't the only thing I saw.

I saw the marid. The great hulk of its healing body and its glittering cluster of eyes meeting my two. Its stinger sliced across the stars like an ebony dagger and its presence in my mind coiled tight one last time, the golden bond between us briefly manifesting.

Then ever so slowly, the tether dissipated. I couldn't fathom how these creatures communicated, but as the marid vanished beneath the black water and slowly unwound from my mind, I would swear it was calling us even.

Dunya peeked up. "Is al-Dabaran gone?"

An excellent question. "I certainly hope so." I cleared the rubble away from where we had sheltered, thanking God for my new strength. The enormous white snake, the insects . . . all were gone, perhaps fleeing the destruction to whatever deeper cave tunnels and chambers they called home. My ruined sword was long gone, but I kept the meteor blade in one hand as I helped Dunya out and pointed her toward the edge of the cave that met the sea.

"Go. I will meet you there. I want to get out of here before that snake decides to come back, but there is one more thing I need to do."

Dunya didn't question me. I watched her pick her way carefully over the rocks. Then I turned to my final task.

Al-Dabaran had ripped out of Falco with a force that had hurled the Frank across the ruined chamber like he was a reed doll. But I could hear his panting breath as I strode across the broken floor. The man who'd intended to remake a land that was not his, with stolen magic he could not understand—the man who had arrived on the blood of butchered innocents and taken even more lives in Socotra—now lay pinned beneath a shattered boulder that had crushed his left leg and pelvis. Blood trickled from his mouth and dust coated his face, his sash of pilgrim badges lying in tatters and his bleary eyes taking in the sight of me standing over him.

"Al-Sirafi . . ." he wheezed. "Come to gloat?"

"No." Falco's wound was almost certainly fatal, promising a more lingering, painful death than I could grant him. But I did not believe in leaving threats to fester, and this fiend had killed enough.

Falco struggled to raise his head as I drew closer. "If you would just listen . . . the things I saw in al-Dabaran's mind— *wait*!" he cried hoarsely as the tip of my dagger met his breast. "Just give me—"

"You have taken up enough of my time." I shoved the blade through his heart.

His gaze brightened with a moment of panic, his body jerking in response. But it was only a moment. Then Falco lay still, blood spreading across his chest.

I wiped the dagger on his cloak and walked away.

Dunya was waiting for me, hugging her knees to her chest as she sat on a flat rock overlooking the sea. The little scholar had shown incredible valor in thwarting Falco the way she did, and I could tell she was fighting to hold that courage, though her entire body trembled when her wide brown eyes met mine.

"Did you . . . is it done?" she whispered.

"It is done." I wrapped an arm around her shoulders. "Come, child. Let's get out of here."

Chapter 33

I did not allow myself to relax even a hair until we were four days at sea. I had spent the past week doing everything I could to ready the *Marawati* for departure, even if we would be traveling at a sluggish pace and against the monsoon; true repairs needed a better harbor and more supplies than we had at hand.

But I wanted to be *home*, desperately. I wanted my child and my family and to set this all behind me—for however long the peris would permit.

Magnun had entreated me to stay, offering use of the well-stocked boatyard and skilled tradesmen back at his base. But I was not eager to try the luck of his comrades twice and told him so.

"Then perhaps you should join us truly," he had suggested with a hopeful glint in his eyes as he packed up the plunder from Falco's camp. "Take the oaths, add your *Marawati* to our fleet, and raid the sea as a proper bandit queen again."

I'd shaken my head, giving an admittedly regretful look at the spoils he'd earned. My people had been permitted to take a few pieces, but I would not renege on the deal I'd struck with the sole nakhudha who'd been willing to help me.

"I'm done with that life, but thank you for coming to my aid." Far more reluctantly, I handed over the meteor dagger. "And thank you for this."

"Ah, ah . . . did I say the loan had ended?" Magnun folded my fingers over the dagger. "You battled a sea monster with that, al-Sirafi. Hold on to it a bit longer, see where it takes you." He winked. "If anything, it means I will have to track you down one day to retrieve it."

I could see a hundred ways being tracked down by Magnun could go badly, but honestly, the Egyptian nakhudha ran a tight ship and seemed like a good time. And it *was* a remarkable knife. Besides, I had four more magical items to retrieve—I could probably use a celestial blade. "Then until we meet again, God willing."

With Raksh aboard again, we ran into blessedly good luck, the wind and current exactly what we needed despite the season.

"Amina, go rest," Dalila said, shoving my shoulder when I began to nod off on my captain's bench. "You have not slept in days."

I shuddered awake, wincing as one of the muscles in my neck twinged in protest at the movement. "I'm fine," I mumbled. "Never better."

"Even your lying is affected. *Go*." She pushed me in the direction of the galley. "Else I will slip a knockout potion in your next meal."

I muttered a curse but staggered away as commanded. The galley was wondrously cool, my cushion alluring. I was taking off my cloak and unwinding my turban when a feline growl caught my attention.

"*Payasam?*" I said in disbelief. The cat had survived the attack on the *Marawati* because of course it had; it was a curse and had already returned to trying to sleep on my face. But the growling, hissing feline hunched in the galley's roof beams bore little resemblance to Tinbu's happy idiot of a pet. "What has you all . . ." I trailed off as I followed the cat's glare.

On the ledge of the narrow window, glittering in a shaft of sunlight, rested a single lime-green feather.

Khayzur.

With a final hiss, Payasam jumped down from the ceiling and tore out the door. A chill ran down my spine, at odds with the warm day and pleasant breeze as I stared at the peri's feather.

Five. The number rang through my head; five Transgressions I was to retrieve. One was done, four more to go. They could be anything. They could be anywhere.

I dropped my cloak and turban and picked up Khayzur's feather. It was cold, buzzing in a strange but not unpleasant way.

Who are you? I wondered. For now that my loved ones were out of imminent danger, my mind had cleared, and in hindsight, it seemed extraordinarily fortuitous that Khayzur—one of the few peris who would save a human—had been exactly where I needed him when I was dropped out of the sky. Where was the line between God's plan and something being too good to be true? Yes, Khayzur seemed kind and had saved my life, but that did not mean I trusted him. I did not trust any magical being.

Even though, as much as I hated to admit it, I might now be one of them.

A shadow fell across me, and Raksh spoke from the doorway. "A gift?"

"A message," I grumbled. "I suspect the peris want to make sure I know they're watching me. They're likely not pleased I destroyed the Moon of Saba myself instead of handing it over."

He plucked the feather from my fingers. "Do not worry yourself over those birdbrained fools."

I smacked his arm. "Maybe I should be blaming *you* for the birdbrained fools. What were you thinking back on the island, suggesting I sign my entire life over to them!"

Raksh frowned. "Was it not obvious?"

"That you were sacrificing me to save yourself?"

"*Sacrifice* you?" Raksh burst into laughter. "Is that what you've been thinking this whole time?" His eyes began to glow. "Oh, Amina . . . no. Not at all."

Nothing that got Raksh this excited was good. "Then what were you doing?"

He dropped the feather and closed the distance between us. "You don't even see it, do you?" he asked, seeming to marvel at me anew. "Amina, I am going to make you a *legend*."

I stilled. That word was very dangerous when it came to Raksh. When it came to me. "What?" I asked in a whisper.

His eyes locked on mine. Without me realizing it, he'd taken one of my braids in his hands, weaving it through his fingers. "A supernaturally blessed warrior tasked with traveling the world and hunting down some of the most marvelous treasures ever created," he breathed, sounding almost reverent. "Do you not realize your *potential*? I am going to spin such tales that your adventures will live on in epic poems grander than that of Antarah and Dhat al-Himma, your name sung in odes to heroes whose mighty feats surpass those of Alexander." Raksh's voice rose in merry delight as he pulled me closer, so enraptured he seemed to forget doing so risked him getting stabbed. "It will be like we dreamed the night we first met!"

The night we first met. I remembered the ill-fated evening Raksh and I had crossed paths. How I had laughed and sighed under the stars, bewitched into revealing my heart. How I wished to travel the world. How I wished to be the *best*, the adventures of the great Amina al-Sirafi told around courtyards and campfires.

"I-I cannot," I stammered. "You heard the peris. They told me to be discreet."

"Ah, but you did not actually strike such an ironclad deal with them. Were they to put consequences into the 'loose agreement under which they would not let you fall to your death . . .'" Raksh rolled his eyes, before a far more cunning expression stole onto his face. "*That* would have been a proper pact with a mortal. They would never admit to such an abomination. And truthfully, there's nothing they can do to stop the spread of human stories: to interfere would be against their own code."

I was completely taken aback. "You *tricked* them?"

"I did! But you need not look so fretful. It's what you want, isn't it?" He kissed my fingers. "You shall have your adventures, shall explore the world and for *righteous* reasons. We heard how dangerous those

Transgressions are: now you will be the one to rid the world of them."
He winked. "Do some good to counterbalance all your misdeeds, no?"

I knew Raksh cared nothing for good deeds; he was merely reading my
heart's desires and using what he sensed for his own reasons. However,
the future he painted so prettily no longer sounded like the ridiculous
dream of a decade ago. I had yet to wrap my mind around what had happened to me on the peris' island, yet to sit and let the implications of my
"not-deal" settle.

But I had dueled with a sea leviathan. Battled a wizard and set free an
ensorcelled lunar aspect.

What else might I do?

Go home and be a mother to your child for as long as you can. And
truthfully that was what I desired more than anything right now, my heart
aching at the very prospect of holding Marjana in my arms. And yet . . .

And yet . . .

I wanted everything Raksh had just purred. If I was being honest,
I wanted *more*. I meant what I had told Nasteho back on the beach in
Mogadishu: I had never stopped being a nakhudha, never stopped being
an *explorer*. It wasn't this accursed demon or spirit of discord or whatever he called himself putting alien desires in my soul: *I* wanted to travel
the world and sail every sea. *I* wanted to have adventures, to be a hero,
to have my tales told in courtyards and street fairs, where perhaps kids
who'd grown up like me, with more imagination than means, might be
inspired to dream. Where women who were told there was only one sort
of respectful life for them could listen to tales of another who'd broken
away—and *thrived* when she'd done so.

I wanted to show Marjana that. Not now. But when she was older,
when it was safer. I wanted to teach my daughter to read the waves and
the night sky, to see her eyes widen with wonder and curiosity when I
brought her to new places, new cities. I wanted to *give* her all that I'd had
to *take*, positioning her to enjoy opportunities I could never imagine.

Was it possible? Could I be an adventuring nakhudha *and* a mother?

Did I even have a choice? For I was obliged to recover four more Transgressions, and a strange niggling guilt gnawed in my belly at that. If I had no choice but to go adventuring, then perhaps I didn't need to delve into the dark, murky part of my heart that wanted to do so for selfish reasons.

Raksh had held his tongue, his eyes flicking back and forth across my face as my mind raced—he was, after all, well practiced in waiting for foolhardy humans to dream their delusions. But watching him do so was enough to shake me from my dreaming.

For I wasn't the only one with ambitions and I recalled another night with Raksh—our last on the peris' island. When my husband and I sat by the fire, watched the sun dip below the ocean, and he got as close to confiding in me as I suspected he was capable of. When he mused with open wistfulness how he'd been created to spin tales and inspire legends.

When he regretted that he hadn't enjoyed the opportunity to do so in a very, *very* long time.

And as Raksh gazed at me with his beautiful, bewitched eyes, the nearest thing I had ever seen to a genuine grin playing over his perfect mouth, I suddenly understood that for all his lies and cowardice, for all the bloody history between us—I had just become exactly what he craved the most.

And because of that, he was never, ever going to let me go.

Kill him now. Before he suspects anything. And yet how could I? He was Marjana's father and I'd just been delivered a very harsh lesson about how little I knew of her magical heritage. Were there other children like her? What happened when *they* grew up? Were there other possible threats to her like the Moon of Saba? I couldn't ask Raksh those questions today, not when I was determined to keep our daughter's existence a secret. But he was still the only guide I had if I ever needed answers about "the spirits of discord" and their kin.

Well, he was my only guide for *now*. Deciding on another path, I settled my hands around his neck. It was an echo, a reminder of how easily

I'd been able to strangle him back on the island, but instead I played with his hair.

"So, what?" I asked with open doubt. "I am to trust you now?"

Raksh shivered and leaned into my touch. "You are welcome to trust me, do other things to me, whatever tickles your fancy. I know we've had some troubles in the past but"—he pulled my body against his completely, rocking his hips into mine—"what marriage does not?"

His breath was hot on my throat, setting my treacherous blood aflame as he pressed a kiss to the edge of my jaw. Ten years. *Ten years* since I'd been touched like this.

You're supposed to be getting rid of him, remember? And yet my hands were already slipping around his waist. I gave his glorious backside a proper squeeze, and Raksh let out a messy sigh. All right, yes. There were some creepy magical ways he wanted me, but on *this* specific desire, we were briefly united.

"Close the door," I said coarsely.

Raksh glanced up with faint surprise. "Truly?"

I shrugged. "If we are to go about this as husband and wife, we should start things off on the right foot, no?"

He kicked the door shut and dropped to his knees. "The wisest of women you are, Amina al-Sirafi."

◆

The asshole was honestly surprised.

"I thought we were turning over a new leaf!" Raksh shouted from the bottom of the raft as we dropped it out to sea. Well, "raft" was perhaps a diplomatic term. But as we had no dunij thanks to Raksh stealing it, the crudely bound platform of broken boards would have to do. He shook the chains around his hands and feet with great indignation. "You let us have sexual intercourse!"

At my side, I felt Dalila and Majed turn to stare at me.

"What?" I flushed. "I needed a way to distract him, all right?" Majed let out an overly judgmental sigh, and I hissed, "We're still married. It's allowed!"

Dalila pinched her brow in exasperation. "Not even slightly the point, Amina."

"You were the one who told me to relax!" Granted, Dalila had obviously been referring to slumber, not shushed sex with my chaos spirit spouse in the ship's cramped galley, but everyone had their own way of unwinding. I turned my attention back to Raksh, tossing down a water-skin and a bag of dates. "Next time don't fall asleep beside me. I'm sure you'll be fine. At least we did not bury you in a chest."

"We probably should have," Majed muttered.

"We could still blow him up," Dalila added. "I have some black powder left."

Raksh writhed furiously in his chains. "You are the most *disloyal* of companions!"

Majed pulled at his beard. "I am normally not one for murder, but are you certain it is wise to let him live? Why *don't* you divorce him?" he asked under his breath as Raksh's raft drifted away. "He can still yell the words if we tell him what they are."

"Because I fear there is more than marriage holding us together," I explained with a grimace. "I don't need him looking into what that might be if a divorce fails to sever our bond. And should Marjana ever need to know about that part of her heritage . . . I cannot kill him. Not yet."

"Amina!" Raksh wailed in the distance. "Don't do this! I can still make you a legend!"

I can do that myself. "Best of luck, truly!" I shouted before glancing at Majed. "Let's speed up."

Majed went to give the orders, filling in for Tinbu, who was being forced to recuperate. But even the sight of my friend resting on my captain's bench, his injured leg propped on a pillow and Payasam on his lap, filled me with guilt. Tinbu had rebroken his already poorly healing leg when he'd thrown himself at Yazid to save my life. We'd set the bone as best we could and I intended to get him to a physician, but we'd all seen the outcome of similar injuries. Tinbu would walk with a limp for the rest of his life, a limp that would undoubtedly make a career as a sailor— already perilous—all the riskier.

"Don't give me that pitying look," Tinbu chided as I joined him, clearly reading my expression. "You saved *me* from being crucified as a brigand, remember? I was repaying the favor."

"I know, I know," I muttered, taking a seat. Around us, the sea seemed to undulate and roll, a great blue watery beast stretching its legs.

"I take it Raksh is floating on a slow not-boat to nowhere?" Tinbu asked, stroking Payasam's head as the cat stared adoringly at him.

"God willing. I have little doubt he'll be back."

Dalila climbed up to join us, rolling her wooden staff between her palms. "Then we are done with the magical world?"

I sighed and pulled Khayzur's feather from my belt. "Not quite."

◆

In the time it took to tell my friends of the happenings at the peri court, some of the sailors began singing. Their smiles, hesitant at first, grew broader as they teased each other over the lovers and wives to whom they were return- ing, children and friends they ached to see, and how wonderful it would be to put into a familiar port. The rhymes were not the ones we chanted when we begged the ocean to be merciful or remembered the many dead lost to storms, but I had no doubt my crew was scarred by what had happened at Socotra; no doubt some of them would slink away once we put ashore to find nawakhidha who might pay less and treat them unkindly—but ones who didn't face off against foreign sorcerers and sea monsters.

For my crew had not emerged unscathed. Three men had been killed— Arjun, a carpenter's apprentice of barely nineteen; Ishtiaq, an always smiling sailor who left three kids in Jeddah; and Bassam, a salty old sea dog who made Majed look young and proudly crowed he'd never spent more than a day on land. Bassam had been swept away during the marid's attack, but we said the funeral prayers for him, then buried Ishtiaq and cremated Arjun according to their rites. A life at sea was dangerous, and though I knew the money and faltering letters I would send to their dependents were always a feared possibility, their souls weighed heavy on my conscience.

But I would keep such sorrows to myself. Right now, the rest of my crew seemed to be healing and though I kept my ear low, I heard no whispers of malcontent that might lead to mutiny.

Among my dearest, however, a new surprise was settling in.

"So you are what . . . some sort of treasure hunter for a bunch of magical bird men?" Tinbu asked after a stunned silence.

"I suspect the magical bird men would squawk that I do not work *for* them—they have all sorts of rules about interacting with humans—but yes. I owe them the retrieval of four more magical items. That was their price for my being permitted to leave the island."

"And you trust such creatures to uphold this deal?" Majed asked. "They tried to throw you to your death!"

"I don't trust them at all. I believe the one who saved me is a good man . . . bird. A believer—whatever. But I also suspect he had his own reasons." I spread my hands. "I had little choice. Even if the peris renege on the deal, it was worth being able to stop the Frank."

"I cannot argue against that." Dalila tilted her head to study me. "The time on the island, you say it changed you? So your strength, the way you were running . . ."

"I am stronger," I confirmed. "*Much* stronger. I was finally able to bloody up Raksh a bit," I added, unable to conceal the relish in my voice. "I haven't noticed any other physical changes, but I can see things. Creatures, the oaths Falco's men made to him as though they were chains, visions of other worlds . . ."

"Al-ghayb," Majed said softly. "The realms of the djinn and such. There are mystics who claim to have gained the same Sight. Holy men and women."

"They were probably better equipped to deal with it than me." I shuddered, remembering my vision of jailed monsters beyond the brass door. Had any of that been real? The bridge? The nasnas? Asif and his accusations? "Though I suspect I'm going to need both magical strength *and* Sight to retrieve these Transgressions."

"You should start training with more weapons," Tinbu said, sounding awed. "Gods, Amina, you could be like some warrior out of yore."

"She's going to need more than brawn." Dalila flashed a conspiratorial grin at Tinbu. "You have a gambler's soul. I take it you are in?"

"In?" I blinked in surprise. "Wait . . . you wish to *join* me?"

"Of course we wish to join you! The knowledge you could stumble upon, the lost potions and tricks of the ancients . . ." Dalila's eyes gleamed. "I might learn things that would make me the sheikha of the Banu Sasan. Those bastards will rue the day they chased me out of Iraq."

Tinbu's expression turned dreamy. "I bet there will be treasure. There has to be, right? The kind of people who go after magical artifacts are always rich in the stories. Surely the peris won't mind if we keep *some* of the mortal wealth." He pressed a kiss to Payasam's straggled fur. "Going to make myself a raja and sweep a certain Adeni merchant off his feet."

My heart rose with a mix of hope and worry. "It is going to be unspeakably dangerous. You'd be putting yourselves at risk for a deal you had no part in—"

"Oh, shut up," Dalila interjected. "We know it's dangerous and can make our own decisions. And you are far more likely to survive, let alone find these hidden artifacts, if we are with you."

I wanted to protest. Perhaps a better friend would. But Dalila was right, and I was learning, many years too late, that I could not control the hearts of those around me. I had lived a daring life. I had fought for my ambitions.

I could not deny others theirs.

"I . . . would be forever grateful if you joined me," I confessed. "We can discuss the matter further when we return to shore. I cannot tell the crew everything, but I want no man brought on unwilling. And I will pay for safe passage to Mogadishu," I added, looking at Majed.

Majed let out an indignant harrumph. "And passage back to the *Marawati* after? The three of you are *not* going off to explore without me. You will get lost in the doldrums and die. And do not give me any guilt trips about responsibility, hypocrite," he said more severely as I opened my mouth to do just that. "You have your family concerns, and I will talk to my wife. There must be a way to make this work so we can see our children."

He could have no idea how much those words stirred my heart. God, I hoped so. No matter what I told my friends, I had yet to make peace in my soul with the cost of this new venture when it came to Marjana. The days and nights I would lose with her, the fears we would both carry when seas separated us.

It was a price with which I might never make peace. It was a *choice* I prayed she might one day understand. Might take courage from when it came to chasing her own dreams.

"Then it's settled," Tinbu declared. "But may I make a suggestion? Should any of us find ourselves in the position where we are being persuaded to cut a deal with a magical creature, let's not. Or at least bring it to the group for discussion."

"Amen to that," I breathed, suddenly feeling lighter than I had in weeks.

There was, however, one more matter. I glanced across the *Marawati*. The men had taken to Dunya, and she was with a group of sailors now, looking shy but eager as Firoz showed her how to make rope and she diligently took notes.

Dalila followed my gaze. "Have you made a decision?"

"Aye," I said heavily. "That I have."

Chapter 34

Salima's courtyard was an eerily still place. Though I stood in the shade of a tall, thickly bladed palm tree, it did little to cut the sweltering air. My shirt clung to the damp of my back, a bead of sweat rolling down my brow. It was too hot even for insects to be flying about, their drone confined to buzzing in the shrubs.

Salima al-Hilli gave no indication of being affected by the heat. She stood with her back ramrod straight, her attention entirely focused on Dunya's letter. She had been staring at it long enough to have read the letter in its entirety at least a dozen times.

She finally lowered the paper. "This is her decision?"

I had not read the letter but had a fairly good idea of its contents. "It is, Sayyida. She seemed very determined. Very capable."

"She's a child." Salima folded the paper into increasingly smaller halves, as though its implications might vanish entirely. "She says I am not to blame you. That you saved her life at great risk to your own, and that she begged you in the name of her father to let her go."

There was movement in the branches above us, a shifting and crackling as though something heavy shifted in the tree to get a better look. I resisted the urge to glance up. Salima had not reacted, and I heard the noise as though it existed in another world, almost dreamlike.

I was beginning to understand what that meant. What it would mean for the rest of my life.

I returned my attention to Salima. "I could not persuade her to come back to this life, Sayyida. I tried. But in spending time with her . . . I came to understand why she made that decision. I think you do as well."

Salima shook her head. "God did not mean all dreams to be chased. Sometimes people must hide their hearts to survive, to honor their family."

"God made us who we are," I said softly. "I have to believe we are to find wisdom in that."

Salima scoffed, but she did not sound disaffected. She sounded heartbroken. "If I threatened you again, would you reveal her location?"

"No," I said plainly. "I gave her my word and she is likely long gone. She's a talented scholar and has an unparalleled gift with languages. People have made good lives with less. God willing, there may even be a day when you two meet again in peace." I steeled my voice. "I suggest you live to see that day, Sayyida."

The unspoken threat lay heavy between us, a long moment of tense silence in its wake. I had not returned to this house without being prepared to put a stop—by any means necessary—to whatever new threats Salima might fling my way. But I was weary of bloodshed and prayed she saw sense.

Whatever was spying in the branches moved again. A shadow darted past my eyes, leaving a scent like lightning and desert dust.

Salima slipped the letter into her belt. "I want you out of my home. You saved Dunya's life, and for that I will not pursue you. I will leave your family in peace—I swear to God. But we part as enemies, nakhudha."

"Understood." I suspected asking for another share of the promised reward would have been pressing my luck, so I didn't bother. Her early payments were enough to get me, my ship, and my people through for now. It was not the life-changing fortune she had promised, but I had seen my life changed enough. Salima's dishonoring of our agreement was between her and God.

Instead, I bowed my head and turned to leave. No one made to escort me, but I had not come this far in my career without being able to retrace my way to an exit.

An exit that was in sight when a copper-hued hand grabbed my wrist.

Unfortunately for the hand's owner, I was still getting used to my new strength. So when I spun on the shrouded figure, ripping free of its grip and slamming it against the wall, I did so with more force than necessary.

The creature hissed, a burst of oddly sweet breath. Whether it was human or something else entirely, I could not tell. It was swathed in a parchment-colored garment, and I could see nothing but a pair of glowing eyes beneath its deep hood.

"For the little one!" it gasped out, shaking a saddlebag.

I frowned but released the creature and took the bag. A glance revealed it was stuffed with books, scrolls, and tools whose purpose I could not fathom. "What is all this?"

The creature made a disgruntled snort, brushing down its clothes. "What I could gather in a short amount of time. The family's work must continue."

I gave it a baffled look. "And who are you?"

The creature glared with its fiery eyes. "Their djinn. *Obviously.*" Then it stepped through a wall and was gone.

◆

The sudden appearance of the al-Hilli's family djinn had delayed me, but I did not tarry further, joining my waiting companions at the beach.

"Are the police behind you?" Majed called in greeting.

I didn't break my stride. "No."

"Soldiers from the governor?" Tinbu asked worriedly.

"Not them either. Salima said I made an enemy, but it seems saving her only grandchild's life multiple times earned me a reprieve."

"Any more reward money?" Dalila nodded at the bag. "That looks big enough to hold a fortune."

"I wish. They are books for Dunya. A gift from the family djinn." Dalila blinked and I sighed. "I can explain on the ship. We will have to make do with what money we have for the moment. We can look into other jobs later.

"But right now there is only one place I intend to go."

◆

Dawn was breaking as we anchored off a secluded beach south of Salalah, the cliffs and ancient fort concealing our arrival.

But not entirely. I may have kept my brother from our family's true vocation and my daughter from my former life, but my mother had watched for the *Marawati*'s sails far too long to forget what our ship looked like. Even before I jumped into the surf, I could see her making her way across the beach, her shayla blowing madly in the wind.

A much smaller, squealing figure raced ahead.

With a choked sob, I charged forward. I was at Marjana's side the next second, catching my daughter in my arms and clutching her tight. I pressed my face against her hair, tears running down my cheeks.

"Oh, my love," I breathed. "My dear little girl . . ."

Marjana buried her head in my neck. "I missed you so much."

"I know, my life. I know." I picked her up with ease, carrying her in one arm as I made my way out of the water.

"Wow, Mama . . ." Awe stole into Marjana's voice. "When did you get so *strong*?"

"Amina!" My mother rushed to cross the distance between us, standing up on her toes to pull me down so she could kiss my cheeks. "Alhamdulillah, God be praised!" Then she drew back and swatted my shoulder with far more force than was affectionate. "*Do you know how worried I have been?* Could you not have sent a *letter*? Did the *Marawati* fall off the edge of the world where there are no couriers?"

I drew my mother into a hug so fierce she had to stop yelling. "We ran into some difficulties; I apologize. But you don't need to worry about any of that right now." I kissed Marjana again, tickling my noise against hers until my daughter giggled. "I am home."

And for the time being, that was all that mattered.

There Was and Was Not a Nakhudha Named Amina al-Sirafi

There was and was not a nakhudha named Amina al-Sirafi who sailed with a cunning crew all over the great Indian Ocean, dashing after magical treasures and talismans, outwitting cruel sorcerers, and battling incomprehensibly powerful creatures from legend. This is her story first, and only one of her many adventures that I hope to relate.

But there was also once a scribe named Dunya. A scribe reborn in a ship's galley between Aden and Salalah.

I ran a hand over my newly cropped hair, the length unfamiliar. I was dressed in a striped thawb Majed had picked out, suggesting it was the type of garment a young scholar from a good but not wealthy background would wear. I placed a cap on my head and wound a length of turban cloth around it. I did not have a looking glass, but God willing, I appeared a jittery if innocuous youth, one of the many young men of intellectual persuasion who take to the sea to travel new lands.

I did not need a looking glass, however, to know that I was grinning from ear to ear.

I stepped out of the galley. The nakhudha had brought her daughter aboard. We were still anchored outside her family's home, and she had been taking various relatives on the *Marawati*, seemingly uncertain at first (though I would never dare utter such a presumption in her presence) and then with much enthusiasm. Marjana lay on the deck watching a pod of leaping dolphins play in the sunlit water, while the cat Payasam sat on her back, batting the tassels of the young girl's rather strikingly well-woven belt.

The nakhudha herself was with her companions, sitting on her bench as they argued over a map. I had never been around any group of people who argued at such length or so loudly. They were deeply intimidating to approach, but Amina must have noticed my arrival, for she glanced up, her black eyes pinning me.

"Jamal," she called, and it took a moment to realize she was calling *me*, my new name having yet to settle. I was not entirely certain it *would* settle, not certain this person was actually me. Dunya was the name my lost parents had chosen, and I suspected I would always have a passing fondness for it. Now as Jamal, I felt equal parts free and terrified, suddenly on the first steps of a journey of which I had only ever dreamed.

But I *was* on it. And for now, that was enough.

"Have you found a spot for your manuscripts?" the nakhudha asked, stirring a steaming pot of fish stew the cook had brought over.

I hesitated. I didn't know what to make of the bag of manuscripts and instruments my family djinn had given to Amina. I didn't know we *had* a family djinn. But considering our misadventures, I suspected she was done with al-Hilli dramatics for a while, so I simply said, "Yes, nakhudha."

Marjana skipped up to join us. "Mama, is it true your scar is from battling a Hormuzi prince?"

Amina snorted, ladling some of the fragrant stew into a wooden bowl. "Who told you that?"

"Uncle Tinbu."

"It was no prince," Amina said derisively. "It was a horse thief with delusions of grandeur."

Tinbu clucked in disagreement. "He had a crown, did he not?"

"A crown with gems made of paste," Dalila cut in. "None of you believed me when I tried to warn you against selling them, and you were lucky to keep your heads for the error. That sultana had the last merchants who cheated her thrown out a window."

Marjana's eyes were now very wide.

I ventured closer, pulling out a piece of parchment and a stylus. "Would you tell us the story?"

Amina rolled her eyes at my supplies. "I know what you're doing, scribe. You will make me into some ridiculous character out of your tales with flowing locks and verses like a poet."

"I would never dare compromise your most . . . unique voice," I promised, picking up a writing board and kneeling near her feet. "But how else will the world know your legend?"

I had meant it as a jest, but Amina went oddly still at the word, an expression I couldn't read flashing across her face as she stared at her ladle.

Finally she glanced up. "Would you tell it in my words?"

"In your words," I agreed.

"Even if they're rude?"

I paused. "Surely the occasional softening of terms or expanded commentary on key topics—" Amina lifted her ladle in a motion far too reminiscent of a dagger, and I quickly changed course. "Right. All the rude words stay."

Marjana had only gotten more excited. She tugged on her mother's sleeve. "Tell us a story, Mama! Please."

"I . . . oh, *fine*," the nakhudha grumbled in the end, clearly won over by the pleading in her daughter's eyes. "But do not talk to your grandmother about any of this, understand? And only if you *eat*; you are all skin and bones of late." She settled Marjana beside her, placing a bowl of stew on her mat, and only after the little girl started putting food in her mouth did Amina al-Sirafi begin her next tale.

But that, dear sisters, is a story for another night.

Glossary

barija (pl. bawarij): a pirate vessel, frequently associated at the time with India

dunij (pl. dawanij): a smaller vessel often used as a lifeboat or to bring cargo and passengers ashore from an anchored ship

jahazi: cargo ship, particularly out of East Africa

muhtasib: a government official tasked with overseeing trade and commerce, as well as proper public behavior

nakhudha (pl. nawakhidha): a ship owner, authority at sea

qaraqir: large deep-sea cargo and transport vessel

qunbar and sunbuq (pl. sanabiq): large cargo vessels

Author's Note and Further Reading

The Indian Ocean is arguably among the oldest seas in maritime history, witness to over five thousand years of humans traveling its shores and crossing its expanse. Pilgrims and pirates, enslaved persons and royalty, traders and scholars. In our modern age, we are accustomed to thinking of continents and land borders; rarely do we see the sea and its littorals as places of shared culture. But long before the so-called European Age of Exploration (an age that would do more damage to existing Indian Ocean networks and indigenous populations than any such incursion before), the ports of the Indian Ocean were bustling, cosmopolitan places where one could find goods and people from all over.

Its medieval history has fascinated me since I was an undergrad, first learning of the accounts of the famous Geniza merchants, members of a Jewish diaspora that stretched from North Africa to India. There was something so relatable and human about these often mundane accounts of normal people's lives: people who weren't sultans or generals, but parents purchasing gifts for their kids' weddings, fretting about in-laws and business decisions, and mourning the sudden death of beloved siblings lost at sea—the sort of connections that make the past seem alive. It was always my dream to write a book set in this world, to pull on the stories that had resonated so deeply, and when I first began, I was thrilled to finally have a proper work excuse to throw myself into research. Indeed, I believe the phrase "I'm going to make it completely historically accurate except for the plot" came out of my mouth at least once.

Reader, I am fortunate that such a delusionally ambitious statement didn't instantly summon my own Raksh. For as I have been reminded again and again and AGAIN, history is a construct, ever-changing and always subjective. Not only does it reveal the biases of its teller, audience, and intention, but also there is often much we simply don't know. While the past decade has seen astonishing developments in the study of the medieval Indian Ocean world, I have no doubt that by the time this book is published, some detail I believed factually sound will be disproved.

I have endeavored to make it historically *believable*, then, trying to balance scholarship with the spirit of the story. There are, of course, plenty of fantasist's touches. Would Amina have realized Aden was balanced on top of a submerged extinct volcano? Doubtful, but it is a setting too fabulous to ignore. Is the Moon of Saba a real legend? Absolutely not: one does not spend one's time reading stories of djinns and demons and then give directions to summoning such a creature in a commercial novel. However, nothing would delight me more than if you were intrigued enough by the history underlying Amina's story to learn more about this world, and so I'm sharing some of my sources. This isn't a comprehensive list—that would be a novella itself—but rather some enjoyable and accessible reads I think fellow history nerds would enjoy.

Let's start with primary accounts (I'm listing English translations here; if you are an Arabic reader, you'll have far better options). I've already mentioned the Geniza traders, and while a great number of books have been written about their lives, a good one is *India Traders of the Middle Ages: Documents from the Cairo Geniza*. Then there are the travelers. Ibn Battuta is the most famous, though slightly later; his lovely recollections of Mogadishu informed descriptions of that city in this book. Ibn Jubayr is more contemporaneous, and though his journeys kept him slightly northward, he had a *lot* of opinions about maritime travel in the Red Sea. Closer to Amina's world is the merchant and would-be geographer Ibn al-Mujawir, whose very entertaining—if occasionally quite scandalous—

trips to Aden, Socotra, and the southern Arabian coast were instrumental. From the perspective of actual seafarers are Abu Zayd al-Sirafi's *Accounts of India and China* and *The Book of the Wonders of India*, a collection of sailors' yarns credited to Buzurg ibn Shahriyar al-Ramhormuzi, a captain who was likely fictional.

If information on the lives of regular people during the medieval period is difficult to uncover, reliable accounts on the lives of criminals, those who often made a living by covering their tracks, can be even more elusive. My favorite primary source is the thirteenth-century trickster's manual *The Book of Charlatans* by al-Jawbarī, several of whose ruses made their way into this text. For felonious tales that skirt the line between fact and fiction, Robert Irwin's *The Arabian Nights: A Companion* offers some of the history behind the collection's famous rogues, and C. E. Bosworth's first volume in *The Mediaeval Islamic Underworld* translates and contextualizes numerous odes and legends about the Banu Sasan. Less whimsical but more telling is the actual criminal activity recorded and studied in works such as Carl F. Petry's *The Criminal Underworld in a Medieval Islamic Society* and Hassan S. Khalilieh's articles on piracy and Islamic law at sea. However, to better understand piracy in the medieval Indian Ocean, one must read far more widely. An entire book could be written just on the place of pirates in modern and historical lore. Both romanticized and villainized, they can be spun as heroic corsairs, justified freedom fighters, or murderous enslavers . . . it all depends on who's telling their story. But in primary accounts and historical studies, much of what I read painted a picture of various groups of people who were often just as part and parcel of the littoral society they lived in as were traders and navies. Alongside Khalilieh's articles, I found the work of scholars such as Roxani Eleni Margariti, Sebastian R. Prange, and Lakshmi Subramanian most illuminating.

To put together the lives of noncriminal citizens and the cities they dwelled in, I relied heavily on Margariti's *Aden and the Indian Ocean*

Trade, Elizabeth A. Lambourn's *Abraham's Luggage*, Yossef Rapoport's *Marriage, Money and Divorce in Medieval Islamic Society*, and Delia Cortese and Simonetta Calderini's *Women and the Fatimids in the World of Islam*. Chapurukha M. Kusimba's *The Rise and Fall of Swahili States* was an excellent guide to the world from which Majed and Amina's mother hailed, and on conflicts farther abroad, I found Paul M. Cobb's *The Race for Paradise*, Amin Maalouf's *The Crusades Through Arab Eyes*, Hussein Fancy's *The Mercenary Mediterranean,* and Graham A. Loud and Alex Metcalfe's *The Society of Norman Italy* helpful in providing context for Falco's character. For a primary source that offers a very different and personal take on Muslim and Christian interactions during the Crusades, I suggest *The Book of Contemplation* by Usama ibn Munqidh. For those who enjoy audio content, I suggest checking out the podcast series *New Books in the Indian Ocean World* and the *Ottoman History Podcast*.

Absolutely nothing bedeviled me like researching anything nautical. From ship details to sailing schedules to life at sea, what I could glean at first largely seemed to contradict other sources; while there's a fair amount of information after the fourteenth century, maritime history in the early medieval and late classical eras is less studied. I did find some gems, however. George F. Hourani's *Arab Seafaring* is a classic in the genre, and Tim Severin's account of the Sindbad voyage, in which a ninth-century vessel was reconstructed and sailed from Oman to Singapore, discusses technology that predates Amina's *Marawati* but is still a delight. Most helpful (and far more recent) is the work of Dionisius A. Agius, in particular his book *Classic Ships of Islam*. This was also a subject for which I relied heavily on academic articles, the scholarship of Ranabir Chakravarti, Inês Bénard, and Juan Acevedo being of note. Yossef Rapoport's *Islamic Maps* is a gorgeously rendered volume that helped me better visualize and understand how Amina would have conceived of the geography of her world, and for a larger overview of the

Indian Ocean in history, I recommend *The Ocean of Churn: How the Indian Ocean Shaped Human History* by Sanjeev Sanyal; *Dhow Cultures of the Indian Ocean: Cosmopolitanism, Commerce and Islam* by Abdul Sheriff; *Monsoon Islam: Trade and Faith on the Medieval Malabar Coast* by Sebastian Prange; and *Oman: A Maritime History* by Abdulrahman Al-Salimi and Eric Staples.

It is difficult to overstate how prevalent what we call "magic" was in the medieval world and how difficult it is as well to remove our modern biases from understanding that. Astrological predictions were the law of the land, relied upon by scholars and sultans, and folk rituals were part of everyday life, no matter a person's religious background. I won't attempt a comprehensive list (especially with some of the most fascinating scholarship currently being done by young academics) but will share that I found *Islam, Arabs, and the Intelligent World of the Jinn* by Amira El-Zein and *Legends of the Fire Spirits* by Robert Lebling very helpful. For a different perspective, I recommend Michael Muhammad Knight's *Magic in Islam*, and for those who enjoy podcasts and Twitter, Ali A. Olomi is a treasure.

So much of this story is inspired by folktales that it's hard to know where to start in recommending them, but I'll begin with what I am asked most frequently: my current favorite edition of *The Thousand and One Nights* is *The Annotated Arabian Nights*. Yasmine Seale's translation is beautiful, and the accompanying art and background information is not to be missed. *Tales of the Marvelous and News of the Strange* as well as al-Qazwini's *Marvels of Creation* are also highly entertaining. You can read English versions of the stories of the epic figures mentioned in this book in Melanie Magidow's translation of Dhat al-Himma in *The Tale of Princess Fatima, Warrior Woman*; Lena Jayyusi's *The Adventures of Sayf Ben Dhi Yazan*; and James E. Montgomery's *Diwan 'Antarah ibn Shaddad*. For even more female fighters, check out Remke Kruk's *Warrior Women of Islam*.

Finally, I would be remiss if I didn't mention the modern authors that started me on this journey: the incomparable Naguib Mahfouz, Radwa Ashour, and Amitav Ghosh. Though I recommend all their books, for stories inspired by the folktales and history mentioned here, I suggest *Arabian Nights and Days*, *Siraaj*, and *In an Antique Land*.

Happy reading!

BIBLIOGRAPHY

Ahsan al-taqasim fi ma'rifat al-aqalim, by Abu Abdallah Muhammad b. Ahmad al-Muqaddasi, translated by G. S. A. Ranking and R. F. Azoo (Calcutta: Asiatic Society of Bengal, 1897).

The Book of Charlatans, by Jamāl al-Dīn ʿAbd al-Raḥīm al-Jawbarī, translated by Humphrey Davies (New York: Library of Arabic Literature/NYU Press, 2022).

A Traveller in Thirteenth-Century Arabia: Ibn al-Mujawir's tarikh al-mustabsir, edited by G. Rex Smith (London: The Hakluyt Society/Ashgate, 2008).

ACKNOWLEDGMENTS

I began writing *The Adventures of Amina al-Sirafi* in March 2020, and if there is any book that took a village to complete, it would be this one. Balancing a pandemic, virtual elementary schooling, and a manuscript that required depths of research beyond anything I could have originally envisioned is an experience I hope never to repeat, and one I couldn't have gotten through without the help of a great many people.

First, to all the historians and academics who took the time to answer my queries, recommend new books and sources, or track down various images and facts about lunar spirits and medieval boats—particularly Laura Castra, aka Plumas, Thomas Lecaque, Sarah Luginbill, Melanie Magidow, Roxani Margariti, Ali A. Olomi, Sebastian Prange, and Amanda Hannoosh Steinberg—you have my eternal gratitude. To my utterly brilliant academic reviewers, Fahad Ahmad Bishara and Shireen Hamza: it was a delight to work with you and I learned so much.

One of the joys of being in this field for a few years now is becoming friends with ridiculously talented fellow writers who will not only keep you sane during the ups and downs of publishing, but also tell you when it's time to kill your darlings and point out battle scenes that defy the laws of time, space, and plot. To my wonderful beta readers and friends: E. J. Beaton, Melissa Caruso, Roshani Chokshi, K. A. Doore, Kat Howard, Sam Hawke, Fonda Lee, Rowenna Miller, and Megan O'Keefe . . . thank you so, so much. May the Bunker crew prosper forever! It was also my privilege to work with a great team of sensitivity readers for this project:

Naseem Jamnia, Phoebe Farag Mikhail, Ardo Omer, and Prity Samiha—I am deeply grateful for your time and guidance.

None of this would have been possible if Jen Azantian hadn't taken a chance on me years ago and continued to be one of the best literary agents in the business: many, many thanks to you and everyone at ALA. I owe an enormous amount of gratitude to everyone at my publishing team for putting my books out into the world and being incredibly understanding with my schedule when Covid completely disrupted it: my editors, David Pomerico and Natasha Bardon, and everyone over at Harper Voyager US/UK, particularly Robin Barletta, Danielle Bartlett, Mireya Chiriboga, Jennifer Chung, Kate Falkoff, Emily Fisher, Nancy Inglis, Amber Ivatt, Beatrice Jason, Holly Macdonald, Maddy Marshall, Vicky Leech Mateos, Mumtaz Mustafa, Shelby Peak, Amanda Reeve, Karen Richardson, Dean Russell, John Simko, Elizabeth Vaziri, Robyn Watts, Erin White, and Leah Woods. For designing covers and art that literally took my breath away, a shout-out to Micaela Alcaino, Ivan Belikov, and April Damon.

Huge thanks as well to all the readers who've supported my books and shared them with friends, I hope you enjoy this new series just as much! Hugs and much love and appreciation to my family, particularly my parents and grandmother, who stepped in whenever I needed help, and my mom, who taught me from an early age how fierce mothers could be. To Shamik, the best partner and spouse I could ask for, thank you for embarking on a new literary adventure with me and figuring out what the night sky would have looked like in 1143—one day we'll understand the mechanics behind the lunar mansions. And for Alia! Thank you for all your assistance, lovebug: you drew the best covers and I could have never created Payasam without your cat expertise.

Finally to the One who has blessed me more than I deserve, I hope I have done justice to the lives of past believers and pray our community continues to find faith in reflecting on Your wonders.

About the Author

SHANNON CHAKRABORTY is the author of the critically acclaimed and internationally bestselling Daevabad Trilogy. Her work has been translated into over a dozen languages and nominated for the Hugo, Locus, World Fantasy, Crawford, and Astounding awards. When not buried in books about medieval seafarers and con artists, she enjoys hiking, knitting, and re-creating unnecessarily complicated historical meals. You can find her online at sachakraborty.com or on Twitter and Instagram at @SAChakrabooks, where she likes to talk about history, politics, cooking, and Islamic art. She currently lives in New Jersey with her husband, daughter, and an ever-increasing number of cats.